Kingdom
CHAOS

Jeff Dixon

Kingdom Chaos
© 2019 Jeff Dixon

Published by Deep River Books
Sisters, Oregon
www.DeepRiverBooks.com

Unless otherwise indicated, all Scripture quotations are taken from Holy Bible, New International Version, Copyright 1973, 1978, 1984 by International Bible Society.

ISBN: 9781632694980
Library of Congress: 2019915955

Printed in the USA

Cover design by Joe Bailen, Contajus Designs

Table of Contents

Twice Upon A Time . . .

The unusual phrase above is not the expected way a story begins. However, those words are necessary to lay the foundation for the once upon a time *yet* to come. By definition, *once upon a time* normally propels you into a story by giving you a starting point. The beginning point is often one that tweaks your imagination and thrusts you forward with expectation and hope. This narrative is no different. However, in this work of fiction we begin with not just one but two distinct stories that are factual. Both of those facts are essential to fully embrace the pages of fiction that will follow. As a result, our story begins with the unusual—*twice upon a time.*

This book is built upon the following factual events in Disney history.

Fact One

Sweat trickled down the back of the young man's neck as he was seated at the controls of Monorail Red on the sticky June afternoon in 1959. Tugging at the neck of the uniform he wore, he glanced at the futuristic wardrobe that the costume department had put the final stitch into just an hour ago. The discomfort he experienced could partially be blamed on the heat of the summer day, the thickness of the fabric in his uniform, and the gnawing concern that what he was getting ready to do had the strong possibility of failure.

The plan had been to drive Monorail Blue, but production was running behind and Blue was not available yet. Monorail Red was operational; however, the train was anything but reliable. As the driver, a young man named Bob Gurr, looked out the sleek, sloped, futuristic window, he knew how difficult getting to this moment had been. Gurr and German engineer Konrad Deller had worked day and night preparing the monorail for its official debut. Debut day was today, June 14.

The routine had been the same for longer than Gurr could remember. They would eat dinner at the Disneyland Hotel, then work in Deller's hotel room to create sketches for replacement parts. Once the sketches were complete, a truck would arrive around midnight, pick up the drawings, and take them to the Disney Studio Machine Shop in Burbank. Engineers would then work all night creating the parts needed based on the sketches and have them redelivered to Gurr and Deller the next morning. The pair would then install them in the train. If ever there was a work in progress, it was the monorail now parked in the monorail station, waiting for the official dedication of this new attraction.

There had been a brief moment of hope the night before, after Monorail Red had finally made a successful loop around Tomorrowland for the very first time. Every other attempt had resulted in a breakdown along the monorail line, and to describe the futuristic mode of transportation as unreliable was an understatement. They feared a crowd would be waiting for the dedication event only to have the monorail unable to make it to the station. Much to their amazement, they had caught a break with a positive test run, and the monorail actually worked. Knowing that the pattern had been hit and miss, they decided to park the monorail in the station for the event, instead of risking another breakdown. Now staged at the station, the monorail was guaranteed to be in place for the television cameras to see. If things went well, Bob Gurr would pilot the monorail out of the station and out of sight, so even if it were to burst into flames, it would be away from the unblinking eye of the cameras.

Gurr sat behind the controls as the entourage made its way toward Monorail Red. Photographers flashing their cameras, crowds that descended on the station, and Disneyland security surrounded the boarding area. The honored guests for the dedication ceremony created a wave of motion as they moved into place. Walt Disney approached the train, along with US Vice President Richard Nixon. Nixon had brought his two daughters, Julie and Tricia, along for this special occasion. Walt's close personal friend Art Linkletter was a part of the group too, along with more Secret Service agents than Gurr could count.

At the appointed time, Gurr fired up the 600-volt DC power so the air-conditioning would cool down the cab for their guests. This would be a great photo opportunity and, hopefully, a bright moment in Disney history. Walt Disney, the Nixon family, and Art Linkletter all climbed into the cab of the monorail. As they waved to the crowds and the cameras looking in, Walt gave the word to the extremely nervous driver that it was time to reveal the engineering marvel of the monorail.

Gurr eased into the journey ever so slowly and smoothly, gliding the train out of the monorail station. Taking deep, calming breaths, Gurr willed the monorail to keep moving, fearing it would break down and ruin the television footage. Once the monorail had cleared the station and made the curve taking it out of the view of the crowd, Bob Gurr let out the deep breath he'd been holding. Now all they had to do was make the loop and return. His relief was short-lived.

Richard Nixon made the observation that the Secret Service, all of them, had been left on the loading platform. In essence, the Disney team had kidnapped the vice president of the United States. At that moment, he was no longer under Secret Service protection. Gurr's anxiety returned with a fury as he continued the journey forward on what was the most excruciatingly tense lap he had ever driven on the monorail line. At one point, he remembered they had only made one successful loop prior to this occasion, but the current ride was even more intense, not because of the fear of failure, but because of the passenger and the security breach that had just occurred.

Finally, the station came back into view, and once again, Gurr let out a slow, controlled breath of relief. The ride was almost over. Secret Service agents now lined the platform waiting for the monorail to return. It was then that one of Richard Nixon's daughters made the request of her father to take another trip around the loop.

Walt Disney leaned toward the driver and said, "Bobby, give 'em another ride."

Walt was the boss, so Gurr accelerated the speed of the monorail through the station. The Secret Service responded by running alongside the sleek vehicle, pounding on the doors and windows as it passed, looking for some way to jump aboard. The design of the monorail, the automatic-door system, and the sealed windows prevented easy access. The agents came to a screeching halt as they ran out of running room on the platform. Monorail Red streaked away from the station, leaving the Secret Service behind for the second time in less than fifteen minutes.

Richard Nixon was delighted at the turn of the events. Those under Secret Service protection often try to steal moments alone where they are not so closely observed and surrounded by security. Walt and Nixon laughed at the turn of events. The trip was more enjoyable because Disney's new attraction worked better than it ever had before. Walt was showing it off, and he knew he had another great draw for guests at Disneyland.

The monorail arrived back after the second loop and this time slowed to a stop. Instantly, the Secret Service moved in to make sure the vice president was safe. They secured the area, closed in tighter, and the passengers moved down the ramp and on into their day. The monorail had been officially dedicated, a national kidnapping crisis of the vice president had come and gone, and Walt Disney had once again created a moment in history that many would never forget.

Fact Two

Donald J. Trump was elected the 45th president of the United States in a stunning victory that surprised pollsters, pundits, and political insiders. Apparently, the only people who weren't surprised were the supporters of the newly elected president and President Trump himself. The billionaire builder managed to turn the political establishment upside down with a brashness beyond what many ever anticipated or expected from the former reality show television star, bestselling author, and real-estate mogul, whose name is a brand recognized across the globe.

The anti-politician shocked voters on election night when he defeated Hillary Rodham Clinton, who most people anticipated would become the first woman ever elected president of the United States. It became clear in the early hours after this upset victory that the landscape of American culture, the political landscape, the predictability of political parties, and the stability of the media suddenly found itself in unfamiliar territory where the commonplace was no longer common, and the rules were about to change. President Trump chose to use his Twitter feed as the way to communicate directly with the American people and as a means to literally seize control and drive the news cycle on any given day. While many believed the methodology used during the campaign season would settle into a more predictable presidential pattern of doing business, the opposite occurred.

Trump supporters loved his brash personality and enjoyed the disruption of the media and political insiders. With the myth of their objectivity shattered, they allowed the chaos to clutter reasonable thought processes and reacted with a venom that revealed a hatred and bias unprecedented in history. Each day the cable networks, mainstream networks, news organizations, and commentators described corruption, collusion, the deep state, conspiracies, and international influence in a disorienting stream of constant banter.

No matter where one's personal feelings landed on the events of the election, it was indeed one of the most divisive elections in the history of the United

States. The resulting split in philosophies and clashing worldviews left people trying to find some middle ground, some way to process the changes, and a way to hold on to their dreams and vision of America.

The Walt Disney World Resort features an attraction that was born in the heart of Walt Disney himself known as The Hall of Presidents. There was a never-built addition to Disneyland in California that was to have been called Liberty Street. This area, as envisioned by Walt, was to feature the rich history of America, including its presidents. Due to a variety of factors, Liberty Street was never added to Disneyland.

As so often is the case, when one dream ends, another emerges. Walt Disney kept working on the creation of the historical show. He began preliminary planning on an attraction to be called "One Nation Under God." The showpiece would be filled with wax figures of all the presidents. Not merely a wax museum, the attraction would be interactive, and the presidents would move, speak, and appear lifelike. The project stalled because the technology didn't exist yet to make it happen. That changed at the 1964-65 New York World's Fair. Walt Disney secured sponsors and unleashed his creative team. As the fair opened, he had created a full-size Audio-Animatronics figure of his favorite president, Abraham Lincoln.

The successful creation and presentation of this Audio-Animatronic figure led Walt's brother Roy to push for the fulfillment of his late brother's dream. The Hall of Presidents is now that dream come to life. It features each of the presidents of the United States and stands as a non-partisan tribute to the ongoing movement of democracy and freedom. President Bill Clinton was the first current president to have a speaking role in the show. In addition, he actually provided one of his own wristwatches for his Audio-Animatronic to wear. The Hall of Presidents is the only other place besides the White House that the Presidential Seal can be displayed. As each new president is elected, the attraction is closed, updated, and the newest president added.

After the election of Donald Trump, the attraction went through the usual changes and reopened featuring the Audio-Animatronic version of the president speaking the words he had recorded:

From the beginning, America has been a nation defined by its people. At our founding, it was the American people who rose up to defend our freedoms and win our independence. It is why our founders began our great Constitution with three very simple words: we the people. Since that moment, each generation of Americans has taken its place in the defense of our freedom, our flag, and our nation under God.

These are the achievements of the American spirit. The spirit of a people who fought and died to bring the blessings of liberty to all our people. Above all to be American is to be an optimist, to believe that we can always do better and that the best days of our great nation are still ahead of us.

It's a privilege to serve as the president of the United States, to stand here among so many great leaders of our past and to work on behalf of the American people.

Shortly after the attraction was opened to the public, the speech was interrupted by a guest at Walt Disney World shouting "Lock him up!" toward the Audio-Animatronic president. The guests around him reacted with horror as they tried to silence him. Some covered the ears of their children as audience members tried to shout the disruption into silence. Guests told the man yelling that he was verbally accosting a robot, that it was not really Donald Trump, and to be quiet and sit down.

The man doing the screaming was Jay Malsky, a former NBC executive, turned drag-show comedian from New York, who has impersonated Hillary Clinton, the candidate Trump defeated in the election, as part of his act. After Disney reopened the attraction, Malsky had posted a picture of Donald Trump's robotic likeness with the cryptic notation, "Are we allowed to say that we want to murder this?"

Eventually, Disney security escorted Malsky out of the attraction, much to the relief and delight of the guests who had simply come to the Magic Kingdom for a vacation, a time of family fun, and to relax . . . in a place that was safe from the political correctness and craziness of the real world outside the gates. One unnamed guest said it this way: "The world has simply gone crazy."

Both of the events mentioned above really did take place, twice upon a time. And those two very distinct factual events now set the stage for the story that will unfold in the pages that await. This novel is a work of fiction, but it is best understood as *faction*. Faction is where fact and fiction collide to form a story that leaves each reader wondering where fact ends, and fiction begins.

Now that we have our facts in place, we have moved past our *twice upon a time* to discover our *once upon a time*. Get ready for an adventure.

Once upon a time . . .

CHAPTER ONE

Danger in the Darkness

Chaos has cluttered our minds. The ability to think has been disabled. These were the thoughts that echoed in his head as he moved silently through the darkness. Sweat trickled down the back of his neck as he tugged at the high collar on the uniform he now wore.

Less than an hour ago, he had descended into the legendary tunnels beneath Walt Disney World's Magic Kingdom, gone to his locker, and emptied it out except for the lone envelope he placed on the shelf. Now he made his way toward the monorail shop, a solitary figure traveling the backstage roadways that were absent of activity at this time of day.

Shifting the backpack he carried from one shoulder to the other, he slowed his pace, but only for a moment. The pack now resettled, he scuffed his feet and continued onward. The predawn morning offered a cooling breeze that pressed against him, making his long walk more comfortable than he had anticipated. As the wind slightly gusted across the gritty pavement, a breeze of thoughts blew through his mind. People, events, and crossroads of the past had all carried him to the road he had chosen to travel this day.

Guiteau, Czolgosz, and Oswald were names that some people still remembered. They were the roster of names that belonged to an exclusive club—each had been a presidential assassin. However, the name he most respected and admired was John Wilkes Booth.

A smile crossed his face as he understood what most people did not. History was lost on the common man. People had lost the ability to think and instead relied on pundits to help them process the world around them. Creative thought and the insight to search for deeper meaning took too much effort for mere mortals. Sound bites and sounding off had replaced sound, thoughtful insight. Their inability or refusal to think had become their greatest weakness and why he had to do what needed to be done.

Sighing deeply, he wished people would understand history. John Wilkes Booth didn't start out to be an assassin. No, that was not his destiny at all. Booth believed President Abraham Lincoln would destroy the Constitution and the beloved South that Booth adored. In order to put a stop to this decimation, Booth put together a team of co-conspirators, who after Lincoln's election in 1864, planned to kidnap Lincoln and take him to Richmond, Virginia.

After Booth had the president in his grasp, he would offer him as a trade for Confederate soldiers who were serving their time in northern jails. This original idea of kidnapping the president evolved into a more elaborate plot to kidnap Lincoln as he traveled in his carriage. The added drama of people finding an empty presidential carriage added a flair to the event that Booth enjoyed. The rest of the plan remained unchanged; Lincoln would be ransomed for the release of Confederates. This he believed would inspire the South and turn the tide of the war, as the North would be rocked by their vulnerability in losing their leader.

Then the unexpected happened. In a moment no one anticipated or predicted, General Robert E. Lee surrendered to General Ulysses S. Grant. For Booth, the days that followed were a blur. He listened as Lincoln gave a speech laying out how the nation would be rebuilt and unified. Booth's blur refocused into a razor-sharp rage against what he saw as injustice. Their plan had to take a much darker and dangerous path.

The brilliant activist actor now planned to assassinate Lincoln along with top officials in his administration. The target list was ambitious. President Lincoln, General Grant, Secretary of State William Seward, and Vice President Andrew Johnson were to be killed the same night, within minutes of each other, by men Booth had found to be like-minded in their concern for the nation.

One of the co-conspirators was instrumental in orchestrating the events that would unfold. John Wilkes Booth was convinced that the simultaneous assassination of four top officials would propel the North and the Republican Party into chaos long enough for the Confederacy to reassemble itself. Most people had no inkling of the motives that Booth brought to that fateful evening in Ford's Theater.

Much to his disappointment, the team he had recruited did not share his resolve or resourcefulness. They all failed in their roles. But Booth did not; history was forever changed with the assassination of President Abraham Lincoln.

Time had erased the commitment and concern that motivated Booth. Today, it was his responsibility to take up the cause to protect and preserve a land that he loved. John Wilkes Booth had been willing to die for this purpose.

Now he found himself in Disney World, walking along the solitary roadway, ready to make the same sacrifice as Booth. However, this time, history would be changed forever.

His smile broadened as his footsteps carried him past the concrete buildings that housed some of the most famous and beloved attractions in what many believed to be a magical world. But he was more learned than the masses. He understood that the magical exteriors were nothing but fantasy, and they only served as distraction from the grim reality that threatened them all. The façades were simply an illusion. From his vantage point, he could see what the world really looked like. Industrial, functional, unfinished, and uncaring painted a more accurate portrait of the world around them. His role was to expose fiction and reveal the facts that would help protect the nation that seemed to be slipping away.

The road curved to the left, and in the distance he could see his destination. The view of the Magic Kingdom behind the scenes, or as they had been indoctrinated to call it, *the backstage area*, was less than spectacular. Plain and ordinary, it reinforced his disdain for the glitz, glamor, and packaging that could so easily distract. And that was how the nation had been lured into this dark place in history.

The election of Tyler Pride as president had been the most shocking and divisive election in the modern history of America. A northern business mogul who had built an empire in tech companies, real-estate ventures, and reality television had used his name recognition, his branding genius, and his personal charisma to stun the entire world as he swept into the White House.

Glitz, glamor, and packaging had been used by the disruptor, along with the campaign slogan, "*It is time for some Pride in America*," to motivate and engage voters from all walks of life. Pride was the ultimate anti-politician. He had shelved political correctness in a brutal campaign season and leveled his angry attacks at the infrastructures, the institutes, and the insiders, creating a political earthquake that continued to suffer damage in the aftershocks of the election.

As he continued his walk backstage, his smile disappeared. His pace quickened as he neared the monorail shop. Thoughts of Tyler Pride clouded his thinking. He, along with others, had hatched this plan on the night Pride was elected because they knew how dangerous he really was. His ideas, his methods, and his policies were already ripping apart the very fabric of the nation. It was time for a revolution, and he had been selected as an instrumental part of it.

A cast member waved at him as he entered the barn. With a hearty greeting in return, he exchanged a good-morning wave and moved on toward his intended stop. Glancing upward, he smiled once again. Monorail Red sat on the track that would travel along the spur line, move into the Transportation and Ticket Center, and then sit on the Epcot line. It was here he would wait for the dawn about to break—and his destiny. How the coming events would unfold was really up to Tyler Pride, but as for him, his choice had been made and his decision was final.

There would be some foolish people who would dismiss the events about to be set into motion and simply label him, and the others, as assassins. But he knew differently. He had been selected for this moment in history. He quickly moved through the mental checklist of the actions about to be carried out. For a brief moment, he imagined what the look on the president's face would be. Ego and arrogance were about to come face-to-face with a harsh reality check. How President Pride would react was really a matter of his own pride.

This could be the first day of revolutionary change, or it might be a day that ended in great sacrifice. No matter the circumstances, the results would be the same. He would be remembered as a patriot who helped save America.

Climbing aboard the front cabin of the monorail train, he opened the compartment below the controls along the back wall, carefully tucking his backpack into the storage area. Taking a seat behind the driver's console, he once again tugged on the collar of his monorail cast member's uniform. Glancing out through the sleek, sloped window, he knew this would be the vehicle he would ride into his future. Not just his future, but into history itself. *History and the passing of time will revere and reveal true patriots.* That is how he wished to be remembered.

CHAPTER TWO

Into the Wilderness

"**Y**ou're riding in an American icon." David Grimsley smiled at his wife, who peered out the window absorbing the sights surrounding them. "Some call them silver bullets, but those in the community just call it living riveted."

Gail Grimsley loved to hear her husband talk like this. David spoke this way when he was most relaxed, away from the grind of his work and on vacation. Pulling their Airstream camper, he'd always give her a brief history lesson that brimmed with pride over their investment and choice of camping vehicles. She had heard him use the phrase "living riveted" on other occasions, but she always nodded as if it was the first time. The distinctive round, silver rivets that punctuated the finish of the camper was the source of the phrase.

She nodded as David continued. "They're long lasting. In fact, some of these campers last as long as forty years. This is a lifetime purchase for us. They're sturdy, durable, and lightweight. Easy to tow, better gas mileage, compact, roomy, and stylish." David pushed his thumb over his shoulder toward the Airstream they pulled behind them. "And best of all, it's made in America."

Gail shook her head and laughed. "Don't say it." She knew her husband was proud of the fact that this brand of trailer had been made in the same plant, near his hometown in Ohio, since 1952. The community had strengthened him with what many would consider staunch conservative roots. That background had gotten him very involved in the last presidential election, and now he often used the campaign slogan that had become part of the American vernacular.

"It's time to put Pride in America again!" He joined her in laughing.

The silver Airstream slowly moved along Fort Wilderness Trail, heading toward their designated camping space in the Fort Wilderness Resort at Walt Disney World. The Grimsley annual camping trip was the highlight of their year. Their trek from Ohio to Florida allowed them a full week at the resort, staying in the same camping area, and using it as their home base for a relaxing, refreshing, vacation getaway.

Fort Wilderness had been one of the first resorts to debut when Walt Disney World opened in 1971. Walt Disney himself wanted people to come and visit his new "Florida Project" and have the option of camping in anything from a sleeping bag to a luxury suite. Desiring to attract people from all walks of life, Walt understood the importance of cost and allowing everyone to experience their visit in the way they enjoyed most.

He also had a great appreciation for the natural beauty of the region and knew this would be a vacation destination many would find attractive as they were able to camp close to nature. Longtime Walt Disney World fans referred to the Disney Fort Wilderness Resort as "Old Disney." Although, like everything else, the area had been improved and changed over time, it still boasted over 750 acres of pine and cypress forests that served as the camping experience of a lifetime in the vacation capital of the world.

"What's our slot number this year?" David asked as he carefully turned the camper off of Fort Wilderness Trail onto Big Pine Drive.

Gail rechecked the map they had been given at the reception outpost. "Cypress Knee Circle—311."

The Grimsleys had stayed at the resort so many times they had established a casual relationship with some of the staff and usually booked their next stay far enough in advance that they could stay in their preferred area of the campground. Winding along Big Pine Drive, they drove past the Meadow Resort area, getting closer to where they would park and set up camp.

When David glanced in the side mirrors of the truck though, he saw a park security vehicle pull up behind them with its lights flashing. Checking the mirror on the opposite side, he pulled the camper to the edge of the lane so the security SUV could pass. Instead of passing, the vehicle pulled to a stop directly behind them.

"I wonder what this is about." David ran his hand through his hair, opened the door, and stepped into the roadway.

Doors opened on both sides of the SUV as two powerfully built men wearing security uniforms emerged from behind the tinted windows. Following her husband's lead, Gail also stepped out of their vehicle and moved toward the two men walking alongside the Airstream.

"Did I do something wrong?" David tilted his head as he moved closer to the pair.

"No, sorry to bother you." One security officer extended his hand to greet them. "Actually, we have a special guest arriving at Walt Disney World, and our security protocol has changed for the next few days."

"Very sorry about the inconvenience." The other officer's tone sounded flat.

The first spoke again. "They were supposed to do a visual inspection of your camper at registration before they cleared you to move through. They sent us to do what they forgot."

"That's different." Gail looked toward David, who nodded in agreement.

"Like I said, we have a special guest, which means we're taking some extra precautions. Sorry for the inconvenience."

"Would it be okay if we took a quick look inside the Airstream?" Security guard number two asked.

"Um, sure." David moved alongside the silver-covered camper, toward the door. "I suppose."

"Thank you. Again, we're sorry for the inconvenience." The more talkative of the security personnel waved his hand toward the door. "After you, please. This will only take a moment."

After exchanging a quick glance, David and Gail stepped inside. David turned as he entered and spoke over his shoulder to the security team. "Whoever is coming to visit must be pretty important to create all this extra effort. Who's coming, the president of the United States?"

Neither man answered. They moved to follow the Grimsleys inside their trailer.

Gail observed the men as they entered behind them. It was then she noticed something that had been bothering her since they were first stopped. She had not been able to put her finger on what was wrong, but something beyond the unusual search was not quite right. She took an extra two steps away from them, challenging the situation. "Isn't it some kind of rule that all Disney cast members have to wear a nametag while they're working?" Her eyes moved from one man to the other. "Neither of you is wearing a name badge. Why not?"

Silence. No answers were forthcoming.

Gail and David's eyes grew wide at what happened next. Gail attempted to scream as David rushed forward. It was too late.

CHAPTER THREE

Through the
Looking Glass

Dark intelligent eyes inspected the reflection in the mirror. Her toned frame filled out the jet-black suit accented by the collared, brilliant-white blouse. Using her fingers, she raked her brunette hair back and held it in place as she studied her image. Wrinkling her nose in disapproval, she let her hair fall to its shoulder length and then shook her head to add body. She continued to fuss with her hair, allowing her fingers to style it again.

Finally, Jillian Batterson smiled and turned away from the mirror. She checked her watch to see how well she was managing her time. Right on schedule. If the rest of the day went that way, she would be shocked. She ran her hands down her jacket and once again turned back to the mirror.

What am I so nervous about?

Thoughts about the upcoming events flew through her mind. The president of the United States was here. Along with the president came the massive amount of security precautions and personnel that had consumed her life over the past few days. Perhaps she was nervous about working with government officials again. Although she had never been a part of the Secret Service, for years she had been an agent for the Department of Homeland Security. Her career had been on what most considered a fast track. Promotions and added responsibility had been the norm for her in the department. Most people who knew her assumed she would rise to the top of the division if she wanted the job. She had believed that as well.

Then along came Disney. The assignment had been simple and important. The investigation of a terrorist threat at the Walt Disney World Resort sent her to Florida. Working with local law enforcement, the task was to uncover a plot to attack the resort, or so she had first believed. Instead, she uncovered a complicated and twisted plot to do something far different.

As she now understood it, Walt and Roy Disney had created a masterful plan of succession if the Disney Company ever needed to implement it. The authority and knowledge of how this was to take place was entrusted to a small handful of Disney Imagineers. Prior to arriving in Florida, she was not really sure what an Imagineer was. It was a term Walt gave to those creative people he surrounded himself with. Part imagination and part engineer. In the world of Disney, the title was revered, and the Imagineers were responsible for creating the worlds Disney fans loved so much.

Somehow, she had managed to live most of her life ignorant of all things Disney. So many of the terms used to describe the theme park were like a foreign language. Imagineering, attractions, rope drops, Fast Passes, cast members, Hidden Mickeys, Extra Hours, and more, all became barriers to her as she tried to understand the world she was forced to navigate. And like most subcultures, each term had its own acronym that made it even more difficult to translate. Yet she had managed to not only survive but thrive and help unravel the mystery of the Magic Kingdom.

What she hadn't expected was *him*, Chief Creative Architect of the Walt Disney World Company, Dr. Grayson Hawkes. Hawk was as frustrating as he was fascinating. In an intense and dangerous situation, she had worked alongside him, protected him, and he had protected her while saving the Magic Kingdom from the dangerous threat. After the investigation wrapped up, she discovered that the elaborate plan Walt Disney created had now been initiated. And the man chosen for the task of leading the company and protecting the legacy of Walt Disney was Grayson Hawkes.

Hawk had disclosed some of the details of that plan to her, and what she learned frightened her and yet captivated her at the same time. Walt Disney was so much more than just an entertainer; he was a visionary and thought leader. His dreams and the secrets he carried had the power to change the world, then and now.

Although Hawk had not told her much, he told her enough to entice her to leave Homeland Security and become head of security for the Disney Company. In a decision that stunned her family, coworkers, and friends, she accepted the Disney offer and now spent her days protecting an entire world. Most believed she simply protected the world of Disney they were all familiar with. In fact, she helped protect and preserve a world that Walt Disney had envisioned and entrusted to Grayson Hawkes.

Jillian stared at her image. Perhaps it was the president arriving at Walt Disney World and the influx of government agents that caused her unease. Maybe it was because she had been away from this level of intensity and national security for two years now. Or maybe, it was her. She had changed since she had arrived at Disney and she knew it.

Somehow, after living in this often-magical world, she feared she might have lost her edge. Was that okay? She found herself laughing more than she used to. She had friends now, people who genuinely cared about her, her life, and her feelings. There was a purpose to her life and the secrets she helped protect, even though she only knew some of them. But they were important enough to give her a purpose deeper than anything she had known before. The secrets she helped protect could have global impact.

Tilting her head, Jillian smiled at her reflection. She wondered if she was a better version of herself. She was kinder, gentler, and softer around the edges, which she liked. But did she still have "it"?

She turned away from the mirror and continued her self-reflection. Advancing toward the door of her apartment, she gathered the items methodically placed along her exit path. Phone, sunglasses, ID, weapon, and key were each picked up and tucked away as she repeated her daily routine. With a deep breath, she opened the door and stepped into the hallway.

Living in Bay Lake Towers adjacent to the Contemporary Resort was a perk of her job. She now made her home in a place most people spend their lives saving to visit for only a few days. The apartment had been remodeled according to her specifications, and it was located just down the hallway from Hawk's executive office suite. As she breezed past the suited Secret Service agent located by the elevator, she nodded, and the nod was returned. The agent stoically kept a wary eye on her as she passed.

The Secret Service had arrived the week before and launched all of the security measures necessary for the arrival of the leader of the free world. She had dealt with the intrusion, the protocols, and the details that were needed to ensure the safety of not only the president, but the first lady and their daughter as well. Although exciting, it had also been exhausting. Even before their official arrival, she awaited their departure with just as much enthusiasm.

She reached the unmarked door and paused, again thinking about how she had ended up here. It was his fault. She blamed Hawk, sometimes kiddingly she told him as much, but behind the joking, the truth was he had been able to convince her to join his team and become head of security for the company. Her day in and day out responsibilities were monumental, but the unwritten and unofficial role was to also protect and take care of Hawk.

She pushed through the doorway and strode briskly across the main floor of the offices that had been created for Hawk in Bay Lake Towers. Much like her home had been, this office was built especially for Hawk after his own arrival at Disney. Originally part of the Disney Vacation Club, one of the multi-floor suites on the penthouse level of the resort was converted for the leader of the Disney Company.

Hawk had told her the office was overkill and tried to avoid going there as often as possible. He preferred walking around the resort. But when business needed to be done, he got there.

Jillian glided through the massive downstairs portion of the office, which included a waiting room, a dining area, balcony, and a spectacular view of the Magic Kingdom. The actual office Hawk used was upstairs. That portion of the suite featured a huge conference room that had the same view of the theme park as downstairs. The waiting area featured art designs created by Disney Imagineers, some models of familiar sites within the Walt Disney World Resort, and a wall featuring some of the pictures, magazine covers, and articles written about the chief creative architect at Disney.

The cover of *Time* featured the headline "There Is a New King in the Kingdom" with a picture of Hawk standing in front of Cinderella Castle. *People* magazine highlighted a photo with the headline "When You Wish Upon a Rising Star." *Entertainment Weekly* placed Hawk in a picture next to Mickey Mouse on a cover that read "Where Did He Come From . . . And Where Will He Take Them?" *Money* magazine showed a smiling Grayson Hawkes dressed in a tuxedo with the phrase "A Hawk Takes Flight and the Mouse Soars," and *Leadership Journal* showed a split cover of Walt Disney and Grayson Hawkes with the words "Work Will Win When Wishing Won't!"

Standing at the base of the stairs, she hesitated before heading up to where she was supposed to meet him. She pressed her lips together and formed a slight grimace before exhaling slowly. Hawk was the reason she may have lost her edge. She blamed him. Not that he had done anything except be himself, but she felt too comfortable around him, too relaxed. And maybe she had grown closer to him than she had planned.

Those feelings caused her to doubt her ability to protect him and keep him safe if need be. Not that she didn't want the attachment, and it wasn't that she disliked the way she felt. It just made her task more difficult. Had she allowed life in this magical world of Disney to somehow cause her to lose touch with the real-world dangers that had threatened him in the past? Based on what she knew, they would threaten him again. If not today, someday. Her main job was to take care of him. Doubt gnawed. Was it possible she was too close to him to do her job?

Taking the first step up the flight of stairs, she concluded that yes indeed, it was his fault. As she often told him, if anything ever went wrong, the responsibility fell on the leader. So if she felt conflicted, she would simply blame him. Nodding, she decided that would work for her . . . for now. As she crested the top of the stairs, she glanced toward his massive office. Seeing it empty, she turned toward the conference room. Entering, she saw him gazing through the glass window wall with the magnificent view of the Magic Kingdom.

CHAPTER FOUR

Revolution
or Resistance

Monorail Red effortlessly glided into the Transportation and Ticket Center, and the switch operation allowed it to transfer from the Monorail Barn line to the Epcot line. Once the track had reconnected, he eased the length of the monorail into the station as a line of Secret Service agents moved into place along the edge of the loading zone. He tugged again at the collar of the high-necked uniform. The neckline was a bad design he concluded. It was cut annoyingly high, and the material made him sweat.

He punched the door-release button and heard the click of the monorail doors opening on each train car. A dark-suited Secret Service agent stepped aboard the front cabin and simply nodded as he explored the area where the driver and passengers would be seated. The driver smiled in return with confidence, attempting not to show his excitement over what was going to happen soon. He had already been through the security clearance needed to transport the president and his family. All of those details had been tediously taken care of. The agent moved relentlessly through the cabin, carefully looking over every inch of the area.

The driver stared out the slanted windows of the monorail as he heard the agent open the storage compartment below the controls on the back wall. The agent reached in and pulled out the driver's backpack. Stepping to the side of the monorail operator, he thrust it out and held it between them.

"This is yours?" the Secret Service agent asked.

"It is," the driver replied.

"Can you open it?" The agent handed the bag to him and waited. "I need to inspect its contents."

"Sure."

The driver fiddled with the zipper, taking longer to open it than he wanted. He was more nervous than he thought. As he finally unzipped the backpack, he saw another agent lean into the cabin. The agent who still watched him looked over his shoulder at the new arrival.

"Be done here in just a moment."

"Here you go." The driver held open the bag.

The agent looked inside. He reached in and moved items around, inspecting the contents. Slowly raising his head, he stared at the driver.

"Have you brought anything else with you into the cabin this morning?" the agent asked.

"No, this is it."

The Secret Service agent smiled. "Okay, then go ahead and zip it back up and stow it. You've been given the itinerary and instructions. You are not to leave this cabin until the president arrives. You are not allowed to exit the platform, go the bathroom, go get something to eat, or leave for any other reason. If you do, you will not be allowed back into the secured area. Got it?"

"Got it." The driver nodded. He had indeed been given the instructions. He knew he was in for a long wait before the president and the first family arrived. "I'm not going anywhere."

"Good." The agent stepped out of the monorail cabin and spoke into the microphone that was tucked into the wristband of his jacket. "Monorail Red is clear. Driver is clear. Cabin is clear."

The driver leaned over and spoke to the agent. "Mind if I close the cabin door? That way the air-conditioning doesn't escape. It will be more comfortable for our passengers when they arrive."

"Close it," the agent snapped without looking back.

After pulling the driver's door closed, he replaced his bag in the storage compartment. He exhaled slowly and sealed the door. After the backpack was secure, he returned to the driver's chair, leaned back his head, and closed his eyes.

It would not be much longer now. All of the planning, all of the preparation, all of the details that had to be worked out were now complete. The only thing missing was President Tyler and his family seated in the cabin with him.

Today was the day the revolution—as he preferred to think of it—or the resistance, as those who were less informed viewed it, would take a more definitive course of action. History would be made soon. He would be revered and revealed to be the patriot he was. He was convinced of it.

CHAPTER FIVE

Hail to the Chief

"It's a big day, huh?" Jillian interrupted, walking through the doorway.

Hawk was lost in thought, gazing out over the picture-postcard view of the Magic Kingdom. Her voice pierced his wandering thoughts and returned them to the present.

"It is." He turned and watched her move across the room to the pot of freshly brewed coffee on the credenza at the far side of the conference room.

She inhaled as she poured herself a cup. "This smells good."

Hawk smiled as he watched her meticulous ritual of doctoring her coffee. An exact amount of cream and sugar had to be added before she would obsessively stir the ingredients into one seriously flavored cup of java. As she mixed the hot beverage, she noticed he was watching her. He often made fun of her as she prepared her coffee because it was always the same choreographed production.

"There, now it's just right." She returned his smile as she took her first sip.

Hawk motioned for her to take a seat. "Is everything ready for the day?" He already knew the answer.

"Yes." She took another sip of coffee. "Everything on our end has been completed, and we've turned over most of the control for security in each area to the Secret Service. We really are just assisting."

"Sounds like a government takeover."

"It is." She nodded back at him. "You know the way the Feds work."

Hawk knew how federal agents worked too well. During his tenure as head of the Disney Company, he had tried to navigate federal investigators and state and local law enforcement, all trying to do their jobs and protect him, while he was trying to protect and keep safe the secrets of Walt and Roy Disney.

There was the original plan of Walt to choose his successor, the spectacles Walt had designed that allowed him to view documents with hidden images that couldn't be seen without the glasses. Walt Disney's diaries, the notebook Werner von Braun had gifted to Walt with a design for what some would see as a gift of power and others would choose to view as a weapon, and there was the painting from Walt's dear friend Norman Rockwell that helped the A.G.A.P.E. unit design and diagram. And those were just the bigger ones. The smaller ones were so numerous even he had trouble keeping them straight. It was exhausting at times. But it was a decision he had made years ago that he had never regretted.

"I know we're ready." Jillian placed her cup on the table with a soft clank. "But the real question is, are you ready?"

"Of course, I am," Hawk said. Today he wore a suit—not his normal attire. His collar was still open, and his necktie was draped loosely around his neck waiting to be tied. He grabbed both ends and began tugging and wrapping it into place.

"I'm not talking about how you're dressed." Jillian stood and moved around the table. Playfully, she slapped his hands away from the terrible half Windsor knot he had messed up. Skillfully, Jillian quickly tied the perfect knot and then briskly tightened the tie against his neck. After taking a step back to inspect her work, she paused and narrowed her eyes.

"What's going on with you?" She crossed her arms. "Ever since this presidential visit was set up, you haven't been yourself."

"What are you talking about?" He moved away from her, retrieved her half-full coffee mug, and handed it to her. "Thanks for your help with the tie."

"You're welcome." Taking another quick taste of coffee, she continued. "Don't think you can get away without a good answer. I asked you what's going on with you. You seem nervous about the president's visit. Why?"

"It's complicated," he said with a wavering smile. "Did I ever tell you that the president is an old friend of mine?"

Her eyes widened slightly as she reached over and slid out an overstuffed conference chair. She lowered herself into it and waited for him to continue.

"I'll take that as a no." He pulled out a chair and took a seat facing her.

"No, you never mentioned that you knew the president of the United States." She smiled casually as if it was a normal everyday event for people to know the president.

"Well, he wasn't the president when I met him." Hawk exhaled deeply. "I met Tyler Pride when he was just your way-above-average business mogul, and he was not involved in politics back then."

She leaned forward. "How did you meet him?"

"It was shortly after my arrival at Disney. He contacted us and wanted to bring his family to the resort on vacation. Like other VIPs, you have to make some extra accommodations. He had just completed his first season hosting his reality show, *The Gambler*, that let people see his philosophy of living—*take high risks and expect high rewards*. The show was a big hit, and his popularity went through the roof. So even back then, he drove our security folks crazy with some of the precautions we had to take."

Hawk again glanced out the window at the Magic Kingdom. "We couldn't even let him walk with his family down Main Street USA. The crowds would just press in on him. While he was here, he negotiated one of the largest deals he ever made with his tech company."

"But how did you meet him?"

"I actually showed his family around the resort." Hawk turned back to face her. "We spent a lot of time together. Then over the past few years, I've had the chance to see him on occasion." Jillian seemed to be waiting for more information. "The family would visit regularly for vacations and getaways. The Walt Disney World Resort is their favorite place in the world, or at least that's what they tell me. I've visited his home a few times, had dinner together, and periodically talked with him on the phone about various projects and deals he would tell me about."

Raising her eyebrows, she now sat back in her chair. "I am impressed, Grayson Hawkes. You really do know the president. You're buddies."

"I wouldn't say that." Hawk shrugged. "Tyler Pride is a very talented and interesting man."

"So . . ." Jillian said softly, "again I ask you, what's wrong? A friend of yours is coming to visit. You should be excited. You've been acting like there is impending doom on the horizon."

Hawk paused and lowered his head a moment before looking back at her. He measured his words carefully. "The president of the free world is coming to visit Walt Disney World. I'm just trying to accommodate all the pomp and circumstance that comes along with that."

"No, your friend is coming to visit," Jillian corrected. "He's still your friend, isn't he?"

Hawk hesitated and sighed slightly before responding. "I guess."

"What's wrong then? What happened?"

Suddenly, their conversation was interrupted by a booming voice from the doorway across the room.

"I'll tell you what happened."

Hawk and Jillian turned to the familiar voice and jumped to their feet as the president entered the room flanked by two agents who stopped at the doorway.

"Hello, Mr. President," Jillian said, looking surprised by his abrupt arrival.

Tyler Pride walked over and strongly shook her hand. After releasing his grip, he moved toward Hawk.

"Welcome, Mr. President. We're glad you're here."

"No, you're not." The president ignored Hawk's outstretched hand and embraced him warmly, patting him on the back. "It'd be easier for you if I never came here. I make your life and your theme park world very complicated. I get that."

As the embrace ended, the president motioned for everyone to sit down. Hawk was always impressed with how Tyler Pride could command respect and take over a room when he entered. It was a gift he had noticed long before Pride ever became the commander in chief. It was a skill that had served him well in business dealings and in negotiations long before his political aspirations came into play.

As they all took a seat, the president looked at Jillian. "I'll answer the question you asked when I came in."

Hawk saw Jillian blink quickly. He knew she had momentarily forgotten what they had been talking about before Pride's arrival. Being in the presence of the president had that effect on most people.

"We're still friends." The president smiled his familiar smile. "Hawk just doesn't like the way I do things."

"Respectfully, sir." Hawk cleared his throat. "I like what you do. The economy is strong. You are a strong leader and strong on defense. You have the country on solid footing globally. I have no complaints about that at all."

"Ah." The president laughed. "You should be the politician. You said you like what I do, but I said you don't like the way I do things. There's a difference."

Hawk smiled and felt a slight blush warm his cheeks. Tyler Pride was smart and had caught exactly what he said. It was another one of the president's strengths in dealing with people.

"I think I missed something," Jillian said, glancing between the two men.

"Hawk doesn't like the way I do things," the president said for the second time. "He doesn't approve of my approach and the way I say things."

Silence swam across the room for a moment, and Hawk felt a line of sweat form along his collar. Breathing deeply, he measured what he was about to say.

"I just believe, respectfully, that when you have the bully pulpit to say things—" Hawk didn't get the entire thought expressed before he was cut off.

"That I shouldn't be such a bully?" The president threw back his head and laughed.

Jillian smiled politely, as if not knowing whether what President Pride said was meant to be funny. She intently gazed at him, watching his reaction.

Hawk nodded in agreement. "Sometimes, sir, you're pretty harsh in the way you say things."

Hawk looked at the president and then at Jillian. She had momentarily frozen at their surprising conversation. He watched her slowly move her eyes from him toward the president.

"Well, maybe it sounds harsh to you." The president smiled as he spoke. "Or maybe I'm the toughest counterpuncher in the history of the presidency." The president turned toward Jillian. "Ms. Batterson, you know the way it works. If there's a fight in the schoolyard, the teacher rarely sees the first punch being thrown. It's usually the student who hits back that gets caught." He tilted his head toward Hawk and then straightened his neck as he continued to speak. "Hawk doesn't like the fact that I hit back. I hit back harder than I get hit. Most people don't expect it. They don't know how to react to it. But that is what America has needed for a long time—a fighter for a president. Someone to stand up and stand strong. So I fight every day for you." Then President Pride turned back to Hawk. "And for you. And for America."

"There are just some days I think—" Once more, the president cut off Hawk's thought.

"That you wish I would be a little bit nicer." The president continued to smile. It appeared he was enjoying the conversation. "Hey, I listened to some of your sermons back from when you were a preacher. You always said that people could change the world."

Hawk was stunned. "You went back and listened to some of my old sermons?"

Prior to his emergence at the Walt Disney Company, Hawk had been a pastor. It was in that calling that he had first met and become friends with one of Walt Disney's own Imagineers, Farren Rales. It had been Rales who selected Hawk to become the keeper of the Disney dream along with all the secrets of the Disney brothers. Hawk was caught between feeling impressed and surprised that the president had taken time to listen to the words he had said years ago.

"Of course I went back and listened. Your faith is one of the things that inspires me about you, my friend." The president rose. The agents at the door instantly moved into their assigned security positions. The president was ready to exit the room. Jillian and Hawk stood as well.

"Everybody wants to touch and change the world, Hawk. You communicated that then and you still do today. The problem is that very few people want to do the hard work to touch and change the world. It's not easy. You have to be tough—sometimes tougher than people want you to be."

Tyler Pride patted him on the back with genuine affection. The president then shook Jillian's hand. "It's nice to meet you, Jillian."

Her mouth dropped open slightly in surprise, causing Hawk to smile. He realized he had never gotten the chance to introduce her officially to the president. Now for the first time, Jillian realized the president knew who she was. Hawk was always impressed with his ability to deal with people.

"Nice to meet you, sir," she responded.

The president did not release his grip on Jillian's hand. He leaned in slightly and whispered, "Why don't you ask Hawk to tell you why he didn't take the job I offered him in my administration?"

Hawk again saw her mouth drop open. The president did have the ability to make people do that. "It's good to see you again, sir," Hawk said. "Really, it is."

Hawk noticed something on the floor next to the chair where the president had been seated. It was small and round, highlighted in red, white, and blue. He reached down to pick it up and saw immediately what it was. He flipped it in his hand. It was a poker chip, emblazoned with Tyler Pride's name and the campaign slogan "*Time for some Pride in America*." It was a giveaway for the people the president met. It played effectively off his image as a gambler and made for a nice keepsake.

"You dropped this, sir." Hawk held up the chip.

"Keep it." Tyler Pride winked and moved toward the door. "I'll see you at Epcot, right?"

"I'll be there," Hawk said.

"Good. I know Kim and Mary will be excited to see you."

As quickly as the president had entered, he was gone. An awkward silence filled the space the leader of the free world had momentarily occupied.

"Wow!" Jillian broke the silence and looked at Hawk. "You really do know the president."

"Yep." Hawk smiled and brought his gaze back to the massive window overlooking the Magic Kingdom. "I know the president."

"And he offered you a job in the administration?" Jillian reached out and grasped his upper arm, turning him toward her. "And you said no? Why?"

Hawk reflected on her question for a moment before answering. He then motioned toward the window and the spectacular view. "I suppose for the same reason that you left your role at Homeland Security. You caught a glimpse of another world that needed to be protected."

Hawk peered into her eyes. "I left my role as a pastor to come to Disney because I believed I was called to be here. I'm still called to be here, so there is no other job I would rather do or could do, no matter who offers it to me."

He knew she didn't completely understand, but it was something that could not be quickly explained. To change the subject, he picked up her coffee mug and walked over to the credenza. "Do you need another cup before we go?"

"No, I'm good." She studied him.

He assumed she was processing what he had just said. "Then let's head over to Epcot. We need to meet the president and the first family for some photo ops before he gives his big speech in front of Spaceship Earth." Hawk gestured toward the door.

The president had decided to grab some vacation time while he used Epcot as the backdrop for a major policy announcement that most believed had to do with world commerce and new American economic policies. Hawk knew that could be true, but there was always a level of surprise and unpredictability where Tyler Pride was concerned. That probably was also a part of his sense of caution about today. He didn't like the fact that one of his theme parks might be where some world-changing event might be announced, especially when he didn't have any idea what that change might be.

Jillian exited the door, and Hawk exhaled loudly. Whether he was ready or not, the day was off to a running start.

CHAPTER SIX

The Chosen

The sun sparkled off the silver panels of Spaceship Earth in the blazing brilliance of a Central Florida morning. Surrounding the iconic attraction was a frenzied bustle of activity as news organizations positioned microphones, cameras, and staked out their personal territory in the designated press area, awaiting the speech by the president.

Space had been reserved right in front of the stage, where a hand-selected crowd of supporters would hear the news of the American Commerce and Trade Initiative, or ACT as it was being referred to. Against the symbolic geosphere, President Tyler Pride would share his plan to invigorate trade agreements and manufacturing to shake up world markets and spark financial growth in American business.

Skeptics believed it was an overreach and feared what it would do to global markets. The president and his cabinet sincerely believed it was a risk worth taking because of the benefit to the national economy and the dependence much of the world had on trading with American companies. Whether or not it would be effective would be revealed in the months ahead.

David Walker finished his brief tease for the morning talk show on the Global News Network. GNN had given him the assignment of covering Tyler Pride since he had first become a candidate for president. It was the push Walker needed to establish himself as the preeminent news correspondent of the network. Once they were off the air, Walker nodded toward John Ware, his cameraman, and returned the microphone to Allie Crossman, his producer.

"I'll double-check the schedule and see if they're running behind," Allie said as she took the microphone.

"Great." David nodded as he viewed the expanding crowd gathering to hear the president. "I can't believe the White House didn't give us a preview of what to expect today."

"That's the fun of covering Tyler Pride, right?" Allie read the stream of information constantly flowing through her cell phone.

David helped John secure their equipment since they would be moving to a different setup for the president's speech.

"Yes!" Allie shouted, startling the two men. Her fist pumped the air as she looked up from the screen of her phone. "We've gotta move, boys."

"What's going on?" David halted in assisting John with the equipment, alert and ready to follow their producer.

David Walker had discovered that in covering the news, and especially this president, being fluid was essential. News cycles changed quickly, but Tyler Pride not only owned the news cycle, he had the ability to control it. The president had a combative relationship with many in the press corps. The worldview that most had held for decades was not the same worldview of Pride and his supporters. As a result, in coverage and in interactions with the administration, contentious moments were more the norm than the exception.

President Pride seemed to love that strained relationship, and Walker believed, although he had not confirmed it, that the president actually took great satisfaction in upsetting the press. Their inability to remain unbiased had resulted in an adversarial relationship with the administration and less than accurate and fair coverage of the news at times.

Walker had determined to rise above it and not get drawn into what he considered unprofessional journalism. He desired more than anything else to tell the truth and communicate the news, good or bad. He believed that fairness and integrity would always have a place and was what people desired. Most surveys agreed with that thinking, and Walker enjoyed being one of the most respected and trusted journalists in America.

"I just got a text from Juliette Keaton. We've been chosen." Allie smiled and motioned for the two men to follow her.

David knew that Juliette Keaton was chairman of the Theme Park Division for the Disney Corporation, but also had spent years as head of communications for the Walt Disney Company. She and Allie were trusted friends and worked closely with the Disney CCA, Grayson Hawkes. Hawkes and Keaton had arrived at the Disney Company at about the same time, and she was now the voice that spoke for the company when there was something vital to be communicated. But David also knew that Allie Crossman had met Juliette Keaton years before the events that brought them to Epcot today.

Moving through the crowd, as he followed Allie weaving in and out of people, he recalled that Allie had been the personal assistant to journalist Kate Young. Kate had an amazing career and was an acquaintance of his through the years. Kate's career had taken a strange turn when she arrived at Walt Disney World to do a story about Grayson Hawkes for the news show *Total Access*. She and Hawkes had become an item, a true media power couple.

It was during that time Allie had first met Juliette Keaton. Over time, Allie had continued to rise through the ranks of various news organizations to become his producer at GNN. He speculated that their sudden rush through the crowd was due to the connection between Allie and Juliette from years before.

A twinge of heaviness touched David as he once again recalled the tragic death of Kate Young. She had been murdered as she exited a monorail here at the Walt Disney World Resort. The world had lost a respected voice, an honest reporter, and a much-needed connection in the craziness of the news world today.

"Let's go." Allie beckoned from in front of them.

David and John followed and eventually broke through the crowd into an area that was protected by an army of law enforcement and Secret Service officers.

"Where are we going?" David asked for the second time, since he had not gotten an answer the first time.

Allie turned, wearing a smile. "We've been invited to stand on the platform of the monorail station as the first family arrives."

Instantly, David knew what this meant. A select number of reporters and cameras would be allowed on the platform. There would be dramatic footage of the monorail streaking along the track, emerging from behind Spaceship Earth, and the president and his family emerging from the cabin. There would be a few dignitaries there, including Dr. Grayson Hawkes, to greet them, and, of course, a few moments to perhaps ask the president some questions. David suppressed a grin because this president liked to talk and usually was great for a sound bite or two. This invitation was definitely because Allie knew Juliette Keaton.

As so often occurred in his business, who you knew and how you treated them really did count for a lot. In this case, it meant close access to the president of the United States. The trio made their way to the base of the ramp that rose toward the landing platform. After security checked their credentials, they made their way through the gauntlet of guardians and ascended the ramp to where the monorail would soon arrive.

CHAPTER SEVEN

Fire and Ice

Craig Johnson listened intently as his earpiece crackled. *Fire and Ice are on the way*. Being on the presidential detail was a dream come true for Craig. It was the role he had signed up for the day he became an agent. As a result, he saw his work as a calling, a sacred task in protecting the leader of the free world.

He knew what the message meant. "Fire" was the code name for Tyler Pride. Each president since Harry S. Truman had been given one. The use of code names was originally for security reasons. With advances in technology during the mid-twentieth century, the potential danger of spies listening in on private conversations became a real fear. Although classified or sensitive electronic communications were now encrypted, the names remained for brevity, clarity, and tradition.

Outwardly, his expression remained stoic, but inwardly, Craig could not think of a better code name for the current president than Fire. In stark contrast to the president, the first lady was code-named Ice, not because of a coldness or aloofness in personality, but because of her graceful ability to cool off and simmer down her sometimes-explosive husband. The first lady's code name sounded like an insult to some, but the agents who worked around them considered it a compliment. To be honest, the agents liked it better when Fire was with Ice, because she helped keep her husband a bit more subdued than when she was not present.

This assignment would accompany the first family on a partial vacation, but as usual, the president never really took a vacation. To the untrained or uninformed critics, anytime the president was not in Washington was somehow misconstrued as him not being on the job. Johnson knew it didn't matter where the president was or what he was doing. Whether it was dining, playing golf, or traveling on Air Force One, the president never took a day off and was always working. This current president had a stronger work ethic than any of his predecessors. He would work into the early hours of the morning, sleep briefly, and then be the first one moving in the West Wing on any given day.

For the Secret Service agents who protected him, this made scheduling more difficult. It seemed, as of late, they were always on the clock as well. Craig Johnson considered it an honor to be among the thirteen-hundred agents at work around the country, but his assignment to guard the president made him one of the elites.

Standing next to the door of Monorail Red, Johnson glanced inside at the monorail pilot seated at the controls. Protocol had mandated that he be positioned there long before the arrival of the president and that the monorail had been secured and inspected before the first family climbed on board. The assignment for this part of the trip was simple enough. The president, his wife, and his daughter had left their wing in the Bay Lake Towers, moved through the interior of the Contemporary Resort, and boarded a monorail. They would take a short ride, along with their Secret Service detail, to the Transportation and Ticket Center, where they would exit the first monorail, walk across the platform, and board the monorail with the red stripe for the next leg of their trip. Monorails were named according to the color of their stripes, so the awaiting transport was known as Monorail Red.

Craig watched as the president's monorail glided over the track curving from the Contemporary to the TTC. Again his earpiece crackled to life, with less distortion this time. *Fire and Ice arriving at TTC.* The monorail came to a halt, and the doors opened. Immediately, three agents stepped out onto the platform. Craig noticed that Jeremiah Stanley was the first one out of the monorail car. As head of the Secret Service, he did not always travel with the president. It was usually on special or extra-important events that he would be on-site with the rest of the agents. The speech the president planned on giving today must be of major importance or potential impact. Johnson continued to survey the platform for any unexpected movement or action.

Stanley motioned with his hand and said something back into the monorail car as Tyler, Kim, and Mary Pride emerged. Kim held her daughter's hand, and both followed the president as he strode confidently toward his position. As he got closer, the president spoke.

"Morning, Craig, how're you doing today?" Pride smiled.

"Very good, thank you, sir," Craig responded.

The president paused as his wife and daughter prepared to enter the front car of Monorail Red.

"Good morning, Craig. Thanks for being here with us," Kim Pride said as she moved past him and entered the cabin of the monorail.

"Yes, ma'am," the agent replied with a nod. The first lady was always very pleasant.

Mary Pride waved as she moved past. "Hi 'ya, Craig."

"Good morning, Mary." Craig Johnson watched her hop past him. She was obviously excited and anxious to start her vacation at Walt Disney World.

The president patted him on the shoulder as he moved past and stepped on board to join his wife and daughter. As the first family nestled into their seats along the arching window surrounding the front of the monorail, the doors shut automatically along the length of each monorail car. As instructed, Johnson closed the door to the driver's compartment and positioned himself beside the monorail, facing outward.

We're clear and good to go. Fire and Ice are ready to move, the voice said in his earpiece. As they had planned, he then turned and knocked on the window of the monorail and gave them a thumbs-up sign. That was the signal to go. Instantly, the monorail silently glided forward and pulled ahead of the platform along the track.

Johnson watched as the monorail moved past, and then looked back down the line where the train had rested, awaiting the arrival of the family. The platform was now lined with agents. Head Agent Stanley walked toward him.

"Good job. Everything went as planned," Jeremiah Stanley said as he moved past him.

Johnson noticed something that seemed out of place. Quickly turning, he cleared his throat to get the attention of his boss.

Stanley stopped and turned toward him. "Is there something you need, Johnson?"

"Yes, sir. I just wondered why we didn't put any agents in the monorail cabins." As soon as he asked the question, he braced himself, knowing that either he should have known the answer or that his question might be misinterpreted as questioning the strategic plan.

Jeremiah Stanley cocked his head and looked at the agents along the platform. Thoughtfully, he hesitated before speaking.

"As the strategy was designed, I'm sure the determination was made that since there was no access to the president's cabin from the other cars in the monorail, keeping them empty would be an excellent buffer and ensure security. And there is one agent riding in the empty passenger section." Stanley moved toward the exit ramp of the platform. "Let's move. We'll reinforce the agents at Spaceship Earth before the speech begins."

Johnson instantly followed. There would be a series of cars waiting for the agents at the gates, and they would move quickly along the secured roadways directly to a parking area at Epcot. The president and his family would arrive at the monorail station of the theme park. Then he would be escorted by agents from the platform to a secure area offstage and, within minutes, be introduced and give his speech in front of the Spaceship Earth attraction. Their strategy now would be to move to that secured area where they would meet the president before he stepped into public view.

As Craig Johnson descended the ramp, he glanced back to where Monorail Red had sat. Although there were no stops along the Epcot monorail line, it just seemed odd that for this short trip there was only one agent traveling with them. He wondered how he had missed that agent getting on board. Perhaps he had boarded from the opposite side of the train. He refocused his attention on the ramp and jogged toward the waiting vehicles.

CHAPTER EIGHT

The Arrival

Thick white clouds highlighted the blue Florida morning sky. David Walker noticed they looked puffy enough to allow a person to bounce from one to the other. It was the perfect setting for a day at Walt Disney World. The sun glinted off the white monorail track that looped toward them.

The monorail was scheduled to arrive momentarily from the Transportation and Ticket Center, and as most events like this one played out, everything would be well orchestrated. The president and the first family would look out of the windows and wave to the crowds below in Epcot as they rode past. The monorail would then arrive at the station, the Pride family would disembark, there would be a few photo opportunities, and if all went well, President Tyler Pride would take a few moments to answer the barrage of questions hurled by reporters.

It was often in these types of question-and-answer settings that the glib commander in chief would create what would become the biggest news of the day as he gave an unscripted, impromptu answer. Those in the president's inner circle would often cringe and spend the next two days doing damage control. However, the unpredictability of the president was one of the reasons he had been elected.

David moved into position along the front line of the secured area set aside for press viewing. There were nearly thirty hand-chosen greeters for the first family standing on the platform where the monorail would come to a stop. He recognized some of them from covering other events. He watched Allie Crossman motion to John that she would be right back. She crossed over the holding area line and greeted Juliette Keaton with a hug.

In addition to the Disney head of the theme park division, whom he had met before, David also made note that Shep Albert stood along the front lines of the select group to greet the president. Albert was in charge of a variety of special projects as David understood his role. He had become a target of an investigation a few years before in a messy situation within the Walt Disney Company that also involved Grayson Hawkes.

A terrorist attack, or so it seemed, had occurred in the Magic Kingdom and done extensive damage. Most of Tomorrowland had been rebuilt. The actual role Shep played and even the threats that had been made on Grayson Hawkes had been disclosed only in the vaguest of terms.

David smiled as he considered that, as familiar as he was with trying to discern stories from limited information, this team that surrounded Grayson Hawkes—led by Juliette Keaton—had become very good at it too. They would survive well in the Washington Beltway, he surmised with respect and satisfaction.

A car pulled up along the roadway below the monorail platform. Secret Service agents met the vehicle and waved the occupants out, clearing them to enter the area. A few of the cameras turned to film the activity, including the one that rested on John Ware's shoulder. Turning his attention to the people now moving up the multi-level ramp toward them, he recognized both individuals.

Grayson Hawkes, wearing a dark suit that seemed to highlight his white, shaggy mop of hair, made his way up the ramp. Hawk interacted with the crowd, stopping to shake a few hands and laughing with those he recognized. The chief creative architect of the Walt Disney Company was known to be a longtime friend of Tyler Pride, so it was not a surprise that he would be here to greet him. David corrected himself. Hawk in his role at Disney would be here to greet any American president, regardless of whether they were good friends or not.

David also noticed the other striking figure walking alongside Hawk. He recognized her as Jillian Batterson, the head of Disney security. With eyes covered by dark sunglasses, her expressionless demeanor made her look more like a government agent than a Disney cast member. Since this had been her background prior to working at Disney, Walker assumed she had been involved with setting up the details of this visit with the Secret Service office.

Both made their way to the top of the ramp and joined the welcoming party. David Walker liked to observe people. It was the part of his job as a reporter he really enjoyed. So he watched the interactions that took place as Hawk and Batterson made their way into position. Batterson had a quick conversation with Pat Nobles, the presidential detail chief for many of the president's trips.

He had heard it rumored that the head of the service, Jeremiah Stanley, was also on-site, although it was unusual for both Nobles and Stanley to accompany the president. Unless, of course, the announcement that would be made in just a short time was far more important than anyone had knowledge of. Walker quickly scanned the small crowd and confirmed that he did not see Stanley among the group.

Hawk stood between Juliette Keaton and Jillian Batterson as Nobles motioned for the agents on the platform to get ready. The press and greeters all turned and fell silent as they watched the glistening monorail with the red stripe slide majestically around the iconic Spaceship Earth and ease its way toward the monorail station.

The monorail slid into place and stopped. Walker moved slightly so he could see the president from a better angle. He allowed his cameraman to move forward to capture the shot as the first family emerged for their day at Disney in the Central Florida morning. Then he noticed something was wrong.

Lurching quickly between colleagues that had not yet reacted, he made his way to get a better view of the front cabin of the monorail train. The door had not yet opened, and there was a baffling flurry of activity as Secret Service agents blanketed the front of the monorail. Usually a respectful distance was honored to allow the president and his family to move and be seen. That was not the case this time. Something was very wrong.

The agents drew their weapons as one stepped to the door of the monorail cab. Walker's mind raced, trying to process the scene unfolding before him. Now from a better vantage point, he saw why the agents had reacted so quickly. There was no one in the cab, with the exception of the lone driver, seated behind the controls staring blankly through the sloped front glass. Surely, the president and the first family were seated in the regular passenger compartments and would emerge momentarily. But why this sudden manic activity?

Seeing John Ware move beside him with his camera running, David leaned in and spoke over the buzz of the crowd.

"Didn't the release say that the president and his family would be riding in the front of the vehicle?"

Ware nodded affirmatively.

"Then where are they?"

David Walker had just asked his questions when out of the corner of his vision he noticed movement. Grayson Hawkes pushed his way through the group of people that had waited with him. Jillian Batterson turned and said something to him, and he motioned her toward the monorail. Juliette Keaton also said something to Hawkes just before she lifted her cell phone to her ear, following her boss as he pushed through the crowd.

David Walker observed this blur of activity as if in slow motion. He turned back to watch as the door to the cabin of the monorail clicked open. Voices yelled, but the sounds were muddled in an uproar of reactions. The distinctive pop of a firearm evoked a scream from the crowd of bystanders. A crimson splatter of blood had struck the interior window of Monorail Red.

Had the Secret Service just shot the driver of the monorail? What had they seen that he had not been able to see? Why in the moments before it happened did the head of the Disney Company leave the platform? What did he know or what had he seen that others hadn't?

Without hesitation, David pushed his way through the stunned and panicked crowd. He found himself at the back of the platform and looked down to see Grayson Hawkes jump into the car that had brought him into the area. As the car sped away, Secret Service agents on the lower level ran to jump into their vehicle parked just out of sight. In a matter of moments, they followed the vehicle that Hawkes was driving, racing out of Epcot.

Spinning around to the monorail, Walker was shoved as people jostled past him. The Secret Service was clearing the platform. Before being forced to move away, he could see the driver of the monorail slumped over the control panel, unmoving. David realized it was the driver's blood that had spattered the interior of the window.

And he would not be moving, ever again.

CHAPTER NINE

Lockdown

Jillian stood next to Hawk and Juliette as they watched the majestic arrival of the monorail at the Epcot station. Sleek and shining, Monorail Red silently curved along the track around Spaceship Earth to reach its destination. She inhaled, momentarily held her breath, then slowly released it. The arrival of the president to the resort had made her nervous, and now the official schedule of events would commence according to their planning.

Hawk stepped forward and leaned in to get a better look as the monorail slid into the station. She wondered why he would be so anxious to see the president's arrival, since they had already had a chance to visit with the commander in chief just a short time ago. A sudden cold feeling radiated from her core as Hawk suddenly turned and shoved his way through the crowd on the platform. Unexpected urgency punctuated his every move. First he moved toward the arriving monorail. Then he backed away from it. Her senses shifted into high alert, and her years of training as a special agent jolted her into action. As the scene around her began unfolding in slow motion, she focused on Hawk.

"He's not in there," Hawk said urgently. "The first family is not in the cab of the monorail."

"Where are you going?" Jillian shouted at him.

"Find out who the monorail pilot is." Hawk motioned for her to move toward the pilot's cabin of the train. "We need to know who he is."

Jillian rushed toward the front of the monorail as the Secret Service agents surrounded the cab of Monorail Red. As she pulled up and stopped to allow the agents to move into place, she heard the voice of Juliette cut through the wall of noise as people began to panic.

"Where's the president?" Juliette shouted in Hawk's direction.

"Gone. Lock everything down," Hawk ordered as he turned away for the last time and ran down the ramp of the station platform.

Juliette lifted her cell phone and gave the word to lock down the resort. She felt her cell phone vibrate as that instruction instantly rippled through the Disney security network. Quickly she grabbed her phone and read the text message that had arrived. It was waiting for her confirmation as security chief to approve the mandate. Tapping her finger on the word CONFIRM, she understood that she had just officially created a nightmare scenario for every resort cast member. The Walt Disney World Resort was now under an official lockdown, and she had set in motion a list of security protocols that most people never realized existed.

Positioning herself behind a Secret Service agent with his weapon drawn, she watched as the door of the monorail clicked open. A man seated in the driver's command chair stared blankly through the front window of the cabin. As Pat Nobles barked out an order for the man to raise his hands where they could be seen, the driver slowly turned. He peered out the door toward the arsenal of weapons aimed in his direction. A smile crossed his face as he quickly lifted his hands, but not toward the roof in a gesture of compliance. Instead, in each hand he held a small-caliber handgun. He aimed one at his own head and with a twitch of his finger pulled the trigger. The explosive pop of the gun was instantly lost in the screams from the monorail landing platform. The driver slumped forward as his life ended. As the agents rushed into the front of the monorail, Juliette caught a glimpse of the driver's expression. He had committed suicide with the smile still on his face.

The driver's compartment flooded with Secret Service agents plunging inside. Jillian shoved her way past the human barricade that now surrounded the monorail. An agent checked for a pulse and confirmed with a shake of his head to Agent Nobles that the driver was dead. Nobles turned toward her, his prominent jaw tense, yet his voice steady and sure.

"We need to shut everything down," he stated. As if it were the easiest task in the world to complete.

"Already done, sir." Jillian stole another glance into the monorail cab as she answered.

"What do you mean, it's already done?"

"Dr. Hawkes gave the word to shut down the parks as soon as the monorail arrived." Jillian turned back to the agent. "The order was given, I confirmed it, and even as we speak, we are locking down the resort."

Nobles' eyes narrowed. Jillian could almost see his mind processing what she had said and wondering the same thing she did.

"Where is Hawkes now?" He looked around the platform trying to spot the Disney CCA.

"Gone."

"Gone, where?" Nobles' eyes locked on hers.

"That, I don't know." Jillian shrugged. "As soon as the monorail arrived, he left."

Nobles momentarily froze as if he suddenly had disconnected from the world for a moment. Jillian had seen the look before and had been guilty of doing the same thing. She realized that Nobles was connected to another conversation in his unseen earpiece. She waited, and then he returned to their conversation.

"I would like to know where he is and want to speak to him as soon as possible," Nobles said. "Do you find it odd that your boss somehow knew what was happening and made his exit just seconds before I knew about it?"

"No."

"No?" Nobles pressed.

"It's just Hawk being Hawk. He has incredible instincts when there's trouble. He has ever since I met him."

"So he knew something was wrong?"

Jillian nodded. "Apparently. And as much as it pains me to admit this, he's usually right."

Nobles turned away, instantly immersed in a flood of decision-making. During their brief conversation, the Secret Service had managed to efficiently clear all the spectators and press off of the platform and were moving them into a makeshift holding area.

She already knew how they'd work the disappearance during their next few hours. They were all witnesses to some sort of crime, an event, a happening that as of yet was undetermined. But each media group had footage of the chaos, each reporter had an angle, and each individual had a perspective on what they had seen. They were all eyewitnesses to the disappearance of the president and his family, as well as the suicide of the monorail pilot.

Jillian again moved back through the barricade of Secret Service agents and allowed her gaze to take in the scope of what was happening around her. Looking down over the railing to the entrance area of Epcot below, she spotted Juliette Keaton standing with a Secret Service agent and speaking with a few members of the press who had been on the landing platform. Shep Albert spoke on his cell phone, standing near the back of the group that had been herded into a quickly secured area. He saw her and waved. She returned his wave, and he shrugged his shoulders as if to ask what had happened. With a shake of her head and a shrug, she let him know she hadn't a clue . . . yet.

Juliette answered her cell phone, receiving the security department's confirmation and the first update of all their action plans. As soon as she had confirmed the order to shut down the resort, a number of protocols had kicked into action. Immediately, in each of the theme parks—the Magic Kingdom, Epcot, Animal Kingdom, and Hollywood Studios—all attractions, restaurants, and merchandise shopping areas were closed.

Cast members were not aware of what had taken place. Hopefully, they were doing what they had been trained to do. Jillian knew this approach would create confusion and even anger among some of the guests. After all, this was their vacation and they were being told their theme park of choice was closed. But as the company had discovered through previous experience, this was the best approach.

Since all of the attractions, restaurants, and shops were closed and locked down, there was no place for the guests to go except into the streets of the theme parks. When the shutdown command had been given, trained security and cast members had moved into predetermined positions at the rear of each area of the theme park. Cast members then joined hands and formed a human wall, and slowly, without touching any guest, began to herd the crowd toward the center of each park, and then toward the front entrance of each park.

Just as soon as the first call ended, her cell phone notified her that she had a text message. It read: CLOSING OFF EACH AREA OF THE MK NOW. The human wall of cast members had started in each area of the Magic Kingdom—Adventureland, Frontierland, Liberty Square, Fantasyland, and Tomorrowland. They now made their way toward the hub of the park in front of Cinderella Castle. They would then move down Main Street USA until they swept people through the train station and out the front gate.

Each guest would be given a complimentary ticket for a return to the theme park at another time. From there, law enforcement and security would move massive numbers of people to their next destination—either a resort hotel, or to wherever they would be staged next.

Jillian confirmed additional texts that each of the other three theme parks and each resort hotel was also in the process of being locked down. She listened as the following announcement was made over the public address system of Epcot:

Due to circumstances beyond our control, Epcot is now closed. Please follow the directions of the nearest cast member.

An army of law-enforcement personnel poured into each resort area, and there would be more to follow. As guests exited the theme parks, Juliette anticipated many would be angered by the orders that they would not be allowed to return to their vehicles.

Every form of Disney transportation had now been dispatched to pick up all guests not staying in a Disney resort to be transported to a designated holding area at ESPN Wide World of Sports. In compliance with the rules and standards needed for a presidential visit, the decision and designation of that location had been made in advance of the arrival. Protocols like this were always put into place in case of a worst-case scenario, but the majority of the time they were never implemented. Most people were blissfully unaware of the possibilities of what might happen. The massive sports entertainment complex had room for guests to be detained. Everyone's itinerary, background, and activities of the day would be checked. They'd have every right to be angry, but there was no other option.

This was officially the worst-case scenario. The unthinkable and impossible had occurred. No one was leaving Walt Disney World.

The constant pinging of texts continued as each guest resort checked in to confirm they were implementing lockdown procedures. Guests of the resort were to remain on the property of the particular resort hotel where they were currently staying. Actual guests staying at the hotels were not going to be as angry, but no one liked to be told what they could or could not do. Chaos reigned. Disney would do its best to mitigate the chaotic circumstances, but they could not make exceptions for anyone. Confirming each message electronically, she felt her heart rate slow, knowing all of their security procedures had been implemented.

"Batterson!" Agent Nobles called to her from across the platform.

Turning back from the railing that had a view of the entrance to Epcot, she now saw the first sea of guests exiting. A line of law-enforcement officers moved the crowd into lines as visitors were herded out toward the massive bus-loading area where guests would board buses to their resort of choice. Today, in this moment, each guest wearing a Magic Band was being scanned and sent to the area where they would be picked up and taken back to their hotels. Any guest that could not offer proof of being a guest on the property would be taken to an area to board a bus to the ESPN location. All things considered, as the first wave washed out of the exit, everything seemed orderly and controlled.

She strode to where Nobles waited, also watching the same migration of people.

"Update?" he asked, as soon as she was close enough for a conversation.

"All is going well. The theme parks are closed, the resort hotels locked down, and every guest who drove will eventually be taken to the ESPN location. There are a lot of people here, so it will take some time, but we can get it done. They will be herded into every space we can put them based on the theme park they were visiting." Jillian sighed. "That will be our trouble spot."

"Trouble spot?"

"Because we're detaining people. We aren't letting them go home." Jillian stated the obvious. "We need to process them as quickly as possible."

"I appreciate your commitment to customer service. But you also used to work for us." He let the statement hang in the air for a moment. She felt an unexpected rebuke in the way he said it. "We have a crisis that's more important than anyone's feelings. President Tyler Pride and his family are missing. This is a national crisis, and it happened in front of every major news outlet."

Jillian looked down at the holding area where invited guests from the platform had been gathered. She knew what Nobles said was true, but it struck her as odd that he was concerned that it happened in front of cameras and the press. That should have been the least of their worries. "As I said, all is going well. The plan is working. We are doing everything according to the procedures we agreed upon." Jillian turned away from Nobles.

"Where are you going?"

"To do my job," she tossed back over her shoulder. "I have my cell. Call me, and whatever you need I will do."

She made her way down the platform ramp. Her thoughts immediately shifted from security protocols to the immediate crisis—find and secure the safety of the president and his family—but she knew there was someone else she needed to find first. She had some of the same gnawing questions that Agent Nobles had expressed. Hawk had, indeed, noticed that something was wrong before anyone else at the monorail platform had time to react. He had been on the move before the monorail doors opened, and he'd exited the perimeter by the time the gun had been fired.

Jillian motioned for one of the security agents at the bottom of the platform to come over. She needed to borrow his vehicle. Walt Disney World was also the world of Grayson Hawkes, and the best hope of finding out what happened to the president would be allowing Hawk room to work. The knotted balls in her stomach churned as she dared to think about what might happen next.

CHAPTER TEN

The Substation

Hawk mashed the accelerator to the floor of the borrowed vehicle. The surge of power pushed him back in his seat with more force than he had thought it would. Rolling his neck and shoulders, he tried to clear his head and think through what might be happening.

The Walt Disney World monorail was a closed system. The monorail train ran on concrete, single-beam tracks that were impossible to access unless you were at a monorail station, the Monorail Shop—the Disney monorail maintenance facility located a short distance northeast of the Magic Kingdom—or a maintenance substation, and there was only one located along the Epcot line.

Swerving around slower-moving vehicles, he realized that most of the traffic in the area had been diverted because the president was traveling in the resort. The wide security net extended way beyond what most people might think reasonable, but with the president in the area, the security team and the Secret Service took extreme care and every precaution to keep him safe. Shaking his head, Hawk wondered what had gone wrong. Clearly, the president was supposed to have been on board the monorail.

As Monorail Red pulled into the station, he had seen inside the cab and instantly knew their worst nightmare had come to pass. There were no passengers in the cab. They should have been easily seen through the slanted front window. Because of his familiarity with the resort, he immediately concluded that the monorail had made an unscheduled stop along the way. He knew there was only one place to stop, and that was his destination now.

As the vehicle exited the Epcot parking lot, the loop to the left carried him along World Drive. He skillfully navigated the confusing road system on autopilot. Walt Disney World was his home, and he knew the roadways like anyone would in their own hometown. Every shortcut, side street, and pathway—marked or unmarked—he was familiar with. He had spent endless hours driving and walking through the resort at all hours of the day and night. It was his hometown, and right now something was not right in his house.

Decision made to take the most direct route, he turned on Timberline Drive. This was the roadway that served as the entrance to Disney's Wilderness Lodge, but Hawk had no intention of going to the resort entrance. Instead, he quickly turned left off the paved road and bounced into an opening behind the tree line. The dense foliage on either side offered him a secluded path.

Squinting, he looked through the windshield and saw the monorail maintenance substation a short distance ahead. The ash-gray concrete structure was nothing but a service zone for the monorail. Hawk could not remember the last time it was actually used. Although slightly visible, it was usually ignored since it was tucked away behind trees and dense foliage. More often than not, guests would never give the structure a second thought as they took in the sights or anticipated their next experience at Walt Disney World.

There was no paved roadway leading to this substation, but the ground was packed hard enough for emergency vehicles to travel along if needed. Hawk continued to search his memory. To the best of his recollection, his most recent visit here had been in the aftermath of a lightning strike along the monorail line, which had caused the monorail to lose power. Rescue crews were able to easily evacuate passengers using the set of steps leading to the landing platform of the small utility station. Lightning storms were commonplace in Florida, but a lightning strike hitting the monorail line was rare. Someone had taken some footage of the evacuation with their cell phone, and the scene was covered by some news outlets. That was the first time many people even knew there was a substation in the area.

The vehicle skidded to a stop. Hawk was out the door less than a second later. Running toward the stairs, he glanced up to the platform. Over twenty-five feet above his head was the landing. Taking three steps at a time, he bounded to the empty platform and explored it with his eyes, looking for something, anything that might give him a clue as to what had transpired here.

Surely, there had been someone from the presidential security detail positioned here. The substation was in the middle of nowhere along the monorail line, but there had to have been someone here. If so, they would have seen what had happened. Hawk moved to the edge of the platform and looked over the railing toward the densely wooded area stretching out before him. Nothing unusual could be seen to the casual eye, but this had to be the spot where the president and his family had left the monorail. His brain raced through other options, but there were none. This had to be the place.

Again, he visually scoured the platform for anything that might give him a clue to what might have happened and how. Powerful engines sounded below him, and he watched as a string of black, armored vehicles followed the same off-road path he had used to arrive at the substation. His cell phone rang. He reached into his pocket. The display read JILLIAN.

Sliding his finger across the screen, he answered. "Hello."

"Where are you?" Jillian asked, her breathing rapid.

"I'm at the Monorail Substation along the Epcot line, just off the entrance road to Wilderness Lodge." Hawk watched as Secret Service agents exited their vehicles, looking up at him.

"I'm on my way there now. Do you know what happened?"

"This is the only place anyone could have gotten off the monorail after they boarded at the Transportation and Ticket Center." The agents at the base of the stairs had drawn their weapons and pointed them at him. "Jillian?"

"Yes?"

"You better hurry over here. The Secret Service has arrived, and they're aiming their guns at me."

"Well, do what they tell you to do. Don't do anything . . ." Her voice trailed off before she finished the thought. "Like you might normally do. They will shoot you."

"Yep, they look pretty serious," Hawk replied calmly.

"Raise your hands and put your phone on the ground," one of the agents yelled at him from the base of the stairway.

Another agent moved up the stairs with his weapon aimed at Hawk. After setting his phone gently on the ground, he raised his hands. A second wave of vehicles now roared toward the substation. Everyone bounced and veered along the off-road pathway to where he now stood with hands in the air.

The agent grabbed Hawk by the shoulder and spun him around. Quickly, he was frisked and checked for a weapon. Finding nothing, the agent grabbed one of his upraised arms and with a twist pulled it behind Hawk's back. He held him securely in place as the other agent raced up the platform.

"What are you doing here, and why did you leave Epcot?" the agent asked.

"The same thing you are. I'm trying to find the president."

"How did you know something happened to the president?" The agent twisting Hawk's arm said as his grip tightened even more.

Hawk raised up on his toes in an attempt to relieve the pressure on his wrenched arm and shoulder. "Since he wasn't on the monorail when it arrived at Epcot, I knew he had to be somewhere. This is the only place the monorail could have stopped."

"And you know that how?" the other agent asked.

Hawk furrowed his brow and leveled his eyes at the agent in front of him. "How do you *not* know that?"

The agent twisting his arm shoved him forward toward the stairway. Hawk attempted to change the angle of his body to release the pressure, but the agent expertly compensated for the movement. The end result was even more painful.

"Down the stairs," the agent barked over Hawk's shoulder. "Now!"

CHAPTER ELEVEN

No Help Wanted

Secret Service Agent Craig Johnson rode in the passenger seat as the car raced toward Epcot. His conversation with the head of the Secret Service, Jeremiah Stanley, ran on an endless loop in his head. He allowed his uneasiness with the way the service had secured the monorail to consume his focus as they drove. A detached voice crackled through his thoughts into his earpiece.

An explosion of multiple voices sent a series of urgent messages. Craig Johnson listened as the conversations were cluttered with panic and confusion. The next voice was clearer and more controlled; it was a message specifically for him and his partner.

"Divert from Epcot. Fire and Ice did not arrive. Transportation and Ticket team en route to Timberline Drive."

Shaking his head, Johnson turned to the agent driving the car, who instantly executed a high-speed U-turn.

"We heard that right, didn't we?" Johnson asked the agent driving.

"Something has happened." The agent concentrated as their speeding car gobbled up chunks of road as they raced toward their new destination.

Through the window Johnson could see a caravan of Secret Service vehicles all converging into a response unit. The car that had been driving in front of theirs had gotten the same information they had been given and almost simultaneously had executed the same U-turn. To his right, a pair of black vehicles moved toward them along a side road. Obviously, they were responding as well. Retracing the roadway they had just covered, they passed other cars in various stages of reversing their direction.

The Disney sign in front of them indicated that Disney's Wilderness Lodge was off to their right. Johnson had memorized the roadway system they had to secure and knew Timberline Drive as the name of the road. The sharp turn of the car caused him to tilt to his left to compensate for their speed as the vehicle made a quick right followed by an immediate left. The second turn carried them onto a hard-pressed, off-road path along a tree-lined pathway. Looming in front of them was a concrete structure that Johnson knew was their destination.

The monorail substation was the only place the monorail could stop along the Epcot loop where passengers could disembark. In fact, they had planned on using this spot to evacuate the president and his family if there was a problem with the arrival destination at Epcot, but there had been no confirmation that the evac plan was in place. There had been no warning at all that something had happened at Epcot to cause the monorail to stop at this location.

Now the calm was broken by all the voices in his ear.

Although a number of voices spoke over one another, a few words had come through crystal clear and caused sweat to run down his back. *Shots fired. Fire is gone. Ice is gone. Clear* and *secure*. The words had managed to break through the mix of messages. The rest became meaningless static. Something had happened to the president.

He tensed as he saw the scene they rolled up on. Two agents with weapons drawn moved a man dressed in a suit down the stairs from the landing plat-form of the monorail. The car bounced to a stop, and Johnson bounded out the door with the driver, who left the engine running. After drawing his weapon, he leveled it toward the agents and the man they hustled down the stairs. He recognized Grayson Hawkes, the CCA of the Disney Company. Arriving at the bottom of the stairs, he immediately became part of the action.

"Hold him," the agent behind Hawkes said as he shoved the CCA toward Johnson.

"Right." He grasped Hawkes by the arm. "What's going on?"

"This is where we believe Fire and Ice disappeared, and for some reason, this man seemed to know that before we did." The agent pulled his cell phone out of his pocket to make a call.

"That is the question, isn't it, Dr. Hawkes?" Jeremiah Stanley said. He had arrived in the caravan of cars racing to this location, part of the rush of agents piling out of cars as quickly as they came to a stop. "Just how did you know this was the place the president and his family were ambushed?"

"It's the only place it could have happened." Hawk indignantly snatched his arm free from Johnson's grip.

Johnson decided to let him go. There were now a dozen agents on-site. Most of them had their weapons drawn. A group had ascended the substation stairs and were investigating the platform level of the station.

"That is a logical conclusion," Stanley said. "I guess what I really want to know is how did you figure it out quicker than we did?"

"I have no idea why I knew something that you should have figured out quicker than you did." Hawk's voice was tense but controlled. "But what *I* want to know is how this could have happened. You guys have turned my resort upside down and inside out with all the security protocols you put in place. But I arrived here and there was not a Secret Service agent in sight. I'm wondering how this area could have possibly been left unsecured."

Johnson listened intently. Hawkes seemed to state the same thing that he had been pondering moments earlier in the car ride to Epcot.

Just then, Jillian Batterson arrived and exited her car, sprinting to Hawkes. Johnson had met her during their briefings and install procedures prior to the president's arrival. She had been extremely helpful, very pleasant, and he found her to be very thorough, which he assumed was due to her past work with Homeland Security.

"Why are you aiming your weapons at Hawk?" Batterson asked, as she stepped next to her boss.

"Just discussing his ability to somehow know where the president and first lady may have been when they disappeared." Stanley shot a look at her, then at Hawkes.

"And I was pointing out that for some reason when I arrived here, there were no agents in sight," Hawk added.

"Dr. Hawkes was just telling me that we should have done a better job in our security." Stanley turned away from Hawk to face Batterson. "What he doesn't seem to understand is this is a matter of national security. The president is missing. I don't have time for lectures, or to listen to his opinion. I need his cooperation. I don't need him running into the middle of our investigation."

Batterson nodded in agreement. "You know you have our complete cooperation."

Hawkes stepped away from the group. "I was not telling you anything. I simply implied it. And to be clear, I did not run into the middle of anything. I was the only one here when I arrived."

"Hold it right there please, Dr. Hawkes." Johnson stepped over to block his path.

Hawkes pulled up short and turned back to where Stanley, Jillian, and a half dozen Secret Service agents stood.

"Where are you going?" Stanley asked Hawkes.

"Up to the platform to see if I can figure out what happened."

"I think we're already on that," Stanley said. "I need you to leave the area."

"You're kidding, right?" Hawkes's face reddened.

"No. Agent Johnson, I need you to remove Dr. Hawkes from this area."

Johnson motioned for Hawkes to follow him. Jillian Batterson spoke up and once again stepped toward Hawkes, before turning back toward the head of the Secret Service.

"Director Stanley, I really think Hawk can be helpful if we will let him," she offered.

"He will be most helpful if he lets us do our job." Stanley brushed past Hawkes and headed up the steps himself. "Johnson, take Dr. Hawkes and former agent Batterson back to the Bay Lake Towers. We have a nightmare on our hands here. You will all be more helpful to us there." He paused. "Johnson, come back here after you drop them off."

Hawkes shook his head. "You can't be serious."

Batterson gently placed her hand on Hawkes's forearm. "Let's go. They have work to do."

Johnson escorted the pair back to the car he had arrived in. The engine was still running, and he opened the door for them both. They slid into the back seat. He quickly moved around and took his place in the driver's seat. He was trying to find something to say that would ease the tension a bit, but he couldn't think of anything. This was the situation that they never wanted to face and had never happened before.

Johnson put the car into gear and headed back across the path toward Timberline Drive.

"So tell me, agent," Hawkes said from the backseat. "Who was supposed to be posted at the substation? And why did the Secret Service lose the president between the Transportation and Ticket Center and Epcot?"

Johnson glanced in the rearview mirror and saw Batterson lower her eyebrows, shooting Hawkes a look that he interpreted to mean *be quiet.*

"Well, who was it? What happened?" Hawkes pressed, ignoring Batterson.

"As the strategy was designed, the determination was made that since there was no access to the president's cabin from the other cars in the monorail, keeping them empty would be an excellent buffer and ensured security. We did have an agent in the passenger section." Johnson's offered answer was eerily similar to the answer he had been given earlier. It was still just as unsatisfying when he said it as when he heard it.

"That isn't what I asked." Hawkes caught his gaze in the rearview mirror and smiled. "I asked who was posted at the substation and how the president could have just disappeared."

"Hawk, the Secret Service is very thorough," Batterson said. "Something unforeseen happened. They will figure it out. But I am sure they were well prepared."

Johnson gritted his teeth. "We don't know what happened yet. But we will figure it out. We really need you to stay out of the way."

"That's what your director just said." Hawkes leaned forward. "If you can't find the president quickly, you'll need my help. Don't be afraid to ask." Hawkes locked eyes on Johnson's reflection.

Johnson looked back at the CCA again in the rearview mirror. Hawkes was not smiling. His face was tense and serious.

"What do you think you're doing?" Johnson heard Batterson whisper.

"I'm offering to help," Hawkes whispered back to her.

Johnson saw the pair lock eyes and communicate something. What the look meant he wasn't sure.

"If someone is lost in Walt Disney World and needs to be found," Hawkes said softly to Batterson, "I'm one of the best people to find them."

Jillian Batterson stared at him. "We're talking about the president of the United States."

"I don't care who we're talking about." Hawk leaned closer to her. "We have a serious situation here. I don't believe they can figure it out without us."

Johnson stiffened. "Believe me, Dr. Hawkes, the United States Secret Service is more than capable of finding the president. We won't need your help. It will be best if you just stay out of our way."

Again, Johnson and Hawkes locked eyes in the mirror. The tension in the car thickened. Silence, then Hawk responded clearly and deliberately.

"The United States Secret Service somehow managed to lose the president on a monorail that runs twenty-five feet above ground between two stations, with only one possible stop in between at a substation. Remember my offer. If you need help, all you have to do is ask."

"Stop it!" Batterson raised her finger to Hawk in an effort to silence him.

After accelerating down North World Drive, the car rapidly came to the end of the road trip. The steady blinking of a turn signal preceded the right-hand turn that carried them into the parking area next to the Contemporary Resort. Johnson pulled the vehicle to a stop in front of Bay Lake Towers. Again, he watched the pair in his rearview mirror as they scooted across the seat to get out of the car. Grayson Hawkes nodded at him, as he looked back at his reflection. Officer Johnson returned the nod and watched the two of them enter the main doors and disappear into the lobby.

CHAPTER TWELVE

On the Air

The media had been escorted to an area designated for their use in the Epcot parking lot. The Imagine lot over the years had become multi-use acreage used for special events and activities. Most often, it was used as the finishing area for the seemingly endless array of wildly popular Disney-sponsored running events. Today, it had been chosen as the best broadcast zone for media outlets covering the presidential visit.

Each network had been given a specific area, which they had then set up with whatever infrastructure they deemed necessary based upon the amount of time and the level of coverage they chose to distribute to their audience.

The Global News Network was nestled into a slot between two mainstream news media outlets. GNN had chosen to simply use the space for remotes and cutaways from their round-the-clock news coverage. Originally, they had planned to use it once during each of their news shows to update whatever President Pride was going to say in his speech. All of those plans had abruptly changed.

Immediately after the arrival of the monorail, there had been moments of confusion and chaos that erupted on the monorail platform. Quickly, the platform had been cleared and the GNN team had been escorted back to this area. The advantage they had in their initial reporting was they had been allowed special access to the monorail platform to cover the president's arrival. No news agency or journalist ever could have predicted what had taken place afterward.

"David, we'll be going live in just a few minutes," Allie Crossman said as she watched John Ware check their satellite link to make sure it was operating properly.

The steady flow of reporters and news teams arriving all around them was hard to ignore, as they prepared to announce to the rest of the world that there was a crisis of global importance at Epcot in the Walt Disney World Resort. Some of the reporters from other news groups stood just beyond the barrier of the GNN setup, hoping to hear what David knew.

No one but GNN had a complete picture of what had actually happened on the monorail platform. The others were set up in front of Spaceship Earth, waiting for President Pride to confidently stride across the platform and step to the lectern to speak.

There had been a manic race to get to their broadcast locations when they heard the sudden announcement that Epcot had been closed. Some had received text messages alerting them to a breaking news story at the monorail station, but because they were packed into tight, specific, secured areas, they were isolated from getting a good sense of what had happened.

The Secret Service and the Walt Disney World Company were silent, offering no information. So, much more than any news organization would like to admit, they were forced to gather information from a rival news agency and then repackage it, using their own correspondents, to make it their own.

David Walker realized that not only was he about to broadcast news, but he had been in the middle of the breaking story.

"We're set, Allie." John Ware hoisted the camera to his shoulder and focused in on David's face.

"Great, thanks." Allie turned back to David. "Are you okay? Had time to gather your thoughts?"

"Yep, I think so." David smiled and slowly exhaled. This was a habit that he usually used before he went on the air live. He had started the practice while he was still in journalism school, and over the years, he had never changed his routine.

"You already know we're one of the few agencies who have a clue what has really happened. After you give your report, then everyone else will be catching up." Allie frowned. "While that would normally be exciting, I have to admit, I'm worried that we're in the middle of something that might turn out even worse than it is now."

"Hey, that's our job, right?" David smiled, trying to reassure her. He shared her sense of dread.

"So did you see what happened to the driver?" Allie softly asked David.

"I didn't have a clear line of sight. I saw the aftermath, the blood, but I can't be certain about what exactly happened." He thoughtfully lowered his head for a moment. "I'm not sure if the Secret Service agents fired first, or the driver committed suicide. However, the driver of the monorail is very much deceased."

"But, of course, we have no official statements to share yet," Allie reminded him.

David looked over his shoulder at the massive sphere of Spaceship Earth. This day had certainly not turned out like they had expected this morning. He wondered how much to share and speculate as he reported. All of those thoughts evaporated into the morning sunshine as Allie began her countdown.

"And we're going live in 5 . . . 4 . . . 3 . . . 2 . . . 1 . . ." She pointed to David.

"This is David Walker, reporting to you from Epcot in the Walt Disney World Resort." Solemn and professional, he spoke into the unblinking lens of the camera. He was framed against the bright Florida morning with Spaceship Earth and the monorail track serving as the background for his report.

"Just a few moments ago, what was supposed to be a highly anticipated announcement in a speech from President Tyler Pride took an unexpected and shocking turn. The monorail in which President Pride, First Lady Kim Pride, and their daughter, Mary, were riding arrived here at Epcot at the monorail station in the distance behind me. As the monorail pulled into the station, it was immediately clear that something was not right.

"As the monorail slowed and stopped, it was rushed by Secret Service agents, who discovered that the first family was not on board. As yet, we have no explanation about *why* they were not on the monorail, but in a tragic turn of events, a weapon was discharged, and the driver of the monorail sustained a gunshot wound.

"The Secret Service, local law-enforcement agencies, and Disney security forces have locked down the area, and we were escorted back to this parking lot, which has been set aside for the media. Epcot resort was immediately shut down. I was on the platform along with my camera operator and producer, and we witnessed the chaotic moments as they unfolded. We had a front-row view of what is clearly a confusing and baffling situation."

David now paused and instantly heard a question asked from an unseen voice that he recognized. It was from one of the hosts of the morning show in New York. GNN had him on split screen with the morning crew to now interview their man on the scene. It was the way he started most mornings. Even as the question was being asked, he could see Allie Crossman shaking her head no in answer.

The host, Harrison Banks, wanted them to show the footage Ware had captured of the monorail and the moments that followed its arrival on the platform. That footage had been requested and given to the Secret Service for their immediate review and investigation. It would be released later, and when it was, it would be aired. But for now, it was considered evidence, and David Walker was a man who took his responsibility seriously. As badly as he wanted to run the footage, he was also willing to comply and help in law-enforcement situations. It was that integrity he brought to his role as a journalist that had garnered him so much respect.

"You reported that the first family was not on board the monorail," Harrison said from New York. "Is it possible they missed their ride to Epcot?"

"That was my initial thought," David said. "When I saw the monorail come into the station without them on board, I first thought they were sending over some agents and that the plans had changed. Maybe another monorail would follow with the president and his family." He looked squarely toward the camera lens. "But the sudden activity as the Secret Service pushed past us and began to lock down the platform led me to realize they had also expected the president to be riding in the front cabin of the monorail like the rest of us."

"So, where are they?" the female anchor from New York, Vickie Wallace, asked.

"That is the question." David pursed his lips. "We just don't know at this time. The Secret Service has yet to give us any additional information. What we do know is that the president and first family were not on board."

"The gunshot that you heard. Did the Secret Service open fire on the monorail driver?" Harrison asked.

"That also is unclear. There was mass confusion in those first few moments. We have some footage that we have not had the chance to review, and we have not been cleared to air it as of yet. The Secret Service is reviewing it, and we will get it to you as soon as we can."

"Is there somewhere the first family might have gotten off the monorail?" Vickie asked him from New York.

"I'm not familiar with the layout of the monorail system. That is a question we are waiting to get the answer to. We believe they boarded the monorail, but even that information is a bit sketchy at this point because, obviously, they were not on the monorail when it arrived at Epcot."

Unknown and unseen by David Walker, GNN had put up a drawing of the monorail system they had managed to find on an online source. The indication was that the express line had no stations or places to stop along the way. As David filled the other half of the split screen, he continued.

"The situation here is fluid at the moment, and we've had no official statements from the Secret Service. Most of the news agencies were waiting for the president's speech at Spaceship Earth, which is the large, metallic structure behind me that resembles a massive golf ball."

"So in essence, David, what you're reporting is that our president is missing, along with his family, at Walt Disney World," Harrison said.

"That is accurate in that to our knowledge, they are missing." Walker tried to state the facts as carefully as he could and still offer some information to their viewers. "The fact is, the media has not been told where the president and his family are; why they were not on the monorail; and why shots were fired shortly after the monorail arrived. As you can imagine, there is a sense of urgency and heightened security measures here, which would lead us to conclude that something has gone unexpectedly and horribly wrong and that it involves the president of the United States in some way."

David heard distortion in his earpiece, and he could not tell if there was some sort of interference or if the anchors and producers might be talking over one another. He had no idea whether they had asked a question or not, so he continued with his report.

"It is the unknown that has created this scenario. By all appearances we have a crisis that involves the president and his family, but I don't want to incorrectly speculate on anything beyond that at this point. There is a lot more we want to share with you, and we are trying to get the information as we speak."

"Thanks, David; we'll get right back to you," Harrison Banks said from the anchor desk.

David waited for a moment, knowing it would take a second for them to break the live feed. When they did, he moved toward Ware, who nodded his head, indicating their report had gone out. Other reporters were calling out to him, trying to get his attention. He waved them off for right now. He also watched reporters from other news agencies broadcast their reports, offering the skimpy information he had just shared. They were reporting based on what he had said and then adding their own spin and commentary. But he and GNN had broken the story to the world. The president was missing, at least as far as they knew, and as of yet, there was little information to share.

CHAPTER THIRTEEN

A Conspiracy

Hawk could feel the stiffness in his shoulders and the muscles in his back stretched taut as he gazed out over the Magic Kingdom. The sun shone brilliantly, illuminating one of the most unusual sights ever in the Walt Disney World Resort. The theme park was nearly deserted. The shutdown of all theme parks and lockdown of the resorts was still in full implementation, but the Magic Kingdom had managed to empty out faster than the other parks on property.

Disney World had only closed a few times since it first opened in 1971. Hurricane Floyd closed the park in 1999. The terrorist attacks of 9/11 in 2001 closed the park, as well as a 2002 power failure. Hurricane Frances, and Hurricane Jeanne managed to shut down the parks in 2004. Hurricane Matthew blew threw in 2016, and Hurricane Irma arrived in 2017.

Hurricane Ginger had been the most memorable for Hawk. His eyes inadvertently traced the monorail track, as he remembered facing that storm on the top of a monorail. He would much rather face a hurricane than deal with the current storm raging over the resort.

Confirmation had just come in; all of the theme parks had been evacuated. The few who remained inside were cast members following through on the security procedures to lock it all down. When the Magic Kingdom closed without warning on 9/11, it took less than thirty minutes to evacuate and close the parks. The evacuation today had taken fifteen minutes longer.

Turning from the glass wall in the conference room toward the voice behind him, he watched Jillian Batterson enter, talking on her cell phone. She ended the call, touched the tips of her finger to her temples, and closed her eyes tightly. Momentarily, she reopened them and locked on his.

"It's chaos out there." Jillian clutched her phone and read a text message that had just come in. "Organized chaos, but still chaos."

"I didn't know you could organize chaos," Hawk said softly.

"We have guests still being bused over to ESPN, and the resorts and parks are all locked down. Our leads have their managers putting plans into place so we can keep folks occupied at the resorts like we would during a storm scenario. The Secret Service is working with the sheriff's department to screen people and keep them occupied at the sports complex. And, of course, everyone wants to know what's going on." She took a deep breath and exhaled loudly.

"You're doing great."

"And how are you?" She ignored yet another text message that pinged her phone to focus on Hawk.

"Worried." He turned back toward the window. "The president and his family have gone missing. But we spent weeks meeting the security standards as instructed. And still they disappeared on the Epcot monorail line in the one place that for some reason was left unsecured."

"What are you thinking?" Jillian sat her phone on the conference room table and pushed it slightly away from her. It was a symbolic gesture that Hawk appreciated. It was as much of her full attention as she could offer him right now.

"I'm wondering how this happened." Hawk stared at her. "How did they miss covering the monorail substation?"

Silence followed as he watched Jillian's fingers tap the tabletop. It was a habit when she was thinking deeply. Hawk had told her she was creating a rhythm track to make her mind work better. After a few moments, she stopped and rubbed her finger lightly over her chin.

"It was a mistake." She reached back across the table to reconnect with her phone, which had pinged twice in those few short moments she had ignored it. "The Secret Service blew it and messed up. It was a mistake—a big mistake."

"Maybe." Hawk leaned forward and placed his hands on the table. He had already come to that conclusion but found it unsatisfying. "They may have made a mistake and left an area uncovered. But what are the chances someone knew where that one exposed place was, so they could stop the monorail and kidnap the president and his family?"

"You don't know that's what happened."

"No, but it makes sense. If the first family got on the monorail at the Transportation and Ticket Center but were not on it when it arrived at Epcot, there is only one place they could have gotten off." Hawk once again stood to his full height. "And I don't think they would have decided to stop there on their own. Why weren't Secret Service agents stationed there *and* on the monorail?"

"We sure can't ask the driver, because he's dead." Jillian eyed him carefully.

"So, where is the president and his family, and who planned their disappearance?" Hawk asked, knowing she was beginning to ask the same questions he had been thinking about.

Their conversation was interrupted by a knock on the door. It cracked open, and they saw Shep peeking in. Hawk nodded that it was okay to enter, but Shep only pushed the door open a little wider and stayed outside the room. He used his body to block somebody behind him.

"Hawk, Jillian, I brought some folks over that want to talk to you." Shep cut his eyes to the side to indicate they were behind him listening. "I hope it's all right. I think it's important you talk to them."

"Send them in." Jillian turned her chair to await who was coming in.

As Shep stepped back, motioning them to come through, Hawk instantly recognized the pair that entered. Samuel "Sam" Reno, President Tyler Pride's chief of staff, and Dana Brown, the president's press secretary, stepped inside. Hawk stood as they entered and motioned for them to take a seat at the table. They nodded and sat down heavily in the chairs. He noted the stress in the lines of their faces.

"Thanks for seeing us," Sam Reno said.

"Of course." Hawk moved around the table and sat next to Jillian. "What's the latest news on the president?"

Dana looked back toward the door and Shep closed it, leaving the four to their privacy. She waited for the door to click shut before she spoke.

"There is no news." Dana Brown clutched her gold cross necklace. "The president, first lady, and their daughter are still missing."

Reno clasped his hands together and allowed his shoulders to slump slightly. "We wanted to speak to you, but we only have a few minutes."

Hawk had never met either of them, although he had seen them so often on television, he felt as if he knew them personally. Both had assumed their very public positions of service when Tyler Pride was elected president. Between the two of them, they had become the most visible and staunch communicators and defenders of the Pride presidency.

"Dr. Hawkes, you're a friend of the president," Reno began. "He speaks very highly of you."

"He also was extremely disappointed when you didn't accept a position with the administration," Dana added.

Hawk nodded. "I was honored to be asked."

"As were we," Reno continued. "Tyler Pride was elected in an era of deep division in our nation. People have become polarized through the years during previous administrations."

Dana added to the description. "But the norm today is to choose up sides based on the issue of your choice."

"I'm familiar with what has gone on. There's no need to replay the election cycle for me." Hawk waved his hand. "I didn't accept a job in the administration because I love what I'm doing here at Disney. I also didn't want to be a constant irritant to President Pride, knowing I wasn't always going to agree with his style or his policies."

"We're not telling you this to replay the election," Reno stated. "We are telling you this because it's important, and we don't have much time."

"You've said that twice," Hawk noted.

"What?" Reno paused.

"You said you only had a few minutes, and then you said you don't have much time," Hawk reminded them. "What is this about?"

"Please, be patient," Dana asked of him.

Hawk looked from the pair toward Jillian, who raised an eyebrow. She was as confused as he was about the point of the conversation.

"Tyler Pride, as you know, is not your typical, politically correct candidate or politician. He blew into Washington and pretty much accused the career politicians of being parasites and challenging them on the way they had been doing business through the years." Reno smiled. "As a result, the political establishment doesn't like him. Some tolerate him, but they don't like him. He's a direct threat to the corrupt insiders who have captured and control our government."

Hawk leaned forward. "Captured and control?"

"Yes," Dana injected as she glanced toward the doorway. "And President Pride has not been afraid to take on the establishment. He's also taken on the media. He's been characterized as a fascist, a racist, and every statement is scrutinized and twisted. The rule of law has become irrelevant for many in Washington. And politically motivated creators of fiction have shaped the truth for many people."

"Our nation is divided," Reno said. "Pride was elected because Americans were sick and tired of politics as is. They wanted a two-fisted, common-sense communicator, who was not afraid of a fight and wasn't ashamed to be called and labeled a proud American. They also liked the fact that he was willing to take risks—high risks. It's the gambler persona he carries. He meant it when he said it was time to '*Put Pride in America*.'"

Hawk smiled. "It did make for a great campaign slogan."

"But that's just it," Dana said, lifting her chin sharply for emphasis. "It isn't the usual rhetoric. President Pride means every word, and he has been like a wrecking ball inside the Washington establishment. But he's threatened leadership at the highest levels because he is not afraid to call them out and accept their pitiful struggle to hold on to power. The appointees of some of the highest organizations in government oppose and even conspire against him."

"Conspire against him?" Jillian said. "How and who?"

"That's just it." Reno looked at her. "You of all people understand how these governmental agencies work. There's the rank-and-file teams who are real patriots, but there is also a leadership network that has risen to power and might have other agendas. Not all, of course. For the most part, the people at those levels are excellent at their jobs. But there are some who love the power and their positions more than they love the people of America."

"That's a pretty serious accusation." Hawk slowly asked the next question. "Who are we talking about?"

"Name it," Dana said. "FBI, CIA, NSA, judiciary, opposing political parties, news media organizations, and Secret Service. Basically, any organization that doesn't like a leader messing up the status quo."

"The president is carefully navigating and leading a divided America. In some ways, we're at the crossroads. Worldviews are in conflict, and he's standing in the gap, protecting the freedom for all of those worldviews to have a real voice while protecting American values and the Constitution."

"Wait, wait . . ." Hawk stopped them. "Go back. You said the FBI, CIA, Secret Service, and others are conspiring against the president. To accomplish what?"

"To remove him from power," Reno said. "And to do so in any way possible."

The words hung in the air for a moment. Hawk again glanced at Jillian, who leaned back in her chair seeming to process the information they had just been given.

"And now Tyler Pride and his family are missing." Dana lowered her voice. "In your resort. And we don't believe in logical and easy explanations."

"This is an inside job, Dr. Hawkes," Reno said.

"You know this sounds crazy." Hawk looked from one to the other. "There is a crisis happening because the president and the first family are missing, but you're suggesting there's a conspiracy within the government that could be behind this."

"It may sound crazy, but you already know better," Reno challenged Hawk. "You have already figured out that there's something suspicious about how the president disappeared. That's why you were at the monorail substation before the Secret Service could get there. And you also know that sometimes the things people dismiss because they sound crazy might just be the first steps toward finding the answers you're looking for."

Hawk leaned closer. "Why are you telling us this?"

Dana answered quietly. "We need your help to find them."

Hawk shook his head. "Why would I be better at this than the feds?"

"This is your world, your kingdom, your playground," Reno said. "The one that was too important for you to leave and move to Washington. You know it better than anyone else, and you know the president."

Noisy voices came from the other side of the door. It suddenly burst open. Pat Nobles, the Secret Service detail chief, strode into the room. He was trailed by three suited agents.

Nobles looked around the conference room table. "Is this a meeting I wasn't dialed in on?"

"No, not at all." Reno pushed back from the table and stood. "Just leaving now. We're trying to figure out how to best help you find the first family and how to help Dr. Hawkes keep his resort intact. If you haven't noticed, we're surrounded by thousands of guests and an army of media members."

"Is there anything we need to make a statement about yet?" Dana asked the detail chief.

"Of course not, not yet," Nobles said. "But we do want information about the monorail driver. Perhaps you can help me with that, Agent Batterson."

Jillian stepped over to him and checked her phone for new messages as she did. "Working on it. I should know who was driving the monorail any minute now."

"As soon as you have it, I need it." Nobles said.

"You'll have it."

"Thank you." Nobles moved toward the door. The Secret Service had an office set up on one of the floors they had taken over for the presidential visit. Hawk assumed it had very quickly become a command center. "Mr. Reno, you and I need to have a chat if you wouldn't mind."

"Not at all." Reno followed him toward the door. "I want a status update on what we're doing to find the Prides."

Both moved out of the doorway quickly and disappeared into the hallway and down the stairs. The three remained silent until the office space surrounding them grew quiet. Hawk turned back to Dana Brown, who seemed to have more to say. Before he could speak, she reengaged him in sharing information.

"I know you don't believe us." Dana pleaded with her eyes. "It sounds far-fetched when we suggest it. But ever since President Pride was elected, there have been so many within the government who are not happy about the results. He is a threat to their predictable power structures. Their dislike and distrust of him runs deep, and he is very aware of people working to undermine what he is trying to do."

"So, what is their plan?" Hawk asked. "The president and his family are missing. Are they going to be killed? Ransomed? What's the end game?" He shook his head. "Like I said before, it sounds crazy."

"I know it does. But think about this." Dana cleared her throat. "There are over thirteen hundred agents in the Secret Service. This includes administrative personnel, snipers, and guards. The White House and Washington, DC are their home field. When we travel, it gets complicated, and things are much more fluid. Outside of DC, we don't have home-field advantage. When we go anywhere, the eyes of the world are on the president, but the eyes of the Secret Service are always on the crowd and the surroundings." She stood, apparently to emphasize her next statement. "The president is gone. His family is gone. He can't just disappear without a trace, because he's the most watched man on the planet. He has to be somewhere. He can't just disappear. It's not possible. Unless someone in or around the government wants him to disappear."

Jillian had answered her phone and spoke softly to someone as soon as Nobles and Reno had left the conference room. Punching the screen and ending the call, she cut off the pair talking.

"We've got him. Or we've got the name of the driver." Jillian smiled.

"Great." Hawk moved immediately to the door. "Do something for me."

"What?" Jillian said.

"Send me the name before you send it to Nobles and the Secret Service." Hawk glanced back at Dana, who smiled at hearing this.

"I can't do that," Jillian said. "They are running an investigation, and we're all a part of it."

"I know that. I didn't say *don't* send it to them. I said send me the information first. Give me a head start before you give it to them."

Jillian's face grew serious. "Why? What are you going to do?"

"Nothing, I just want a head start." Hawk tried to reassure her with a smile.

Jillian rocked on her heels and studied the floor for a moment. Finally, she raised her head, tightened her lips, and nodded at him. "Five minutes. You better know what you're doing."

"You know better than that." Hawk laughed and stepped into the hallway. "I'll just make it up as I go."

As he moved to the head of the stairs to exit, he overheard Jillian speaking to Dana.

"That's what he always does and what I'm most afraid of."

CHAPTER FOURTEEN

Finding the Driver

"**I**'ll just make it up as I go." Jillian heard Hawk's words as he moved out of the conference room and descended the stairway.

Turning, she saw Dana rub her hand across her chin, her eyes registering her baffled thoughts as she watched him leave.

"That's what he always does," Jillian said with reassurance. Then thought better of it. "And what I'm most afraid of."

She scanned the information on her cell phone; the name of the monorail driver was Edward Fenn. As she scrolled quickly down the screen, she read his employment record. At first glance, his file was fairly unimpressive and clean of any items noted by supervisors where he might have been written up for some minor employment infraction. As she continued her quick read, she also made note of one item that stood out. It had actually been the one she was looking for. Fenn had a locker in a cast-member room.

"Hmm," she said aloud.

"Find something interesting?" Dana asked.

Jillian raised her head and realized she had gotten momentarily lost in reading the information on her screen.

"Yes, maybe." She held her finger on the information on the screen, waited for the copy option to be displayed, copied what she was looking at, and then forwarded it to Hawk's cell phone. It was against her better judgment, but sometimes her better judgment and her instincts were known to battle one another. This was one of those times when her instincts might actually help Hawk plan his next move.

"Can you share what you found?" Dana again interrupted her thoughts.

"Yes." Jillian walked over to the massive window and watched as Hawk exited the building and hurried across the parking lot. She knew where he was headed. They had taken this walk together more times than she could remember. Leaving the Bay Lake Towers, they would walk across the red-brick sidewalk, cross the street, and then move directly to the gates of the Magic Kingdom resort. The walk was less than ten minutes when you strolled leisurely. Hawk wasn't running, but he walked faster than normal. She realized he could make it to the gates of the Magic Kingdom in less than the usual ten minutes; he would cut the time in half. That was the five-minute head start he had asked her for.

"The dream job of any Disney employee is to become a monorail pilot. It's almost an iconic position." Jillian continued to watch Hawk disappear from view below. "The Disney World Transportation team runs with the philosophy that getting there is part of the fun. Disney World Transportation cast members are often the first representatives of the resort guests encounter."

Dana smiled. "It must take a special person to make a great first impression."

"It does." Jillian ran a hand through her hair as she turned back from the windowed wall toward Dana. "To get the job of monorail pilot you have to do more than just say it's your dream job. You have to convince someone in the interview process why you would be good at it. You have to have a compelling reason you think the job is a good fit for you." She paused and looked back out the window, confirming that she could no longer see Hawk and that he had not been followed or created any unusual attention as he left Bay Lake Towers.

"You have to be a bit fearless. A monorail is over 200 feet long and carries 360 guests at a time. The lives of those guests are in your hands. That kind of responsibility is not for everyone. Your driving record has to be clean. The hours are incredibly odd and long. Ultimately, you have to work at a high-performance level." Jillian paused. "So, the man that was driving Monorail Red this morning has been working with the company for over five years, has a clean and unimpressive record, but nothing glaringly wrong or that would draw attention to himself."

"And he was screened before he was selected?" Dana asked.

"Yes." Jillian softened her voice. "His name was screened by everyone involved."

"Who is it?"

"His name is Edward Fenn."

"So we need to dig into his background and see what might have been missed."

"Of course." Jillian looked down at the screen of her phone. "But there is one thing that is a bit odd. It's a little thing and probably means nothing, but it might be something." She wrinkled her nose as she thought. "Edward Fenn is a monorail pilot. His locker room and break room are located at our transportation barn; it's where we park trains and monorails. Yet, according to his file, for some reason he has a locker in a cast-changing area underneath the Magic Kingdom."

"And that is odd because . . .?" Dana now rose to her feet.

"It's odd because it's not normal. There's no reason for him to have a locker there."

"And where is Dr. Hawkes headed now?"

"I'm not sure. If I were to guess, Hawk is off to check out the locker."

"So he's going to help us find the president?"

"Of course he is." Jillian smiled. "We will all do our best to help find the president. And now, I need to forward this information to Detail Chief Nobles and escort him to the locker room."

"But that's where you said Dr. Hawkes was going," Dana said with a distressed expression.

"Yes, but I also told the Secret Service I would give them the information." Jillian lowered her voice. "Don't you want me to give them the information?"

Dana hesitated. "Yes, I suppose so. But as we told you, this power struggle has some deep tentacles. I don't trust many of those who surround the president these days."

Jillian considered her words. "I think we have to trust the Secret Service. As a matter of fact, I'm obligated to give them the information. It's the right thing to do and the only thing to do."

"Yes, I suppose it is." Dana nodded in agreement. Then she hung her head.

"Look, I gave Hawk his head start." Jillian inhaled deeply. "If what you suspect and fear is true, if there is some conspiracy at work here, Hawk doesn't let things like that get in his way."

"What do you mean?"

"It's complicated." Jillian raised an eyebrow and exhaled as she sent the information to Nobles with a note to meet in the lobby. "Hawk has an interesting history. But you were correct, this is his world. He is the best person alive to navigate it, and if there is something or someone lost in Walt Disney World, there is only one person alive who you want looking for whatever or whoever it is—Grayson Hawkes."

CHAPTER FIFTEEN

The Underground City

Walt Disney was taking a walk through Disneyland in California when he spotted a sight he couldn't forget or ignore. A cowboy moseyed through Tomorrowland on his way to work in Frontierland. There weren't any other options for this cast member to get to his post, but the sight jarred Walt. He knew that a cowboy didn't belong in his world of the future, and more importantly, he knew that for his guests, the illusion he had worked so hard to create was shattered. It was at this moment the need for an alternative was born, and the original idea for the Utilidor was created.

In the very early planning stages of The Florida Project, it was determined that the Utilidor, which meshes together the idea of utility corridors into one descriptive word, was going to be an essential element in fixing the Disneyland problem in the Florida theme park. The design would eventually be called Walt Disney World and include an incredibly complex, underground tunnel system for cast members and maintenance personnel to travel beneath the park unbeknownst to guests.

When the Magic Kingdom was under construction, Imagineers drained Bay Lake (a natural lake that existed on the property) and dug out the man-made Seven Seas Lagoon that wows guests in front of the Kingdom. An enormous infrastructure was built that contained walls reaching fifteen feet high and formed a massive structure that was destined to be buried. All the silt and debris from Bay Lake and the material from the lagoon were used to cover the structure. They used more than seven-million cubic yards of earth in the process. Once the hallways were covered, the Magic Kingdom was constructed on top of the structure beneath. The tunnel infrastructure was nearly nine acres large, with

392,000 square feet of space. Beneath the Magic Kingdom, an underground city had been formed.

This underground city was about to have a visitor, as Hawk made his way through the Main Street Station and glanced toward his apartment on the corner of Main Street USA. He had lived above the Main Street Fire Station in a specially designed living space since he assumed his role with the Disney Company. Many described it as "the ultimate perk." Although his office in Bay Lake Towers also contained a large living space, he liked the smaller apartment that allowed him to look out his window onto Main Street USA. As he entered the security checkpoint, it was assumed that was his destination. It was not.

After bounding up the steps to the Town Square Theatre, Hawk pressed against the doors to enter the lobby area. Quickly stepping through the lobby, he moved into Tony's Town Square Restaurant and headed toward the kitchen. The isolated eatery echoed with each footstep as he exited the dining area and passed through the kitchen doors. His destination was the stairway behind the kitchen that would allow him to descend into the Utilidor tunnel system. The ash-gray walls of the tunnels were something he had gotten used to over time. The bright and vibrant colors that brought so much life to the Magic Kingdom above were lost in the very industrial and functional infrastructure below.

Following the hallway in front of him, he took a right at the corner and continued forward. On his left, he passed the Main Street Breakroom, which had obviously been evacuated quickly in the aftermath of the disappearance. The television was still playing, there were half-empty paper cups on side tables, as well as the remnants of someone's breakfast.

Just beyond the entrance to the restrooms, the hallway intersected a large branch that moved off to his right. Hawk knew it would carry him below Tomorrowland, but there was a more direct tunnel to get him where he was headed. Main Street Base and the Labor Central office were on his left as he ran out of hallway and cut over to the tunnel next to him. He looked for the next intersection of the underground system. Quickly, he arrived and stood at the point where he once again had to choose a direction. The tunnel to his right would run directly under Main Street USA, his destination in the bowels of Disney World. He had used it many times before, and he hoped it would give him a few extra minutes, which he was convinced he needed.

The text he had gotten from Jillian gave him the name of the monorail driver, Edward Fenn. The note she included suggested there was nothing unusual about his employment record on the surface. Hawk smiled, as he was convinced that for Jillian to have made that summary statement, she was more than convinced that his record—by all readily available and reasonable research—was clean.

Later, security would take a deep dive into his employment record. That's where they would find something they might never have seen because there had been no time for it yet. It was the second text that had sent Hawk on this mission. Jillian had told him that Fenn had a locker, Utilidor MLR 1865, which caused him to instantly have someplace to go and something to do.

He broke into a jog down this straight tunnel. He was running on the main street below the main street of the Magic Kingdom. Along the roofline, various pipes were tucked away overhead, each with a specific function. This complex underground network allowed many of the necessary things it took to run a theme park to be hidden from the eyes of each guest. The Utilidor had accomplished what Walt had envisioned years before in Disneyland. Hawk slowed his pace as he neared the end of the tunnel. Thinking quickly and anticipating that Jillian had sent the same information to the Secret Service, he wanted to get to the locker before they had a chance. He played out the possibilities of how they would enter in his mind.

In front of him was the Revenue and Currency Control Area just before the cut-through tunnel he needed could be found. But at that particular intersection, he was just a few feet away from the main Utilidor entrance, the Mouseketeeria (cast dining area), and the Disney Learning Center. This is where the Secret Service would enter; it was the main entrance.

He dodged to his right and took a slightly longer way toward his destination. If they were close, it would keep him out of sight. Breaking into a run once again, he moved behind the Character Zoo, and then followed the hallways to the left toward the stairways that allowed cast members to enter various sections of Fantasyland. As he intersected the next hallway, he pumped his legs, drove to the left, and headed for the next opening where tunnels would meet.

The tunnel to his right allowed him to race past the entrance to the Women's Locker Room area and the Kingdom Kutters (the cast-member barber shop). With a shove he entered the Men's Locker Room, known as the MLR. Catching his breath, he was pleased he was still alone and there was no other activity in the Utilidor. Now inside the locker room, he paused and listened for any noise.

"Hello?" Hawk's voice echoed off the metal cabinets and concrete floor. There was no response, but he tried again. "Hello, is anyone in here? We have evacuated the area. Is anyone still in here?"

He waited and heard nothing. Cautiously walking through the room, he glanced down each line of lockers with benches spaced uniformly so people could sit if they needed to. After visually inspecting each row, he found himself alone and satisfied that no other person was in the area. Now he looked for locker number 1865. The first locker alley he moved down was labeled with lower-numbered lockers—not what he was searching for.

After rounding the end of the metal fixtures, he moved down the next row, reading numbers so fast he momentarily forgot the one he was looking for and moved passed it. Realizing his mistake, he paused, backed up, and spotted it. Locker number 1865 was right in front of him. Hawk took the lock in his hand and realized he had no way to open it. It was a keyed lock, one distributed by the company for the cast member to use. There was a master key to open the locks in case of an emergency. This would qualify as an emergency, but Hawk had no idea where to find a key to the lockers if he wasn't with Disney security.

Running his hand down his face, he considered that Jillian would know. But that would take too long, and he had no way of knowing where she was or if she was free to talk. Hawk scanned the area for something heavy enough to break the lock but didn't see anything helpful. So he ran back down to the end of the locker line and looked toward the exit door. Mounted on the wall, easily accessible, was a heavy fire extinguisher.

After covering the distance to the door in a few steps, he hoisted the extinguisher off the hook that suspended it and weighed it mentally as he moved back to 1865. Carefully lining it up, he drove the bottom edge of the extinguisher along the top edge of the lock. An explosion of sound bounced off the metal canyon walls surrounding him. Before the echo died, he struck the lock a second time, and then a third. On the third strike, the lock popped open.

The fire extinguisher hit the floor and rolled away from where he stood. Hawk grabbed the lock and wrenched it sideways, releasing it from the door. A quick flip upward on the closing unit opened the locker. He peered inside. A quick visual inventory revealed what he did not expect. It was empty, except for one item nestled on the shelf as if waiting for someone to discover it. The envelope was unmarked on the outside, thick, and sealed. Hawk didn't hesitate. He flipped it over in his hand and tore it open.

CHAPTER SIXTEEN

The Most Powerful Disappears

Leaning over and staring at the video playback screen in the makeshift mobile control area inside the GNN tent, David Walker realized he was holding his breath. Consciously making an effort to exhale, he glanced away from the screen and realized he was not the only viewer who seemed breathless. Allie Crossman, John Ware, and Juliette Keaton were all as mesmerized by the footage as he was. He moved his hand, hitting pause on the control panel and evoking a startled reaction from the others.

"Hey!" Allie said, the pitch of her voice higher than usual.

"What's a matter?" John asked.

David knew his cameraman was anxious to see the footage that had just been returned to them by the Secret Service. John Ware had captured this action at the platform in Epcot when Monorail Red had glided to a halt. The tape was about to become the most viewed footage in the world over the next few hours. Unlike the shaky videos captured by cell phones that had surfaced in the last thirty minutes, this footage had been captured by Ware's professional and steady hand. They were viewing the footage of a serious and important event.

"Look." David cut his eyes toward the other members of the media who were nonchalantly milling about. "The other media reps here know we have some kind of footage. Their networks have been airing the YouTube video snippets that people captured at the monorail station, but not one of those videos shows anything except confusion and people getting shoved around." Nodding toward the screen, he continued, "This video is going to show us something. John had a clear view of what was happening."

"And I kept the camera running until the Secret Service stepped in my way," Ware said.

"Just take a deep breath," David suggested. Everyone relaxed a bit. "And no matter what, don't let your faces react to what you are about to see, or every news agency in the world will know we've got something spectacular."

"Which is footage they don't have," Ware said.

"Exactly. But like good team players, we'll give them access to it." Allie reached down to press play on the control set. "*After* we have aired it, reported on it, and branded it with our exclusive label."

The footage showed the monorail slide into place and stop. The camera shifted slightly as Ware moved closer to the edge of the crowd and zoomed in to get a shot of the first family stepping out into Epcot. He had captured a clear view of the front of the monorail as Secret Service agents rushed forward. The black-suited security detail surrounded the sleek cab and in perfect focus, it showed clearly that each and every one of the agents had their guns drawn and aimed toward the monorail. The camera revealed there was only one person visible inside the cab, the driver. And the first family was nowhere to be seen.

The door opened, and for a brief instant, the footage showed the monorail driver turning to look through the open door. The agents moved forward, then the camera lurched to the side when Ware had been pushed or shoved by people on the platform. The steady cameraman had obviously been knocked aside by either a bystander or an agent, and the footage was of an indistinguishable moment as the camera lost its clear view of the monorail. When Ware's camera found another angle, this time shooting through the front window of the monorail, the driver was slumped over the controls, a red splatter pattern now visible on the interior of the monorail. An unidentified hand then moved into view of the camera lens, covered it, and forced the camera down, ending the footage.

"Wow," Allie said in a subdued tone. "That is powerful footage."

David understood that she was trying to underreact to what she had just seen. As he lifted his eyes from the screen, he could see rival news organizations watching them watch their exclusive footage. The privacy of the tent did not allow anyone else to see, but in the competitive world of news programming, it would be a matter of moments before one of the agencies would break a story that there was footage coming soon and that the event had been captured on camera.

"You're going to air this?" Juliette said softly to Allie.

"Yes, of course," Allie said. "Is there a reason we shouldn't?"

"Because it shows or partially shows someone dying in a monorail," Juliette stated as a matter of fact.

John Ware tensed. "Are you afraid of bad public relations?"

"No." Juliette turned on him. "I'm afraid it is in bad taste. Someone is dead. You have captured it for the world to see. Maybe the world doesn't need to see it."

"It's news," Ware said. "It's what we do."

"Look, I know this is gruesome, but we can't hide it." Allie's voice cracked a little. "The world will see this footage, whether we want to show it or not. It's our job."

David tried to ease the tension. He realized that for the Disney Company this was an image that broke the carefully crafted illusion they worked so hard to create. Walt Disney World was a world away from the world, perfectly safe, perfectly fun, and to coin a phrase from a classic Disney film, practically perfect.

Their footage shattered that illusion of a practically perfect world. But the bigger story was the disappearance of the most powerful man in the world and his family. It was a national crisis. The president had gone missing, and the footage they captured was now part of that story. He would report on it and add the narrative to the footage with restraint and integrity, but they would allow it to be seen.

"Juliette, maybe I could get a statement from you for our next report. That way, you can add a word or two on behalf of Disney that might ease some of the graphic visuals people will see."

Juliette's face tightened ever so slightly. A smile, sincerity struggling to overcome condescension, relaxed some of the lines of stress. "I don't think so," Juliette said without wavering. "I have no official comment on behalf of the company at this time."

"I understand that," Allie said. "But it might be good if you could say something that would help our viewers process—"

"I noticed that Grayson Hawkes left the platform in the midst of the confusion." David had decided that asking now might be his only opportunity. He feared that this source might be on the verge of shutting them out of the information stream. "Why did he leave? Where did he go?"

"You will have to ask him." Juliette smiled. "When the time is appropriate, I am sure he will make a statement for Disney as well."

"It seemed to me that Dr. Hawkes was actually moving off the platform before anyone else knew what was happening. He left before the monorail opened, and he certainly was gone before the driver got shot." David continued his questioning. "How did he know something was wrong before even the Secret Service was able to react?"

"Again," Juliette said, turning to leave, "you will have to ask him that yourself."

Allie reached out and grasped Juliette's arm. "I'm sorry, Juliette. We're just doing our job."

"I know," she replied. "And I am doing mine."

Juliette walked to the edge of the tent and paused. The three remaining behind the viewing monitor watched as she turned to them. "Thank you for letting me view your footage before you air it."

"Of course," Allie said.

David realized they had reached an impasse, but he wanted to communicate respectfully and leave the exchange on the best note possible. "Juliette, thank you for your help," he said. "This is an important story. The most powerful man in the world has gone missing in your resort. We have to report it. That's why I asked those questions. It just looked like your boss knew what was going on faster than the Secret Service did."

Juliette listened, dropped her gaze to the ground, then turned it on the three newspeople. Stepping back toward them, she shook her head as if trying to decide if she should say what she wanted to say. Once again, she glanced toward Spaceship Earth looming in the background, then took another step forward and spoke softly enough that no one outside the tent could hear.

"I understand your questions and realize you have a job to do. I'm not offended by them." Juliette gave them a half smile. "I do want to make a statement, but it has to be off the record." She paused, and her smile disappeared. "I'm terrified that the president and his family are missing at the moment. But you have made one error in your summation of what might be going on and what you are implying in your questions. The most powerful man in *this* world, Walt Disney World, is my boss."

She inhaled deeply and sighed. "And if Dr. Grayson Hawkes does know something about the disappearance of the president, then that is the best news possible for the president and his family. It doesn't matter what he knows or when he first knew it." She again paused. "Allie, as I said, and I know you understand, this is all off the record." With that, Juliette Keaton moved away from the tent and was immediately assailed by other news organizations bombarding her with questions and requests for an official statement.

David watched as she graciously waved them off and made her way to a secure area at the edge of the press-and-media zone. He waited until she was out of sight before speaking. "Okay, Allie, what was all of that about?"

"What do you mean?"

"What do you know about Dr. Hawkes, and why is he possibly the best news for the president and his family?"

Allie shook her head, apparently deciding not to answer his question. "We need to get ready to cut in and go to broadcast." She pointed toward the monitor. "Let's figure out how to package this for our next report. The world is about to see the footage we captured."

CHAPTER SEVENTEEN

An Empty Locker

Hawk held the ripped envelope in his hand and turned it over, allowing what was inside to cascade into the palm of his other hand. A piece of paper fluttered away and gently floated toward the ground, drifting on unseen currents of air. An oversized coin hit his palm with more weight than he had anticipated, and another slip of paper, this one smaller than the first, came to rest on top of the coin.

Instead of picking up the paper on the ground, he first turned his attention to the two items in his palm. The first was a small Post-it-note-sized paper. It was aged, like the page of an old book that had been long forgotten on a shelf. Six words, apparently written on an old manual typewriter, were centered perfectly on the brittle square:

Allen Never Found Stevens or McKay

Hawk quickly memorized the phrase and then uncovered the coin beneath the paper in his hand. It was not actually a coin, but instead, it looked as if it was designed to be a medal or medallion of some sort. Silver in content, it also appeared very old; the date read 1780. If the date was correct and the coin was original, its age alone would make it valuable. On the top, it featured a pipe held in place by a set of wings. Studying the coin, he looked at the image on the first side. A colonial period individual shared a peace pipe with a Native American while they both sat under a tree. Emblazoned around the top of the coin were the words HAPPY WHILE UNITED.

Baffled, Hawk tilted his head to one side and wrinkled his brow. He flipped the coin over. This side had letters surrounding the image of a warrior, sword drawn in one hand, clutching a spear in the other, standing victorious over an enemy. The word *Virginia* was written directly above the warrior.

Hawk recognized this side of the coin as an early version of the Commonwealth of Virginia's official seal. It had changed over the years, but this could have been the 1780 version. The words formed by the letters surrounding the medal sent a chill down his back. *Rebellion to Tyrants is Obedience to God.*

Instantly, he remembered a piece of history he had stashed away in his brain long ago in some history class. A knack for remembering random details was one of his traits that at times had been useful and at other times distracting. The modern version of the Great Seal of the Commonwealth of Virginia included the Latin phrase, *Sic Semper Tyrannis*, meaning "thus always to tyrants."

The chill had been caused by the phrase being used at a very memorable event in American history. On the night Abraham Lincoln was shot at Ford's Theater in Washington, DC, John Wilkes Booth leapt on the stage and cried out, "Sic Temper Tyrannis!" Now, with the president missing, Hawk was frightened to ponder the significance of the connection. Jarring his mind back to the moment, he remembered the piece of paper that had fluttered to the floor. Bending down to retrieve it, he recognized what it was instantly.

It was an old ticket out of a Walt Disney World Ticket Book, specifically an E-Ticket. These ticket books had been retired with the opening of Epcot in 1982. A single admission and attraction ticket had replaced this style of coupon.

Back in the day, Disney sold what had been called Adventure Ticket Books. They contained the transportation ticket, an admission ticket, and a particular amount of individual ride tickets. Most attractions required a separate individual ride ticket that was identified on a letter scale from A to E. The tamest rides in the park, such as the Main Street Vehicles or Cinderella's Golden Carrousel, required an A-Ticket. The best rides and the most advanced rides, like Jungle Cruise or 20,000 Leagues Under the Sea, required an E-Ticket. The booklet would contain anywhere from seven to twelve tickets depending on when you purchased them and how much you paid for them.

This E-Ticket listed attractions in Adventureland. Pirates of the Caribbean and the Jungle Cruise were both popular and featured audio-animatronics, which the guests loved then and now. Tomorrowland featured one E-Ticket attraction when the ticket had been sold—Space Mountain. Fantasyland offered It's a Small World and 20,000 Leagues for guests, and Frontierland allowed the ticket to be used for the Country Bear Jamboree. Liberty Square included two main attractions according to the ticket—the Haunted Mansion and the Hall of Presidents.

Hawk made note of the presidential attraction listed. He was certain that was not a coincidence. On the back side of the ticket, someone had scrawled some words in blue ink that were almost illegible. Hawk squinted, trying to bring them into better focus. His mind slowly read each word, trying to connect it into some type of sensible phrase: THE RESISTANCE HAS RISEN.

His mind tried to freeze each of these discoveries into some mental lockdown box where he could process what they meant. He didn't know yet, but he was convinced they could not be random. These contents had meant enough to Edward Fenn, the monorail driver, to store in his personal locker. Hawk looked around the room as he wondered why Fenn would have a locker in this area at all.

Suddenly, the door of the locker area crashed open with startling urgency, and the room quickly filled with men in dark suits. The Secret Service had arrived, flanked by Walt Disney World Security and the Orange County Sheriff's Department. They poured into the room. Some had drawn their guns, and the once-empty locker room became quite crowded. Hawk recognized the agent from earlier in the day, Craig Johnson, who had his firearm drawn and aimed at him. From behind this mass of law-enforcement agents came a voice.

"Okay, you can put the guns down," Jeremiah Stanley said as he broke through the group.

Hawk saw not only Stanley, but also Detail Chief Pat Nobles, followed closely by Jillian, whose jaw was set tight as she locked eyes with him.

"Once again, Dr. Hawkes, you have managed to insert yourself into the middle of my investigation before I could get my team on-site." Stanley stepped in front of Hawk and leaned closer. "Tell me why that is."

Hawk exhaled and stepped back, creating space between himself and the head of the Secret Service. "I was just trying to be helpful."

"Really?" Stanley barked. He extended his hand for the items Hawk held. "Somehow, I don't see it that way."

"Instead of telling us about Edward Fenn first, you informed Grayson Hawkes, didn't you?" Pat Nobles said to Jillian.

She shrugged slightly, never breaking eye contact with Hawk. "He is my boss."

"Yes, indeed he is." Stanley interrupted the conversation as he examined the items Hawk handed to him. "By touching all of these, you may have contaminated any forensic evidence they might have contained."

"Sorry," Hawk said.

Stanley offered a sarcastic smile. "Thanks, that means a lot to me."

"Anytime."

Jillian rolled her eyes and sent Hawk an unspoken message to stop talking. Hawk watched Stanley carefully examine each of the items from the envelope just as he had done. After he looked at each one, he handed them to Agent Nobles, who examined them as well. Next they were deposited into an evidence bag that had been produced by one of the agents.

"Do they mean anything to you, Dr. Hawkes?" Jeremiah Stanley inquired.

"Not really. An old piece of typewritten paper, an old E-Ticket with some words scribbled on the back, and a coin of some sort. Granted, it is an old coin with what I guess is the Seal of Virginia on it, but they seem kind of random if you ask me."

"I don't believe they are random at all," Stanley said. "Anything but random if you want my opinion. After all, they were found in the locker of the last person to see the president and his family just before he killed himself." Stanley eyed Hawk suspiciously. "Was there anything else in the locker?"

Hawk stepped away from the open locker to give him access. "Not a thing. See?"

Stanley stepped forward and looked inside. "You will understand if I am slightly skeptical."

With a nod of his head, Stanley motioned for Hawk to be searched. Agent Johnson stepped up and spun Hawk around toward the row of lockers on the opposite side. After forcefully shoving him toward them, he patted Hawk down. Then he spun Hawk back to face him. "Empty your pockets."

While Hawk was being searched, Agent Nobles turned to Stanley. "Do the items mean anything to you at first glance?"

Stanley watched as Hawk emptied his pockets and clumsily dropped his wallet, keys, and cell phone into Johnson's hands.

"Well, Dr. Hawkes is correct. The coin is an old one that has the Seal of the Commonwealth of Virginia on it. The date says 1780. I would suspect that if the coin is genuine, it's extremely valuable. The papers mean nothing to me." Stanley now nodded for Hawk's personal items to be returned.

"Dr. Hawkes, I believe that Jillian Batterson told you about the locker before she told us. Of course, that would have given you a head start to get here. As a matter of fact, I would guess that we took the long way since Jillian was our guide. That gave you time to get here, look inside the locker, and see what was in it before us." Stanley rubbed his forehead before continuing. "What I want to know is why. I want to know why you seem to be just a step ahead of where my team is and why you seem intent on blocking my way when I am trying to find the president and his family."

"Like I said, I was just trying to be helpful." Hawk smiled.

"Sure you are." Stanley sounded unconvinced. He motioned for everyone to leave, and the agents and officers in the room began to exit. People drained out of the doorway as quickly as they had come in. In a few ticks of the clock, the only people that remained were Hawk, Jillian, and Jeremiah Stanley. As the three looked at each other and the quietness emerged from the activity of everyone leaving, Stanley turned to make sure they were alone. Satisfied that they were, he cleared his throat.

"Is there someplace close by where we can speak?" He looked toward both of them. "We need to have a quick chat."

CHAPTER EIGHTEEN

A Matter of Trust

Jillian watched as Hawk moved away from the row of lockers, brushed past Jeremiah Stanley and then herself, and headed for the exit. She tried to read his face for some indication of what he was feeling, thinking, or doing. He swung open the door and held it for the pair, who stepped back into the silent hallway of the Utilidor. Motioning them to the right, Jillian took the lead, followed by Stanley, and then Hawk.

"Let's take him to DACS," Hawk said from behind them.

DACS was the Digital Animation Control System. This high-tech powerhouse served as the nerve center that operated the bulk of the Magic Kingdom. DACS was responsible for making sure audio-animatronic characters stayed on cue in attractions, controlling when stage doors opened and closed, and making the stages elevate and lower. It even automated when curtains raised and opened.

Although it had been part of the original Magic Kingdom design, there had been numerous upgrades and improvements over the years. Off-limits to everyone, including cast members who had no responsibility for being there, few pictures existed of the area, and most eyes would never see it. DACS was a marvel of imagination, technology, and innovation both then and now. It had held all the controls for the Magic Kingdom until attractions began to be added outside the berm as the resort eventually spread out and expanded.

Hawk swiped his ID to unlock the door and motioned them through. Jillian led them in and moved down the rack of workstations to the right, spun, and waited for Stanley and Hawk to follow. Hawk pulled out a chair on wheels at one of the stations, rolled it toward Jillian, and then did the same for Stanley.

After they sat down, Stanley glanced around the room, taking in his surroundings. "Very impressive. I wish I had time for a tour."

"I think you have more important things on your plate right now," Hawk said.

"Most definitely." Stanley leaned forward and trained his gaze on Hawk, ignoring Jillian as if she was not in the room. "Dr. Hawkes, I've heard a lot about you. President Pride is a big fan of yours. He trusts you. He wanted you to be part of his administration."

"And you?" Jillian interjected.

Stanley tore his attention from Hawk. Turning toward her, he did a double take. "And me, what?"

"Do you trust Hawk? The president does, but up to this point he has been searched, shoved around, and treated like a suspect. So, I ask you again, do you trust him?"

She thought she caught Hawk smiling as she asked the question, but when she turned toward him, his face showed no emotion.

"Of course I don't." Stanley turned back to Hawk. "As I told you, Dr. Hawkes, you keep showing up at my investigation scenes."

Hawk opened his mouth to speak, but Stanley held up his palm to stop him.

"We have another mutual friend, I've discovered," Stanley continued. "Former Sheriff Cal McManus is an old friend of mine. We actually went to the academy together in Quantico. I got a call from him a few minutes ago, offering any help he could give. Then he said something that was more than a little odd."

Hawk raised an eyebrow. "Really?"

"Yes. He told me that if something was happening here in Walt Disney World, you had an unusual set of gifts and a way of doing things that might be helpful to me. He was vague about what those gifts were and exactly what he meant. But he implored me to let you help in any way you can."

"McManus is a good man." Hawk smiled. "I always thought he was a great judge of character."

"Well, I'm not convinced. And I'm still not so sure about you."

Hawk grew serious. "I promise to help you find the president. Tyler Pride and his family are old friends of mine, and I'll do anything I can to help find them."

"Again, that's not how I see it." Stanley pointed his finger at Hawk. "To this point, you've done everything to get in my way. I've seen very little help from what you've done, but I see great potential for harm. My job is to make sure the president of the United States does not get hurt." Stanley paused, and after a stare down with Hawk, he turned to Jillian. Then back to Hawk.

Breathing deliberately and taking his time before exhaling, he continued. "I'm willing to let you do whatever it is you do in this world of yours, but I will not let you interfere in my world. I expect and demand your full cooperation. Or I will have you arrested." Stanley leaned back in the chair and smiled. "Do I make myself clear?"

Hawk's eyes narrowed. Jillian tried to read what he was thinking.

"We're clear," he replied curtly.

Rising to his feet, Jeremiah Stanley nodded and turned toward the door. Jillian rose to help him navigate his way back through their underground world. Abruptly, Stanley turned and brought her up short. "I've got this. I can find my way out."

Stanley once again addressed Hawk. "We have set up what we think is a reasonable perimeter and will start working our way back toward the last-known point where the first family stepped onto the monorail. That would be the Transportation and Ticket Center. We assume, just like you, that there was an unscheduled stop at the monorail substation. It's included in the search zone."

Jillian cleared her throat. Stanley turned toward her.

"Do you want me to mobilize our security staff to help in the search?"

"No." Stanley moved toward the exit door. "I want your security people to keep your guests out of my way."

And with those words, the head of the Secret Service powered his way through the doors into the Utilidor. Staring toward the now-empty doorway, Jillian heard Hawk's chair creak as he leaned back.

"Thanks," Hawk said.

"For what?"

"For giving me a head start and taking the feds the long way to the locker room."

"Of course." She smiled and tossed her head to the side. "I always enjoy obstructing a federal investigation into the disappearance of the American president. We both can be arrested for that. Jeremiah Stanley wasn't kidding. He'll do it, too, if we get in his way."

"Relax," Hawk reassured her. "We are helping, and we will continue to help."

"How?" She took a step closer to him, tucking her hair behind her ears.

Jillian felt a sense of inadequacy again. The sense that she might not be as sharp as she used to be waged a battle within her heart and head. As a former federal agent in her previous life, she completely understood Agent Stanley's frustration with her current boss. But the softening around the edges of her personality had allowed her to give Hawk the head start. She had purposely taken her time in getting the law-enforcement team to the locker room, enough room for Hawk to do whatever he was trying to do.

Hawk stood to face her. "Are you okay?"

Jillian shook her head. "No. We're dealing with a critical situation here. And I'm trusting you to have some sort of idea about what's happening." She closed her lips into a tight line and paused before continuing. "But I already know you don't. You have great intentions of being helpful, but you are making it up as you go along, ticking people off. And you're getting ready to do something that will get you in trouble." She looked him directly in the eyes. "And you are going to ask me to help you do it."

Hawk gave her a half smile but did not hesitate to answer. "Yep!" He walked past her, opened the door, and looked both ways to make sure Stanley was gone. He eased himself back inside DACS when he was sure they were alone.

"Yep?" She lifted her chin and tried to relax her tense neck muscles. "That's all you have for me—yep?"

"Yep." Hawk smiled. He reached into his pocket and flicked an object toward her. "And this."

Focused on the object, she thrust out her hand and captured it mid-flight. Closing her manicured fingers into her palm, she reopened her hand and saw what Hawk had thrown to her. It was small and round, highlighted in red, white, and blue. A poker chip, emblazoned with Tyler Pride's name and the campaign slogan "*Time for Some Pride in America*." The Gambler— the United States president—had dropped the chip in the office earlier this morning.

She looked at it closely and then at Hawk. "This is what you picked up off the floor this morning?"

Hawk nodded.

"You told him, 'You dropped this, sir.' And he told you to keep it."

"Exactly." Hawk's face grew serious. "Flip it over."

Jillian turned over the campaign-giveaway poker chip. Written on it were two words in black ink and printed in bold capital letters—*HELP ME.*

Jillian read the two words over and over again until they tumbled and took a free fall through her brain. The already intense situation had taken an unexpected twist that nearly caused her to lose her mental balance. She quickly recovered, now trying to process what the words might mean.

Hawk stood with his shoulders back and chin raised. "So, what do you think, Agent Batterson?" Usually, he called her that when he was teasing her or trying to get her to overreact. This time, Hawk wasn't teasing.

"Tyler Pride sent you a message?" Jillian was thunderstruck at the power of two handwritten words on a piece of plastic.

"It appears so. It struck me as odd when I picked it up in the office. I saw the words, but Pride was leaving and told me to keep it. Then he confirmed that I would be seeing him later, so I was going to find a moment to ask him about it."

"But, of course, he never arrived."

"No, he didn't."

"And when you didn't see him in the monorail, you knew something had gone horribly wrong and where it happened."

"You're giving me too much credit." Hawk shrugged. "I knew before anyone else there was only one place to stop a monorail between the TTC and Epcot. So that's where I headed."

"So why didn't you mention this to Jeremiah Stanley?" She leaned against the workstation beside her, turning the poker chip over and over in her hand. "This is evidence."

"Yes, it is. But evidence of what?" Hawk leaned back next to her on the workstation. "After Sam Reno and Dana Brown paid us a visit, I began to wonder just who Tyler Pride needed help from. I almost showed the Secret Service the poker chip at the Monorail Substation, but they saw it when they searched me and gave it back. They did the same thing when they searched me in the locker room. They think it's just a campaign giveaway. They didn't even notice the note."

"So, you don't think Jeremiah Stanley can be trusted?"

"Well, you just asked him if he trusted me. He doesn't. Why should I trust him?" Hawk nudged her playfully with his shoulder.

Smiling, she replied, "Because he's the head of the Secret Service and, well, you are just you." She returned the nudge.

Jillian looked at the poker chip, reading the words over again. *Help me.* The president was the most powerful man in the entire world, so why did he feel like he needed to ask Hawk for help?

"Look, 'trust' is a big word, and there are only a few people I really trust in this world." Hawk hesitated as if he wasn't comfortable being so transparent. "My life is pretty simple."

Jillian laughed out loud. "Your life is a lot of things, but simple is not a word that even begins to describe it."

Hawk didn't laugh, but simply nodded in partial agreement with her assessment. "Fair enough, but it's pretty simple when it comes to who I trust." He glanced off in the distance, closed his eyes, and then continued as he reopened them. "Tim and Juliette, Jonathan, Farren Rales, and you. That's it."

Jillian knew each of the people in Hawk's inner circle very well. Tim and Juliette Keaton were some of Hawk's dearest and closest friends, as was Jonathan Carlson. Juliette and Jonathan had served on a church staff in Celebration, Florida, before he recruited them to follow him to the wonderful world of Disney.

Farren Rales was the Imagineer who had drawn Hawk into the mysterious and sometimes magical world where Hawk now flourished. Farren had been one of the original Imagineers, hand selected by Walt and Roy Disney to ensure that the company and the legacy of what the Disney Brothers had started would continue.

But she realized one name was not on his list. Shep Albert had also been with Hawk through the years. The relationship Shep had with Hawk was close, had been very close, and then there was a moment that had nearly destroyed both of their lives. All had been painfully forgiven, but as often happened, trust was never reestablished right away. Jillian sensed it created an emptiness in Hawk that forced him to often be more cautious and closed around Shep than he wanted to be. On more than one occasion as she had become aware of what had happened, her counsel had been to give it time. Their relationship would get better. She had no idea if she was right, but it was the best she had to offer.

"So, you have five close friends you can trust," Jillian said. "That's not too bad; it's more than most. And the people you mentioned really care for you, and you can trust them. No doubt about it."

Hawk pushed himself off the workstation. He walked toward the door then paused, turning to look back at her. She still leaned against the workstation, eyeing the poker-chip cry for help nestled between her fingers.

"Come on, let's go." Hawk motioned for her to follow.

"Where are we going?"

"To find the president and his family. And as we do, you'll find out something else."

"Really?" She was curious to see what Hawk might be planning as a means to find the first family. Her curiosity was contained by slight twinges of dread. More often than not, when Hawk got involved in things, the unexpected became the normal and the consequences were not always what they might have hoped.

"And what might this something else be?" She blinked as she moved toward the door with him. "I would think finding the first family would be more than enough."

Hawk looked at her and appeared to ignore the question. He tilted his head and smiled. "Let's go," he said softly.

"No, hold on." Before they exited DACS, she reached out and grabbed him by the arm. "You didn't answer my question. What is this something else you think we are going to find?"

Hawk turned away from her, but she did not release her grip on his arm. He faced her. Leaning in close, he spoke in a soft, gentle voice. "I didn't say we were going to find out something else, I said *you* were going to find out something else." He smiled and waited.

"What am I going to find out?" She felt herself grow tense, awaiting his response.

"I've just noticed that since we've been getting ready for this presidential visit you have been tense dealing with all of these government agents. You used to be a federal agent yourself. You're wondering if being here at Disney has made you soft. Maybe you've lost your edge in this world of magic and pixie dust." He smiled kindly. "And now something bad has happened. You're wondering if you're as tough as you used to be back when I first met you, if you still have your edge, if you can still get the job done."

Each word peeled back another layer of how she'd been feeling. Her thoughts swirled so quickly she couldn't get one to slow down long enough for her to process it. How had he known? And did he know the rest? She looked at him, knowing her body had gone motionless while he spoke. She had started her day with the very struggle he had just outlined, with the exception of her conclusion that it was his fault. He hadn't mentioned that at all.

"I . . . uh . . . well . . ."

"Don't worry." Hawk smiled reassuringly. "You still have your edge, and your instincts haven't melted away like ice cream on Main Street USA. You still have it . . . whatever *it* is."

This time he pushed through the door into the Magic Kingdom's underworld, leaving her mind racing. The door closed behind him, leaving her alone in DACS, still frozen in place. Instantly, the door clicked open, and Hawk pushed his head through.

"Jillian? We've got to go find the president."

CHAPTER NINETEEN

No Comment

No *comment, no comment, no comment* were the only comments David Walker got from anyone connected to the Pride administration. The Secret Service had no comment, the press secretary had no comment, and on the local level, The Disney Company and the Orange County Sheriff's Department had no comment. Their president was missing, and no one seemed to have any information to share about it.

Leaning back in a folding chair underneath the GNN media tent, David scrolled through the news items appearing on the touchscreen of his smartphone. He shook his head as he quickly scanned, not reading beyond the first paragraph of most of the reports that had started to come out. He had held the belief that, in a crisis, it was best to get out in front of it, and if people were smart, they would get out relevant information first before others could create their facts or spin it beyond control.

Even now, his long-held theory that when there was a vacuum of information, there would always be some voice trying to fill that space with noise, was being proven true. It was clear to everyone that something was terribly wrong at Walt Disney World. There had been no explanation at all offered for why President Pride and his family were not on the monorail when it arrived at Epcot and why the driver of the monorail was now dead. With each flick of his finger across the screen, he could read how people were crafting and creating their own narratives of what happened and why.

Various stories were being floated by some that Tyler Pride had fallen victim to an assassination attempt organized by a foreign government irritated at his pro-Israel stance, which had caused more than a few sleepless nights for other

Middle Eastern leaders. There was a smattering of reports suggesting that Pride and his family were actually taking a vacation on the taxpayers' dime and the entire disappearance had been fabricated. According to one article, this was just another example of Tyler Pride's total and complete disregard for the American people. David chuckled at the slanted reporting. If there was one thing he was convinced of after covering the candidacy and presidency of Tyler Pride, it was that he passionately loved America.

David slowed his browsing to read some of the reports being offered by some of his cable-news competitors. They dripped with sarcasm and an intense, almost venomous dislike of President Pride. A part of David understood their hatred. Pride had the ability to make the press corps extremely angry. Normal decorum in White House press briefings was no longer predictable. The press seemed to go after the president with a complete lack of respect for the man and the office. And the president seemed to relish those battles and would hit back at the press with a force that most newspeople had no experience handling. As a result, the press often looked petty and silly, and the president and his staff came off looking like bullies and hard liners, but that seemed to feed the supporters of the president even more.

One of David's competitors had made a statement on-air that having the president missing was a good thing for the nation. He actually suggested that if Pride was never found, the nation would be better off. David scoffed at his colleague's take and angle. In his mind, his colleague was no longer a real journalist but had been reduced to the ranks of an apologist pundit for the rival political party of the president.

David continued scrolling and found an entire other world of reporting that came mostly from Internet sources. These were the reports that were suggesting, no not merely suggesting, insisting they had evidence of a deep-state conspiracy. As he scanned through them, he read theorists explain why they thought the evidence showed that the FBI, the NSA, the CIA, and various other military agencies were operating a shadow government.

According to these conspiracy theories, there was a New World Order that believed the nation was being drawn into a One World Government and a One World Currency that would eventually control all of the nation's assets and power. They offered a variety of reasons why President Pride was the anti-politician and therefore a threat that needed to be eliminated so this deep-state plan could move forward. The reports also suggested that the mainstream media was a player in these plans, and their unfair reporting conspired to turn public opinion against the president.

David Walker raised an eyebrow and pondered whether any of these theories could be true. They all presented a strong argument; however, he was skeptical of their evidence and facts. As a journalist, he refused to get caught up in the popularity of personality when it came to his work and reporting the news.

As for the president, David had believed Pride would be explosive and bombastic in the White House, which had proven true. He had known that most of his colleagues would hate the president because of his anti-political, independent bent. But in fairness, the president was hated by both Republicans and Democrats. He was the Gambler who had defied the odds and become the most powerful man in the world.

Pride *prided* himself, and as always, his last name would lend itself to an intended pun, that he owed no political party, no power group, no special interest, and no financial backers for his rise to the White House. Politicians were losing their minds not knowing how to deal with the leader of the free world who always kept his cards close to his chest, wasn't afraid to bluff, and then in the next breath went all in. He was a risk-taker in a city and community infested by people who lived their lives by the numbers in political polls and the pressure of pundits.

David had always tried to report the real story, the real facts, and leave the decision about how to process it to his viewers. The trend in cable news had morphed into so-called journalists telling people how they should think and feel about a story. He strongly disapproved of their methods. He didn't know for sure, but at some level he believed the president could see this and appreciated the fair shake he gave the commander in chief. As a result, Walker had scored a few exclusives with the president and had hoped to again on this trip. But for right now, no one knew where the president was.

He was troubled. He turned his head and looked over toward Spaceship Earth. He knew where the president was supposed to be, when he was supposed to be there, and what should have happened. None of that had taken place. However, in the aftermath of the morning's events, the White House had said nothing, the Secret Service had offered nothing, the FBI had offered nothing— no one was saying anything. This was the soft soil for conspiracies to take root and grow. Maybe he too was pondering those conspiracy theories too much.

But the events of the day lent themselves to thinking about strange, unexpected, and diabolical theories. There was no evidence to disprove the thoughts, and some events actually reinforced them. What had happened to President Pride? Where was his family? Why were their usual sources of information silent?

Inactivity was driving him crazy. Allowing his chair to rock back toward solid ground, he looked over to where Allie Crossman was buried deep in concentration reading something on the screen of her phone.

"Allie?" David called to get her attention.

She looked up and responded by not responding, waiting for him to continue.

"I need to be doing something."

She placed her phone on the table beside her. "What do you need to be doing?"

"I need to be working, digging, trying to find a story here."

"It would appear to be a pretty big story here." She motioned in the air around them. "I think you have plenty to do telling this one."

"That's what I'm talking about." He leaned forward. "We don't really have a story yet. We have no information, and it doesn't look like we're going to get any for some time. I need to be doing something. I was wondering if you could get in touch with Juliette Keaton again for me."

"Sure." Allie reached over and picked up her cell. "I can get in touch with her. She's pretty good at responding . . . most of the time."

"Great." David stood and looked around at the frenetic activity in the media zone. "I'd like a few minutes to talk with her again."

"Why? What are you going to ask differently this time?" Allie had worked with David long enough to know his pattern. David realized she had already figured he was going to take a different approach to find the story in this situation.

"I want her help." David smiled at Allie. "She told me earlier that if I wanted to know why Grayson Hawkes left the monorail station so quickly, I'd have to ask him myself. I want her to get me an audience with the most powerful man in this world."

CHAPTER TWENTY

An Emergency Call

Engine Co. 71 was nestled on a corner of Main Street USA. Firefighting enthusiasts loved the hidden gem in Walt Disney World's Magic Kingdom. It had a prominent location right next to City Hall and was officially called the Town Square Firehouse. Any guest who took the time to visit would see sports props and details that told the story of an early-1900s fire department. The company number 71 paid homage to the year the Magic Kingdom opened. The most significant part of the decor though was the tribute to the brave men and women of firehouses near and far. On display in multiple glass cases were hundreds of local firehouse patches donated to Disney from firehouses across the country.

As Walt Disney World was being created, the inspiration for Firehouse 71 came from the West Coast—Disneyland Fire Department 105 in the original park located in Anaheim, California. That fire station was rich in Disney lore. Its second story was a charming apartment used by Walt Disney and his family. Now a time capsule honoring the memory of Walt Disney, the apartment had been left and maintained in the very condition it was when Walt passed away. A light is always left on in its window in Walt's memory and honor.

Inside Walt Disney World, this bit of history was not lost on Grayson Hawkes. Once he became head of the company, he began a remodeling project on Main Street USA, which led to the creation of an apartment above Engine Company 71, right on the corner, similar to the apartment Walt built in Disneyland. Hawk's version of the apartment involved some creative planning and forced perspective that allowed him, along with a willing and excited team of Imagineers, to create a large living space that was carefully hidden along the top of the existing structures.

As time went by though, more and more guests realized that the chief creative architect for the Walt Disney Company actually lived in the Magic Kingdom. It was a daily occurrence for people to congregate at the base of the steps leading up to his doorway, waiting for a picture or an autograph. Especially fortunate guests might catch a glimpse of Hawk sliding down the fire pole that connected his living room in the apartment to the bottom floor of the fire station. The Main Street Firehouse was now a special destination for many to take pictures.

In a practical sense, the firehouse was located next to a gate simply called Car Barn. The barn was the starting or ending point for the Magic Kingdom's parades. Many guests lined the street at the base of Hawk's apartment, unofficially referred to as the Hawk's Nest, to watch parades. On many evenings, guests who were paying attention could look up at the second-story window and see Hawk watching the parade as it passed his home on Main Street USA.

Juliette Keaton paused at the bottom of the metal stairway on the right side of the firehouse. Glancing around her, she was struck by the absence of activity in the Town Square. It wasn't actually the absence of activity; it was the abandonment of the square. Even when the parks were empty, there was still some activity, but not today. This was a lockdown unlike any they had ever experienced. It was certainly the most unusual since she had been promoted to chairman of the Theme Park Division.

Her promotion came in the aftermath of the attack on the Magic Kingdom, which had resulted in portions of Tomorrowland being blown up. The pressure in the days after the attack on Walt Disney World was tricky to maneuver, so she transitioned from her role as head of communications to head of the Theme Park Division while they rebuilt and reimagined the new look of Tomorrowland. There was so much of the new job and responsibilities that she enjoyed, and it had given her family—Tim and the kids, Jason and Beth—some opportunities to travel the world and spend time in all the Disney resorts.

But for the last few weeks, she had gotten much more involved in the communications world again as they prepared for President Pride's visit to Orlando. Right now, she was glad to be away from the media area at Epcot and climbing the steps to the Hawk's Nest.

A few minutes ago, Juliette had received a call from Jillian, asking if she could slip away and come to the apartment. This was exactly the escape she needed. She turned the doorknob and entered, never bothering to knock. Before closing the door behind her, she glanced back one more time at the isolation of Town Square. Jillian was seated at the table next to the window, and she waved as Juliette stepped inside.

"Hey." Jillian smiled warmly as Juliette took the seat across from her at the table.

"Hi. What are we doing here?"

Jillian slid the campaign poker chip toward her. It scraped lightly across the table's hard wooden surface, and then she removed her hand and allowed Juliette to see it. Juliette looked at Jillian, then back at the poker chip on the table before picking it up. Her eyes widened as she read the two words written on the back of the chip.

"Help me?" Bewildered, Juliette looked at Jillian. "What does that mean?"

"It means that the president needs our help," Hawk said. His voice came from the direction of the bedroom. He stepped into the living room area wearing a pair of jeans, long-sleeved shirt with the arms rolled up to his elbows, and athletic shoes. No suit this afternoon.

"Where did you get this?" Juliette asked.

"From Tyler Pride, of course." Hawk slipped into a chair at the table and picked up the poker chip, flipping it in his fingers.

"The president dropped it when he came by the office this morning," Jillian said. "Hawk picked it up and asked him about it. The president said to keep it and then left."

"So, you think President Pride was asking you to help him because he knew something was going to happen to him?" She felt her pulse increase slightly; she already anticipated his answer.

"Maybe, maybe not, but something did happen to him and his family." Hawk inhaled deeply, shook out his arms, then his hands. "So we're the ones who will have to find the president."

"And how are we going to do that?" Juliette scanned their faces.

"We have some clues to help us get started." Hawk passed the chip back to her.

"A campaign poker chip?"

"No, the clues we found in Edward Fenn's locker," Hawk said.

"Who is Edward Fenn?"

"The monorail pilot of Monorail Red," Jillian said.

"The president's monorail?" Juliette let the words sink in and then perked up as she realized what they were telling her. "You found something in his locker?"

"A few things," Hawk replied.

"What? Can I see them?" Juliette's fingers fidgeted, waiting for them to show her what they had found.

"No, you can't," Jillian said with disappointment. "The Secret Service confiscated them as evidence."

Juliette looked at Hawk. "So, you found something in Edward Fenn's locker?"

He nodded yes.

"And you got there before the Secret Service and opened it?"

Hawk gave her a half smile. "Bingo."

"Why did the Secret Service not get there before you did?"

"Because I gave Hawk a bit of a head start." Jillian grinned sheepishly.

"Ah, and then the Secret Service got there and took what you found," Juliette surmised.

"They did," Hawk confirmed.

"And was the Secret Service upset that you got there first, opened the locker, saw some type of evidence, and maybe contaminated any clues they might have been able to find there?" Juliette studied Hawk.

"They were not pleased." Hawk grimaced. "But I did have time to see what was in the locker."

Juliette crossed her arms and leaned back in her chair. "And?"

"I found two pieces of paper and an old silver coin." Hawk leaned his elbows on the table.

"What were they?" Juliette waited, trying to stay patient and calm.

"That's the same thing I'm wondering." Jillian now crossed her arms, mirroring Juliette's posture and staring at Hawk. "But as of yet, the keeper of secrets is keeping it a secret."

Hawk propped his cheek against his fist and allowed his gaze to drift outside the window toward Main Street USA. Juliette had seen this gaze many times before, and she knew he was trying to put together the pieces of a puzzle scattered across his mind.

Hawk reviewed with them what he had found. "There was a vintage coin dated 1780, with the seal of the Commonwealth of Virginia on it. There was an E-ticket from a Walt Disney World ride book that said, 'The resistance has arisen' on it, and a piece of old paper with the message, 'Allen never found Stevens or McKay.'"

"You know what they mean?" Juliette expected him to say yes.

"No."

"No?"

"No, not yet." Hawk stood up and paced from one side of the apartment to the other. "But I'm working on it."

Juliette watched him pace. After giving him a moment, she decided it was time to ask a question that she dreaded the answer to.

"So, the Secret Service has asked you to help them find the president?"

"No, they really want him to stay out of the way." Jillian smiled as she said it. "He keeps beating them to places they want to investigate first. They are not happy with him."

Juliette turned on Jillian. "But you were the one who gave him a head start to the locker, right? So you're helping him tick off the Secret Service."

"Technically, that is true," Jillian said. "But I'm not happy about it."

Sighing deeply, Juliette turned back to Hawk. "Why are you not helping the Secret Service? Do you think they had something to do with the disappearance of the first family? They're assigned to protect them."

"Maybe."

"What do you mean, maybe?" Her frustration was growing.

"We had a visit from the president's chief of staff and press secretary," Jillian said. "They tried to convince us there's a group of people in Washington conspiring against President Pride. They said a deep-state plot has been hatched against him."

Juliette's mouth opened in astonishment. "And you believe them? Did they offer evidence? Did they give you something else to go on?"

Hawk's silence answered her question.

"So, what are you going to do? You have a 9-1-1 message handwritten on a poker chip, and you're getting ready to slide down the fire pole, jump on a rescue truck, and race off to do what?" She was being overdramatic, and she knew Hawk hated that. But she was trying to make a point and understand what his plan was, or if he had a plan at all.

Hawk looked at her and shook his head no before taking a seat on the couch. "We have a missing president, we have a missing family, a poker chip asking for help, a dead monorail driver, and some vague clues along with a coin to go on." Hawk closed his eyes and rubbed his temples. "That's all we have, so we need to figure out what it all means."

Juliette looked at her friend. She already knew that if this was, indeed, some sort of conspiracy against the president and the country, Grayson Hawkes was the one person who you'd want to figure out what happened. But she also knew that if what Jillian and Hawk said was true, finding the president would be dangerous, and they could trust no one.

As if he knew what she was thinking, Hawk interrupted her thoughts. "Where's Jonathan?" he said.

Jonathan Carlson was head of the Entertainment Division of Walt Disney, but more importantly one of Hawk's inner circle. If things were going to get complicated, she knew he wanted him close. Sadly, she did not have good news for him.

"He's in Tokyo. They're finishing up the new fireworks show this week. So, he's not here to help."

"Okay." Hawk was silent for a moment and then began to think out loud. "Juliette, I need you to figure out a little bit more about this deep-state conspiracy theory and if it's true. According to what we were told, Washington insiders, power players, and the mainstream media are working together to undercut the president."

"Undercutting and working against him is one thing." Juliette tapped her finger on the table. "But kidnapping him or worse? That's a whole other level of evil." She took a breath. "If they have killed him and his family, they will kill anyone who gets too close to the truth. But if they've kidnapped him and his family, what's their end game? There have been no ransom demands."

"No ransom demands that we know of," Jillian interjected. "If there has been, it won't be made public, I can promise you that."

"And we're not telling the Secret Service or the FBI about this, or anyone else, because we're afraid—"

"Because we don't yet know who we can trust," Hawk said. "So, maybe if we can find out what's going on, we can actually be of some help."

"You really think that President Tyler was trying to give you a message on that campaign poker chip?" Juliette wanted confirmation. She had been with Hawk long enough to trust his instincts; they were usually correct. As much as it pained her to admit it at times, he did tend to be right—a lot. But in this case, she wanted to slow him down enough to make sure he'd thought through this well.

The implications of their conversation were staggering and frightening. The possibility that some very powerful people within the most trusted and necessary segments of the government might somehow be involved in a plot to hurt, undermine, or unravel the effectiveness of the American president was unbelievable.

"Yes, I think the president was asking for my help." Hawk looked at them both. "And, in essence, he was asking for our help."

"All right, I'll see what I can find out." Juliette stood up and headed for the door. Then she stopped, turned around, and walked back to them.

Reaching out her arms, she gave Jillian a hug, then gave Hawk one as well. As she hugged him, she said, "Be very careful."

"I will. I'm always careful, aren't I?" He smiled at her.

"And that is the attitude I know and love, and at the same time what terrifies me." Juliette stepped back, a smile of determination on her face. "I'll let you know what I find."

When she reached the door, Hawk's voice interrupted her leaving.

"You know, we probably should assume that any communication we have might be monitored in some way. So unless we are face to face, let's keep the communication vague and cryptic. Let's use Disney references to communicate anything that we can. Just be careful, and hopefully, we can stay a step or two ahead of whatever might be going on around us."

Juliette didn't turn back to look at him. "I'm not sure what that means."

"I'm not either. I guess I'm only saying, you be careful too."

With a nod, she was out the door. As she descended the stairs, her cell phone rang. Looking down at the screen, she saw it was a call from Allie Crossman. She slid her finger across the screen to answer.

"Hello, this is Juliette." She listened to the voice on the other end of the call as she walked across the Town Square, with Cinderella Castle looming at the other end of Main Street USA.

CHAPTER TWENTY-ONE

On the Dock

Craig Johnson pushed his way through the thicket of trees that separated him from the waterfront. It would have been easier to walk back around through the parking lot, circle the back of the building, then reemerge on the far side of the warehouse. But easier would have taken time and patience. Both of those were in short supply in his personal tank right now.

The events of the day replayed on a continual loop in his mind. Each moment, each conversation, each detail kept repeating over and over. Something had gone horribly wrong, that was now evident, but what had they missed, or more importantly to the safety of the first family, what had *he* missed? He knew he was just one of a team of agents, but this is what they did. They were now dealing with the impossible scenario that had instantly become their present reality.

Shoving away the last barricade of branches, he emerged on the concrete pad between two storage buildings on the waterfront, where a series of boat slips created orderly docking spaces for a portion of the Walt Disney World Transportation boat fleet. Other agents had been assigned to investigate the train and monorail barn, where Monorail Red would have been housed before the president's arrival. But he and a handful of agents were assigned an offshoot area connected to, but not a part of, the main hub of activity.

This was a working Disney marina used for the fleet of boats that provided transportation and service for the Seven Seas Lagoon and Bay Lake resort areas. The private tributary just off of Bay Lake allowed Disney to dock the many watercrafts that were an often overlooked but essential part of the transportation system connecting the various resort areas at Disney.

Johnson rolled the tension from his shoulders and focused on the task at hand, the job he had been assigned. He was to search the dock and through the warehouses along the marina front for any signs of the first family or what happened to them. Convinced he was not a part of where the real investigation was happening, he picked up his pace once he was clear of the foliage and walked the docks along the water's edge. Wooden pilings protected by rubber barricades ensured the boats would not be damaged and could remain secure. There were ten boats of various sizes tied off in the docking area, gently bobbing in the dark lake water.

As the scenes of the day continued to repeat in his head, the one conversation that seemed to fill up any empty space was the one he had with Grayson Hawkes, who had become a major distraction in their early investigation. Yet Hawk's words were bouncing in his brain over and over again.

"So, tell me agent," Hawkes had said over his shoulder from the backseat of the car earlier. "Who was supposed to be posted at the substation? And why did the Secret Service lose the president between the Transportation and Ticket Center and Epcot?"

Those were the questions that had initially annoyed him, but the lack of answers to those questions now simmered in his gut. Instead of being on the front lines and investigating the monorail station, he was stuck out on the waterfront, exploring the docks and warehouses. How could the president and his family have gotten from the monorail to the boat docks? His bosses wanted to be thorough, but he was convinced that this part of the investigation was pointless. What was not pointless was answering the question the chief creative architect of the Disney Company had asked.

Sun sparkling off the water sent bright chips of light against the metal door on the warehouse. Gripping the handle, he discovered it was unlocked, so he shoved it open harder than necessary. It clanged against the doorstop and echoed through the dark, cluttered building. This was a maintenance shop for the fleet of boats that operated in this area of the resort. The racks of parts, tools, ropes, canopies, life preservers, and the faint smell of engine oil proved this marina shop was an unspectacular and unhelpful place to investigate the disappearance of the president and his family. He heard the sound of ropes creaking as they pulled taut, then loosened, as the vessels bobbed on the surface of the water.

Moving through the line of shelves, he eased his way past them and looked out the window toward the other agent who had been exiled to this island of boathouse boredom. The agent outside was sweating profusely in his black suit, baking in the Florida sun.

He placed a hand on the metal shelf beside him and surveyed a row of boats on racks, obviously in dry dock. Each of the boats seemed to be in various states of repair or disrepair—some covered, some uncovered, and some partially covered by heavy cloth tarps that allowed a musty smell to float over this section of the warehouse.

His eyes moved past the row of boats and back down the aisle of shelves to his right, beckoning him to continue his walk through the canyon of marine material lining both sides. Scratching the back of his neck, he stepped methodically down this new walkway but halted abruptly. Slowly turning back toward the area he had just searched, he retraced his steps to the edge of the shelf line, once again looking at the row of boats. His earpiece crackled, and he heard a voice speak to him.

"Johnson, update on marina area." The voice was that of the site commander for the area. Moving his wrist closer to his mouth, he answered.

"All clear. Still searching the warehouse along the dockside." Johnson allowed his gaze to once again cover the expanse of the building. "A few more places to look, but for now, all clear."

"Speed it along. This is a big resort, and we have a lot of ground to cover." The commander's voice came back into his ear. "When you have cleared the area, I'm sending you to Bay Lake Towers. The detail chief wants to keep a set of eyes on the offices in the tower."

Johnson clenched his teeth. He understood what was happening. He was being sent to the Bay Lake Towers to babysit Grayson Hawkes. His fists tightened in frustration as he moved toward the row of boats. Reaching out, he tore back the cloth cover on the first boat in the line. A wet, musty smell greeted him, but there was nothing out of the ordinary. This was a waste of time. The next boat in line was open, with no cover. He leaned up against the side of the boat and peered over into the bow. Empty except for a toolbox that had been left partially opened because a hammer handle had managed not to make it back into the tray inside. The third boat was also uncovered and after a closer examination, also empty.

"Just finish up and get out of here," Johnson whispered to himself as he moved toward the next boat.

This boat was similar to the first one he had seen. Twenty feet in length, it was used to transport guests, he assumed. The front of the boat was covered with a heavy tarp, just like the boat he had inspected earlier. Gripping the tarp to pull it back, he was surprised when it didn't budge. Repositioning his grip, he once again gave it a tug, only to find the tarp unwilling to budge. Stepping back, he looked closely at the tarp and tried to find the edge of it. His fingers traced the cloth material. The edge was secured, fastened into place with what appeared to be nails.

Tilting his head, he looked closer and confirmed his discovery. Not being a nautical man, he had not spent much time around boats or the water, yet he thought this was odd. Why would you would nail a cover on a boat that was nestled inside a protected warehouse in dry-dock? What kind of repair would require that? Looking back toward the boats he had passed he remembered the toolbox in the second boat and the hammer handle protruding from it. After retracing his steps, he jumped up, scaling the side of the uncovered boat, flipped open the toolbox, and retrieved the hammer. Leaping back over the edge, he now moved back to the tarpaulin that refused to budge.

He slid the claw end of the hammer under the seamed edge of the cloth and pulled until he felt the nail release. It clanged to the ground. He moved to the next nail and did the same thing. He broke a sweat as he pulled out each nail from the tarp-covered boat. What was so important the cover had been nailed into place? He had always heard that you didn't need to drive nails into a boat anyway; it just didn't make sense.

Finally, enough of the nails had fallen to the floor to allow him to grip the edge of the cloth. He heaved it away from the body of the boat. Now that it was removed, he stepped up to look over the edge into the bow.

A shoe protruded from what appeared to be another tarp laid across something in the belly of the boat. Johnson pulled himself up quickly, landed inside the boat, reached down, grasped the cloth cover, and ripped it back. Scooting backward, he knelt down and looked closely. Moving his wrist toward his mouth, he activated the microphone and spoke slowly and clearly so there would be no mistaking what he was about to say.

"Site Commander, this is Johnson." He paused before continuing. "We need to get a team into the marina warehouse. I have discovered two bodies hidden in a boat."

CHAPTER TWENTY-TWO

Someone in the Hub

Jillian and Hawk stepped off the metal steps descending from his apartment above the fire station, walked along the sidewalk by the Emporium, and slowed before stepping out into Town Square. Hawk thought about how the three clues he found in the locker might fit into some type of pattern that made sense. Aware that Jillian was staring at him as they walked, he slowed and turned to face her.

"Yes?" he asked.

"I was just watching you think and wondering if you really believe this." She looked directly into his eyes as she answered.

"Believe what?"

"If there really is some deep-state conspiracy among the power players in Washington brazenly out to harm the president?" Her eyes widened.

"I know it sounds far-fetched," Hawk said. "But I have found that what seems impossible isn't really impossible at all. The impossible is just something that hasn't been done before, but it could." He shook his head. "So, this is an impossible situation that might be happening. I guess the thing that has me stuck is the idea that it might be possible . . . but is it probable?"

"Okay, I can see that." Jillian shifted her stance. "So do you really think this conspiracy idea is probable and possible?"

Hawk thought about her question while looking toward the center of Town Square. His focus came to rest on the flagpole in the center of the square.

"Look around, Jillian." Hawk waved his hand to emphasize their surroundings. "This is Main Street USA. It's built to take our guests back to the turn-of-the-century small town in America. But it's a place where there are boundless possibilities. Everything in the design captures the heart of the American spirit that reminds us that anything can be accomplished." He smiled. "This is America, and the glass is always half-full. Anything can happen."

They stepped into Main Street from the curb and moved toward the Train Station. The streets were deserted, which was a bit disorienting in broad daylight. Seeing the Magic Kingdom empty was something Hawk saw every night after closing. But during daylight hours, the constant stream and buzz of crowds moving along the street gave the park life. Right now, it was deadly quiet.

"You know how the government works today, Jillian. There are a lot of great people just like you, trying to do their jobs, and who see their work as creating a better America for people." He shrugged as he continued. "Our founding fathers were statesmen. We don't have those anymore." Hawk sighed heavily. "Instead, we have politicians who are more concerned with power for their party than they are about representing the people, the very people who elected them." He glanced up at the flag. "And now we have a president who doesn't align with either party, elected by Americans who felt like they didn't have a voice and no one who cared about them anymore. And the political machines don't like it."

"But if you think Tyler Pride is a statesman like leaders in the past, why didn't you go and work with him?" Jillian asked.

He laughed. "I didn't say Tyler Pride was a statesman. Anything but. He's a disrupter. He likes to provoke, and he likes to make people uncomfortable. It's his style. He truly is a gambler." He paused, adding, "But he does love this country. In some ways, he gives the government a chance to reset and reboot itself. He exposes politicians and power players for what they are and *who* they are at the core. That terrifies them because it might cause them to lose what they crave the most—power and control."

Silently, Jillian scanned the street, then lifted her head and locked eyes with him.

"If what you said is true . . . then it's probable that the impossible has happened."

Hawk nodded in agreement. He understood how difficult it was for her to wrap her head around the idea that many politicians cared only about themselves. She was the product of an environment of faithful, committed, government service. There was a loyalty that came with that commitment, and it was hard to have that structure shattered at the edges by a segment of leaders who liked to work in the shadows. He also knew that although she was willing to believe it could happen, she did not want to and would look for ways to disprove it. He appreciated that.

As he watched the conflicting emotions on her face, he noticed her eyes quit focusing on him and shifted to something over his shoulder in the distance.

"What is it?" he said without turning.

"Not what, *who*." Jillian's face no longer showed emotion. "Don't turn around yet. There's someone standing near the hub in front of Walt and Mickey's statue looking this way. He's watching us talk right now."

Hawk restrained the urge to spin and see for himself. "Is he Secret Service?"

"Could be." Jillian smiled a fake smile, trying to look nonchalant. Hawk noticed she never took her eyes off the person she had spotted. "But the agents usually wear dark suits or blend in so well undercover, you never notice them. This guy is dressed in black military fatigues, dark shades, and a cap."

"Military?" Hawk asked, still wanting to crane his neck to take a look for himself.

"Or law enforcement."

"That makes sense."

"No, it doesn't." She smiled again, never allowing her gaze to leave the subject. "We're looking for a missing president and his family. Secret Service, government agents, law enforcement are involved, but no one is running around solo. They work in teams and search methodically." She waited, still watching. "You're the only one going rogue. That's more your style." She smiled and tilted her head as if they were having a normal conversation.

Hawk knew she was calculating what to do next. Curiosity was smothering him, and he realized that if she didn't say something else, he would have to turn and look for himself.

"Hawk, he's just standing there, watching us. I can tell he knows I've spotted him, even though we're trying to look nonchalant. But he's standing stock-still in front of the statue. Let's casually turn and walk down the street toward him. Let's see how he reacts."

"Finally." Together, they turned slowly toward the hub.

Hawk studied the man Jillian had described. The fatigue-clothed figure continued to watch them as they strolled by the Emporium and walked toward Cinderella Castle. It was then that the man in military garb broke eye contact and bolted to his right, racing across the hub toward Liberty Square. Reflexively, both Hawk and Jillian broke into a run as soon as the man moved.

"I think he knows we were coming to see him," Hawk said.

Jillian sprinted next to Hawk, keeping up with him. "Ya' think? Let's catch him and see who he is and what he's doing."

Each step hammered home the questions bouncing through Hawk's mind. Who was this guy? Why was he shadowing them? And why had he run when he and Jillian headed his way? Hawk realized quickly that because of the man's head start, there was no way they could catch him. They couldn't even keep him in sight.

Jillian was fast, but Hawk speeded up, putting some distance between them as they reached Casey's Corner. Hawk slowed and motioned for Jillian to veer off to her left into Adventureland.

He yelled over his shoulder. "Maybe we can catch a break if I chase him back your way. If I do, don't let him get away. Prove to me you haven't lost your edge," he teased as he sprinted away.

"Why don't you see if you're fast enough to catch him?" Jillian smiled, turning to run across the bridge into Adventureland.

Hawk now glanced to his left and tried to pick up his pace. He moved away from Cinderella Castle, crossing the wooden bridge into Liberty Square, the land that brought many elements of colonial America to life. He trained his eyes on the structures around him, searching for the man.

The Dutch Amsterdam-style buildings were the first he came to as he crossed from the hub. Seeing no one, he continued his run into the Williamsburg Georgian-style architecture of Ye Olde Christmas Shoppe and past the replica made from the actual mold of the Liberty Bell, which brought him to an intersection where he had to decide which way to go next.

To his right, the flavor of New England architecture wound down along the waterfront to Fantasyland. Off to his left, the rough-hewn replicas from the Northwest Territory stretched toward Frontierland. Scanning his surroundings for any movement, he knew that if the trespasser had taken the left toward Frontierland, he'd run into Jillian. If he had turned to the right, there was no way Hawk could catch him. Left was the best option. If he guessed correctly, he would be chasing the fleeing man right toward Jillian . . . *if* they made the right choice. This was their best shot to apprehend the guy.

Racing along the pathway where Liberty Square morphed into Frontierland, Hawk slowed his pace, giving himself time to look into any alcove where the man might hide. If Hawk sprinted toward the end of the path, it would carry him beyond Splash Mountain toward a back entrance to the park that was used by cast members. As he neared the Country Bear Jamboree attraction, he caught a glimpse of movement out of the corner of his eye.

The man in black had been hiding in the path that cut through into Adventureland behind the wooden barricades to the left of the Country Bear entrance. He broke from his hiding spot as Hawk neared and ran across the wooden walkway into Adventureland between Aladdin's Magical Carpets and Aloha Isle, next to Walt Disney's Enchanted Tiki Room. Hawk adjusted his direction.

It was then that Hawk saw Jillian dash into the scene. Racing around the front of the magic carpet ride, she lowered her shoulder as she acquired her target. Leaving her feet, she hurled her body like a missile into the side of the man in fatigues. When she blindsided him, they both grunted as they fell on the red-paved pathway in front of the Tiki Room. The man shook his head, rolled to his side, and got to his feet before Jillian could recover from the impact.

As Jillian slowly rose to her knees, Hawk ran toward them, but knew he would be too late to help her. The man in dark clothing reached over and grabbed Jillian, snatching her into the air over his head with amazing strength. Then he threw her like a rag doll into the foliage along the entrance to the Tiki Room. He watched in agony as Jillian flew over the fence, through the plants, and into the stream of water running across the designed landscape. After tossing her into the plantings, the attacker stole a quick glance over his shoulder at Hawk, then left Jillian lying in a crumpled heap. He sprinted toward the steps descending into the Jungle Cruise.

Hawk slid to a stop and reached into the stream to help Jillian.

"Leave me here. Get him!" she snapped, as Hawk fumbled to help her out of the greenery.

He hesitated.

"Go!" she yelled. "Now!"

Hawk reluctantly left her to give chase. As he did, he realized his delay to help Jillian had allowed the black-clad man to regain any distance he had given up as they had converged on him. Seeing the queue line to the Jungle Cruise, Hawk guessed this was where the man had headed. Leaping over each roped barrier, he headed to the docking departure area of the attraction. The man was in the water, moving away from him around the first corner of the waterway that carried you into the jungle. Looking both ways, he decided to grab one of the boats along the far side of the dock. He leaped aboard and quickly turned the key. The engine fired to life. Unfortunately, it would take a moment for the boat to warm up before he could put it in gear.

The thirty-one-foot boats used in the attraction had been inspired by the film, *African Queen*, and normally would be loaded with passengers. Instead, Hawk had chosen a maintenance craft. Shorter than the passenger boats, with a tighter turning radius, this boat was normally left in an off-stage canal area to the left of the docking area.

Walt Disney himself had designed the original concepts for this attraction. As a result, Hawk had spent a lot of time learning to operate it. Although most guests never realized it, the passenger boats were guided by submerged tracks under the surface of the water. The watercraft he left the dock in, on the other hand, was free floating and used for a variety of reasons on any given day. Today, he needed the faster craft to give pursuit.

The muddy look of the water on the Jungle Cruise attraction was actually man-made, but today he wished the water was clear. If the man he chased submerged himself under the foliage that hung over the river, Hawk might lose him. But he couldn't change the color of the water.

Located behind the attraction was a pumping station that supplied all the water for the ride. Then a special dye was dispensed into the water by a waterfall. Each day as the attraction prepared for opening, the boats made their way around the rivers and acted as floating blenders, mixing the dye through the water.

The dye served two purposes. It gave the water a more realistic look and also hid the fact that the boats were on tracks and concealed the mechanics of the animatronic animals. Since the Magic Kingdom had been open before it was locked down, the water was already mixed and murky. Floating around the bend where he had seen the man wading through the shallow brown water, Hawk scanned the river and the foliage as well. He knew their black-clad interloper could easily disappear into the dark jungle.

CHAPTER TWENTY-THREE

Going AWOL

Jillian staggered to her feet, kicking through the foliage. She climbed over the fence and fell onto the pavement in front of the Enchanted Tiki Room. Her limbs felt heavy, and she struggled to sit limply on the pathway gathering her thoughts. It had all happened so quickly.

She had been running and searching throughout Adventureland, looking for the man wearing black fatigues. As she slowed her pace to make sure he wasn't hiding in some alcove, she heard commotion in front of her on the other side of Aladdin's Magical Carpets. Then she saw the man they were chasing—on the run, presumably from Hawk. But the man was so focused on who was behind him that he failed to notice her. Taking her chance, she shifted into a dead sprint and circled to the left around the flying carpet attraction. When she rounded the corner, she knew her strategy had worked perfectly. The man in fatigues still did not know she was there.

Fixing her gaze on her target, she had sent herself flying into him. The man never saw her coming. She hit him so hard she felt like she'd bruised her shoulder. But she knew they would catch him and find out who he was. Blinking back the pain of the collision, she watched in disbelief as he got back to his feet. Willing herself to move, she tried to get up, but she reeled from the force of crashing into him.

That's when the man grabbed her and hoisted her high into the air. How could he not be hurt? Her limbs felt like jelly. With resignation, she realized she was in trouble. Tossed to the side, she helplessly waited for yet another hard impact, which hurt more than the first. When Hawk arrived and tried to help, she had insisted he continue the chase.

Jillian rubbed her eyes and tried to refocus on her surroundings. The man was incredibly strong and resilient. He had not only absorbed the best attack she could muster, but he had shaken it off quickly and been able to throw her aside as if she were a discarded toy. Who was this man? What would happen to Hawk when he found him? *If* he found him?

Spinning around, she once again tried to regain her footing and stand. Wobbling, she managed to get up and felt her strength slowly returning. Now dripping wet, she reoriented herself to the problem. They had headed toward the Jungle Cruise. Each step she took toward the stairway in front of her pushed back the pain she felt. Jillian's elevated pulse pumped blood back into her aching muscles, and she prepared herself mentally for whatever she would face next.

Moving into the queue line, she reached down and unclasped the rope barriers that were used to funnel people back and forth as they waited to board the attraction. The Jungle Cruise area was heavily themed with period artifacts, tools, gear, photos, and more. It had been created to resemble an outpost where an exploration of the jungle rivers might be booked and was divided into four main sections that might be opened or closed in sequence to accommodate crowd fluctuation. The ropes she unfastened would take her directly to the dock.

Normally, the long line was designed to wind about so that guests could view the decorations as they waited. As she moved past them, she ignored them all. Silently, she crept beside the office of Albert Awol, the fictional Jungle Cruise boat captain and disc jockey for the Disney Broadcasting Company. Considered the "Voice of the Jungle," he broadcasted everything from news to quizzes and weather, and served as a disc jockey for the station, filling the airwaves with music from the 1930s Depression era.

Jillian had learned a great deal about Disney in her time with the company and knew this was one of the original attractions that had been in place when Walt Disney World opened. Like other attractions, it had inspired a film based on it, which had only increased its popularity with the guests. Hawk had often told her to slow down and observe the story that could be found in the details. Right now, she didn't like the story they were trapped in, and the surroundings put her on edge.

Arriving at the dock, she didn't see any movement—no signs of life. Boats lined the dock. None of them seemed to be missing or out of place. Where had Hawk gone? As she stood on the edge of the dock strategizing about what to do next, her cell phone vibrated, breaking her train of thought. Snapping it off her waist, she saw the number; it was the main line for Disney Security.

"This is Batterson," Jillian said, answering.

"This is Joel Habecker. I was told by the Secret Service to locate you."

Jillian knew Joel. He had been with the company for nearly three years, working in security. His supervisors spoke very highly of him, and he was in line for a promotion before the end of the year.

"Okay Joel, you found me. What does the Secret Service need?" Jillian continued to stare toward the other side of the river, looking for any signs of life.

"They need you, ma'am," Joel said. "There has been a discovery at the maintenance marina off of Bay Lake."

Immediately, Jillian swallowed hard. She knew that marina was in the same area as the monorail and train maintenance areas. The Secret Service was scouring the locations near there, looking for clues related to the plot of the dead monorail pilot and anything else that might help them find the first family.

"Did they say what they discovered?" Jillian tore her eyes away from the shoreline and calculated the best way to get to the marina.

"No ma'am. They just said they needed you there on site as soon as possible."

"Thanks, Joel. I'm on my way." She ended the call.

The loading dock of the Jungle Cruise was isolated. Hawk was nowhere to be seen, nor could she see the man they had been chasing. She stepped back, continuing to look at the river as it wound off around the corner and into the distance. Taking another step back, she knew she had to leave now. Turning, she retraced the pathway she had created by opening the rope barriers.

Once again passing the office of Albert Awol, she tapped the icon on her phone to call Hawk. Jillian knew his cell would be on silent and would vibrate an alert. He tended to keep his phone on silent most of the time so he wouldn't be interrupted. In this case, she knew that if he could answer, he would. As the phone rang and she waited for him to pick up, she worried he might have found their mystery man and something bad had happened.

Jillian paused and considered going back, ignoring the call to the marina. Looking back over her shoulder, she inhaled deeply and then exhaled slowly. Her encounter with the guy in fatigues was causing some pain and stiffness as she tried to move. Ignoring the aches, she told herself that she had to do her job, and she had to get to the marina. Hawk would call when he got the chance. She heard his familiar voice ask her to leave a message.

"Hi, you've reached Hawk. Can't get to the phone right now. Sorry about that. Leave a message and keep chasing your dreams." The notification tone let her know it was time to record her message.

"It's me. Call me back, please."

Hawk was AWOL, not where she had hoped or wanted him to be. He would call and check in. She just knew it. She just wished she knew where he was.

CHAPTER TWENTY-FOUR

The Falls

The Magic Kingdom's Jungle Cruise was based on a similar ride that opened with Disneyland in 1955. Drawing inspiration from a series of short documentary films by Disney called True-Life Adventures, Walt had originally hoped to use real animals in the attraction. That would be problematic though, since animals couldn't perform like he envisioned.

It was more practical to use a form of audio-animatronic creatures. Hawk realized as he made his way through the rivers of the Jungle Cruise that as the theme park had been evacuated, the usual shutdown procedures had not been completed. In many ways, the attraction still operated as it normally would, except there were no guests.

His boat steadily made its way down the Amazon River, passing several large species of butterflies, fluttering around Inspiration Falls. The spiel of the skippers of the attraction echoed in his head as he passed, noting that the reason they were called Inspiration Falls was to inspire you to go deeper into the jungle and further down the river. Hawk's eyes explored the foliage, looking for any indication of where the man in fatigues might have gone.

His watercraft now motored past the abandoned pygmy village, abandoned because of the massive snake that was curled up in the tree along the river. The skippers would quiz the guests on the attraction, asking them if they knew what kind of snake it was. They would give them a hint. The name began with the letter p. Inevitably, someone would yell "python" and the joke was now set. The skipper would correct them harshly and say, "No, the correct answer is plastic!" Then the guests would be reminded that the snake wasn't real. It was a Disney attraction at its best.

Now he moved past the trashed camp area, where gorillas had creatively gotten the engine of a Jeep to turn over. He then slowed as he prepared to make his transition into the Nile River. When he passed the enormous African bull elephants threatening each other from opposite sides of the river, they reacted as if he was guiding a tour boat. Sensors had been placed along the route that activated various actions and sounds from each setting for guests to enjoy. Ignoring the elephants' activity, he now guided the boat through the African veldt.

Shifting the boat into neutral, he slowed and drifted at the base of Schweitzer Falls, named after the famous explorer, Albert Falls. Normally, the river tour would wind to the right and carry the guests through additional scenes. Hawk studied the falls and tried to orient himself as to where he was in relationship to backstage areas beyond the berm.

Shifting the boat back into gear, he decided to steer to his left, allowing the portside of the boat to set his direction. As he did, he noticed an unusual movement to his right. Branches that snapped back into place as if they had been pulled aside for someone to pass through. Guessing that he had once again found the man in black fatigues, he pushed the throttle on the watercraft wide open, and the boat wedged itself on the shoreline.

Hawk jumped out and followed the path through the faux jungle, cutting to his right as he saw more movement. In front of him, nearing the top of the hill, was the man in fatigues. He followed. As he scurried up the slope to catch him, the man turned. He grabbed Hawk like he had Jillian moments before. Hawk twisted to his left away from the attacker's grip. Quickly he lifted both arms to pry himself loose from the robust man he fought. The man's dark sunglasses were oversized, and his facial features nondescript, but Hawk tried to find anything that might make him identifiable.

A punch sailed toward Hawk's jaw, and he jerked sideways, allowing the punch to sail past his cheek. The force behind the blow threw the attacker slightly off balance. Hawk lowered his shoulder and slammed into his opponent's ribcage. The man fell, and Hawk followed him. They both crashed out of the foliage into a stream of rushing water.

Feeling the sudden sensation of water rushing over him, Hawk tried to focus on where they had landed. He knew in a matter of seconds; they were on top of Schweitzer Falls. Slogging to his feet, Hawk grappled with the man in fatigues. Both men were having trouble gaining their footing as the water surged past them, making its way to the edge of the man-made cliff.

Hawk shoved the attacker backward toward the jungle foliage and was surprised how little his adversary actually moved. The burly man hurtled toward Hawk. As he did, he remembered the strength the man had shown when he hurled Jillian over the fence and into the bushes. Now Hawk discovered firsthand how powerful this person really was. He stepped aside to avoid the body slam.

Undaunted, Hawk moved in again, looking for an opportunity to land a punch. Or maybe he needed to figure out a strategy of putting the attacker on the ground and subduing him. Jabbing a fist forward, Hawk connected with the chin of the man. Once again he was shocked that the guy barely reacted. The pain in Hawk's fist sent a warning signal that this opponent was brawny enough to take anything he could dish out.

"Who are you?" Hawk's breath was ragged, as they squared off against each other.

The man remained stone-faced as he threw another punch. This one nicked Hawk's jawline. The glancing blow sent him stumbling to the side. His feet slipped in the water rushing over the rocks, and before he could regain his footing, the attacker loomed in front of him. Hawk strained to his feet.

"Leave this alone!" the man in black fatigues yelled, as he threw another punch toward Hawk's chin.

Again, Hawk jerked his head to the left, almost escaping the blow, but causing him to lose his balance. Hawk's feet slipped out from underneath him. As they did, he reached out and tried to grab hold of his assailant. His hand grasped nothing but empty space as he realized he was no longer on stable ground. He twisted his body in the air as he fell backward—off of Schweitzer Falls and into the river of the Jungle Cruise below.

Tumbling downward, he prepared his body to absorb the coming impact. If there was any good news for him, it was that below him was the deepest portion of the shallow river that ran through the attraction. But Hawk knew it would hurt when he slammed into the water and the river bottom below.

The words of his attacker still echoed through his mind. *Leave this alone.* Who was this guy he had chased into the jungle, and how was he involved with the disappearance of the president?

All of these thoughts drained from his mind as he hit the water.

CHAPTER TWENTY-FIVE

To Tell the Truth

The luxury offices inside the Bay Lake Towers were spectacular. David Walker had the privilege over the course of his career to travel the world and see more than most people would ever see in a lifetime. He had been blessed. But as he waited in the reception area of Grayson Hawke's office, he had to admit he had never seen an office area quite like this one. And never had he been in one like this with a such a stunning view. Staring out the window, he could see the monorail line stretching from the Contemporary hotel toward the front gates of the Magic Kingdom. As he gazed at this unique world that spread out before him, he had to admit he was impressed.

"Wow," he said to Allie, who sat on the sofa. "That is some view."

Allie Crossman got to her feet and walked over to the window next to him. "That's what I thought when I visited this office for the first time a few years ago. But this really is not his office. His working office is upstairs across from an oversized conference room with the same view. The office is loaded with Disney memorabilia."

"I hope I get to see it," David said, eyeing the stairs.

Allie had placed the call he had requested to Juliette Keaton, requesting an interview and audience with Dr. Grayson Hawkes. He was surprised that she hadn't said no, but as Allie pointed out, Juliette had not agreed to the interview either. Instead, she asked them to meet her here. They were picked up and escorted by Disney Security and members of the Orange County Sheriff's Department. At Juliette's instruction, they did not bring a cameraman with them. John Ware had remained in the media tent city in front of Epcot.

"I'm not sure what's going on or what we're about to hear." Allie continued to stare at the amazing view. "Juliette was very interested in your integrity."

"My what?" David turned to face her.

"She wanted to know if you were a reporter with integrity. She's aware of your reputation, but she was very interested in whether your reputation was just public-relations hype or whether you really were a journalist that took pride in what you did for a living . . . that you wouldn't settle for less than the truth."

David cocked his head. "What did you tell her?"

"The truth." Allie smiled, piquing David's curiosity. "I told her you were cut from the same cloth as Kate Young." Allie lowered her head. "I told her there was no way I would work with you if you were not a truth teller."

"I take that as a high compliment." David smiled. "As a matter of fact, it may be the best compliment I've ever been given."

He and Allie had known each other for years now, but there were times he forgot the trek her life had taken in the past. Years before they met, she had been the assistant to Kate Young, the host of *Total Access*. The investigative news program won numerous awards, and Kate won just as many for her journalistic work on it. One of their assignments brought them to the Walt Disney World Company to do an investigative piece on the mysterious leader of the company, Grayson Hawkes.

It was a bit of a strange assignment with the end result morphing into a very complicated and complex story that even now, most people couldn't understand. It was also the start of a very public relationship between Kate Young and Grayson Hawkes that had ended tragically when Kate was killed by an assassin here at the Walt Disney World Resort.

The relationship between Kate, Allie, and Juliette Keaton was forged in some very troubling days and tense circumstances. The relationship today between Allie and Juliette was reinforced by tragedy. By Allie's own admission, she was an acquaintance of Dr. Hawkes, but she had a strong bond with Juliette. David had seen it on display in their stay here during the presidential visit and now again over the last few hours.

David knew how close Allie and Kate had been. Their relationship was dicey at the outset of their work together, but over time, they became fast friends that went beyond a relationship between coworkers. He remembered vividly Allie telling him about the words Hawkes had shared at Kate's funeral and the impact they made on her own life personally. Those experiences had forever intertwined her life here at Walt Disney World, making it much more than just a vacation resort.

Hearing footsteps coming down the stairway, they turned. Juliette descended the steps and entered the waiting area. Appearing confident and in control, she greeted them and motioned for them to have a seat. They quickly settled in. David noticed that Juliette's smile tried to mask some of the pressure he knew she was under. It wasn't every day the president and his family disappeared. He wanted to talk to Hawkes and drill down into the details.

"Before we get started, I have to tell you something." Juliette leaned forward. "Dr. Hawkes is not here. You do not have an interview scheduled with him." She paused, seeming to gauge their reaction. "Yet."

"I thought that's what we agreed to," David said calmly.

"No, I don't believe it is," Juliette corrected him. "I agreed to speak with you about setting up an interview with Grayson Hawkes. But if you want to leave, you are more than welcome to."

The three sat in silence for a moment. Allie turned her head to watch David. She obviously wanted to stay, but she appeared to be waiting for him to make his decision. Allie nodded at him and smiled.

He turned back to face Juliette. "Then why are we here?"

"So we can talk about getting you the interview you want," Juliette said, her face brightening. "It is not my intent to be deceitful, but there is a need for me to be careful. I have spent some time talking with Allie about you and the work you do."

"I heard."

"Good." Juliette glanced at Allie, then back to David. "Then you understand my concern. There are a lot of individuals in your line of work who tend to make themselves the story or tell the story they prefer to tell rather than the truth. According to Allie, who I believe to be truthful, you are only interested in the truth as well." Juliette paused. "So what I am prepared to offer you is a truthful give and take. If it goes well, I will get you the interview you want with Dr. Hawkes."

David scratched his chin. "A truthful give and take. Hmm, it sounds like you have something you want from me. I thought I was the one asking you for something. I thought that was the reason we were invited here."

Juliette grinned. "Consider this a bonus. And if everything goes well, you might just get the interview you want."

David looked at Allie and considered the offer. There was a part of him that was proud that his reputation had gotten him this meeting. There also was a part of him that wanted to shove back in frustration because he had the sense he was being manipulated. Now he again turned his gaze on Juliette, who had relaxed a bit and eased back into her seat, waiting for him to respond. But it was Allie who spoke first.

"David, I think you should see if you can work with Juliette. I trust her. We wouldn't be here if there wasn't something important to discover." Allie leaned back in her seat as well.

Obviously, they were both waiting for him to decide what he wanted to do or say next. He cleared his throat, inhaled deeply, and then cleared his throat again. He realized there was no camera to record this, so he reached into his pocket and pulled out his cell phone.

"Can I record this conversation?" He slid the recorder onto the table next to his seat.

Juliette smiled. "No, you may not. We are going to have an off-the-record conversation first."

"Seriously?" David raised his eyebrows.

Juliette nodded. "Yes, seriously. What would you like to know?"

David thought for a moment. He picked up the phone and returned it to his pocket. Juliette seemed cautious as she watched him. He held his cell up for her to see.

"I didn't hit record, I promise." He pocketed his phone again.

"Just wanted to make sure."

"Where is Dr. Grayson Hawkes right now?" David asked. That was not really the most pressing question on his mind, but he decided it was good to throw out an easy one first.

"I have no idea."

"Really?"

"Really," Juliette said succinctly. "We are being truthful as agreed. I have no idea where he is."

"I asked you earlier why your boss, Dr. Hawkes, left the monorail platform so quickly at Epcot. Where did he go? It's as if he knew something was wrong."

"Which do you want to know?" Juliette showed no emotion.

David was puzzled. "Which what?"

"You asked three questions in what you just said. So before I answer, I want to know what you are asking." Juliette paused before continuing. "Are you asking why Hawk left so quickly? Are you wanting to know where he went when he left? Or are you asking if he knew something was wrong? As I said, there are three questions in there somewhere."

David nodded. "Yes."

"Yes what?"

"Yes to all three questions."

"Fine." Juliette didn't break eye contact with him. "Hawk left because he realized the president and his family were not on the monorail as we had been told they would be." She then raised her hand with two fingers, indicating she was now answering the second question. "He went to the first place he believed they might have exited the monorail."

"Wait, I thought the Epcot monorail line was an express route."

"It is."

"So . . . there is a place they could have gotten off the monorail?" David clarified.

"I didn't say that," Juliette said. "I have been instructed not to talk about that topic at this time." She now raised her third finger, indicating she was now moving on to the third question. "Yes, he believed that something was wrong. It is obvious from all that has transpired, especially from the footage you captured and have aired, that something was seriously wrong. Hawk just knew about it a few seconds before everyone else did. He has very good instincts."

"And all of this is off the record?"

"Yes," Juliette said softly. "That is your fourth question."

"I have more." David was now fully engaged. His mind tended to ask questions and connect answers rapidly. Every piece of information drove him toward the next.

"Do you know what has happened to the president and his family?"

"No."

"Do you really not know or are you just not allowed to tell me?"

"No, I really do not know."

"Does Grayson Hawkes know what has happened to the president and his family?"

Juliette thought and carefully answered. "I don't believe he knows what has happened to them."

"You don't believe he knows what has happened?" David asked to clarify.

"Yes, I don't believe he knows." Juliette smiled. "As I told you, I have no idea where he is right now."

"Do you know what he is doing?"

"Generally, yes . . . specifically, no, I don't."

David huffed slightly. "Is this the way you are going to answer all the questions I ask?"

Juliette again smiled and measured her response. "If you mean, am I going to answer all your questions truthfully, the answer is yes. As promised."

David shook his head.

"I believe I have now allowed you to ask ten questions, which I have answered for you."

David took a moment to recount them in his head.

"I think I promised you a truthful give and take, Mr. Walker, but to this point, you are doing all the asking and taking every answer I give."

"So what do you want from me?" David asked.

"And the reporter in you once again has asked me another question." Juliette's tone was scolding. "What I want is the same you asked of me. I want you to be truthful with me."

"About what?"

"Question twelve, I believe."

"Stop that."

"Okay." Juliette looked him squarely in the eye. "Are you aware of the stories that suggest there is a deep-state conspiracy against the president of the United States?"

David's mouth fell slightly open. He was stunned at the question. Of all the things he had expected from Juliette Keaton, it had not been this. He eyed her carefully. He had not figured her to be a conspiracy theorist.

"Why would you ask me that?"

Juliette stood to her feet, brushed off her skirt as she did, and then turned toward Allie.

"Great to see you, Allie. I will have security escort you back to the media area at Epcot." She then turned toward David. "Mr. Walker, you answered my question with a question. That is not what we agreed to in this off-the-record conversation. We said we would answer truthfully. I have answered everything you asked. You may not be satisfied with the information, or that it was off the record, but it was truthful as we agreed upon."

She walked toward the stairwell. "Apparently, you do not have the integrity Allie believes you to have. You did not do what you said you would do." Juliette started up the stairs.

"Wait!" David hurried toward the staircase. "Wait, wait, wait . . . just relax for a minute. I'm a journalist. I ask questions. That's what I do. I'm sorry . . . really sorry. Your question surprised me."

"So as a journalist, you don't expect to hear the unexpected?" Juliette again turned to climb the stairs. "I'll have to remember that."

"Hold on . . . please."

Juliette stopped and once again turned to him. She stood midway up the staircase.

"I have heard of the deep-state conspiracy theory. As a matter of fact, chat rooms, social-media sites, and web-driven sources right this minute are talking about a scenario that believes the so-called deep state orchestrated the disappearance of President Pride. They're saying the deep state is taking over control of the government by eliminating the president." David looked up at her. "So, the answer is yes. I have heard of it."

"Do you believe it?" Juliette asked him, waiting for an answer.

David pondered her question carefully before answering. "I want to answer your question with another question." He smiled that smile that viewers were very familiar with across the world. "I want to ask if *you* believe in a deep-state conspiracy . . . but I won't ask." He held out his hand in a gesture of truce. He didn't want her to walk away. "I will tell you that although I'm familiar with some of the thinking, I'll admit that I'm skeptical. It seems extremely far-fetched."

Allie now stepped toward the staircase.

"Juliette, what is this about?" Allie frowned. "Do you think that's why the president is missing?"

"What I think doesn't matter." Juliette slowly walked back down the stairs.

"I just want it on the record that Allie asked the question, and you answered her. So she gets to ask questions, but I don't?"

"Right." Juliette pointed at him. "And that was yet another question. You just can't stop."

"Sorry." He hoped their conversation was back on friendlier footing.

"I have it from some very solid sources that there is something to this deep-state theory," Juliette spoke softly. "I don't know what, and I don't really understand all of it. From what I have been able to ascertain, the previous administration attempted to cripple the candidacy of Tyler Pride because he was such a disruptive threat to the political system as we know it.

"Their plan failed, so they moved into phase two—to remove him from office. Essentially, a coup. They never believed he should have ascended to the presidency at all. He was a threat to the establishment. As a result, a small group of people within agencies of the government exceeded their power in order to target somebody they didn't want in office . . . somebody they believed would never be elected."

David wondered where in the world she got her information. She made the crazy things he had been reading from fringe sources sound almost rational. Perhaps because he had never heard anyone say it out loud before. Juliette Keaton seemed like a rational, sane, smart person, yet she succinctly described the conspiracy theory that was floating around.

"Most people consider that to be nothing but paranoia or a fear-mongering campaign," David finally responded.

"And the elite media goes, 'Oh, that's an exaggeration.' And either on purpose or by accident they become part of the conspiracy, or they become a part of the coup attempt because Tyler Pride threatens their morality, their worldview, or their ideology." Juliette remained expressionless. "And as a result, it never gets reported, talked about, or investigated because it sounds too crazy to be true." Juliette came down one more step toward them. "David Walker, you don't know whether it's true or not. You believe it is paranoia or just too outlandish to be true, because no one would crave that much power or that much control. Or perhaps your peer group can't find any room to believe such a story, so as a result it's never really pursued."

David listened to what she said and tried to process it. Quickly, he tried to categorize her words see if there was some reasonable, rational, and reliable way he could explain away the theory, with something other than a dismissive, *that's crazy*.

"But as I said, Mr. Walker, I will be truthful with you. So here is the truth." Juliette stood at the bottom of the landing, facing them both. "The president and his family are missing, and no one seems to know where they are. I can tell you that we hit every single security protocol the Secret Service asked of us, and then some, to ensure his safety.

"The first family managed to disappear on an express monorail line that we all believed was secure. It is absolutely impossible for the president to be missing, but yet he is. That is not an exaggeration; that's what happened. The impossible apparently wasn't so impossible after all. Perhaps you should change the way you view the deep-state conspiracy as being impossible to being improbable."

David thought about what she had just added to the stream of information.

"You asked me earlier if I believed it. To be honest, as I have been consistently, I am not sure. I think it is highly improbable. But right now, I don't have any other answers to explain what happened, so I have to at least investigate the improbable. That's why I agreed to speak with you. I hoped you might be willing to investigate it as well. Because honestly—there's that word again—I don't think any other credible journalist is doing so." Juliette paused. "So, as I said, I don't really believe it. But right now, the improbable is the most plausible explanation I can find. If I'm wrong, then I am sure that you won't hesitate to tell the world I am crazy."

"I wouldn't," David said.

"Sure you would." Juliette laughed. "But who would believe you? I live in a world of pixie dust and imagination." Juliette grew serious once again. "But what if I'm right? What if there is some type of conspiracy unfolding here? How will we ever know the truth?"

CHAPTER TWENTY-SIX

Dripping Dry

Sitting on the dock, Hawk leaned back against the pair of crates bundled with some barrels by the Disney Company, just as though they were real cargo ready to be shipped—all part of the illusion. He turned his head and read the addresses marked on the crates. One read "Thomas Kirk, Esq., M. Jones, Cartographers Ltd. Field Office, Island of Bora Danno." The other was addressed to "Kenneth Annakin, Director of Imports, Wyss Supply Company, Colony of New Guinea."

He slowly felt his soggy mind kick into gear as he remembered that these two jungle crates were a reference to the Disney movie *Swiss Family Robinson*. Tommy Kirk played Ernst Robinson in the 1960 film, then later played the title character in the 1964 movie *The Misadventures of Merlin Jones*. James MacArthur, the actor who played Fritz Robinson, later played Danny Williams, or as he was called Danno, on the original *Hawaii Five-O* television series. The second crate referred to Ken Annakin, the director of *Swiss Family Robinson*, and Wyss Supply, which was a tribute to the author of the original book, Johann Wyss.

Hawk thought the fact that he was able to remember what seemed like meaningless detail was a good sign, a sign that he had not sustained any serious damage when he had collided with the bottom of the river. The names were details, and details were sometimes important in the world of Disney. Another idea slowly began to creep over his drip-drying thoughts.

When he fell from the top of the waterfall, he had been stunned at first and had to fight his way back to the surface and then drag himself to shore. As he pulled himself onto dry land, he knew the man in the fatigues was long gone.

He had even stolen Hawk's boat. Hawk was sure he would find it in the boat storage area adjacent to the attraction and was confident the man had fled out through the backstage buildings.

Frustrated, Hawk blamed himself that he had not been able to subdue his attacker and figure out who their stalker was. He was convinced that whoever it was had vital information that he needed in order to help President Tyler, but he had run into a buzz saw when he chose to tangle with him. If he had the chance for a rematch, he would come up with a better strategy. His body ached and he was still soaking wet from his fall into the river, but there was no real damage that would not heal with time. For that he was thankful.

Looking around, he wondered what had happened to Jillian. He had been terrified that she had been badly hurt when she was tossed aside. But he knew she was strong and resilient. However, he was also surprised she was nowhere to be seen. Reaching into his pocket, he grabbed his cell phone. Although it was in a state-of-the-art protective case, he rarely had good luck with cell phones. He usually lost them, or he managed to break them. He fully expected to see a blank screen when he pushed the button to turn it on, but to his surprise, the screen lit up. Quickly, he tapped the icon with Jillian's picture on it and listened to the message she had left for him.

"It's me. Call me back, please."

He immediately hit the callback option and waited for the phone to ring. Finally, she answered.

"Hawk, are you okay?" Jillian said.

"Yes, and what about you? How are you feeling? I was worried you were hurt bad."

"I'll be sore tomorrow, but I'll live. Where were you? I came to the Jungle Cruise and couldn't find you."

"It's a long story. Where are you?"

"I'm at the Bay Lake Maintenance Marina. We have a situation. Are you sitting down?"

"Yes, why?"

"We have two bodies. Both deceased. Shot."

"Is it—?"

"No, it's not the president or his family. They appear to be guests."

"How? What?" Hawk stammered, as he realized she was telling him that people had been murdered at Walt Disney World.

"They were found by a Secret Service agent while looking for any clues about the president. So we also have the sheriff's department here. This is all under federal jurisdiction, but the murder of the guests, or the presumed guests, will be coordinated between the FBI and the Orange County Sheriff's Department."

"We need to know who they are." Hawk pushed himself to his feet. "There's no way this is not connected to the Tyler family's disappearance."

"You didn't answer me earlier. Where are you?"

"Still at the Jungle Cruise." Hawk was now moving back into Adventureland. He now remembered that they were going to communicate carefully in veiled conversations, trying to use some type of Disney code to relay messages. It must have been the fall, because he hadn't remembered that as he called Jillian back as soon as he heard her message. He had to keep his head in the game and his wits about him. If anyone was monitoring their conversations, it was too late now for this one.

"You're there? Did you get that scumbag who tossed me into the bushes like he was throwing out the trash?"

"No, well I had him for a minute, but then things went badly."

"How badly? Are you all right?" He could hear the concern in her voice.

"I got thrown off the top of Schweitzer Falls. It stung a little, but I'm fine," Hawk reassured her.

"Who was that guy?"

"Don't know. Just something else we need to figure out." Hawk was now making his way past the Jungle Navigation Co. LTD Skipper Canteen, a dining area themed after the Jungle Cruise.

"I'm about done here. I'm going to let someone from Disney Security coordinate with the sheriff. The FBI doesn't want to play nice and has informed me they don't need my help or the help of my wannabe law-enforcement staff," Jillian said, her words laced with disgust. "I'll come and get you."

"No, I'll come to you. Stay busy there—find out what you can." Hawk now moved past Bwana Bob's, the souvenir stand named in honor of Walt's friend, Bob Hope. "I'll run by the apartment to change and then come get you."

"But I think—"

"See you soon. Stay put." Hawk abruptly ended the call, thumbed through his contacts, and then touched the screen to call Juliette Keaton.

Picking up his pace as he strode past the Crystal Palace, he quickly moved under the alcove and past Casey's Corner, turning onto Main Street USA.

Juliette answered on the first ring. "Hawk, where are you? What's going on? Have you spoken to Jillian? We have a situation."

"Yes, I just spoke to her. I heard about the discovery." Hawk changed the subject. "I wanted to follow up with you about that item you were researching." He was still concerned about how they were going to communicate with each other. He felt he could keep their conversation generic enough to not raise suspicion. Although the very thought of someone listening in made him more paranoid than he dared admit.

"I've been busy. I have someone working on it and doing some additional research for us." Juliette was also being purposely vague, which Hawk appreciated.

"And you think that person will be helpful?"

"It was a calculated risk. But based on what we talked about earlier, I was able to make a compelling argument with enough intrigue to pique their curiosity." Juliette once again generically summarized, "I think it might work."

"Great, keep me posted," Hawk said, as he had now made his way down to the corner by the Emporium. Turning toward his apartment, he mapped out what he would do next. "I'm going to pick up Jillian. I'll be in touch."

"Hey Hawk, I feel like I say this to you all the time." Juliette paused. "But this time, maybe more than ever, be careful."

"You too." Hawk ended the call and bounded up the steps to his apartment.

CHAPTER TWENTY-SEVEN

What They Know

Jillian watched the coroner carefully examine the surface of the boat where the two bodies were discovered. It was her own personal observation that led her to believe that the cause of death was by gunshot and at close range. Although they had not given her the chance to get too near the scene, she was able to observe. And based on her experience, what she saw aligned with that conclusion.

As officer after officer moved in and out of the marina area, she tried to imagine how or why this deceased pair had ended up here stuffed into a boat. The obvious conclusion was that they were placed here with the belief that their bodies would not be discovered for a long time.

Jillian had been on the phone with Joel Habecker to see if anyone had been reported missing. Today of all days was the worst to ask that question. Since the four theme parks had been unexpectedly shut down and guests transported all over the resort, there were a number of people who had not been reunited yet with friends or family. Hourly, the figure changed since reunifications were taking place as soon as Disney could figure out who was where on the property and how best to return them to the rest of their group. They had talked about this nightmare scenario and trained for it, but that wasn't the same as experiencing it in real time. There were lots of people missing right now.

Jillian stepped outside and glanced up as she heard the sound of a boat coming around the point and entering the alcove. The speedboat rapidly decelerated and nestled alongside the dock. Each post on the dock had a life preserver hanging from a hook and between each post were anti-slip rubber mats that allowed people to step from the boat to the dock without losing their footing. Grayson

Hawkes sat behind the wheel of the boat and waved her over as the engine continued to idle.

He extended his hand to help her down into the boat. As she moved, pain shot through her hip, a reminder of her flight through the air just a short time ago. Evidently, Hawk noticed her wince and how gingerly she stepped into the boat and took her seat. "Hey, are you sure you're all right? You took a nasty fall."

"You mean I took a nasty throw," she corrected. "How are you? You fell off the falls?"

"I took a *nasty throw* over the falls. That guy is strong. We need a better plan if we meet up with him again."

Hawk kicked the boat into gear and banked it hard to port, swinging it around to exit the marina. Jillian grabbed the seat to keep from falling out and then steadied herself as the boat moved out onto Bay Lake.

"Where are we going?" she asked.

"Fort Wilderness." He looked back at her, his brow furrowed, and stared at her longer than she thought necessary. "Are you sure you're okay?"

"Hawk, yes, I'm fine. It just hurt when I landed on the other side of the fence in those bushes, that's all."

"I was worried." He smiled at her and then looked back out over the water as they zipped across the glassy lake.

Bay Lake was about thirty-five feet deep and a little over a mile across. The speedboat was fast, and Jillian noticed that Hawk wasted no time taking in the sights as he usually did. She had been with the company long enough to know where she was. The triangular-shaped lake connected with the Disney-made Seven Seas Lagoon by a water bridge on the west side.

There were two islands in Bay Lake—the largest, Discovery Island, was located in the center of the lake. Discovery Island operated as a walk-through wildlife sanctuary from 1974 until 1999. The original dock, as well as some of the attractions, could still be seen on the shoreline. This particular island intrigued her, and she wanted to explore someday. Hawk had shared stories about the times he had spent on it, but she wanted to take some time and really see what was there. She never seemed to find the time. The smaller of the two islands, Shipwreck Island, was located between the Contemporary and Wilderness Lodge resorts in front of the water bridge.

Hawk banked the boat around Discovery Island and past the legendary shoe tree of Bay Lake submerged in water to the base of the canopy. When you looked closely, you noticed there were objects hanging from the branches of the tree—shoes, dozens of shoes hanging by their shoelaces. Adorning the tree like Christmas ornaments, they represented a tradition cared for by cast members. The tree was the unofficial final resting place for the shoes of retiring cast members. Today, the tree was reserved for the shoes of retiring Seven Seas Lagoon and Bay Lake boat skippers.

The boat bounced over the water again as Hawk banked the boat hard to starboard and ran it up next to the dock.

Killing the engine, he immediately moved to the side and leapt to the dock. Pausing there, he extended his hand to help her. Normally, she might not want or need his help, but the pain in her hip still bothered her. She'd need to take a couple of ibuprofens to get through the rest of the day. Jillian took his hand and felt his fingers close around hers, assisting her to the dock.

"What are we doing here, Hawk?" Jillian asked, as they made their way down the lengthy wood-planked dock and across the white sand beach toward the Fort Wilderness Resort Campground. The beach was a gorgeous recreational area. She knew the resort was home to one of Hawk's favorite restaurants. They had eaten many meals at Crockett's Tavern on the lower level of Trail's End Restaurant. The tavern was loaded with memorabilia from the life and world of Davy Crockett, including a six-foot bear. The food wasn't fancy, but it was wholesome. Hawk would eat there more often if it weren't for the crowds of people who always seemed to interrupt their dinners. Surely, he wasn't planning on getting something to eat right now.

Hawk glanced over at her. "The Settlement Trading Post is up ahead. I've got a hunch."

"Sure, what are we looking for?"

"Do you remember the words we found on the old piece of paper in Edward Fenn's locker?" They stepped onto the porch area of the camp store and souvenir shop.

The Settlement Trading Post resembled an old trading post where you could stock up on supplies that you might need on any trip into the wilderness. A large porch area surrounded two sides of the post, equipped with oversized chairs and checkers if you wanted to pass the time before you hiked deeper into the woods.

"Yes, the paper said someone didn't find somebody." Jillian tried to remember the details. "I didn't get to look at it very long. The Secret Service scooped it up pretty fast. After all, it was evidence."

"True, but I do know what it said. It said, *Allen never found Stevens or McKay.*"

"And you know what that means?"

"Not really, but I think it's more of a location than anything else."

"And that location is?"

"Here," Hawk said. "Fort Wilderness. We just need to be sure. That's why we're here."

Her adrenaline stirred inside as she realized they might be on the verge of making a discovery. She felt her step lighten and momentarily forgot about her pain. As they stepped onto the porch, Hawk gestured to the walls alongside the trading post.

"As always, the Imagineers decorated a location while at the same time told a story. If you take the time to find their clues, it can be fun. When I heard the names, they sounded familiar. It took me some time, but I finally remembered what they were. I was looking at the crates on the dock of the Jungle Cruise, and recalled the names stamped on them are part of the story, or a sub-story, that Imagineers often tell. The names on the old paper are familiar. I think they have something to do with the notices on the wall of the Settlement Trading Post." Hawk motioned for her to move to the far end and start looking. "Read the signs. We're looking for the names Allen, Stevens, and McKay."

Quickly, she moved along the wall, and for the very first time in all of her visits here, she took the time to notice what was hidden in plain sight. The Troy Ballston and Saratoga Coaches were opening a new and faster stagecoach line to carry passengers from Saratoga to Lebanon Springs. This old advertisement for a stagecoach company fit in so well in the surroundings, she had never taken the time to read it. But that was not what they were looking for.

"Here!" Hawk said excitedly, as he pointed to the notification on the wall. "$300 reward for information leading to the arrest of Curly McKay, dead or alive, for armed stagecoach robbery. Reward being offered by the marshal. That's it, McKay. Allen never found Stevens or McKay. This is the McKay in the clue."

Jillian went back to exploring. She found something, read it, and scratched her head. "Hawk, here is another. But I don't get it."

Hawk moved next to her and read the poster on the wall. "Wanted: $250 reward for the capture of Bart Allen for cattle rustling. Last seen in Dark Canyon with gang. Notify nearest Law Officer."

"If this is the Allen in the clue, why was he looking for Stevens and McKay? The marshal was looking for *him*. Are you sure this is right?"

"I'm not certain," he said, "but keep looking. The names are here; we just have to make sure," Hawk pointed to another poster. "Here's another one. It reads, 'Wanted for stage holdup, B. H. Stevens.' That's our Stevens that Allen never found. It seems as if Stevens and McKay were stagecoach robbers."

"So why didn't Allen find them or why was he even looking?" Jillian continued to explore the wall, searching for a clue. She saw another notice and bit down a smile. They'd very possibly just found what they were looking for. "Hawk, come here. See this sign? It says, 'Reward. We will pay $1,000 reward for information concerning the person or persons responsible for the death of investigator Jim Allen.'"

"That's why Allen never found the men who robbed the stage. Because he was dead." Hawk nodded, trying to piece together the puzzle.

"But this means something, right? All the names are here."

"Yes, it does. In some ways, whoever took the president and his family pulled off the equivalent of a stage robbery. They managed to stop a moving transport vehicle, this time a monorail, and take the cargo—the people—off and disappear."

"But why leave the clue? Why? That makes no sense."

"It doesn't, unless you really believe that you will never be caught. And this is really as much a clue as it is a message. Someone was trying to communicate with Edward Fenn in some type of coded message, using Walt Disney World clues." Hawk paced across the porch, looking toward the campsites.

"And it means?"

"I think it means there's something hidden here at Fort Wilderness." Hawk turned to her.

Jillian smiled, ready to keep searching. "Or *someone* hidden here at Fort Wilderness."

"Yes, I think so." Hawk looked around at the expanse of the natural setting surrounding them. "It's big, plenty of places to get lost or lose someone. All we have to do is figure out where."

Jillian continued to stare at Hawk because something else had dawned on her. If she was honest with herself, she didn't like the realization that it might be possible. Hawk noticed her staring and turned toward her.

"What?"

"I don't think anyone else in the whole world could know enough about Walt Disney World to have figured out that clue," Jillian reasoned. "So whoever put that coded message together never could have guessed that you would figure it out. In other words, they didn't count on you getting involved."

"Maybe so, maybe not." Hawk shrugged. "But we figured it out."

"Yes, we did. But that also means that whoever designed that clue knows a great deal about the resort. That makes what we're trying to do that much tougher."

Hawk thought about what she said. He looked down at the ground and then stood up just a little bit straighter. "You're right. It might make our search for the president and his family harder. But it doesn't mean they know the resort that well. They logged their time preparing, researching. They had some inside information, or . . . in other words, they know what they know. But they don't know what we know. So, if anyone can unravel this, we can. Right?"

Jillian remembered when she first met Hawk. She had not liked the swagger he displayed. Now she saw it as one of the characteristics she liked the most. His confidence gave her confidence. Hawk brought her back to the moment as he continued to speak.

"We need a vehicle." Hawk hunted for anything around them that might be available to borrow. "We have a campground to search."

"We're going to search the entire campground?"

"Of course we are." Hawk moved toward the restaurant next to the playground area. "It will be easy."

"Nothing about this will be easy. There's a lot of ground to cover."

"Yes, but remember what we're doing," Hawk said as he picked up his pace. "We have a campground full of people all around us. That's what we expect to see. So, we're looking for the one thing that's just a little out of place, that doesn't fit, that doesn't quite make sense. If we can find that, we may find another clue that gets us closer to the president."

Jillian watched as Hawk opened the door of a maintenance truck. The small pickup had the logo of the Walt Disney Fort Wilderness Campground emblazoned on the doors. She climbed into the passenger seat. Hawk tilted down the visor. The truck keys fell into his lap. She smiled and shook her head.

"How did you know those keys were there?" Jillian was impressed and surprised.

"I guessed." Hawk turned the key, and the engine kicked over.

"Seriously, you guessed?"

"Not really. The cast members who work here at the campground usually leave the keys hidden behind the visor. These trucks are not assigned to individuals. They're assigned to work projects, so whoever needs the vehicle can usually take it."

"I never knew that."

"They don't know what we know, remember?" Hawk put the pickup truck into gear.

They don't know what you know. And that makes me feel better.

CHAPTER TWENTY-EIGHT

Web Search

Juliette sat in her office and perused the words on her computer screen. She had decided to grab a few minutes and take a crash course on the conspiracy theories that circulated on the Internet in regard to Tyler Pride. Stunned by the number of articles the search engine had given her to choose from, she tried to carefully select a few that seemed more credible than others. Again she was reminded of what she had heard so many times from different people—don't believe everything you read on the Internet.

She was fascinated with the vast array of sources with various opinions on the presidency of Tyler Pride. The first article she spent some time with made a case for the ascension of Pride to the presidency. The author of the article suggested the previous presidential administration had been corroded with corruption, fickle and weak in foreign policy, and had managed to massacre the economy. They had handpicked the successor to the highest office in the land and were convinced their candidate would win. The power of the president's personality and popularity would carry the chosen replacement into office. Or so it was believed.

"Hmm . . ." she said to no one, as she tapped a manicured nail against the space bar.

The next article laid out the reasons the economy was in shambles. People had quit looking for jobs because there were none to be found. Many had turned to working additional part-time jobs just to make ends meet. The economy was on life support, and people were told to accept this economic climate as the new normal.

Pausing to run her fingers through her hair, Juliette realized that her job at Disney had exempted her from this tough economic world. She had no idea if all she was reading was factual. She sensed the truth lay somewhere in between the lines, but the world she lived in was the vacation destination of the world. Their profits remained strong. The company had not seen the downturns mentioned in this article.

Another article focused on the diminished American culture and how a melting pot was a metaphor for a society where many different types of people blended together as one. America was often called a melting pot. Some countries were made of people who were almost all the same in terms of race, religion, and culture. America was different, and that was good. However, the article then suggested that many of the people who now came to America refused to become part of the American Experience. Instead, the article said, America was simply melting and losing the identity and the character that had kept her strong through the years.

Juliette sighed as she scanned the next article, about how religious freedoms had been trampled upon. She continued to read and found articles that sounded the warning alarm about losing the rights granted to citizens in the US Constitution.

The next article was a lengthy read about all the terrorist groups active across the globe. They all seemed to have two enemies in common—America and her ally, Israel.

Against this backdrop, the surprising election of Tyler Pride had stunned the political establishment. Some of the articles suggested that his arrival happened at just the right time in history, just as many seemed to believe that President Pride would unravel the world with his arrogance and dogmatic belief that America had to lead the world through strength. Juliette collected information rapidly and tried to figure out whether it was really possible there were people so enraged by Tyler Pride that they would attempt to remove him from office by any means possible.

As she continued to scan and search, Juliette began to see that the dislike for Tyler Pride was not just limited to Republican and Democrat. It was a sweeping hatred that seemed to be shared willingly by media organizations. It dawned on her as she read that most of the articles she found were either missing the point or ignoring the point on purpose. Tyler Pride was a conservative, but he was not a Republican or Democrat. He was an independent, an outsider, a populist, who in essence had risked a great deal to enter the political fray. A gambler who had managed to shock the world and become president.

The evidence that was being offered ranged from the FBI having an operative as part of Pride's presidential campaign, to accusing him of working with foreign governments to rise to power. Never had a candidate been so universally disliked by so many Washington insiders and media, yet the results were too important to ignore. He had been elected by the American people in one of the most stunning and unexpected upsets in all of election history. Personally, she liked the man and his family. Juliette recalled some of the times the Pride family had visited the resort back when he was just a reality show star and a tech mogul. She would have never guessed he had political aspirations.

Placing her elbows on her desk, Juliette rested her chin in her hands and mindlessly looked at the screen. Thinking back, she remembered the visit Tyler Pride had made to see Hawk right after the election. The campaign had been brutal. The language used had been abrasive, and the road to the White House had been a no-holds-barred political brawl. Pride had wanted Hawk to come work with him and help him restore pride in America . . . or that's how he explained it to Hawk.

When she discussed it with Hawk, he laughed it off and said he never really considered taking the post in the president's cabinet. But she sensed there was more to it than that. Hawk liked Pride. They were friends, but she knew how much Hawk had struggled watching his friend destroy his opponents and roll over them with aggressive force. She heard Hawk say on more than one occasion that being a bully was no way to get things done.

And yet, the results were that Pride was elected and there were many positive signs of growth and change happening in America. She had a sense that the bitter dislike and partisanship blinded objectivity for far too many.

As soon as the election was over and Pride was sworn into office, the cries of removing him began. His win had also opened the door for the longest election cycle in modern history, as immediately his political opponents began lining up to run against him in the next election season.

Juliette's instincts about David Walker from GNN seemed to be correct. Allie Crossman's endorsement of him had helped, but as she researched now, she could see a pattern in his reporting that was balanced. Walker was not afraid to report bad news as it related to the president. Yet at the same time, he was willing to report good news as well. Unlike many of his colleagues in the industry,

Walker still seemed to want to get the real story right. She wondered if he struggled with the information he saw each day as much as she struggled with what she was reading now.

A flash of light radiated across the surface of her screen. The bright light then dimmed, and a soft glow announced the arrival of a blank screen. It had fritzed out with no warning. She glanced over to the power light on the computer and saw it was still on, however, her screen had disappeared. Absently pressing keys and sliding the mouse back and forth did not bring it back to life. She crossed her arms and stared at the black screen. Her computer had just died.

A knock on the door diverted her attention. There was no one else in the office suite. Everyone had been dispatched to other locations to help and fill in whatever gaps there were. Juliette walked briskly toward the door and turned the knob, swinging the door open. Standing there was a man wearing a black suit, black tie, white shirt, and dark sunglasses. He smiled and extended his hand.

"Hi, I'm Craig Johnson, United States Secret Service. You must be Juliette Keaton," he said as he stood outside the doorframe.

CHAPTER TWENTY-NINE

Searching the Woods

Hawk and Jillian drove down on Fort Wilderness Trail in the direction of the check-in area of the main entrance. The Reception Outpost was where each guest began their wilderness adventure. The two-lane paved road cut a civilized path through Disney's version of a rugged wilderness. The campground was massive, but it was one of the most state-of-the-art luxury campgrounds in the world.

Slowing the vehicle, they turned as they reached the outpost, and now they faced the opposite direction of where they had just come from. The engine idled. Hawk looked out across the hood of the little pickup truck. Jillian peered at the road ahead, then shot him a look. He could tell she was about to say something.

"Are you thinking, or are you lost?"

Hawk smiled. "I'm not lost."

"That's good, I was hoping you didn't hit your head when you took a dive off the falls and forget what you were doing."

"No, I really was just thinking." Hawk looked at her. "I said earlier that something has to be out of place. Something out here is not quite right. All we have to do is find it."

"Then let's go find it." Jillian motioned for him to get moving.

"I'm not sure where to go and look." He allowed the truck to roll forward slowly.

"We're looking for something that's not right—that doesn't fit." Jillian repeated their earlier thoughts. "So to find it, do something that doesn't make sense."

Hawk nodded and slowed at the first intersection they came to. The sign pointed to their left, indicating a road called Peacock Pass. Steering to his left, he drove through the cabin section of the campground.

A good portion of the 750-acre pine and cypress forest of Disney's Fort Wilderness Resort & Campground was left as natural as possible. Evoking the timeless beauty of the American frontier, the resort teemed with deer, ducks, armadillos, and rabbits. Trails, swimming holes, and bathhouses were seamlessly tucked into the surroundings. The cabin section offered guests the experience of pioneer life with all the conveniences of home. Loaded with rustic charm, these log cabins were private and spacious, and there was row after row of them.

The short distance down Peacock Pass brought them to their first turn. Taking the truck to the left, they traveled the loop called Willow Way. Each loop of the resort was numbered, and along each loop were cabins or campsites for guests.

"Look for something, anything that seems out of place," Hawk said. They each looked out the windows.

Silently, they traveled Willow Way, which eventually wound them back to Peacock Pass. Making a left, the next loop was Heron Hollow, and they repeated their process of searching. There was nothing out of the ordinary. The Wilderness Swimming Pool was on their left as they came to the intersection of another loop. Again turning down the pathway, Hawk and Jillian wound their way through each of the cabin sections along the Peacock Pass route. Loop after loop—Moccasin Trail, Cedar Circle, Settler's Bend, and Arrowhead Way—all proved to be the same endless row of cabin campsites.

The truck came to a stop at the edge of the street, and Hawk had to either go straight across into Bobcat Bend or choose to explore the loops of Big Pine Drive.

"What do you think?" he asked as they studied the view.

The search had been uneventful and was taking a long time. Jillian pointed to the right. "If we go this way, where do we end up?"

"It's all more of the same—loops of cabins or campsites."

She nodded in understanding. Investigative work could be time-consuming and tedious, and this was destined to turn out to be both. Hawk waited for her answer. Jillian looked to the left, and with a tilt of her head, indicated for him to turn the truck in that direction.

"Are you sure?"

"No, I have no idea," Jillian said in surprise. "Do you think we need to go another way?"

"I'm just giving you a hard time." He smiled. "I just know we figured out what the clue on the paper meant. It was a notification that something was here at Fort Wilderness."

The truck slowly traveled and came to the intersection of Spanish Moss Lane. Turning the truck into the next loop, this time they were greeted by mobile homes and more traditional campsites. The cabins were a form of glamping. This area was used by those who either traveled in RVs or preferred a more realistic camping experience. It was longer and covered more ground than the cabin loops, and yet nothing seemed out of the ordinary. Eventually, they wound their way back to the end of the loop and turned right again.

Immediately, the terrain looked a little different.

"Where are we now?" Jillian slid forward in her seat a little bit and peered through the window. The forest grew denser on either side of the vehicle as they drove. Hawk saw nothing but took a moment to explain.

"This road runs down to a place called Creekside Meadow. It's often used by scouting groups and camping clubs. When it's full and the occupancy is high, it's a tent city. There's a bathhouse and a waterfront connected to it. The road will actually be blocked ahead of us as guests can only go so much further down this way." He pointed ahead of them. "Once we get to the end of the guest area, the roadway cuts back over toward the Wilderness Lodge. This is a service road." Hawk slowed the vehicle and then brought it to a full stop.

Saying nothing, he put the gearshift into reverse and eased the truck back a few feet before stopping once again. Jillian looked out the window, following Hawk's gaze, and spotted what he was looking at. A silver Airstream camper was parked under a clump of trees, partially hidden from view, and almost unnoticeable—except it was isolated in an empty area of the campground.

"That is out of place," Hawk said, pointing at the silver-riveted camper. "Most definitely out of place."

"Let me place a call and see if anyone is supposed to be assigned to camp here." Jillian said as she reached for her phone.

"No, don't. Not yet." Hawk reached over and held her hand to prevent her from calling. He leaned closer to her before continuing. "If someone is listening in, we don't want to let them know what we're doing or where we're at."

Nodding in agreement, Jillian looked back toward the silver, bullet-shaped recreational vehicle. "Then what do you want to do?"

"I want to check it out and see why it's parked here." Hawk looked around and then put the truck in reverse again, slowly backing up. "That area is primarily for tents only. It's highly unusual for a camper to be parked there, unless it was the hub for a large group. The Airstream is sitting all by itself. It's partially hidden, which makes me think that someone doesn't want to be noticed. And did you see there's no vehicle attached to it, so it can't leave? It's like it's been disconnected and abandoned."

The truck turned and retraced the roadway they had driven before. Big Pine Drive took the pair back to Fort Wilderness Trail. Hawk turned the truck to the left and made his way down the main entrance route of the campground. Passing the Meadow Trading Post and recreation area on the right, he pulled into the loop on the left. This loop numbered in the 900s and was called Quail Trail. He slowed as they made their way past the campers parked there and finally brought the truck to a stop on the side of the roadway.

"We walk from here," Hawk said, as he slid out of the front seat. "We'll have to cut through the woods. There's a bridge that will take us over a small creek, and then we should be able to come up through the trees behind the Airstream."

"And get a closer look?" Jillian followed his lead.

"Exactly." Hawk noticed how Jillian reached toward the small of her back. "Is something wrong?"

"Reflex. I keep reaching back for my handgun, but with all the security protocols, I haven't been able to take it with me like I usually do. I haven't even had the chance to retrieve it from the safe at my place since this all started." Hawk knew she had been frustrated and furious about some of the security restraints the Secret Service had demanded with the president on site, even among Disney security. She didn't like it, but she had abided by it because she was sensitive to the rule-setting process they needed to go through to keep the president safe. He'd forgotten she didn't have her weapon on her and wished she did. But for now, they would go see what they could find.

Trudging carefully through the woods, they crossed the bridge and now moved through the densely wooded forest. Disney had recently done an extensive clearing out of much of the undergrowth due to hurricane damage. It was a constant battle to let the forest grow wild but still keep it trimmed in case of a catastrophic storm event.

Breaking into the clearing, they now moved slower, trying not to snap branches on the ground as they picked their way toward the next bunch of trees in front of them. Hawk crouched down behind a tree and motioned for Jillian to do the same. Just beyond this next clump of trees, in the next clearing, was the side of the silver Airstream.

The thin, light smell of pine trees pushed past them as they knelt behind the trees, looking across for any sign of activity around the sterling camper. Hawk sensed that Jillian had grown tense as if getting ready for a fight. His heart beat faster too. He exhaled trying to calm himself so he could think. He feared that if they had found something important, they were either getting ready to make a startling discovery or to find themselves in a conflict with someone who didn't want them to make that discovery.

Both options caused a bit of angst. Then the thought wandered across his mind that this also might be a great deal of anxiety over nothing but an Airstream camper parked badly.

"I'll circle around the back of the camper; you move around the front." Hawk's voice was now a whisper. "If there's no one out here to stop us, when we get to the door, let me go in first. Hang back until I give you an all clear."

"No, why don't you let me go in first. I'm the head of security and I am supposed to keep you safe. You hang back and I'll give you an all clear." She too whispered.

"I need you to wait outside. If there's someone inside and they get past me, you have to stop them." He turned to look at her. "So we go with my plan."

"Wait, if I go in first and they get past me, then you can stop them. There's no difference."

"There's a big difference." Hawk smiled. "We go with my plan because you work for me and that way you can tell everyone that you tried to stop me, but I wouldn't listen. If something bad happens to me, everyone will believe that I didn't take your advice and got myself messed up. That way, your personnel file will still be clean with no bad marks or poor performance reviews." Hawk started to move. "That way you won't lose your end-of-the-year bonus." He chuckled and waved her off in the other direction.

"You're kind of a jerk sometimes, you know that?" She smiled and followed him.

"Yeah, but you can't speak to your boss that way. That will definitely go into your file and become part of your permanent record." He chuckled.

CHAPTER THIRTY

Trailer Trash

Jillian crept toward the front of the Airstream, staying low so she could not be seen if anyone were to look out the windows. This model had large, tinted windows that wrapped around the front end, giving it a retro-spaceship kind of look. She slowly moved out beyond the tongue of the trailer where it would be hitched to whatever vehicle would have been used to tow it.

Noticing the ground beside her, she hurried to get back to a safer position. Being out this far in front of the camper left her exposed and easier to spot than when she hugged the side of the RV. She saw tire tracks from the vehicle that had pulled the camper into this place. The angle in which the camper was parked seemed to indicate it had been shoved quickly into this spot with the intent to keep it hidden as much as possible and then abandoned.

Jillian also noticed that as it was backed into place, it had snapped the branches of some trees that were hanging lower than the camper could slide under. It was unusual for someone to so blatantly disregard the potential for damaging their camper.

Clearing the front, she saw Hawk sliding along the side of the camper after rounding the back. He had taken the same approach she had, staying low and trying not to be seen. Watching him, she was reminded again of how amazed she was at his ability to remember and notice detail. That's how they had ended up here. Jillian had told him on more than one occasion that he probably would have made an incredible investigator or agent. He was fearless, brave, smart, and had an overwhelming desire for good. He believed he could change the world.

Although she usually feigned that it irritated her and that he was just too good, this was another part of him she had admired enough to leave her position with Homeland Security to help him protect the secrets of Walt Disney. Amazingly enough, what they were doing now had nothing to do with those secrets, or if it did, she had not figured out the connection.

Hawk motioned her to wait. She was on one knee, just to the right of the only door on the camper. Hawk was now on the opposite side of that door, getting ready to make the move to open it.

"One . . . two . . ." he mouthed to her without saying a word out loud.

On three, he moved quickly and slid his hand to the side of the door latch, and with a hard tug, he popped it and the door swung open. Before it hit the side of the camper, he was up the step and inside. She moved into the door opening, hanging back and making a barricade in the doorframe if anyone decided they were going to come out.

Listening closely, she heard Hawk moving in the camper.

"Hawk?" she called out as she could no longer hear him stepping through the living area of the camper.

"Clear." His voice carried through the doorway. She stepped up and inside.

Hawk stood at the back of the camper. A quick glance allowed her to inventory the surroundings. The Airstream was nearly thirty feet long, which she had surmised as she moved around it outside. The side entrance door had brought them into the lounging couch area immediately to their right and the galley kitchen area to their left. The dining area was opposite the galley. The table was empty, and the interior continued the retro, sleek silver style that the exterior suggested. This was a well-kept, well-loved, well-used RV.

Motioning her to move forward, Hawk was getting ready to open the door to what she thought was the lavatory. He once again reached slowly toward the door latch, slid his hand behind it, and with a tug opened it. It was empty. He now moved forward to another set of doors—a closet or wardrobe she assumed. As he reached for the door, a thump came from behind the door.

He pulled his hand back; the unexpected noise having startled them both. Jillian had taken a half-step back.

Hawk shook out his hands as he once again reached for the wardrobe door. Quickly, he opened it and stepped in front of the opening to see what was inside. His eyes widened, and he reached in. Jillian rushed to his side and felt a fluttering in her stomach as she now saw what, who, Hawk reached for. First Lady of the United States, Kimberly Pride was folded in a heap inside the closet.

Hawk cradled her body, pulled her out, and sat her on the floor of the camper. Her hands had been bound and tied to her ankles, causing her body to bend forward over her knees. The angle had prevented both her arms and legs from being able to move, and any attempt would have caused pain, and the discomfort of no mobility would have been intensified. There was another rope around her neck, pulling her head forward and drawing it down until her chin was resting on her knees as well.

Jillian could not remember ever seeing this type of restraint in all her years of investigations. The unusual technique rendered the victim uncomfortable and completely immobilized.

A piece of duct tape covered Kim's mouth. Her eyes were wide with fear but also laced with tears of relief. Jillian went to work unraveling the network of knots that had been used with the ropes as Hawk gently pulled back the duct tape from her mouth. The tearing sound was followed by a gasp of precious air. For the first time since her kidnapping, the first lady could breathe unencumbered.

Her gasp was followed by a question. "Where's Mary?" Kim Pride said, with wide eyes. Tears flowed down her cheeks. The second question came just as quickly. "Where's Tyler?"

"We don't know." Hawk placed his hand behind her head, trying to comfort her.

Jillian released the rope that had pulled her head forward, and she gingerly sat up. Once that rope was loose, the others released quickly, allowing her to finally stretch out her limbs,

"Take it easy . . . don't rush . . . give it a minute to get your blood flowing," Hawk said gently.

She turned toward him. "What do you mean you don't know where Mary and Tyler are?" She reached out and grabbed Hawk by the shirt. "You have to find them."

"We will. We're trying. We just found you first. You need to tell us what happened if you can."

Kim rested her head on his chest as she cried.

Jillian eased back and sat down next to the first lady. "I would love to make a call to let someone know we found her, but I'm hesitant."

"You should be." Kim turned toward her. The pitch of her voice was elevated. "I don't know who we can trust anymore."

Jillian looked toward Hawk, whose eyes had widened at her words. A quick shake of his head confirmed that Jillian would not be calling anyone yet.

"Here, Kim." Hawk eased an arm behind her to help her get up. "If you can, let's sit you on this couch, and you can tell us what happened."

Jillian rose to help her as well and noticed that she still gripped Hawk's shirt. What the first lady had lived through had been traumatic, and she was terrified. Her hand trembled as Hawk reached up and urged her to release his shirt. She took a seat on the couch. Jillian reflexively reached over and took Kim's arm and rubbed it to encourage the blood to start flowing again. Now that she had let go of his shirt, Hawk did the same with the other.

"Can you tell us what happened?" Jillian gently squeezed the first lady's arm while continuing to rub it.

"We left the Transportation and Ticket Center on schedule." Kim looked at Jillian and then to Hawk as she spoke. "The monorail was the one with the red stripe. Mary was so excited. Red is her favorite color. She asked her dad how long his speech would take and if she could ride Test Track when he was done." Kim sniffed as a tear trickled from the corner of her eye. "Tyler told her he would see what he could do to make it happen."

Jillian thought she heard something outside and held up her hand to silence them. Easing up and over to the door, which was still open, she peered out, looking both ways. Nothing. She hoped it had only been the wind. "It's okay."

"We had just ridden down the monorail track into the trees," Kim said. "We were laughing and having fun, making plans for the day, when an alarm sounded, and the monorail slowed down. Then it stopped."

"Where did it stop?" Hawk leaned in.

"Someplace where they work on them, I guess. It wasn't a station. It was more like a maintenance place. We sat there for a moment or two before Tyler stood up and went over to the door. He got the angriest look on his face. He told us to run as soon as the doors opened!" Kim sobbed. "The doors opened, and there were two men. They shoved Tyler backward—hard! He went flying all the way across the monorail car and hit the doors on the other side. The other man grabbed Mary and told me not to scream. To come with him if I didn't want her to get hurt." Kim stopped to take a breath. "I begged him to let her go."

"Then what happened?" Jillian asked.

"Then Tyler got up and punched the man who had pushed him. The guy fell to the floor, and Tyler rushed the other one who had Mary. Then the man Tyler hit used some sort of stun gun on my husband, and he slumped to the ground. The man kicked him in the head." Tears streamed down the first lady's face. "Tyler didn't move. I got up and tried to rush over to him, but the guy grabbed me and put a blindfold on. I think Mary also. They dragged us down the steps and into a car." Kim's eyes widened at the memory. "I was screaming, and the man slapped me and told me to be quiet or I would never see my husband again. I didn't scream anymore."

"So you didn't see what happened to Tyler and Mary after they blindfolded you?" Hawk stated the obvious, but he wanted to make sure there wasn't any other detail she had missed.

"No, the car drove away, and it seemed like we were never going to stop. The car bounced when it left the road, and then I was manhandled into this camper. They tied me up and took off the blindfold, then shoved me into the closet. I heard Mary crying and started to scream her name when they slapped duct tape over my mouth. Then they closed the door to the closet." Kim caught her breath. "The next thing I saw was the two of you."

Jillian patted her shoulder. "Did you get a good look at the men who stopped the monorail and attacked you?"

"Sure, but there's not much to describe—military looking, strong, dark hair. They wore dark sunglasses that hid their features some. Black fatigues—the kind where you don't want to be seen at night."

Jillian looked up at Hawk and could tell he had the same thought she had. They had met one of the attackers. So what had he been doing on Main Street USA at the hub?

"Kim, you have to trust us. We're going to get you out of here," Hawk said.

"You have to find Mary and Tyler," Kim cried. "Hawk, Tyler wanted to tell you something. He said he needed your help and would talk to you today. I know this sounds crazy, but I don't know who we can trust anymore."

Hawk again looked at Jillian before softly saying to Kim, "What did he want to tell me?"

"I don't know." She hung her head. "He wouldn't say."

"That's all right," Hawk said. "Do you have any idea who did this?"

"Scum!" Kim nearly spat as she spoke.

"Scum? What scum?" Jillian raised an eyebrow.

"Scum is what Tyler calls the power-abusing, no-scruples, Washington political insiders. He is always saying he's trying to scrape the layer of scum off

Washington so the good people below that layer can do what they're supposed to do. But he says the scum likes to run. You get rid of some of the layer, and it seeps back in and tries to take over. He calls them scum." Kim left her mouth open and breathed heavily. "Hawk, I don't know who the scum is and who isn't."

"Kim, we'll do our best to keep you safe and find Mary and Tyler." Hawk got up and peered out the door. "But first we need to get you someplace safe."

Jillian followed his lead and moved to the doorway. Reaching out, she grabbed Hawk by the arm above his elbow and gave his arm a squeeze. He turned back to face her.

"Why do you think she was left unguarded?" Jillian asked.

Hawk rubbed his chin. "Maybe because they were convinced no one would find her. Or they planned on coming back later."

"That's what I was thinking too. But it also might mean that there's only a small group at work here, and they don't have enough manpower to pull off everything they planned."

"The problem is we don't know the good guys from the bad guys."

"You mean, we don't know who the scum is."

CHAPTER THIRTY-ONE

Off the Record

David Walker rubbed his eyes and slumped into his chair. He was seated in the media area and had spent the last hour pushing and pressing his sources for information. He realized that with some of these trusted sources, he may have just burned some bridges that he could never cross again. He had been specific, testing them to see if they had any knowledge of some deep conspiracy against the president. He wanted to see if there was any evidence they could offer to prove such a claim.

Now he was troubled. Some had scoffed at the notion, others had not. The ones who had spoken to him off the record gave him details that were prompted by his driving questions—most never asked by the press. Some of these sources seemed overly eager to share the information, as if they had been wanting a chance to let their feelings, observations, and even fears become public. He had given them a chance to vent, if only for a moment. What troubled him was that now he had more speculation and conjecture than fact and proof. Yet, as tempting as it might be to share what he had unofficially been told, he would not compromise his principles. He needed at least one source he could put on the record to verify the information.

Maybe the challenge Juliette Keaton had given him was valid. He was now willing to see a truth that he wasn't before. It seemed so unlikely, but that was the problem she had laid down as a challenge for him.

"Well?" Allie Crossman walked over when he ended his last call. "What are we into here?"

"I'm not sure, Allie," David admitted. "It still sounds crazy, but the sound of crazy is not as loud as it was before."

"What does that mean?"

"It means, I don't know." David shrugged. "It could be something, or it could be nothing."

"And?"

"And what?" David looked at her, his brow furrowed. "I still have nothing real—no hard evidence—just a bunch of rumors."

"Well, you need to decide how you're going to approach this, because there's a guest coming over to see you."

"Who?"

"Dana Brown." Allie pointed across the parking lot at the woman who approached.

The president's press secretary walked past the other media tents directly toward theirs. The line of security keeping the media back from the main walkway had doubled on her approach. It was clear Dana Brown would not be speaking to the rest of the media or taking their questions. She nodded at him when she entered the tent. David noted lines of stress creasing her pleasant face. Dana walked directly toward him, stood in front of him, smoothed her dress, and asked if she could take a seat.

David rose to his feet, apologizing. "Excuse me, of course, please take a seat."

Dana sat down and rolled her neck and shoulders before speaking. "I understand you have some questions for me."

"I've got a *lot* of questions." David motioned for Allie to move John Ware into position with his camera.

Allie shook her head in the negative and mouthed the word, "No."

David's eyes widened, and he turned back to the press secretary. "So I take it this is an off-the-record conversation?"

"Is that a problem?"

"No, it seems to be the story of all my conversations today." He sighed.

"Well, if you have nothing to ask off the record, I have things to do." Dana leaned forward to get up. "Allie led me to believe you wanted to talk with me."

"I do." David motioned her back in the chair. "I just don't know exactly how to have a conversation with you."

Dana tilted her head. "That's intriguing." She relaxed in her seat.

"I'm aware the president and his family are missing."

"As is everyone here, I presume." Dana motioned to the many press tents surrounding them.

"But there has been no official word yet," David said, stating the obvious.

"You mean there has been no official explanation yet," Dana corrected. "I am always intrigued at why the press always wants an official word on the obvious, when what they really want is an explanation. But they get feisty when I won't give them a word on what they already know, and the explanation is not what they want to hear." Dana smiled as she often did in the middle of a press briefing. "Why is it that everyone is so interested in telling the story they want to tell instead of the real story that needs to be told?"

"I suppose that's true." David knew at some level she was correct. She dealt with the bias of the press every day. "I guess because we—the press—believe we know what the people should hear and what they want to hear."

Dana continued to smile. "And what about the truth?"

There was that word again. David thought carefully about what he wanted to say next. He decided there was no easy way, and since this might be his only opportunity, he had to ask.

"This is off the record," he said.

"Of course. Nothing I say to you will be verified, and if you claim that it is, or I verified it, you and I will never speak again. That's how off the record we are right now."

David glanced at Allie, who nodded at him to continue. He realized that Allie had been working, as she always did, behind the scenes to get him in the best position to find and tell the story. So this was it.

"Do you have reason to believe there is a conspiracy responsible for the disappearance of the president and the first family?" David stared at her, waiting for an answer.

Dana smiled, made eye contact with Allie, and then addressed David. "It would seem that it would have to be a conspiracy of some sort if the president and the first family are missing. It's the only logical explanation."

Dana got up, nodded toward Allie, and then turned away.

David stood and followed her, whispering, "Who is it?"

Dana stopped short, turned on him, and looked him dead in the eye. "Figure it out, then tell the real story."

Dana Brown left the tent. Many times, he had seen her walk out of the press room as reporters yelled out questions they knew she was never going to answer. Although he had the urge to do so now, he knew there would be no more answers coming. She had just unofficially confirmed for him what he had needed to know. Now what was he going to do with that information?

CHAPTER THIRTY-TWO

A Dead Computer

Jillian entered Juliette's office suite without knocking. It was the open-door policy that Juliette shared with her, Hawk, Shep, and Jonathan. Fully expecting to see Juliette on the phone or working on her computer, she pulled up short when she found Secret Service Agent Craig Johnson seated in the chair across from her desk. As she entered, he stood.

"I'm so sorry, Juliette," Jillian said. "I should have knocked."

"It's fine." Juliette cut her eyes to the Secret Service agent.

"I'm glad you showed up," Craig said. "As a matter of fact, maybe you can help me. I'm trying to locate Dr. Hawkes. My superiors asked me to check in with him and see if he has any ideas, leads, thoughts, or has been able to decipher the events of the day."

"You mean you're supposed to check *up* on him, not *in* with him," Jillian corrected.

"I wouldn't put it that way. But I was tasked to speak with him." Craig smiled. "Could you tell me where he is, please?"

"I can't." Jillian smiled. "I really can't. I don't know where he is right now. I hope to hear from him later. If I do, I'll try to let you know."

"All right, I will take that as a no," Johnson said, eyeing them both suspiciously. "I'll count on you letting me know when you hear from him."

Johnson moved across the room without another word and let himself out. Both women waited until he was gone. Juliette walked softly to the door and leaned against it, listening for any sounds in the hallway, then turned the lock. She strode quickly back across the room and motioned for Jillian to take a seat.

Juliette sat down in the chair beside her and spoke in a hushed tone. "You won't believe what happened," she began.

"I was working on my computer, digging into the evidence for a conspiracy against the president, and then my screen just went blank. It died, not like I had lost a connection to the Internet, but more like something decided my computer didn't need to work any longer. The screen has gone black, it won't reboot, and I can't turn it on or off. It's really weird. Then just after that happens, the Secret Service agent shows up at my door."

Jillian looked toward the computer, then back to Juliette. "So what have we found out about this deep-state conspiracy?"

Juliette ran her fingers lightly through her hair. "I read some strange stuff. The only articles with credibility were written by GNN reporter David Walker. I have a friend who is the producer, and I trust her. I suggested he push his sources and find out if it could be true. I have a feeling he'll come up with something." Placing her hands in her lap, she leaned forward. "What have you been doing? Where is Hawk? You know, right?"

"Actually, I don't know where he is." Jillian leaned closer and spoke in a whisper. "But we found the first lady."

Juliette gasped. "Is she alive? Is she hurt?"

"More or less." Jillian half smiled. "She's alive, shaken up, and terrified, but she's not significantly hurt. No real damage done, but if we hadn't found her, she would have been in real trouble. She wants to know where her family is."

"Where did you find her?"

"Stashed away in a camper in Fort Wilderness." Jillian licked her dry lips and continued. "I asked Disney security to do a quiet search, making sure everyone we have registered is in their cabin or campsite. I gave the instructions as part of the ongoing search for anything out of the ordinary."

"And you are doing this because?"

"I have a feeling the camper she was tied up in was borrowed from someone. I fear it may be the two dead bodies we found in the maintenance marina. If we can find out who is not in the right spot in the campground, we may find out the identity of our victims and add another piece to this crazy puzzle."

"That's smart." Juliette nodded. "Good job."

"Thanks."

"So, where is the first lady and Hawk?"

"That I really don't know. He said he would hide her somewhere she would be safe until we could figure this all out." Jillian pursed her lips. "I told him it would be risky not to let someone know where she is. The problem is, who do we trust? Kim Pride was pretty insistent they suspect there are people, she called them scum, out to get Tyler. She wants *us* to find her daughter and husband."

Jillian could sense that, like herself, Juliette was weighing the wisdom of not telling anyone they had found the first lady. By keeping her hidden and by having knowledge of where she was, they were obstructing the search. Juliette nodded, and Jillian knew she understood and was willing to go along with whatever plan Hawk was putting into action.

"Of course, so what's the next step?" Juliette asked.

Jillian moved around the desk to inspect Juliette's computer. She absently clicked the mouse, touched the screen, tried to reboot it, and had the same luck Juliette was having.

"Hawk said he would let us know where to find her. He also said he had an idea of where he was going next. I'll tell you, Juliette, it's wicked scary how he's able to put clues together in his head. The stuff he connected was so random, and yet it made sense."

"That's what he does."

"He said he would use Disney Code to communicate with us, so we'll just have to wait." Jillian shrugged at the dead computer.

Juliette smiled. "So, you didn't lie to the Secret Service. You don't know where Hawk is right now, and you aren't sure what he's up to at this moment."

"True, I don't," Jillian said. "What I'll do now is send our security team to the campground, get them moving as fast as they can, and we'll try to track down that info. I'll keep you posted. I just wanted to see if we had any evidence or leads on the possible conspiracy yet."

Just then, a faint beep emanated from the computer, and the screen came back to life. Glowing and illuminated, it was the same home screen that always appeared. The Disney logo was screen center, and all the icons surrounding it represented work files on Juliette's computer. They looked at each other and then back at the computer.

"That's odd," Juliette moved around the desk next to Jillian and looked at the computer.

"I'll say." Jillian shook her head. "My suspicious side says your computer's meltdown was no accident. Someone is monitoring what you look at on your PC. They didn't like it, and they killed it for you."

"Do you think they're monitoring our conversations?"

"Well, that's a little tougher. We swept the office for listening devices just before the president arrived."

"But if the Secret Service did the sweep, and they're in on it . . ." Juliette glanced around the room as if looking for a listening device.

"No, after the Secret Service swept the office, I swept it again. It's clean."

"Wait, why would you do it again?" Juliette asked with obvious confusion.

Jillian hesitated to tell her, then decided to let her know. "It was Hawk's idea. He knew I didn't like the way we were being shut out of the preparations for the president's arrival. He didn't like how intrusive and disruptive it was having the first family as guests, so he had me sweep all of our offices just to make sure Big Brother wasn't listening in."

"Why did he do that?" Juliette wondered out loud. "Did he suspect something was going on?"

"If he did, he didn't tell me." Jillian headed toward the door. "Keep me posted on what you find. I'll do the same." She opened the door, looked into the hallway, then closed the door and mouthed the words silently. "Be safe." She smiled and exited the office.

CHAPTER THIRTY-THREE

A Faraway Galaxy

On the edge of the galaxy, between the Unknown Regions and Wild Space, there is a long-forgotten planet named Batuu. Batuu's largest village is a settlement known as Black Spire Outpost, which was a thriving destination for those who would prefer to go about their business unnoticed. This was the connection place for various scoundrels, rogues, and smugglers, and recently, whispers reporting sightings of people associated with the Resistance.

The bad news was that rumors of the Resistance had drawn the attention of the First Order, who were eager to stomp out any remaining flickers of opposition to their absolute control. There was a conflict coming, and in the midst of it was an exotic outpost surrounded by a beautiful landscape dominated by the petrified remains of towering ancient trees, from which Black Spire Outpost drew its name. A long-gone civilization had left ruins behind on which the modern village was built.

It was a village not only beautiful but dangerous, because it was a village of secrets, built upon secrets, buried below other secrets.

Hawk eased himself into the world within a world. The reimagining expansion of Disney's Hollywood Studios had incorporated two of Disney's most valuable assets—the world of Pixar and the world of Lucasfilm. The result had been Pixar Toy Story Land and then what some considered the most amazing and immersive expansion ever, a *Star Wars* themed land called Star Wars: Galaxy's Edge.

Attention to detail in the Black Spire Outpost was as intricate as anywhere in the world of Walt Disney theme parks. The worldwide fan base, the heightened expectations, and the creative forces of Lucasfilm and Disney Imagineering had put a great deal of pressure on everyone involved to make sure this attraction did not disappoint and could live up to the hype that surrounded it as it was built. It had not disappointed and more than lived up to the hype.

Savi's Workshop, the Droid Depot, Oga's Cantina, Docking Bay 7 Food and Cargo, Dok-Ondar's Den of Antiquities, and the Toydarian Toymaker were all creatively themed shopping and dining areas filled with amazing surprises and details for guests to discover. When the land opened to the public, the response had been so overwhelming that cast members actually had to limit the number of people inside to handle the traffic flow. It was never empty, the way it was now. Hawk realized as he made his way into this world that he was seeing it in a way that others only wished they could.

After safely hiding Kim Pride, he quickly went to work on the next of the clues he had discovered in Edward Fenn's locker. The names of Allen, Stevens, and McKay had been familiar enough on the old parchment paper for him to make the jump to Fort Wilderness. The coin still had him confused. But the more he thought about the remaining clue—the E-Ticket with words written on it—the more he realized he needed to search Disney's Hollywood Studios.

The green-colored E-Ticket had listed what were considered the top-tier attractions for each land. In the early 1980s, these tickets had disappeared, so this one captured the Magic Kingdom world from a bygone era. It was a long time ago, and a world that now seemed far away.

His original thought was the obvious one. The two attractions listed in Liberty Square as E-Ticket attractions were the Haunted Mansion and the Hall of Presidents. He had instantly thought the Hall of Presidents might be the place where he could find something. But that was too obvious, considering how well written the other clue had been.

But because the ticket was from long ago in a place that was now very far way, his mind thought back to the familiar tagline of *Star Wars*—*A long time ago in a galaxy, far, far away.* It wasn't much, but it had stuck in his brain. But that wasn't what had convinced him about where to search. The Hall of Presidents was important. It was a reminder that this search revolved around the president of the United States. But the words on the E-Ticket persuaded him where to search next. The phrase, *The Resistance Has Arisen*, meant something very important. Almost too easy, he thought.

As a result, he now traveled into the outskirts, where cast members preferred and were required to go about their business unnoticed. But because the clue seemed too easy, he worried he had made a mistake, or maybe was walking into a trap. Proceeding into the queue line, he slowly and cautiously walked through the rocky cliffs of Batuu.

The color scheme of this world had an official name, but Hawk had always insisted it looked the same color as a baked loaf of bread, so he referred to it as fresh-bread beige. The mud-shaded ground, marked with soldiers' footprints and droid tracks, offered a detail that guests instantly loved. What many guests didn't know was that the track marks had been made from the actual R2-D2 from the movie, *A New Hope*.

Now sliding into the forest cover, he stuck to the pathway until it came to some caves, which led to an opening into the heart of the Black Spire Outpost. The ruins were now the home of a Rebel camp. Hawk knew the storyline had been designed to create the illusion that the Rebels, along with the First Order, were all nearby, searching for something important.

At this point, he veered off the usual path reserved for guests. The attraction named Star Wars: Rise of the Resistance mirrored the clue he carried in his mind. The attraction was a complete immersive experience in which guests boarded a starship and then were captured by a Star Destroyer, put into a hanger, an interrogation room, and onto a second ride vehicle—a trackless car. Finally, they experienced an epic battle with Kylo Ren. Guests flocked to this ride.

But Hawk had no intention of entering the attraction. Instead he stuck to the edges, abandoning the usual guest areas, and headed toward a backstage zone that split the Rise of the Resistance attraction with the Millennium Falcon: Smugglers Run attraction. The epic flight simulator took guests on the ride of their lives on one of the most famous space vehicles of all time. Standing with his back against the wall, he felt the coolness of the cappuccino-shaded rock and closed his eyes, calculating his next move.

The Millennium Falcon was the fictional starship featured in the *Star Wars* franchise. The modified YT-1300 Corellian light freighter was most often commanded by Corellian smuggler Han Solo and his Wookiee first mate, Chewbacca. The highly modified YT-1300 was durable and modular and touted as the second-fastest vessel in the Star Wars universe. The Falcon gained fame for the Kessel Run. In the original *Star Wars* film, Solo brags that the Falcon made the Kessel Run in "less than twelve parsecs." Most moviegoers missed the importance of Solo's remark and the problem with his description. The parsec was a unit of distance, not time, so that fact was debated by fans and, ultimately, explained many films later.

In *Solo: A Star Wars Story*, Solo's Kessel Run is explained in detail, providing the reason for the twelve-parsec boast. Solo made many calculated jumps into hyperspace to avoid killing the crew. Traveling through hyperspace was not a straight line and required careful navigation to avoid stars, planets, asteroids, and other obstacles. Because no long-distance journey could be made in a straight line, the fastest ship was the one in which the pilot could plot the most direct course, thereby traveling the least distance. Using the memory module of a damaged L3 droid in the ship's navigation, Solo took a "shortcut." Chewbacca suggests the real distance was closer to thirteen parsecs, but Solo insists, "Not if you round down." And so, the twelve-parsec claim was verified.

Now, here in Disney's Hollywood Studios, guests could see, explore, and pilot the fictional spacecraft on adventures of their very own. Hawk loved this addition to the theme park. As he studied the spaceship in front of him, a smile crossed his face as he suddenly realized the obvious. The Millennium Falcon was an infamous smuggling ship with compartments where the pilots could hide contraband and escape detection when needed.

If he was right, something or someone might be on board. Looking both ways, Hawk determined he was alone. He progressed toward the ramp that carried a person up into the bottom of the ship. This version of the Falcon was part model, part display, part of the attraction, and partly functional in some of the details that had been included. Now safely on board, he listened carefully for anyone moving in his vicinity. Sliding to his right, he could see the illuminated flooring panels. He remembered that one of them could actually be removed, just as they had in the film. It was used primarily for storage, but it also hid a secret compartment that could be used as a showpiece if they needed to make the setting look even more authentic.

Standing aboard the Falcon, he racked his brain to remember which of the panels could be removed. He knelt down and turned one of the handles only to find it did not move. Crawling forward to the next panel, he did the same. Gripping the handle, he turned it slowly and it clicked open. Now moving off to the side, he pulled up on the hinged panel, revealing a storage compartment below. As he opened it, he immediately saw the little girl lying inside.

Hands taped together, ankles taped together, and a piece of tape around her mouth, the wide-eyed and terrified Mary Pride looked up at Hawk. When she recognized him, tears streamed out the corners of her eyes.

Hawk jumped into the cargo hold. As gently as possible, he pulled the tape from her mouth.

"Dr. Hawkes, you found me," Mary Pride sobbed. "Where are my mom and dad?"

"I'll take you to them, but first let me get you loose." He gave a reassuring smile, trying to comfort her. "Do you know who brought you here?"

"It was a man dressed in a black military outfit," Mary said. "He told me to be quiet and stay here, or I would never see my mom and dad again."

Hawk helped her sit upright. "Did he hurt you?"

"No. I was just scared."

"Well, I think you were very brave." He helped her to her feet. "Are you okay to walk? I'll take you to your mom."

Her eyes widened. "What about my dad?"

"I still need to find your daddy. But I'll take you to your mom before I do."

"I want to go with you to my dad!" she cried, as they stepped up and out of the cargo hold.

"Like I said, you are very brave, Mary," Hawk whispered. "But I need to make sure you and your mom are safe first. It's what your dad would want me to do."

Hawk carefully replaced the panel, closing the cargo hold. Motioning for her to follow him, they made their way through the interior of the Falcon. Hawk paused momentarily as they advanced to the edge of the ramp.

"Stay here until I make sure the coast is clear," he whispered. Slowly, he walked down the ramp. At the bottom, he glanced left and right but didn't see any movement. He waved at Mary to follow him down the ramp. As she reached the halfway point of the ramp, Hawk heard the sound of voices behind him.

Immediately, he raced up the incline of the ramp, scooped Mary into his arms, and hoisted her back inside the Millennium Falcon. "*Shh* . . . someone's coming!"

Together, they raced to the front of the ship and slid into the command chairs on the bridge so they could peer out the window. Hawk knew that with more light outside than inside the spacecraft, they could sit and watch without being seen. At least he hoped that would be the case. Hawk watched two men dressed in black suits and dark sunglasses enter the Black Spire Outpost.

The men appeared to search the area quickly, not stopping or looking closely at any specific place. Hawk realized he had not had enough time to get Mary away from the Falcon. If they knew where she had been hidden, they would come to check on her. And if they did, he needed to come up with a plan. Otherwise, they would be cornered and trapped.

"Do you recognize those two men?" Hawk whispered.

"No," she said softly. "I think they're Secret Service guys."

"I think you're right. Are you sure you've never seen them before?"

Mary narrowed her eyes at them as they walked, talked, and searched the surrounding area. They walked quickly past the Millennium Falcon. She shook her head from side to side as if she were afraid they might hear even a whisper since they passed the starship so closely. The men walked quickly toward the backstage area and out of sight.

"I can't tell if they're good agents or bad agents," Mary whispered.

Hawk was puzzled. "What do you mean good agents or bad agents?"

She looked at him. "There are some of the Secret Service guys around my dad who don't seem to like him very much."

"Those guys tend to be pretty serious about their jobs, so I guess they might look angry."

"No, it's not how they look. I know they're really serious," she explained. "I hear them talking about Dad, and sometimes they say things about him that are kind of mean. They don't know I can hear them or that I'm paying attention. But if they don't like my dad, I don't like them. Those are the bad agents."

"Are there a lot of bad agents?"

"Just a few." Mary kept her eyes trained on the place they'd last seen the agents.

Hawk thought about what she said. He was also mystified by why the two agents had traversed the area so leisurely. They had been looking about as they proceeded, but they never slowed down, never deviated off their course, and only did a visual inspection as they walked. They weren't seriously looking for anyone or anything. He wondered why.

If this little girl was right, even she had picked up on the fact that there were some on the inside of the White House who didn't like her dad. He still found it difficult to believe in a Washington conspiracy, but with each passing moment it was the only theory that made sense.

Now he had to keep his promise to Mary and get her safely to her mom. To pull that off, Hawk needed to spirit her off the Falcon. Instead of moving into the backstage area like he'd planned, he would have to work his way out of the

Studios by heading out the front. They ran the risk of being seen, but he saw no other option.

Hawk turned to her. "Okay, Mary, we need to get you out of here. Stay as close to me as you can. I'll take you to your mommy just as fast as I can."

She smiled. "I'm ready. Let's go."

Hawk motioned for her to follow him off the Falcon and through the Black Spire Outpost.

CHAPTER THIRTY-FOUR

Meet the Press

The largest shimmering, freestanding sphere on the planet was about to serve as a backdrop for the historic press conference. Spaceship Earth loomed above them at one hundred and eighty feet in height. It was massive. As David Walker waited for the speakers to take the podium, he remembered something that had been included in their press packet about Spaceship Earth. Actually, it wasn't the biggest thing in Epcot.

According to the press materials, the entire sphere could be contained in the saltwater tank of the Seas with Nemo and Friends. He also found it fascinating that Spaceship Earth was comprised of two spheres. The first one contained the actual ride; the second was a sort of "shell," located outside the first sphere. The two-sphere design allowed rainwater to be gathered in a gutter system. In the event of rain, rather than water streaming down the sides onto guests below, the water was actually absorbed into the first sphere through small openings in the surface, then channeled into the World Showcase lagoon through the gutter system. The practical design of this location, originally the site of the president's speech that never happened, meant there was no chance of the speech being rained out even though it was outdoors.

The stage that had been set up for President Pride's speech was left unchanged, except now the entire press corps had assembled for a press conference to give the world some official information about the events that had taken place today. David's instincts told him they would not be given much information they didn't already know or hadn't already surmised. But people needed official statements, and that's what they were about to get. His mind whirred around the other story.

He knew there would be no mention of any inside conspiracy, although he was beginning to see mounting evidence that pointed in that direction.

Allie tapped him on the shoulder and signaled they had less than a minute until the press event began. On cue, the stage filled with an impressive lineup of administration officials and agency representatives. They were not all going to speak, but the show of force and solidarity was meant to reassure the public that everything was going to be fine. The situation was contained and under control.

David realized the government's response had been a forced decision. One of the press organizations had released an unconfirmed report that the president had been kidnapped, the monorail driver had committed suicide, and there were a number of terrorist organizations taking credit for the events of the day. Based on what he knew, terrorism wasn't in play, although it could not be completely ruled out, but the information had been intentionally leaked by someone who knew enough to get some of the story right. This was response and spin by the administration team.

Dana Brown, the president's press secretary, positioned herself behind the podium and began the briefing. "Thank you for gathering on such short notice. As most of you know and have already reported, an event took place here at the Epcot Resort this morning involving the president, the first lady, and their daughter, Mary. I am going to turn the podium over to Chief of Staff Samuel Reno to explain more."

Dana stepped back as Sam slid into position behind the podium. He usually spoke from notes on index cards and did so this time as well. Taking the small stack of cards out of his pocket, he quickly fidgeted them into place.

"President Pride had planned to give a speech this morning that we believed would be vital for the American people to hear. President Pride planned to cover a variety of topics, and many of you had speculated on what he was going to say. I've been briefed on your reporting. Some of you were in the ballpark, but most of you created a false narrative of what he intended to say . . . as seems to be your habit."

He paused and narrowed his eyes, his face reddening slightly. Reno looked like he was about to unleash an angry rant at the press, which he had done on occasion during his time as chief of staff. Instead, he took a deep breath, clenched his jaw, and continued. David believed he was angry that a number of the organizations had reported as fact what had been shared in the leak. GNN had chosen to delay their report, waiting for clarification. After this press conference, no matter what was said, they would have to report the unconfirmed information as well.

"President Pride's speech will be scheduled for a later time. As many of you know from firsthand accounts and from the reporting about the footage captured this morning at the monorail station, the president and his family were not on the monorail when it arrived here at Epcot. Gunshots were fired. I want to confirm for you that President Pride, Kim Pride, and Mary Pride were not involved in that shooting and were nowhere near that encounter. So, for all Americans who were concerned about what they have heard or what they might have seen with the limited video footage that has been released, I can confirm that the president and his family were not shot in that exchange."

Hands immediately went up as a number of reporters wanted to ask more questions that they might never have the opportunity to do at this presser. David had not raised his hand; he knew there were more speakers to follow.

Reno continued, "At this time, I want to recognize Jeremiah Stanley, head of the Secret Service."

Stanley stepped to the lectern and gripped it on both sides. David could see his knuckles turn white as his intense grip tightened. Looking down at the podium, he inhaled, hesitated, and then began to speak.

"As Mr. Reno explained, the first family was not on board the monorail when it arrived at Epcot this morning. President Pride, his wife, and his child boarded the monorail at the Transportation and Ticket Center as planned. However, they were not on board when it arrived here at Epcot.

"The driver was the only person on the monorail when it arrived. The Secret Service drew their weapons on him as the doors opened in order to secure it. The driver is now deceased, and we are currently trying to ascertain what happened to the president and his family. The Walt Disney World Resort has been temporarily closed as we conduct our investigation."

There was a powerful and audible reaction from the press corps, as he imagined there were in homes across America as they absorbed Stanley's words. While the press now punted decorum and yelled out questions, Stanley waved them off and left the lectern. Dana Brown strode back into place and uttered the phrase, "Any questions?"

"To be clear, Jeremiah Stanley just verified the president is missing?" a reporter from *MSNBC* asked.

"Yes, you heard what Director Stanley said," Dana flatly answered.

"Do you know where he is?" the *MSNBC* reporter followed up.

"We are currently trying to ascertain that, as Director Stanley stated."

A volley of questions followed. Many questions were drowned out by competing reporters, but the ones Dana could understand wanted clarification. David knew not a great deal more information would be shared.

A reporter from the *New York Times* was called on next. "When you say you are trying to ascertain where the president is, are you suggesting he has been kidnapped?"

"That is not what we have said," Dana responded and then pointed to a reporter from *Fox News*.

"Where is the vice president currently located, and has he now taken presidential authority?" The reporter was basically asking who was in charge of the country.

"The vice president is aware of the events of the day. He is working from his office in Washington, and he is monitoring the situation and is fully capable of doing anything that needs to be done in the administration during this time," Dana said.

Vice President Chris Ware often found himself having to defend the president or explain the president's position on a variety of topics. Unlike the president, he was at home in political circles and had served as a United States Senator from Florida. Many believed he would be a better president on the world stage than the man he worked for. David also sensed that on many issues, based on past statements and voting records, behind the scenes Ware was not always on board with the president's agenda. However, on the public front, he was a good soldier and always held to the administrative line.

"Did President Pride give you any indication that he had changed his plans on this trip or the agenda for the day?" a reporter from *CNN* asked as he was recognized.

"No, the plan was not changed by the president."

"Why did it take you so long to confirm what many of us were already reporting?" a correspondent from the *Washington Examiner* yelled out without being recognized.

"We always strive to be transparent with you." Dana leveled a cool gaze on the gathered reporters. "Many of you have been reporting information that is not factual and have chosen to fill in the gaps with your own narrative. The president has been fairly strong in suggesting you do that more often than not. We wanted to tell you what we could tell you at this time. What you choose to do with the truth is up to you. The president is missing along with his family. Thank you. We will give you more when we have something to share."

Dana Brown turned and walked away from the podium despite a barrage of questions that she did not slow down to answer. David watched as those on the podium filed down the steps away from the stage. Included at the far end of this official delegation had been Juliette Keaton, obviously representing the Disney Company. As they began to move, David repositioned himself to get close enough to the steps to make eye contact. As they did, he motioned for her to come over to where he was now standing. Juliette made her way to him, smiling as she approached.

"Mr. Walker, how can I help you?" Juliette asked. "And by the way, I appreciate you keeping our conversation from earlier confidential. Now you can officially report the first family is missing."

"I'm a man of my word," David said. "I also wanted to tell you that I've been working on the angle of this story that you suggested to me. I have found out some interesting things that tend to confirm some of the suspicions we spoke of."

Juliette leaned in closer to make sure she was not overheard. "I appreciate you doing that and not reporting on it . . . yet."

"To be honest, I don't really know what to do with it yet," he confessed.

"Have Allie set up a time for us to talk later." She began to move away. "I can't do that right now, and we can't talk here."

David Walker nodded and watched as she and the rest of the contingent retreated behind a barricade into a secure area and then disappeared into the theme park. He took in a deep breath and realized this was now an official national crisis. President Tyler, Kim Tyler, and Mary Tyler were officially missing, and the Secret Service of the United States just confirmed that they didn't know where they were. If the news reports were crazy before, they were about to discover an even louder version of craziness.

CHAPTER THIRTY-FIVE

Find a Way Out

The dedication plaque in Disney's Hollywood Studios reads, "The world you have entered was created by The Walt Disney Company and is dedicated to Hollywood—not a place on a map, but a state of mind that exists wherever people dream and wonder and imagine, a place where illusion and reality are fused by technological magic. We welcome you to a Hollywood that never was—and always will be. Dedicated by Michael Eisner, CEO of The Walt Disney Company May 1, 1989."

The Studios, as cast members often called it, had always been a work in progress. During the early years, the approach had been to make it a working movie studio where guests could immerse themselves into the world of filmmaking. Later, as production became too cost prohibitive for studios to work in a Florida setting, while the bulk of major production still happened on the West Coast and in New York, the studio evolved into a theme park with movie-based attractions. The most recent evolution had invigorated The Studios with new life as Disney-owned Pixar allowed for the creation of a Toy Story Land, and Lucasfilm properties allowed the *Star Wars*-themed land, the very land that Hawk and Mary Pride were now trying to escape without being seen.

As soon as the two Secret Service agents disappeared into the backstage area, Hawk took Mary's hand, and they made their way out of the Black Spire Outpost. Moving from Galaxy's Edge, they entered Toy Story Land. Interestingly enough, the first attraction they passed in this area of the park was the Alien Swirling Saucers, more spaceships.

The pair stepped carefully along the edges of the pathway, using natural obstacles to stay hidden. They arrived at the Slinky Dog Dash. This mind-stretching rollercoaster had been built upon a background story of a boy named Andy from *Toy Story* fame, who put together his Mega-Coaster Play Kit and created a ride featuring one of his most special toys—Slinky Dog. This attraction took up a large footprint in Toy Story Land, and Hawk used the queue line and sight breaks to their advantage as they moved past it. Pausing near the entrance, he knew that although they could stay close to the edge of the path, they would be more exposed in the next leg of their escape.

Hawk looked back and smiled at Mary. "We need to run a little bit now. If you have trouble keeping up, let me know, okay? See those buildings ahead of us? We'll make a dash for them. Are you ready?"

Taking a big breath, Mary nodded yes.

"Hang tight to my hand. Here we go." Aware that Mary's stride wasn't as long as his, Hawk began to jog.

Mary did a good job keeping up, even at his brisk pace. Hawk thought about where they needed to go next and mapped the route in his head. The course he believed would work best would carry them to the edge of Pixar Place and intersect the walk toward the Animation Courtyard. As they neared the intersection, they ducked under the covered entrance to Walt Disney Presents. With the key already in hand, he reached over and unlocked the door, easing it open to let them inside.

Still jogging through the empty walk-through attraction, Hawk noticed Mary had slowed. He looked back. She was distracted by the scenes, pictures, and memorabilia from the life of Walt Disney. Originally, this area had been known as One Man's Dream and been an attraction long before he became head of the company. Hawk had also spent time wandering through the exhibits and getting lost in the world of Walt Disney the man. He understood Mary's fascination and curiosity. Even more so now as the keeper of the secrets Walt and Roy Disney had left behind for him. In some ways, the mementos here kept him connected to Walt's life.

A few years ago, Hawk had removed some of the displays that had been a part of what Imagineer Farren Rales put in place to protect Walt and Roy's secrets. Hawk had been able to navigate the details and find the hidden items. After their discovery, Hawk had chosen to preserve some of the artifacts and store some of the items in other places. Many had been returned to the official Disney Archives. Others had ended up in his private collection. Yet he had been adamant that the presence of Walt in the studio theme park not be lost. Many of the displays had been improved and changed, including the feature film that honored the life and legacy of the Disney brothers.

Hawk gave Mary a moment and let her look through a glass window at a desk Walt had carved *WD* into as a schoolchild. Tapping her on the shoulder, he startled her back into the moment. "We have to keep moving, sweetheart. Maybe your mom and dad can bring you here later."

Weaving through the attraction, the pair silently crept into the theater area, then used the exit that would carry them behind a gift shop. Once they reached the end of the gift shop, Hawk knew there was a chance they might be spotted as they passed through the gateway back into the center of the park. Keeping up the pace and staying close to the walls of the buildings, they got ready to enter through the massive gate.

"When we get through the gate," Hawk explained, "we'll go left and head toward the Brown Derby Restaurant. We'll enter through the front door and exit through the back."

Sweat trickled down Mary's cheek. Hawk knew she was tired. "Ready?" She nodded as he took her hand. "Let's run."

Immediately, they sped up. Hawk glanced around as they jogged toward the Brown Derby but saw no signs of anyone looking for them. The Studios appeared deserted, but he knew differently. Even though they were some distance away now, he had already seen two agents. He also knew there had to be more of them combing the area. They were looking for the president, and they had no idea where he might be.

Cutting past the entrance to the Brown Derby, they slid inside to find a darkened dining area. Motioning for Mary to stay close, Hawk hurried into a backstage hallway toward a set of doors that he knew would lead them across Sunset Strip. If his plan worked, they would slip inside a set of shops and make their way to the main entrance of The Studios. Thank goodness, their trip across the strip remained uneventful. For the first time since they left the Millennium Falcon, Hawk thought they might actually get out of The Studios.

The Trolley Car Café always had the sweet smell of fresh-baked pastries and roasted coffee since it featured a Starbucks stop for guests. Once inside, he reached behind the counter and grabbed a cookie for Mary. A smile crossed her face as she promptly bit off the chocolate-iced ear, sending a smattering of crumbs cascading to the floor. She closed her eyes, smiling as she chewed, and

Hawk gave her a moment before tapping her on the shoulder and signaling for her to follow him again.

The Celebrity 5 & 10 was the next shop that would allow them to cover most of the length of Hollywood Boulevard within the confines of a closed-off shopping area. Reaching the end of the line of interconnected shops, Hawk looked through the glass doors across the street at Oscar's Super Service. This faux gasoline station was the outpost for renting strollers and wheelchairs and picking up packages.

In a quick dash, they crossed the street and ducked behind the old-style gas pumps. Now they would have to run through the next expanse of open space to exit the front gates of The Studios. Hawk leaned against the pump, looked Mary in the eyes, and carefully explained what they were about to do next.

"There's no good place for us to hide on the way out of here, Mary," Hawk whispered. "So we need to run as fast as we can out the main gate and then toward the Skyliner. Okay?" Hawk continued to scan their surroundings for anyone who might be in the vicinity.

"Okay, I'm ready." She breathed deeply.

Hawk and the president's daughter raced from behind the pumps, leaving the Crossroads of the World entrance booth in the distance behind them. Moving through the gate, Hawk released a turnstile, making it easier for Mary to wiggle through and past it. Now they broke into a full run, heading toward the lake in front of them to the entrance of the Disney Skyliner, a gondola system that ran from Hollywood Studios and connected to Epcot, Disney's Art of Animation Resort, the Pop Century Resort, the Caribbean Beach Resort, and the Disney Riviera Resort.

On it, guests could be transported conveniently through the sky in colorful gondolas between resorts and some theme parks. It also moved a number of people on a steady stream of passenger cars, which eliminated a little bit of the congestion on the Disney transportation system.

Sprinting past the tram unloading area, Hawk caught movement out of the corner of his eye. Over his shoulder, he saw a black vehicle parked along the edge of the guest pick-up and drop-off area. The onyx doors on either side of the car swung open as two black-suited men emerged, each wearing a pair of dark sunglasses. Hawk didn't need to see their eyes to know they had been spotted. He reached back and took Mary by the hand again, willing her to run faster, but knowing she could not.

He began to look for some way of escape and realized they had reached the point of no return. The only place to go was the Skyliner Station. Since the attraction was still running even though the resort was locked down, they would be the only passengers.

Looking over his shoulder, Hawk saw that the two men, Secret Service agents he assumed, were closing in on them. They bolted forward, Mary running as fast as her legs could carry her. Their feet pounded up the ramp toward the gondola boarding area. Again, he glanced back. If his plan was going to work, it was going to take a minor miracle.

CHAPTER THIRTY-SIX

The Chase Is On

Craig Johnson heard the news blasted through his earpiece. Striding toward the front doors of the Bay Lake Towers, he prepared for the blanket of Florida heat that would greet him as he pushed his way outside. Once he cleared the doorway, he turned to his left and broke into a run to get to his car. As he did, he saw Jillian Batterson eyeing him as she walked across the parking lot where she had exited her own vehicle to head inside the towers. He slowed, took a breath, and yelled out to her.

"Batterson, where's Disney's Caribbean Resort? What's the fastest way to get there?" He continued running toward his vehicle.

Jillian broke into a jog in his direction, then increased her speed, angling to intercept him before he reached his car.

"What's happened?" she shouted.

"Your boss has Mary Pride," Johnson said. "And he's trying to elude two Secret Service agents."

"At the Caribbean Resort?" Jillian now matched his stride.

"That's where they're headed. How do I get there fast?"

"It's better if I show you."

Johnson didn't know if she was surprised by the news that Hawkes had found Mary or not. He also hesitated to take her with him because he didn't know if she would be a help or a hindrance if they were able to catch up with her boss. However, she was the best Disney map he had available and he was in a hurry.

"Get in." *I'll probably regret bringing you with me.*

"Go that way." Jillian pointed toward the exit to the parking area. "You won't regret giving me a lift. I can get you there faster than anyone else."

"Funny, I was just thinking that I was going to regret letting you in the car."

Jillian flashed a smile. "Turn right. You need to punch it. We've got some distance to cover."

Johnson realized she too had no idea where Hawkes was at that moment. She wanted a ride to get to where he was, and Johnson assumed the reason was to assist the man if he needed it. He turned the car and accelerated rapidly as they wound their way out of the parking lot, past Space Mountain and past the Tron Coaster on the perimeter of the Magic Kingdom.

"This road will take you to the back of the Magic Kingdom, close to where you were earlier, then we need to take a left and cut across the property," Jillian said.

"So, did you know your boss had managed to find Mary Pride?"

"Not until you told me."

"Why would they be headed to the Caribbean Resort?"

"I'm not sure. Who saw them?"

Without answering her question, he said, "They're climbing aboard the Disney Skyliner and that's the next stop from Hollywood Studios, isn't it?"

Jillian nibbled her bottom lip. "Yes, it is."

"So again, why would he be doing that?"

"Again, I'm not sure." Jillian looked at him. "I knew Hawk was looking for the first family. Apparently, he found Mary. That's a good thing, right?"

Johnson felt an edge to the question. He observed her out of the corner of his eye as the car made the left and raced down the open road ahead of them. Another black agency car joined them in the road race to the resort. He finally answered her question.

"Normally, I would say it's a good thing. But it seems like your boss is running plays from his own playbook and working against the Secret Service."

"Maybe, just maybe, he doesn't trust you." She pointed for him to turn again.

Hearing her words, he almost missed the hand gesture instructing him to turn. He cut the wheel hard, and they both got tossed slightly in the seat as the car skidded into the turn and then straightened out. Ahead of them was the security entrance to Disney's Caribbean Resort.

"Why wouldn't he trust us?"

"I think he offered to help you find the first family earlier. Apparently, that's what he's doing," she said matter-of-factly.

"I believe he was told to stay out of our way." Johnson fell in behind another car. "Where is this car in front of me headed, any idea?"

"If Hawk and Mary are riding the Disney Skyliner, then they'll arrive at this Skyliner Station location. From here, they can change gondolas and head to the Animation Resort or go the other direction to the Riviera Resort and Epcot."

"That's not going to happen."

"Agent Johnson, earlier today you told Hawk that the Secret Service was more than capable of finding the president and his family." Jillian stared at him. "You were pretty clear when you said that, and I believe you told him that you would not be needing his help."

"I remember that." He could feel her stare, but he chose not to look over at her. Instead he concentrated on his driving.

"You heard our conversation that if there was someone, especially the president of the United States, missing at Walt Disney World, there was no one better to find him than Grayson Hawkes."

"I remember that as well."

"And again, I remind you that you said you did not need his help." Jillian smiled slightly. "Yet here we are. The Secret Service has not been able to find anyone, and Hawk, according to what you told me, has managed to find the president's daughter without you or your team."

"If the reports are true, why is he running from the Secret Service?" Johnson pulled the car to a halt in front of the station.

"Either he doesn't know it's the Secret Service who is chasing them . . ." Jillian opened the door and then paused. "Or, like I said before, he doesn't trust you. If that's the case, maybe you should ask yourself why."

Johnson opened his door and watched as Jillian raced ahead of him into the station. The nagging doubts Johnson had pushed to the back of his mind earlier emerged again—questions about why there had been a breach, an opening where the president could disappear, and who might have known it was there. He shook his head, spoke into the microphone hidden in his wrist, and notified the command that he was now on sight. He joined the other agents who were arriving and flooding into the Skyliner Station waiting for Mary Pride and Grayson Hawkes to arrive.

CHAPTER THIRTY-SEVEN

You Can Fly

The Disney Skyliner, featuring over three-hundred gondolas equipped with onboard audio, offered commentary similar to what guests heard on other Disney transportation vehicles. Covered in reflective panels to absorb and offset the blazing rays of the Florida sun, each ride vehicle featured a Disney character with distinct detailing, making each gondola its own unique vehicle. Each was equipped with wooden bench-style seating that could fit up to eight passengers and transport thousands of people each hour.

The gondolas never stopped, but instead kept moving as they entered and exited the station, similar to the design of famous Disney attractions like the Haunted Mansion. The concept was originally presented to Walt Disney as he looked for ideas for his community of the future. He not only hired the creator of the technology but paid to advance and develop it for use in the themed resort areas, to mobilize and move people efficiently and effectively.

Hawk felt the lift of the gondola as it left the Hollywood Studios station for the Disney Caribbean Beach Resort. The ride vehicle would soar sixty feet into the air and travel at eleven miles per hour toward the next stop. That meant he would have less than five minutes to put his plan in motion. Heart hammering in his chest, he wedged a queue-line pole into the door of the Skyliner to keep it from closing all the way.

As Hawk and Mary's gondola, which featured Pluto on the window, continued to climb, he leaned against the back window, watching as the gondolas lifted in sequence behind them. Three vehicles back, two Secret Service agents climbed aboard. Their gondola rose along the cable, crawling toward the sky. He reasoned they would have alerted someone that they were chasing himself and Mary, and he assumed there would be a reception committee waiting for their gondola to arrive at the Caribbean Beach Resort. If that was the case, things were just as he had planned.

Hawk's heart sank in his chest as he prepared for what he would do next. Committed to what he had designed, he reached over and grabbed the pole wedged into the doorway. Pushing on it and leveraging it to the side, the door slid open, allowing an increase in the warm breeze blowing into the gondola cabin.

Now came the hard part. He stood in the doorway and looked out over the expansive view of The Studios disappearing into the distance. Swallowing hard and holding his breath, he stretched to grab the top edge of the gondola above the door. Trying not to think about how far in the air he was, he lifted himself off the floor with his arms and did a pull-up that suspended him in the air hanging onto the side of the gondola.

Arms straining, fueled by adrenaline, he slowly and purposefully pulled himself up as high as he could until he was looking over the top of the Skyliner car. Legs now dangling, he realized that if he lost his grip, there would be no way to fall back into the gondola. At this point, he was fully committed, no matter what. Swinging his legs up, he tried to catch a heel on the top edge of the ride vehicle. He missed, and his legs swung backward, their momentum threatening him to lose his balance and grip.

His knuckles turned white as he waited for his body to stop swinging. Then, without a moment's hesitation, he attempted the same maneuver again. This time, his heel caught, and he used both his arms and legs to climb to the top of the gondola car. Flinging his body flat against the top, he felt the breeze whip through his hair. He caught his breath.

Getting up on all fours, he looked and could not see if the agents three gondolas back had reacted to his climbing on top of the Skyliner. He was certain they had. He imagined they were stunned and trying to figure out what he was doing. In a sense, he was trying to do the same.

Slowly he stood up on top of the gondola and tried to steady his legs, which were wobbly with anxiety, and rose to his full height as the Skyliner floated through the Disney sky. He turned to see where he was and realized he had to execute his plan now. The support poles that held the cable for the ride system were coming up on his left. From the vantage point on the ground, this had seemed like a good idea, but now on top of the gondola, he had second thoughts.

The pole, similar to any sky-bucket or ski-lift support pole, had a ladder that ran from the ground to the top for use in an emergency or for maintenance.

One, two, and then he jumped off the gondola into the air. Momentarily, he felt weightless, floating toward the ladder on the side of the pole. His brain quickly reminded him that he was jumping toward a pole that was coming at him fast enough to hurt when he hit. Not only would the impact hurt, but he had to keep his wits about him in order to grab the ladder. All those thoughts disappeared in a numbing collision with the metal ladder on the side of the pole. He tried to grip a rung of the ladder with his right hand but missed. His left hand grabbed the rung beneath, but he could not get his fingers wrapped around it as his momentum had suddenly changed from sideways to downward at the impact.

His right wrist and hand found their way into a space between the rungs, and his hand took hold of the ladder, slowing him down. His left hand found another rung to hang onto. Quickly, his feet found a rung to stand on. He had done it, and he was still alive. He had leaped from the Skyliner to the support pole as his Pluto-character gondola was carried away.

As he hung on the ladder, he turned to his right and saw the gondola car with the two agents looking out the door at him. Their expression was a hard-to-read mix of what he interpreted as disbelief, frustration, and confusion. Watching their car drift past him, he descended the ladder, rung by rung, toward the ground.

By now, the agents had called ahead to inform those waiting at the Caribbean Beach Resort that Grayson Hawkes had jumped out of the Skyliner to avoid capture, leaving Mary Pride in the gondola car.

Hawk smiled as he continued down the ladder. Still trying not to look down, he was astounded his plan had worked, although he'd hit the support pole with greater impact than expected. He would be covered in bruises by morning.

As Mary and Hawk had raced up the ramp, he had helped Mary over the retaining wall on the other side of the station entrance, hidden behind a trash receptacle. She had never boarded the ride at all. Hawk on the other hand had made sure he was seen getting in, standing up the entire way. He had been careful to look back at the agents to make sure they had seen him as he lured them onto the Skyliner. As it left the ground into the sky, he had worried that if another agent was close or only one of them had followed, they would find Mary. But both agents stepped onboard in chase mode. Now he was pleased neither agent had been daring enough to duplicate his escape. If his plan worked, they were convinced he had abandoned Mary Pride on the Skyliner car.

Reaching the ground, he broke into a sprint back to the station to pluck Mary from her hiding place. Then he would take her to her mother, where they could both be safe. Then the only thing he had to do was find and rescue the president of the United States.

CHAPTER THIRTY-EIGHT

Making Conclusions

Jillian tried to stay out of the way and remain invisible as Secret Service agents rushed into place at the Skyliner Station in the Caribbean Beach Resort. This particular station was the busiest of all the Skyliner Stations, serving as the connection point for guests traveling to other resorts and the theme parks.

Agents lined both sides of the loading area as each gondola car pulled into the station. Dropping out of the sky and descending quickly, the vehicle would slide into the station, its doors would open, and guests could move in and out of the vehicles quickly and efficiently. Today, there were no guests exiting or boarding the gondola cars, and Jillian felt the tension in the air as they waited for Hawk and Mary. Her heart beat faster and her neck felt tight with dread. What was Hawk up to?

To her right, she could see that a row of agents was listening and receiving some sort of message in their earpieces. Reading their expressions, she could only assume it was bad news. Craig Johnson looked over at her, shook his head, and frowned, indicating something was wrong. He stepped away from his post and strode over to where she stood.

"That was interesting," Craig said as he walked closer.

"What's interesting?"

"There was an incident on the Skyliner after it left Hollywood Studios," he said grimly.

"Go on."

"Grayson Hawkes climbed out of the gondola car, leaving Mary Pride inside the vehicle. He climbed on top of the ride and jumped off of it."

Jillian raised her eyebrows. "Hawk jumped off the top of the Skyliner? To where? For what reason?"

"To escape, of course," Johnson said. "He knew they were spotted and being chased by two agents. That's how we knew where they were. The two agents got on the Skyliner three vehicles behind them, and they watched as Hawkes jumped off."

Jillian's fingers twisted a lock of hair before she caught herself and stopped. "Is Hawk all right?"

"I have no idea. He hit the support pole after jumping off the gondola. It's a long way down, a long way to fall, and pretty desperate if you ask me."

"Desperate?"

"Yes, because he knew he had been spotted. He was afraid of being caught. Hawkes had the president's daughter, and they were running from the Secret Service. It appears our suspicions about his involvement are true."

"That's your conclusion?" Jillian's voice sounded strained in her ear. "No wonder you guys lost the president and his family."

She turned and began to walk away. She had to find Hawk and see if he was hurt, or . . . She shuddered at the thought. Trying to figure out the best way back to The Studios, she was interrupted by Johnson following her as she stepped to the edge of the station.

"No wonder we lost the president and his family? You have something you want to tell me?"

"Your conclusion that Hawk had Mary Pride, and therefore must have been the one who took the first family, is naïve and more ignorant than you realize. My default conclusion is that Hawk must have found her, but apparently he's not sure who he can trust, because as I said earlier, you lost them." Pointing her finger in his face, she added, "And if you had done a better job securing them in the first place, they wouldn't have been kidnapped."

"So you think Hawkes is helping us?"

"No, I don't think that at all." Jillian again turned to walk away.

He grabbed her upper arm. "Then what is he doing?"

"He's helping the president," Jillian said, looking down at his hand. He released her arm.

The agents standing on the platform tensed as a gondola featuring Pluto entered the loading area. They rushed to the side of the platform, and the door automatically slid open. Immediately, an agent bounded inside only to stick his head out of the door and announce, "It's empty. No one inside."

Jillian smiled, struggling to suppress a laugh, as she turned away from Johnson and descended the steps to exit the loading platform. Behind her she heard the Secret Service giving an all-clear verification. The gondolas were empty. She tried to mentally recreate what must have happened. Hawk had pulled off the impossible . . . again. He had gotten on the Skyliner without Mary and jumped off, fooling the Secret Service. She knew he had Mary Pride and was on his way to reunite her with her mother. But she also knew Hawk wouldn't let anyone know until he was sure it was safe to send them a message.

Jillian raced into the parking area and saw a Disney maintenance vehicle parked alongside the curb. She opened the door, stepped inside, and flipped down the visor. The keys dropped into her lap. She smiled again, remembering that Hawk had showed her this trick earlier. She then realized she needed to implement a new policy, prohibiting this practice. It was a great way to steal their vehicles and terrible for security. But she would do that later, when this was all over. For now, it was the easiest way to find Hawk.

As she accelerated the vehicle through the parking lot, she wasn't sure where she was going because she wasn't sure where *he* was going. Her apprehension needed a release. Pausing at a traffic light, she whispered softly to herself.

"Hawk, where are you? What are you up to? Now that someone knows you've found Mary, they officially know you're looking for the president too, which means the clock is ticking faster. You may not have time to find him."

Her phone buzzed, and she reached down to answer it. The name on the readout was Joel Habecker. She slid her finger across the touchscreen. "This is Batterson."

"Jillian, this is Joel. I think we have something." He paused, and it sounded like he was shuffling through his notes. "Apparently, we have a campsite that's supposed to be in use, but it's vacant now."

Jillian knew this might be the information she was looking for. When she had set up her security team to check the Fort Wilderness Resort Campground, she had been specific to verify that everyone who had checked in was where they were supposed to be. Since she and Hawk had found the first lady tied up in the Airstream stashed in an unauthorized area, Joel's missing camper could be the one that had been stolen. Jillian turned the wheel and headed to the campground.

"There's a camper, registered to a David Grimsley, that is supposed to be on Cypress Knee Circle, slot 311," Joel said. "The camper is not there, and it looks like they never set up camp."

"But they did check in?"

"Yes, that is confirmed—a party of two. They're regular guests here, according to our records."

Jillian's heart sank. "There's a good chance it was David Grimsley and his traveling companion who were found at the maintenance marina earlier." She paused to think. "See if any of our cast members know who Grimsley was traveling with. The other body found this morning was female. I would assume it was his wife, but let's see if anyone knows and remembers them—maybe get her name."

"Will do," Joel said. "Do you want us to look for the missing Grimsley camper?"

"We recorded what kind of camper they were staying in, didn't we?"

"We did. It's policy. It's an Airstream."

Jillian needed to stall to give Hawk a little more time. She exhaled softly and then gave her next set of instructions. "Let's not start looking too hard for the missing Airstream yet. I'm headed that way. See if you can get the woman's name, and then we'll give the information to the sheriff."

"Got it." Joel ended the call.

Sighing, she looked at her phone. Again touching the screen, she decided to text Hawk. Thinking carefully, she decided generic texting would be best. She ran her finger across the letters and typed, *U good?*

Almost instantly came his texted reply: *Never better.*

The tension in her neck and across her shoulders released immediately when she read his response. It was the confirmation she needed. Hawk was fine and carrying out whatever plan he had in that genius brain of his. Her phone buzzed again as another text arrived. Glancing down, she stared at his words:

Gone AWOL/check news/Aero Eastern

Blinking, she read and reread the message. It was code for sure—the Disney Code Hawk had said they should communicate in. However, he was really the only one who knew this kind of detail, lingo, and shorthand way of sharing information.

Slowing the vehicle, Jillian decided to change direction. Accelerating into a U-turn, she sped the opposite way, toward Bay Lake Towers. If anyone could help her understand this message or figure out what Hawk was trying to tell her, it had to be Juliette. Apparently, she had been wrong earlier when she thought the clock was speeding up. They were not on that clock anymore; they were now using a stopwatch. And they'd have to do whatever they were about to do fast.

CHAPTER THIRTY-NINE

Echoes of the Past

David Walker fixed his gaze on his tablet screen and flicked through the articles he'd immersed himself in. Every word and photo crossing his screen plunged him deeper into dread that something horrible may have happened to the president of the United States. He glanced nervously to his right and then his left from his seat in the Outer Rim Lounge. Located on the fourth floor of Disney's Contemporary Resort, he had a spectacular view of Bay Lake, but his focus was dialed into his research.

David shook his head and reminded himself to stay calm. Slowly, he closed his eyes and told himself to stay objective and not get drawn into the tentacles of the beast of conspiracy he was currently researching. Although at this point, the only official word he'd heard was that the president and his family were missing. But the research told a different story, that the government was soft selling the severity of what was going on. The more he researched conspiracies and plots against the president, the more frightened he became of how easily it would be to dismiss the connections as nutty theories and ignore the signs that something could be horribly wrong.

David had finished his latest update for GNN and as always had tried to be as objective as possible. He stuck with the facts as he explained them to his viewers. He had become aware from Allie that some of their competitors in the media world had not done that. Some outlets seemed to blame the president himself for his disappearance. They pontificated, as they did on a daily basis, that the man was corrupt and evil. Their reporting reflected an attitude that almost conveyed that whatever had happened to him, he had coming. In David's mind, they weren't journalists at all. They had no place on-air, peddling that kind of fear and misinformation to the world.

Other news outlets were kinder but could not help playing up the drama, suggesting that the president's disappearance could have a ripple effect across the world and that the enemies of America were watching and waiting for his demise. David understood that if something had, indeed, happened to Tyler Pride, the succession of power was in place. The government would not fall apart. As in any crisis or tragedy, there was a plan.

Personally, the possibility that a deep-state conspiracy existed against the president bothered him a lot more. Although easily scoffed at and dismissed by most, there was a mountain of evidence to prove a plot—enough to give him pause and cause him to consider the potential truth.

Eventually, his research filled in details about the death of Abraham Lincoln and some of the strange things that happened and *didn't* happen when the former president was assassinated. The eerie articles he had just discovered caused a chill to run up the length of his spine. It was unprofessional of him to be influenced by the spooky information he was reviewing, yet that's how he felt as he read on.

Abraham Lincoln's vice president was Andrew Johnson, and some believed he was involved with the assassination of Lincoln by John Wilkes Booth. As David read, he ran across information that said approximately seven hours before shooting Lincoln, Booth dropped by the Washington hotel where Vice-President Andrew Johnson lived. The desk clerk informed Booth that neither Johnson nor his private secretary, William A. Browning, were currently in the hotel. Booth wrote the following note: "Don't wish to disturb you. Are you at home? J. Wilkes Booth."

As David scanned this information, he decided to continue reading. Browning had testified before a military court that he found the note in his box later that afternoon. He wondered if Vice-President Johnson and John Wilkes Booth knew each other. His answer came, if he could believe the source, in the 1997 publication of *Right or Wrong, God Judge Me: The Writings of John Wilkes Booth* edited by John Rhodehamel and Louise Taper. The editors suggested that Booth had previously met Johnson in Nashville in 1864. As an actor, Booth was appearing in the newly opened Wood's Theatre. More details emerged from author Hamilton Howard in *Civil War Echoes*, published in 1907, that while Johnson served as the military governor of Tennessee, he and Booth were seen in each other's company.

Could the vice president have been involved in the Lincoln assassination? If so, how had he missed the suggested links that made him a part of such a conspiracy? His American history studies in high school and college might have mentioned it but never explored the real depths of the possibilities.

Mary Todd Lincoln felt Andrew Johnson was involved. On March 15, 1866, she wrote to her friend, Sally Orne,

> *That, that miserable inebriate Johnson, had cognizance of my husband's death - Why, was that card of Booth's, found in his box, some acquaintance certainly existed - I have been deeply impressed, with the harrowing thought, that he, had an understanding with the conspirators & they knew their man . . . . As sure, as you & I live, Johnson, had some hand, in all this . . .*

Not only did the wife of Abraham Lincoln believe it, but at the time some members of Congress also thought Johnson was involved, and a special Assassination Committee was established to investigate any evidence linking Johnson to Lincoln's death. Nothing suspicious was ever found by the committee. However, there were some in political circles who never believed that the evidence they found was complete and thorough. The same Congress that did the investigation would impeach Andrew Johnson a year later.

David sighed. Some things didn't change over time. Another move of his finger across the screen found a note from the book, *A Threat to the Republic: The Secret of the Lincoln Assassination that Preserved the Union*, as author Jerry Madonna argued that Johnson gave assistance to Booth's escape from Washington.

But the conspiracies ran even deeper. One theory attempted to make the connection that Booth assassinated Lincoln because of the Roman Catholic Church. As David read, he found that they suggested because of Lincoln's legal defense of a former priest against the bishop of Chicago, the church wanted him eliminated. The theory was enhanced by evidence that John H. Surratt, the son of Mary Surratt, fled America and ended up in the Vatican, seeking refuge as a Catholic.

John Surratt had been a close contact of Booth and after Lincoln was assassinated, had quickly made his way out of the country. As officials looked for him, it was believed that his mother Mary had been an accomplice and had been involved in the plot to kill the president. Eventually, she became the first woman ever executed by the federal government. David shook his head and just couldn't read any more about a pope's involvement in the assassination of an American president. That was a road too far.

The problem for David was that there seemed to be no end to the stream of information suggesting many more people of the time never realized that surrounding events played a role in Lincoln's assassination.

Another name that kept resurfacing was that of Secretary of War Edwin Stanton. Conspiracy theorists believed he was directly involved in Lincoln's death. Allegedly, not liking the policies and plans of the president, Stanton wanted him out of office. On the day of the assassination, Ulysses S. Grant had been expected to attend the play *Our American Cousin* with the Lincolns. If Grant had attended the play that night, the guards with General Grant never would have allowed Booth to enter the State Box at Ford's Theatre. The reason Grant did not attend was because an order by Stanton had changed his plans for the evening.

David continued to read the case against the Secretary of War. It was alleged that Stanton knew conspirators were meeting at the Surratt boarding house, and he had denied the president's request for a bodyguard on that evening. Stanton's actions certainly seemed suspicious and revealed an ulterior motive. He failed to alert security at the Navy Yard Bridge, over which Booth escaped. There were mysterious interruptions of telegraph communications, and some believed he arranged to have Booth killed before being brought to trial. Some suggested that he tampered with evidence by removing pages from Booth's diary.

David leaned back in his chair and rubbed his eyes. Those who loved Tyler Pride often compared his presidency to Abraham Lincoln's. Although history revealed and remembered Lincoln as heroic, many of the mysterious events surrounding his death had been dismissed as not being possible or realistic. David had always believed that. But now he wondered. Could it be that people could disdain and even hate another leader so much they would do anything to seize power, especially if they believed their cause was just?

Lincoln had led the nation at a time of intense division, and as a result, a radical plot was put into motion to eliminate him. Different circumstances, different times, different divisions, but was it remotely possible that a conspiracy might be the reason for the president's disappearance, along with his family, today? And beyond that, could it be that those behind it were actually members of the federal government? These thoughts raced through his head quicker than he could process them. He stood, rubbed the back of his neck, and stared out the window at Bay Lake for a few moments.

Then, shutting down his tablet, he reached into his pocket for his cell and called Allie Crossman, who answered on the first ring. "Allie, did you get me a meeting with Juliette Keaton yet?"

"Not yet," Allie admitted. "But I have been and will keep on trying."

"I imagine she's swamped right now," David acknowledged.

"Yes, but I'm sure she will want to talk with you." Allie grew silent and David waited for her to pick the conversation back up. She must be distracted by something. "The network wants you back on the air for a live report in less than an hour."

David pondered for a moment as he thought about how he would ever get to the point of broadcasting the real story on air. Especially if any of the conspiracy undertones turned out to be true. And how would he ever be able to decipher what was real and what was not? Everyone in every news agency wanted to get an angle on the breaking events of the day.

Some networks, theirs included, were now covering this story with nonstop, round-the-clock news and commentary. None of the so-called news anchors had time to actually fly to Florida, so they were relying on their Washington-based correspondents, traveling with the president, to give them information. Now some of the local Central Florida news reporters were on the scene and able to contribute their insights and reports into the worldwide broadcasts.

"David, are you still there? I said you're on again in less than an hour."

He tuned his attention back to Allie's voice on the other end of the conversation. "I'll be ready. Thanks."

Slowly, David sat down, stretched his legs, and let all the reasons for a simpler explanation for the president's disappearance roll through his mind. He reasoned that the act was evil and criminal, but there had to be another explanation that didn't involve a sinister government conspiracy. But the doubts kept pushing their way back, filling the emptiness inside. He tried to convince himself not to believe in conspiracy theories. Sadly, he seemed to be failing.

CHAPTER-FORTY

Cracking the Code

Jillian watched as Juliette pushed her way through the glass doors and stepped out onto the breezeway of the Contemporary Resort. This patio area allowed guests a beautiful outdoor viewing spot to look at the Magic Kingdom, but conversations were frequently interrupted by the monorail entering the resort hotel directly overhead. As Juliette approached, Jillian felt like bounding on her toes but tried to remain calm.

Rubbing her hands together, Juliette stepped next to her. "What have you got?"

"This." Jillian showed her the text message from Hawk.

"Gone AWOL-check news-Aero Eastern." Juliette read the message out loud after looking around to make sure they were alone in the viewing area.

"This is the Disney code stuff you guys always use, right?" Jillian asked.

Jillian had not been a big Disney fan before Hawk had convinced her to take a job with the company. She had learned a great deal and had a huge appreciation for the world of Disney—she now understood the culture—but he didn't have a real sense of the details and storytelling that seemed to endlessly fascinate her boss.

"Yes, I'm sure this is a coded message Hawk sent to you." Juliette leaned forward. "Do you have any idea what it means?"

"No," Jillian admitted. "Not a clue."

"Don't worry," Juliette said. "There's no one who understands this kind of communication like Hawk does. As a matter of fact, his ability to figure this kind of stuff out is why we're all here."

"So what do you think we should do?"

"Try to think like Hawk thinks."

"I'd prefer not to." Jillian smiled. "That might get scary."

"I can understand that," Juliette said. "My guess is that he's trying to tell us where Kim and Mary Pride are, or maybe where the president is. He may have found him as well."

"The words of the text seem random."

"I promise you, if Hawk sent this, they are *not* random."

"Then can you help me figure this out?" Jillian asked.

"Hopefully." Juliette looked away toward the Magic Kingdom. "Hawk always says not to overthink this kind of stuff. When you overthink it, you become paralyzed and can't move."

"Got it . . . no overthinking . . . So we start with *gone AWOL*."

"AWOL, absent without leave," Juliette said slowly, fiddling with her earring. "I believe Hawk would recognize how difficult this might be for us to figure out. So there's a pattern to it. It's linear, I think."

Jillian said nothing as Juliette spoke. She was playing the two words over and over in her head, allowing them to tumble through why they might have meaning that was anything but obvious. As she was thinking, she saw Juliette slightly raise her head with a questioning look.

"When was the last time you saw Hawk?" Juliette asked.

"After we found Kim Pride. He said he would take her to someplace safe, and then I came here to see you." Jillian thought back over the events of her day. "You know, I remember thinking Hawk had gone AWOL earlier when I couldn't find him at the Jungle Cruise. Of course, I saw him again later, so that couldn't be it."

"Don't disregard that so fast." Juliette held out her hand. "Did you tell him that? Did you use that phrase with him?"

"No, I don't think so. If I did, I don't remember."

"Then why does it remind me of something?" Juliette took a short, three-step walk away and then paced as Jillian watched and waited.

"Gone AWOL, check news," Jillian said.

"Don't skip ahead." Juliette stopped. "Remember, Hawk is feeding this to us one thought or clue at a time. The second one won't or can't click until we get the first one right."

"Sorry, I went AWOL for a moment." Jillian giggled.

Juliette stared at her with a stern expression.

"What? I know it wasn't that funny, but it was a little bit humorous."

"No, you said you thought Hawk went AWOL at the Jungle Cruise. That's it," Juliette said as she headed toward the door.

"That's it? What's it? The Jungle Cruise?" Jillian fell into step behind Juliette.

"Yes, the Jungle Cruise," Juliette said, as they walked with purpose across the breezeway toward Bay Lake Towers. "Let's take a walk into the Magic Kingdom. The walkway to the entrance will be easier and faster. We'll get inside the park, hit a stairwell, and then take the Utilidor to Adventureland and the Jungle Cruise."

"The Jungle Cruise is the clue?"

Their strides picked up quickly as they exited through the entrance of Bay Lake Towers. Moving across the parking lot, Juliette explained to Jillian why they were headed to the Jungle Cruise.

"Remember seeing the office in the queue line of the Jungle Cruise?" Juliette said.

Jillian nodded. "Sure, I saw it earlier today."

"That is the office of Skipper Albert Awol, a fictional character that is part of the backstory of the Jungle Cruise. Hawk knows all of these backstories, so this has to be what he was talking about." Juliette picked up her pace even more. "Awol is the voice of the jungle, the broadcast voice that entertains guests as the disc jockey for the station. Albert Awol's office is located in the queue line of the attraction. Albert himself is not inside the office, but there are many of his personal items inside, including boots, hats, firearms, gear, and other stuff."

"So if Hawk is saying he's AWOL, he wants us to get to the Jungle Cruise and then check news once we get there."

"Exactly."

Jillian smiled at Juliette, pleased that her friend might have figured out the first part of the clue.

"And you know what the second part of the clue means?" Jillian asked hopefully.

"I have no idea." Juliette's smile faded as she shrugged. "But we can't figure out the next step until we take the first. So let's get to the jungle."

CHAPTER FORTY-ONE

Flip a Coin

Hawk ran into the empty Liberty Square. Convinced that Kim and Mary Pride were now safe, he turned his attention to figuring out where the president might be. By now, Jillian would be trying to figure out the clues he had given her. He imagined she would have recruited help she could trust, which meant Juliette.

Now he could focus on the meaning of the coin. The oversized silver coin featured the seal of the Commonwealth of Virginia. That had been obvious, but as always, the details would matter. The words emblazoned on the coin read, "Rebellion to Tyrants Is Obedience to God." The phrase was the motto of Virginia. "Rebellion to tyrants is obedience to God" was a motto suggested, but not used, for the official seal of the United States. Jefferson eventually appropriated it for his own seal, Hawk remembered. The source of the motto was never known for certain but may have originated with Benjamin Franklin.

The phrase meant more than that to Hawk. A chilling detail from history that he also remembered was that John Wilkes Booth was reported to have shouted, "Sic semper tyrannis" after shooting President Lincoln on April 14, 1865. The phrase, meaning "thus always to tyrants," did more than suggest his disgust and feelings toward the president who had ended the long Civil War.

In Hawk's mind, the coin and the phrase on it were not in Edward Fenn's locker by accident. Perhaps he fancied himself as the same type of misguided ideologue as Booth, convinced he had been chosen somehow to carry out a horrific act. Hawk knew that evil masked itself in a variety of forms. Driven by a sense of urgency, he searched Liberty Square with a slow, purposeful gaze, looking for anything that might be helpful.

Standing next to the Liberty Bell, in the center of Liberty Square, Hawk was surrounded with snapshots of the history of America. The Liberty Bell in the Magic Kingdom had been cast from the same mold used to create the original. Although many never realized it, this meant the size and shape of the bell were identical to the historic Liberty Bell.

The breeze carried the sound of the flags that flapped in the air around him—one flag for each of the original thirteen colonies. His gaze taking in the buildings, he noticed the shutters. Most people never thought about the fact they were not hung quite right. These shutters were hung at an angle, very much on purpose. Colonial shutters were typically hung on leather straps. This would cause the shutters to sag slightly at the top, creating a lopsided look.

Hawk knew the shutters in Liberty Square were hung on metal hinges for stability, but the Imagineers wanted to mirror this authentic detail and set them at a slight angle anyway. He shook his head to clear it. There was something that he was missing on the coin—the meaning of it—and somehow by seeing the slightly off-kilter shutters, he was reminded to change the angle of his thinking about the meaning of the coin. Sometimes the details inspired him.

Standing under the branches of the Liberty Tree, he glanced up at the thirteen lanterns hanging from the branches, again representing the original thirteen colonies. Many towns featured a Liberty Tree, where the business of the day and ultimately the fight for independence would be inspired. To his left was The Liberty Tree Tavern that served up Americana food in six dining rooms, which drew their themes from the names of key people in that area including Benjamin Franklin, Thomas Jefferson, John Paul Jones, Paul Revere, Betsy Ross, and George Washington. Memorabilia from Virginia was displayed in some of them, yet that could not be it.

The image on the flip side of the coin was that of a colonial man sharing what Hawk thought was a peace pipe with a Native American. The words "Happy While United" were stamped on the coin. Hawk assumed the coin was something that must have been presented as a gift to represent a treaty that had emerged around 1870.

He chuckled as he realized that if the coin was genuine, the value had to be in excess of a hundred thousand dollars. Maybe he had been wrong about Edward Fenn, and the coin might have been nothing but payment for his role in the president's disappearance. Sneering slightly at this new awareness, Hawk stepped out into the middle of Liberty Square. If this was only about money, then the coin wasn't a clue, and his thinking was flawed. It grated him that he might have missed the meaning.

He snatched his thoughts back from self-doubt. The coin meant something. The other items in the locker had been clues; this one had to be as well. He hurried across the open area to the Liberty Square Riverboat dock, where the Liberty Belle, a steam-powered paddle wheeler, would take guests on a journey on the Rivers of America. The ship was a reproduction of the boats that ferried people up and down the Mississippi, Missouri, and other rivers in America.

The journey flowed through Frontierland and around Tom Sawyer Island. Splash Mountain and Big Thunder Mountain Railroad were viewed from the riverboat ride, then around the corner, the river bent and swept the passengers into the wilderness of Frontierland. The trip allowed guests to see a Native American village, Wilson's Cave Inn—a reference to the Davy Crockett television series—forests with woodland critters, and a shack alongside the river where Alligator Joe fished for dinner.

Mark Twain narrated and pointed out highlights along the way, peppered with historical perspectives, all said with the author's wit and whimsy.

Looking out across the water, Hawk released a slight gasp as his thoughts tumbled together into place. The coin was a map, connecting ideas that would give away the destination. Virginia and Colonial America had been easy because of the seal, the date, and the words on the coin. The image of the Native American and the colonialist had been tougher, but that was where the more subtle secret had to be. The riverboat carried guests past the only place where the image on the coin might take place—across the river in the Native American village. It would have the kind of meeting place for an event like the one depicted on the coin. If he was right, he needed to find a way to the village on the other side of the Rivers of America.

He pondered his options as he stood on the dock. There was no way to reasonably commandeer a riverboat, plus it was impractical. He could only reach the area quickly either by water or by entering the other side of the village along the train tracks. He instantly set his direction toward the Frontierland Train Station. He would walk along the tracks, which would help him avoid detection. They would lead him into the wilderness area and eventually into the Native American village from a vantage point that was only seen from riders aboard the Walt Disney World Railroad. If he was right, there was something or someone waiting to be found inside that village.

Stepping quickly through Frontierland, Hawk decided not to enter the tracks from the train station but instead behind the Big Thunder Mountain Railroad attraction. Jumping over the barrier and moving along the mine-car track, he reversed the direction most guests would normally travel. The attraction was going to be a part of the originally planned Western River Expedition area. The mountain in the middle of the attraction, to Hawk's right, was where the story unfolded.

Miners discovered gold back in the late 1800s on Big Thunder Mountain. This caused the town of Tumbleweed to boom, and mine trains were installed to transport the ore. Locals claimed the mine was protective of the gold within and anyone attempting to mine its riches would fail. So there had been many disasters, but the trains continued to operate. Yet they seemed to run on their own, and runaway trains could be a major hazard. On a normal day, the queue passed through the Explosives Magazine Room. A guest then followed the instructions for the cranks and plungers contained therein to trigger some explosions of their own creation on the mountain itself.

Hawk slid past the attraction and then behind it, trying not to draw the kind of attention to himself that might set in motion a different type of disaster sequence, one where he was running again from the Secret Service. In a matter of moments, he passed the attraction and entered the heavily wooded area of the train track. The woods were strategically placed to create sight breaks between the train and other activity in the park, but for him the sight breaks were necessary and needed. Sticking to the edge of the track, he quickly moved into the outskirts of the Native American village. It was time to see if his hunch was correct.

CHAPTER FORTY-TWO

Check the News

Juliette and Jillian made their way down the steps toward the entrance of the Jungle Cruise. Carefully taking the time to look behind them to make sure they had not been followed, they stepped into the queue line. As they did, they heard the soundtrack for the queue line playing.

"When we emptied the park, everything was not shut down. So the soundtrack is still playing," Juliette said as they walked inside.

"I guess I was so focused on finding Hawk and a little dinged from the attack, I missed it or didn't pay attention earlier." Jillian tried to remember the details of her last visit to the docks of the Jungle Cruise.

They wove their way into the waiting line, looking for something that would connect them to the clue again. "Gone Awol/check news/Aero Eastern" had to mean something in this area of the Jungle Cruise. Juliette had been quick to figure out the Albert Awol portion of the clue. As if on cue, the soundtrack confirmed what they had concluded as the words came over the speakers lining the queue area.

"This is Skipper Albert Awol, the Voice of the Jungle, broadcasting on the DBC to all points unknown. If you're within the sound of my voice, you are listening to AWOL Airwaves on the DBC."

"We've got the first part of the clue right. So now we have to check news, whatever that means," Juliette said over her shoulder as they looked at all the artifacts on display in the faux office area of Albert Awol.

The faceless voice of the narrator again came over the sound system. "Here's today's River Tip from Skipper Bill on the Congo Connie. Bill says, 'If it rains in the jungle, who cares? That's why they call it a rain forest.' Thanks, Bill."

Jillian rolled her eyes at the corny line. "Maybe we should have turned the background soundtrack off."

Juliette smiled at her. "Listen close. There may be a clue in what he says." She shrugged. "You never know what Hawk was thinking or trying to tell us."

Supplies that would be needed on a jungle river voyage lined the roofline shelves along the queue area. Jillian slowed down and began to read each of the markings on the boxes, crates, and packages. She glanced over at Juliette, who was still studying the office area looking for anything that might help.

"Check news," Jillian said. "That could mean a lot of things."

"Any travelers who may need to exchange foreign currency during their voyage needn't worry. There are banks all along our rivers," Albert Awol said over the radio airways.

Jillian came alongside Juliette and studied the large map on the back wall of the office. Marked *Jungle Cruise Trading Co.*, it gave imaginary routes that their boat cruises might travel.

Albert Awol spoke again. "Instructions on how to dock a half-sunken boat will be given this Tuesday morning at Loading Dock Number One. Due to reasons that are more than obvious, these maneuvers will not be open to the public."

"Hawk could be a captain on the Jungle Cruise," Jillian said as she continued to study the map.

"A skipper. The Jungle Cruise has skippers, not captains," Juliette corrected.

"Same thing."

"Actually, it's not."

"Seriously?"

"It's not . . . but it doesn't matter," Juliette said. "The Jungle Cruise has skippers and Hawk has been one."

"What? Really?" Jillian once again realized there was a lot she didn't know about him.

"Sure. He has done it for fun," Juliette explained. "Every once in a while, he will slide aboard one of the boats and give the guests a tour. He knows most of the jokes, makes up some of his own, and it turns into a real surprise."

"He does it for fun?"

"Yes. He also does it because, according to Hawk, Walt Disney used to often check out the attractions by dropping by and taking an unexpected trip with the guests. He does that kind of thing more than anyone realizes," Juliette said.

Albert Awol interrupted their search of the area with his broadcast. "Last week, the river pilot's license test was given to thirty Jungle Cruise skippers. Congratulations to all those who passed. The remaining twenty-nine pilots may take the test again next month."

"Jillian began to walk to the other side of the queue area. I don't think what we're looking for is in the office."

"I think you're correct," Juliette said. "But it's here. I know we're right."

Jillian read the announcement from the Elephant Safari Company on the wall and again saw nothing that was helpful. She flexed her fingers as she relocated her search to the next area, more determined than ever to figure out what clue was hidden here. She continued to look at the endless collection of suitcases that had been left by and for travelers on the Jungle Cruise placed on shelves throughout the queue area. A slow shake of her head displayed her disbelief at all of the possible places something could be hidden in the array of stuff surrounding them.

"Attention all travelers," Awol said over the radio. "If your name is added to the missing persons list at the end of your cruise, please accept our most sincere apologies. Thank you."

At that moment, an old case caught Jillian's eye. Nestled on a shelf, next to a blue-metal coffeepot, the old sooty case sat on the wooden shelf, high above the ground, out of the reach of guests. A glass jar sat in front of it, and a brown-leather saddlebag lay across the top of it. Jillian smiled as she read the white block letters—CBS NEWS.

"Juliette, I found something," she called out.

Juliette rushed to her side and joined her enthusiasm. "That has to be it. 'Check news,' the text said."

"So, do you think something is in it?" Jillian asked.

"Not sure." Juliette tilted her head. "You know, it's interesting that it's even included in the artifacts. Disney owns ABC, not CBS, including their news divisions. Why in the world would that even be there? It's so out of place."

Jillian now scanned the shelves next to the case. She could see a crate, a scale, a basket, maple syrup, a brown jug of Dad's Root Beer, a lantern, a couple of colored glass jars, and an oversized rusted can lying on its side. On the top was the brand Aero Eastern Motor Oil, with the outline of an airplane in the center of it.

"There." Jillian pointed a manicured finger toward it.

"That's it!" Juliette said. "Now where is the clue?"

Jillian allowed her eyes to examine the shelf closer. She squinted as she fixed her focus on the can tipped on its side. Propped on top of another jar, the mouth of the can was open, and there was something inside. She glanced toward Juliette, who also saw what she was looking at. Juliette winked at her and followed with a confident nod.

Jillian then stated the obvious. "It's just out of our reach. We need to get up there to see what's in that can."

They both looked around them. Juliette found a crate—a box used as a prop—sitting next to the edge of the water along the dock. Grabbing the rope handle, she dragged the crate slowly across the queue area. Jillian fidgeted as she waited, wanting Juliette to hurry, but she knew if Juliette moved any faster, the dragging crate would make a considerable amount of noise. Caution was still the best course of action.

Once they shoved the crate in place, Jillian hopped up on it. It gave her the extra height she needed. Reaching into the can, she grasped a piece of paper tightly in her fingers, pulled it out, and stepped off the crate. Juliette leaned against her shoulder as she unfolded the paper. As it opened, they both saw it was a note in Hawk's handwriting. Another clue.

The key that you need is found in Dread. If these had been here, she wouldn't be dead.

Both women read the clue silently. Juliette turned away and began to pace. Jillian watched for a moment and then returned to reading the clue. She reminded herself that to understand this, she had to think like Hawk would think. The clue was a puzzle to solve. It had been created to make it difficult to figure out, and if anyone without some working knowledge of Disney detail found it, they would never decipher it.

Jillian noted a few words in the clue: key . . . dread . . . these . . . dead. Her years of working for Homeland Security had involved some encryption work, and she had trained in pulling out phrases and words that might have special meaning. But how to tie these together would be difficult. If Juliette could add her special blend of Disney knowledge, they might be able to figure this out.

Juliette stopped pacing and turned, wearing a smile. "Hawk is sending us to the Haunted Mansion," she said with a gleam in her eye. "I have a feeling we need to start in the queue line. It's time to pay a visit to the Dread family."

Dread had been one of the key words Jillian had made note of.

"The Dread family?" Jillian walked quickly with Juliette in the direction of the attraction.

"Yes, the Dread family is a part of the background story of the Haunted Mansion here in Walt Disney World. Hawk has told me the story before; he thinks it's a fantastic detail and loves it. I wish I had paid better attention to the details when he told me about it."

"Do you know enough or remember enough to figure it out?"

"We'll know once we get there," Juliette whispered.

The two women climbed the steps and hugged the edges of the walkways between attractions. They would travel through Adventureland into Frontierland, and then sneak along the porch of the buildings back into Liberty Square to get to the Haunted Mansion.

CHAPTER FORTY-THREE

The Search

Hawk now stood in the re-creation of an Indian village. The russet-shaded ground created a carpet on which teepees dotted the landscape. Animatronic figures and statues also provided glimpses into Native American life, with scenes of cooking, cleaning, trading, and fishing that guests would see in passing as they rode the train. He had observed before that guests did not get a good a view from a distance. Since they passed so quickly, not as much detail had been placed in the village as he would have hoped. He was reminded once again that it might need a bit of reimagining. One day, he would get around to putting a team of cast members on that task.

But now the mission at hand was to find the president, if he was here. The coin had pictured a place where the Native American and the colonist might have used a peace pipe to seal a deal or agreement. That could have happened in a village like this perhaps, if it were real. Hawk studied the teepees and decided to peek inside each one. The interiors of these tents were used primarily for storage of non-essential items that would not be easily damaged in extreme weather conditions.

The dwelling closest to the train track was tan in color with blue highlights. Reaching over and pulling back the flap of the teepee, he saw nothing but boxes, which had been shoved against the back wall of the tent. Stepping away, he traveled to the next one. This teepee was larger than the first, featured more elaborate paintings on the sides, and had what was supposed to be an animal skin drying in the sun. Repeating the process as before, he pulled back the tent flap only to find it completely empty. Drawing his eyebrows together, he walked toward the next one.

Slowing his pace, Hawk realized he had not been doing a thorough job of watching his surroundings. He dropped to one knee and rotated his gaze first toward the tree line, and then back toward the railroad tracks. Satisfied no one had found him yet, he edged carefully to the next teepee. This one featured four statues that portrayed Native American men negotiating a deal of some sort. They were holding the fur skins of animals, and the four men were facing each other in pairs. This would make an appropriate teepee for someone trying to stash the deal-making president. Hawk closed in on it slowly. The teepee was trimmed in red and yellow and the entrance was on its far side, away from the train track, preventing any passersby from seeing inside.

Grabbing the flimsy flap of the teepee, he jerked it back and momentarily stepped backward at what he saw inside. The president was tied up and hunched over. The ropes were secured to a stake that had been driven into the center of the teepee. The knots and the rope had been positioned very much like the way he and Jillian had found the first lady. Tyler Pride's eyes opened wide as he caught sight of Hawk. Instantly, Hawk fell to his knees next to the commander in chief and loosened the gag around his mouth.

"Have you found Kim and Mary?" the president asked in a hoarse voice.

Hawk worked on the ropes binding him. "Yes sir, they are safe." He smiled and offered a soft thank-you to God as he continued to unravel the knots.

"Are you sure they're safe?"

"Yes, sir, I am sure they're safe."

"So you got my message?"

"I did, but I didn't really understand it at first," Hawk admitted.

"I knew you would figure it out and that I could trust you," President Pride said as Hawk loosened an arm.

"I put Kim and Mary somewhere no one can find them. But I've sent Juliette and Jillian to recover them and move them while I looked for you. Kim told me you were concerned about people in the government trying to do you harm." Hawk's fingers worked quickly to untie the ropes. "To be honest, it all seems a little much to believe."

"I understand. Finding out there's a conspiracy that threatens to overthrow the presidency is usually the stuff of movies and fiction," Pride said as another arm was now loose. The president worked to untie his ankles as Hawk removed the last rope securing him to the stake. "But it is real, I promise you."

Hawk gave the president an abbreviated rundown of what had been taking place since he had disappeared. He spoke fast and could see Tyler Pride taking it all in. Another gift the president had that worked well for him—he had a wickedly fast ability to process information. Hawk gave him all the details he thought were important, because for Hawk, his planning had been so focused on finding the members of the first family, he had not slowed down enough to think through all the complications of keeping them safe.

Finally, the president was free of his bonds, and he stretched out on the ground to get the blood flowing back into his extremities. Hawk waited, as he couldn't imagine how painful it would have been for him, forced into that position. After Tyler Pride was able sit up, Hawk stood and extended his hand to help him. Pride grasped his hand firmly, and Hawk pulled him to his feet. Tyler pulled Hawk in and hugged him tightly.

"Thank you for finding my family," the president said, choking back tears. "And for hiding them."

Hawk remained silent until the president released his grip and quickly wiped his eyes. Standing now to his full height, Pride smiled and chuckled softly.

"It feels good to be set free."

"I'm sure."

"So, what's your plan, Hawk?" the president asked.

"Well, like I told you. I found Kim and Mary both tied up in different places. They're safely tucked away. Jillian and Juliette are on the way to find them, and then I'll figure out how to get you all back together as quickly as possible." Hawk glanced out of the teepee to make sure the coast was still clear.

"That sounds good except for one thing," Pride said. "I want to stay away from Kim and Mary. I'm the target here. If you can keep us separated until we end this thing, they'll have a better chance of keeping out of harm's way. I don't have to worry about them, because you've hidden them, not my enemies. I don't trust anyone but you, Hawk."

Hawk thought about this for a moment. "Until *we* end this thing?" Hawk cleared his throat. "Just how are *we* going to do that?"

"*We're* going to stash me someplace safe so that I can share the evidence I've gathered with you. I want to dismantle this conspiracy and expose the scum behind it once and for all." The president thrust out his chin as he finished. "Does that work for you?"

"Yes, Mr. President."

"Good, then let's get out of here." The president waited before continuing. "Where are we going?"

"Some place safer than this teepee. Whoever kidnapped you and your family know that I've found Mary and Kim, so they have to know they're running out of time. I'm surprised they haven't moved you."

"Well, don't be too surprised," Pride scoffed. "I have evidence that makes a lot of people look bad, very bad. The real question is, are they bad enough to have orchestrated this plot? The downfall of these power-hungry vermin is that they're way too arrogant. If they know you've found Kim and Mary, they will deduce you've just been lucky. They won't believe you're smart enough to find me here."

Hawk shook his head. "I don't believe in luck."

"I know that," Pride said. "So take me somewhere I can hide out, and we'll figure out what to do next. Along the way, you can brief me again about what's been going on. I need more details this time."

"Brief you?" Hawk rolled his eyes. "You make it sound like a cabinet meeting, sir. We don't have time for a briefing. Why don't I catch you up after you're safe?"

"Fair enough." Pride patted Hawk on the back. "I'll follow you."

The president of the United States of America and the chief creative architect of the Walt Disney Company stepped out from inside the teepee and jogged through the Native American Village toward the Rivers of America.

CHAPTER FORTY-FOUR

The Dreaded Demise

The howl of a wolf greeted Juliette as she entered the queue line to the Haunted Mansion. She walked briskly beside Jillian through the arched entrance and under the outdoor canopy, where the waiting area for the attraction began. The mansion itself was in the gothic style reminiscent of the eighteenth-century Hudson River Valley structures.

The most recent redesign of the queue made it an interactive experience for guests. Gravestones and crypts distracted guests as they waited, because the line could be long on peak attendance days. Since the park was shut down, it took the pair no time at all to traverse the line to the point they were looking for. This was one of the most amazing interactive experiences a guest could have in a queue line and one that most guests would never realize was available to them.

Of course, Hawk knew that, and he'd known they would be able to figure it out. That's why they were here. The sounds of a wailing ghost wafted down the poorly kept lawn on the exterior of the mansion. The lawn and haunted house itself were intentionally left in dire straits to add to the air of mystery.

"Here we are," Juliette said.

Jillian examined the series of granite busts mounted on the top of podiums in an arc, facing the guests where they would normally wait in line. "This is the Dread family."

Juliette watched Jillian run her meticulous gaze over each bust. She tried to remember what Hawk had shown her when they had examined these a long time ago. She remembered he had been very excited and told her the grim story about the family that made an entirely fitting background for the Haunted Mansion.

243

"Jillian, the Imagineers designed a murder mystery in this area for guests to solve. It has to be the clue Hawk left us. *The key that you need is found in Dread. If these had been here, she wouldn't be dead.* As I said, I present to you the Dread family." Juliette waved her hand toward the statues in front of them.

Jillian stood in front of each bust and read the plaques attached to the podiums introducing each family member. She pointed at one, looked back at Juliette, and then back to the marker.

"This is where it starts," Jillian said. "Uncle Jacob was the first to go. His epithet reads, 'Greed was the poison he had swallowed. He went first, the others followed. His killer's face he surely knew. Now try to discover who killed who.'" Jillian smiled and shook her head. "So the hunt is on. Who killed who?"

Juliette stood next to the Disney security chief as they looked at Uncle Jacob. "Greed was his downfall. Notice the treasures he's holding. But details matter. This is what the Imagineers meant to create. While it seems to be a play on words—Greed was the poison he had swallowed—this is also meant to be taken literally. That is our clue."

Jillian nodded at her, obviously listening, while she explored the other epitaphs. She stopped in front of a man sculpted with a snake wrapped around his neck and shoulders.

"Bertie, who has a bottle of poison on his epitaph. He killed Jacob. Bertie's pet serpent provided exactly what he needed—poisonous snake venom—to kill off Jacob and take the treasure for himself. Bertie killed Jacob," Jillian announced.

Juliette smiled as she watched the former government investigator working the mystery as a real case. As the head of Disney security, it was easy to forget how amazing Jillian's investigative skills were. She had been very good in her role at Homeland Security. Hawk had done a great job in recruiting her to join the team at Disney. It was the important and world-changing secrets that Hawk was given by the Disney brothers that had convinced her how badly she was needed at the company.

"But, obviously, Bertie didn't last too long," Jillian said. "The inscription on his epitaph says he was an avid hunter and expert shot, but in the end that's what he got." She continued around the arc to examine the other statues. Rubbing her hands together, she looked up at Juliette and smiled.

"You can easily find the weapons of choice for this dreaded family." She pointed to the plaque on the statue of Aunt Florence. "Aunt Florence shot Bertie dead. She has a gun on her epitaph marker."

Juliette was now fully engaged in the mystery right in front of them. "Bertie had the inheritance until Aunt Florence realized that her husband was dead! Because Bertie killed Uncle Jacob, Aunt Florence realized that the fortune was missing."

Jillian picked up the narrative. "So, determined to take back the fortune and avenge her husband's death, Aunt Florence shoots Bertie, a fitting end for an avid hunter with an expert shot."

Juliette looked toward Jillian. "Now two members of the Dread family are dead, and the inheritance lies in the hands of Aunt Florence."

"But that must not have lasted very long," Jillian added as she kept exploring. "Aunt Florence's plaque shows a revolver and reads, 'Never did a dishonorable deed, yet found face down in canary seed.'" Jillian drew her head back and traced her jawline with her finger. "I would think that murdering Bertie was a dishonest deed."

Juliette thought for a moment and suddenly remembered a part of the story that would be helpful to them now. "I remember now. Hawk spent an entire day years ago explaining this to myself, Shep, and Jonathan. We spent all day in the Haunted Mansion. I remember this detail about Florence."

"Okay, so tell me."

"Aunt Florence ties into the greater Haunted Mansion story. The Haunted Mansion was owned by George Hightower, the last of Constance's husbands."

"Wait, wait, wait . . ." Jillian held up her hands. "Who is Constance?"

"Constance is the famous bride who appears in portrait form in the stretching room and then in the attic of the Haunted Mansion. She keeps killing her husbands by cutting off their heads."

"You mean that spooky bride-ghost-looking thing with the axe in the ride?" Jillian furrowed her brow.

"Yes, that is Constance," Juliette said. "Sorry . . . the story has a fairly detailed backstory. I can't remember all of it, but upon George's death, depicted in the stretching room as having died by an axe to the head, the mansion had no heirs to transfer ownership to. George's dad, George Sr., was married to a woman named Daisy Dread. Daisy's sister was named Florence, as in Florence Dread, our current holder of not only the wealth, but the deed as well."

"So the play on words is that she never did a dishonorable deed, as in action, and even though she killed Bertie, it was to honor the death of her husband, Jacob." Jillian continued to read and look at the displays. "Never did a dishonorable deed, yet found face down in canary seed. That is a tough way to go."

Juliette watched as Jillian studied the bust of the twins and read, then reread the plaque on display. Jillian snapped her fingers. "It was the twins. They managed to murder Aunt Florence." Jillian pointed to the plaque. "See the dead bird? They had the weapon of choice—poisoned bird seed. Look closely at the statue; there's the bag full of seeds. The twins murdered Aunt Florence."

"Wellington & Forsythia Dread are now dead." Juliette considered their headstone marker and read the words, "'Departed life while in their beds, with identical bumps on their heads.' Wow! They didn't survive either."

"Greed does that to you." Jillian stood in front of the last bust. "Which now leaves us with one suspect, Cousin Maude." Jillian pointed to the remaining statue.

Juliette leaned over and read the epitaph. "She should've been the sole survivor and recipient of Uncle Jacob's fortune, but it seems that she too came to an untimely demise."

Jillian watched closely as Juliette read the words on the podium.

"'Our sleeping beauty, who never awoke the night her dreams went up in smoke,'" Juliette said. "That means they all died."

"And the clue Hawk left us said, *the key you need is found in Dread*. So these busts are the key we need to move forward. The last part of it said, if these had been here, she wouldn't be dead. So what would have kept Cousin Maude from dying if they had been somewhere else? What's 'they'?"

"Her dreams went up in smoke," Juliette said slowly. "So she must have died in a fire."

Jillian walked around to the back of the statue. She smiled and waved for Juliette to join her. Quickly, Juliette followed and saw what Jillian had spotted. Women in Maude's time would use anything they could find to pick or puff up their hair. Unfortunately for Cousin Maude, she chose to use matches to pick up her hair on the night of her death. There, woven into the hair pulled up on her head, were three match sticks.

"As she slept, they rubbed together, and she ignited," Jillian said. "Mystery solved. Actually pretty interesting for a theme-park waiting line."

Juliette nodded. "That's why Hawk thought it was interesting and he was so enthusiastic when he took us through the mansion. But now, the rest of clue—*if these had been here, she wouldn't be dead*."

Jillian nibbled on her lip, tapped her toe, and looked at the ground. Juliette loved watching the wheels in Jillian's head turning. She smiled and remembered the number of times she had watched Hawk try to figure out clues like this. Now Jillian was doing the same. Hawk would have had fun watching them try to solve the clues. But knowing Hawk, they weren't done yet.

"Juliette, if Maude wouldn't have had the matches in her hair, they would have been stored in a kitchen or by a fireplace. Is there a fireplace here?" Jillian asked.

"Yes, there's a famous one—right inside the door."

CHAPTER FORTY-FIVE

The Crazy Split

Hawk and Pride swam across the Rivers of America. Their heads barely broke the surface of the water as they slowly moved along, trying not to create any ripples or traces of motion. Although many of the areas were shallow enough to stand and walk, they stayed low in the water and crept their way across the river toward Tom Sawyer Island.

The island was often considered a minor attraction at the Magic Kingdom. It was easy to see from a distance but also easy to miss since the only way to get there was by raft, or by swimming as they were now doing. Hawk had a special connection to this island. Part of it stemmed from the adventures he had personally experienced here, but the other was because of its connection to Walt Disney.

The original Tom Sawyer Island opened to the public at Disneyland Resort in 1956. What had made the place so special was the creation of it. Walt loved the work of Mark Twain. As they were building it, Walt felt unsatisfied with the island's original design. Days before construction was set to begin, he took the plans home and reimagined the landscape design, creating the inlets, coves, and overall shape the island is known for today.

Walt Disney himself envisioned Tom Sawyer Island as a place for parents to relax and recharge, as well as a place for the kids to explore a little without the watchful eye of parents as a necessity. He created an island to escape inside, within the world of his theme park. It was that escape that Hawk needed to take advantage of now, if only for a few moments.

The president followed Hawk's lead, pulling himself up out of the water and onto the dock that faced Big Thunder Mountain Railroad. As they got up on the planks of the dock, Hawk looked over. "How are you doing, Mr. President?"

"Good. Great actually," Pride responded.

They scrambled to their feet and disappeared into the giant-sized playground geared for kids and inspired by the famous works of author Mark Twain. On an island filled with dark passageways and caves to explore—an old mine; a bouncy, rope bridge; a barrel bridge—Hawk chose to head to a familiar spot for him, the old-fashioned fort named Fort Langhorne. The fort was named in honor of Twain's real name, Samuel Langhorne Clemens. Once inside Fort Langhorne, they had their first chance to slow down and catch their breath.

"We should be safe and out of sight here . . . for a moment anyway," Hawk said.

"Thanks. So where are we headed from here?"

"At this point, I'm trying to find places to go that no one should be looking in. But I don't feel confident enough to hunker down too long in one place. For the short term, I think we need to stay on the move until we can figure out our best plan of action."

"I can live with that."

"That's what I'm banking on," Hawk said with a smile. "But we risk being spotted when we're on the move. We won't always have the cover of alligator-filled rivers to hide us."

The president looked back momentarily in the direction they had come from. "There were alligators in the water?" Pride said with feigned anger.

"There are alligators in every waterway in Florida," Hawk said. "We even find them in our water fountains."

Tyler Pride burst into muted laughter. The chuckling continued as they took a seat inside one of the rooms of the fort. As they sat down, Pride leaned forward and spoke in hushed tones.

"So tell me, Hawk. I know you said Kim and Mary were fine, but how were they really? How scared were they? Are they going to be all right?" Pride displayed genuine concern, not as the president, but as a husband and dad.

"Sir, I think they will be fine." Hawk looked off in the distance and then continued. "Kim was pretty shaken up. She was also angry and scared to death that something happened to you and Mary. Once we freed Kim, just like you, her first thoughts were about finding you."

"And Mary?"

"Well, Mary is . . . well, Mary," Hawk said, and once again Pride laughed. "She was glad to be rescued and determined to come with me to help find you. She's a tough little warrior. You can be proud of her."

"I am, and I love them both."

"I know, sir," Hawk said. "What happened? Why did someone do this to you?"

Pride took a moment and almost unconsciously placed his hand over his heart, then he looked at Hawk and smiled slightly.

"My election, I believe, was a turning point for our nation." Pride paused and smiled. "Now don't tune me out. These are not talking points I'm getting ready to dump on you."

"I didn't think that," Hawk said.

"Well, most people do."

"No, one of things that sets you apart is that you tend not to have talking points."

"Is that good or bad?"

Hawk thought this and decided to lighten up the moment by adding a humorous spin to his response. "I suppose that depends on the day."

Pride laughed. "Fair enough."

Hawk was struck again, as he always was in the presence of the president, by the ease the man had around people and in making conversation. It was a skill Hawk had always struggled with.

"It's no great surprise that America is divided down the middle, Hawk. There are those who consider themselves progressive and those who consider themselves conservative. Both groups have some very valid beliefs about the way the country should be run." Pride paused. "But the problem is, we've lost the ability to find common ground. Instead of being able to respectfully disagree, we've become disrespectfully disagreeable. And there's a big difference in the two."

Hawk nodded. "I guess I've never heard it put that way, but you're right."

"Of course I am. I'm the president," Pride said with a smirk. "Just kidding about the being-right-because-I'm-president part, but I am right." He cleared his throat. "When I announced my candidacy, everyone mocked me and concluded I was a joke. There was no way I could win. I didn't have any great loyalty to either political party. In the past, I had contributed to both parties and some of the major players. As a result, they didn't know what to do with me."

"I remember."

"So while everyone who was in power was writing me off, I knew what they didn't."

"Which is?" Hawk said.

"That there was an America out there that was fed up with politics, political correctness, and having the values and mandates of an elite minority shoved down their throats. They hated that those doing the forcing didn't believe Americans were smart enough, wise enough, or informed enough to know what they wanted."

"And so you ran on a platform to give them what they wanted?" Hawk raised an eyebrow.

"Of course not," Pride corrected. "You know me better than that. But I was in touch enough to understand what they wanted. And I determined that if I could not give them what they wanted, I could work like a dog to give them what they needed."

"Isn't that what most politicians do?"

"Not at all. Most politicians promise to give you exactly what you want." Pride smirked again. "Then after they get your vote, they give you what *they* want. And none of it is what people need."

Hawk thought back to the brutal election battles of the Pride candidacy. Although he had never thought about the run for the White House in those terms, he could see it. He wasn't sure he agreed with the president's methodology, but the thought behind it was sound.

"And you won. You shocked everyone," Hawk said.

"Yes, but I haven't forgotten that my election was *the* election when people went to the polls to fight for their future. They were fighting back the only way they could—by voting. They were worried about their children and their grandchildren and they knew they couldn't trust politicians anymore. So we all lived through what most media analysts called the craziest election ever, where the guy who never had a chance of winning stunned the world and became president." Pride smiled. "But you know what most of this scum has missed?"

"What's that, sir?"

"While they were calling the election the craziest ever, it was really about bringing sanity back to America."

Hawk smiled and thought about what the president was saying. He stood and walked to the door so he could look out toward the gates of the fort. Hawk knew if someone came in, there was an escape tunnel that they could use to slip away. He had used it before and could do so again if needed. But as he pondered the president's words, and he knew they were sincere—he never doubted that— he had to comment.

"President Pride, if you haven't noticed, you didn't bring sanity back to America. People are still pretty crazy about having you as president. We're still divided." Hawk leaned against the doorframe.

"I suppose, my friend, that has everything to do with how you really view the world." Pride stood to his feet. "I agree, the nation is divided, but it's not crazy. The only ones who are really crazy are the political elite, the celebrity elite, the media elite, and the small minority who believe every piece of garbage those groups utter. They're crazy because I've exposed them for what they really are, and they have lost their minds. They're deranged."

Pride laughed. "But most Americans are thinking again and are hearing for the first time another way of looking at the world. They don't mindlessly believe the junk the media is spewing out. They know their own individual lives are better than they were before I was elected. However, it seems that the political elites have decided to eliminate me."

Hawk nodded.

"Hawk, think about it. Are the people who come to visit your resorts crazy? They come and spend their life savings on the vacation of a lifetime. They don't care what politicians are doing. They just want to enjoy life, embrace freedom, and have a chance to chase a dream, an American dream. They want someone who cares about them to make that happen.

"I've had it all. I've had the chance to live my dreams, and I don't need anything from anyone. I simply want to give back and give others the chance to have a better life." Pride's wet feet squished in his shoes as he sloshed to the doorway. "I guess I'm kind of a reset button for our nation."

"Why didn't you use that as your campaign slogan?"

"And waste a good phrase like Put Pride in America?" Pride playfully pushed Hawk out the door. "I'm not crazy, or at least not yet. The media will tell you I am, but I'm not."

"I've never considered you crazy." Hawk motioned for the president to follow. "We're headed to the other side of the island. I need a place for us to hide for a short time before we move again. I also need to make sure that Jillian and Juliette have found Kim and Mary."

"I'm ready."

The two struck out together and slowly made their way through the tree-covered pathways toward the barrel bridge.

"Are you ready to take another swim, sir?"

"I can't wait. I love alligators," the president said as they came to the edge of the bridge. "Hopefully, if I look good to eat, they'll spit me right back out when I punch them in the nose. It works on sharks."

Hawk grinned.

Slipping back into the Rivers of America, they floated quietly, swam, and managed to stay beneath the water, with the exception of their faces. Slowly, they took deep breaths and drifted beneath the surface of the water toward the riverboat dock.

CHAPTER FORTY-SIX

Where the Air Is Deathly Still

The portrait above the fireplace in the foyer drew Jillian's attention the moment she stepped into the front room of the Haunted Mansion. Only flickering light illuminated the darkened chamber. The chandelier, with its broken crystal strings woven through cobwebs and layers of dust, gave the room a distinctly eerie atmosphere that was heightened by the sudden drop in temperature. She shivered. The Haunted Mansion was a classic Walt Disney attraction, and every version, improvement, and renovation of this beloved stop for guests had made it better and better.

Usually, the first stop in the foyer was a brief one for guests. It was basically a glorified holding area as cast members allowed the allotted number of people to enter one of the mysterious stretching rooms.

Guests would huddle together waiting for the room to fill, but Jillian and Juliette had more room to look around and examine the room. Jillian's eyes were drawn to the portrait hanging over the fireplace. The picture of the master of the house, Master Gracey, aged and became a skeleton right before her eyes. Creepy. The fireplace flickered, and the flames cast moving shadows that danced across the floor.

This attraction hadn't been shut down completely either.

"This room is spooky," Jillian said, approaching the fireplace directly. "I know it's not real, but it still creeps me out every time I walk in here."

"Disney Imagineering at its best," Juliette said, following her. "It's amazing. They're always adding something new, or tweaking a feature, or creating a little mischief to make this place more fun and frightening."

"This fireplace has to be the next part of the clue," Jillian said. "If these would have been here, she wouldn't be dead." She dropped to one knee and ran her hand along the inside edge of the fireplace opening. "Matches belong by a fireplace, even if it's just a special effects fire."

"If it were real, we couldn't reach into it, so I, for one, am grateful that is nothing but a fake-fire effect," Juliette added.

"Duly noted."

Jillian caught Juliette glancing over her shoulder toward the door behind them. She stopped searching and listened. Not hearing a thing, she turned to Juliette.

"Did you hear something?"

"How could you not in here?" Juliette laughed.

The soundtrack continued to loop over and over again. Jillian wished she could shut them all off.

The voice of the ghost host repeated in his echoing voice, "Whenever candle lights flicker . . . where the air is deathly still . . . that is the time when ghosts are present, practicing their terror with ghoulish delight."

Juliette stood and silently drifted back toward the front door. Jillian watched her with a mix of curiosity and concern.

"Seriously? Did you hear something?" Jillian whispered, standing as well and abandoning her search. Juliette placed her ear against the door.

"I hear voices," Juliette whispered. "On the other side of the door."

"Do you think someone saw us come in here?"

"I don't know. I don't think so."

"I scoped out our approach, and I didn't see anyone," Jillian said.

She placed her ear against the door, like Juliette, and listened intently. While trying to convince herself there was no one there, the handle of the door suddenly rattled. Someone was trying to open it. Juliette let out a surprised gasp, hushed but audible, nonetheless. Startled, her eyes opened wide. Both women stepped back from the door. As Juliette stared at the handle, Jillian raced back and continued her search of the fireplace. Her hand again traced the edge of the opening. Along the top and one side, she found nothing.

"I locked the door behind us when we entered." Juliette said softly. "But if someone wants in bad enough, it won't be a problem."

Jillian hurried as she searched the other side of the fireplace opening. She felt a small package. Leaning down and sticking her head into the opening, she saw it was taped carefully along the inside of the fireplace, out of sight, yet clearly out of place. The plain brown paper wrapping contained something. This had to be what they were looking for. Again the door of the Haunted Mansion rattled. Now it sounded like someone had inserted a key in the lock. It would open any moment.

Juliette stepped over to Jillian and touched her on the sleeve. With a finger to her lips to remain quiet, she motioned for Jillian to follow her. They disappeared through a dark curtain, which led them into a hallway.

"Someone is after us." Jillian was stating the obvious. "Which is the best way out of here?"

"Down this hallway, and then we enter the load area of the attraction. We can only get out through the interior of the Haunted Mansion."

"Are you serious?" Jillian slowed slightly as they ran down the hallway.

"We'll be harder to find inside, and we can take a look at what you found." Juliette smiled. "Are you scared?"

"I ain't afraid of no ghost." Jillian returned to their earlier pace as she clutched the package in her hand.

The queue area was still. The Doom Buggies that normally ran nonstop inside the walls of the mansion were motionless. Quickly, they scooted past them and into another hallway, where the ride normally began. Juliette led them past the portraits and toward the library.

"I think I heard the door open as we ducked into the load area," Jillian whispered, quickening her pace. "It has to be the Secret Service. They're watching us, or at least searching for us, because they still have no idea what we're up to. They think Hawk knows what's going on, and by default, we know too. Or that's what I'd be thinking if I was them."

"That's the impression I got from Agent Johnson earlier," Juliette said. "As a matter-of-fact, it wouldn't surprise me if he was the one following us."

Jillian shrugged. "If you don't have any solid leads, you go with the closest thing you have to a lead. And that would be us."

The shadow on the piano plunked out a frightening tune as the keys played without being touched. The darkness, the music, and the glowing lights made this a scary backdrop to their escape. Jillian couldn't help but be tense.

Juliette let them into the disorienting stair room, where stairways were set upside down, sideways, and would lead to nowhere. Glowing footsteps appeared on each step and then disappeared into the darkness. In the distance, Jillian heard voices—not ghostly soundtrack voices—but real voices talking. It sounded as though two men were after them, but she had no intention of finding out for certain. They kept running as quietly as possible.

Juliette slowed her pace and then pointed into a long, seemingly endless hallway with a candelabra floating in the middle of it. The illusion itself was simple, done with string and mirrors, but it was intense and looked very real.

"We're going down this way?" Jillian asked. Her nerves tingled.

Juliette nodded. "There's a door on the side at the end of the hall that's real. It opens into a backstage area that will connect us to the Ghost Effect Room."

"Where?"

"Remember? Beware of hitchhiking ghosts? That room." Juliette plunged down the dark hallway.

Jillian trusted her knowledge of how the layout worked. For her, the inner workings of these attractions were not as fascinating as they were to her friends. She had enough knowledge of how they worked and knew her own shortcuts to navigate them in the need of a security scenario, but beyond that, she trusted Hawk as her tour guide. Now she was thankful that Juliette shared that Disney passion as well.

Juliette opened a black-painted door, letting some dim rays of light pour into the hallway. They both stepped quickly through the opening and sealed the door behind them. The dank ash-colored walls around them could have been a part of the attraction itself, not the backstage area.

Jillian took advantage of this hiding spot to once again listen carefully to their surroundings and get her bearings. "So, this brings us out near the unloading zone of the attraction?"

"Yes, we're near the end of it now."

Jillian was planning an escape route. "How far do we have to go to get into the Utilidor?"

"Once we exit the Haunted Mansion, we can run over to the Harbor House. There's an entrance to an auxiliary tunnel beneath it."

"Good, but first let's take a look inside this package and make sure we found Hawk's next clue." Jillian wet her dry lips as she tore the wrapping open.

The brown paper unwound around a solid object made of metal. After a few layers of the paper peeled away, she knew it was a key. Which is exactly what the clue had promised when it told them they would get the key that they would need. But taped to the key was another note, this one folded neatly and tucked along the edge of the key so it could not be missed or discarded with the brown wrapping used to hide it. Running her nail along the edge to peel back the tape, she opened it. Holding it out so they could both see, Jillian's eyes ran across the words written in Hawk's handwriting:

Walt's dad can watch and listen as he keeps them safe.

Jillian glanced at Juliette and waited for her to nod that she was done. When she did, she rewrapped the note around the key.

"He left us the key. That's the last clue," Juliette said.

"So now we have to figure out what it opens."

Jillian needed to think strategically. If they could get out of the attraction and across the pathway to the Harbor House, they could disappear into the Utilidor. That would get them out of sight for a few moments while they figured out where to head next.

Without a word, Juliette stepped back into the attraction, and they made their way past the stationary ride vehicles until they came to the mausoleum. Jillian saw a stairway on the side of the tunnel, and she followed Juliette up the steps quietly until they entered the unloading area of the attraction.

As they hurried along the unmoving, automated walkway designed to move people at the same speed as the Doom Buggies, Jillian decided they needed to create a diversion and confuse the men who followed them. She stepped toward the ride-control system. There was one that could be operated from the loading area and one in the unloading area.

While she didn't know the layout of the attractions like Juliette did—after all, Juliette was the director of theme park operations—she had been around long enough to learn how to power up an attraction and bring it online. She smiled as she thought about two Secret Service agents walking through the dark hallways of the Haunted Mansion when all of a sudden, the Doom Buggies started to move. It would startle them, not scare them, but surprise them, nonetheless. It also would give them an extra few moments to make their getaway.

Jillian threw the switch and punched the illuminated green button. Instantly, the Doom Buggies began to move. As they did, Jillian led the way out the door and away from the Haunted Mansion.

CHAPTER FORTY-SEVEN

Unconfirmed Reports

David Walker watched Allie Crossman shake her head as she spoke into her cell phone. She had taken the call from the network a few minutes ago, and David knew what it was about. John Ware had found out about what was going on and delivered the information moments before the first of their rival networks broke the story. While Allie was on the phone, both he and John had been checking with every contact they could get in touch with to verify the source of this breaking news report, but the far too common response they got was *unnamed sources*.

Allie's call ended abruptly, and David followed close on her heels as she made her way through the news tent and stepped up into their satellite truck. He closed the door behind them. She slumped into the seat, sighing heavily. David sat in a chair next to her.

"That bad?" John asked flatly.

Allie looked at John and then at him. He remained silent, waiting for her to tell him the bad news he had surmised from her end of the conversation.

"I guess you already know what the higher-ups are saying, David," Allie said, again shaking her head in disbelief. "The network wants to know why we haven't broken the news that every other agency seems to be leading with this hour."

David leaned over and put his hands on his knees. "I have an answer for you. I know what they said, but just for your sanity, tell me, what story do they want us to lead with?"

"The news that Dr. Grayson Hawkes, the chief creative architect of the Walt Disney Company, is a person of interest in the disappearance of the president and the first family," Allie said, eyes blinking rapidly as she spoke each word.

"Well, that is news," David agreed. "Except for the fact that there is no cred-ible source that has been named for the origin of that report."

"So everyone else is leading with an unsubstantiated report that the boss of Disney has kidnapped the president and his family," John said. "And the network wants us to run with that."

"The GNN position is that every other news agency seems to be running with the story and we have nothing," Allie said. "I was told, either run with the story or run with something better and bigger."

"And true?" David added.

"True would be good." Allie rubbed the back of her neck. "I tried to explain that we were on the verge of what might be the biggest story of the year, but then this came out."

"It's unsourced," David said. "I just checked in with the White House, and they have no confirmation. The FBI has offered nothing, the Secret Service has offered nothing, and the local sheriff's department has no comment. The only people commenting on the unsubstantiated rumor is the rest of the media. They're taking a bit of information that may or may not be true and running with it."

"And if the information can't be confirmed, then the source is a leak," Allie said. "An unverified leak."

"So what do we do?" John asked.

"Let's go to air." David stood.

"Now? Right now?" Allie asked. "And say what?"

"Trust me." David walked over to the small mirror and checked his appear-ance, preparing to go on the air.

John Ware immediately opened the door of their truck and stepped out into their makeshift setup with Spaceship Earth as their backdrop. After jostling with the camera stand, he finally positioned the camera and checked cables to make sure they would have sound.

Allie followed David out of the truck as he jotted down a few notes for the live broadcast.

"You're not going to report on some deep, dark conspiracy, are you? We have no validation on that one, either," Allie said over his shoulder.

"I said, trust me." David smiled to reassure her. "Get us set up to break in live, please."

Allie got on her phone again and hopped back into the truck. John, now in position, gave David a thumbs-up. As soon as the network wanted the live feed, he was ready. Allie stuck her head out the door and looked once more at David. He gave her a reassuring nod, and she popped back inside. David heard the audio feed in his earpiece as the anchor desk in New York cut away. He looked into the camera lens and began his report.

"This is David Walker with some breaking news to share with you from Central Florida. The latest information that is surfacing is coming from unnamed sources and unconfirmed reports. Grayson Hawkes, the chief creative architect of the Walt Disney Company, is reportedly a person of interest in the disappearance of President Tyler Pride and his family. This stunning development has been breaking over the last few minutes. We've heard the reports and have been trying to get official confirmation about the alleged crime perpetrated by Hawkes. However, the FBI, the Secret Service, the White House, and local officials have all denied or made no comment on this rumor.

"While some of our rival news organizations and outlets have been touting this as a confirmed fact, in reality, it has not been confirmed, and no credible source has been found. The story is nothing more than mere speculation. In fairness, we've made calls to numerous Washington officials, as well as local law enforcement, trying to confirm the leak before reporting it to you. But because other news organizations have been reporting the story as true and confirmed, we felt the need to give you the information and set the record straight with the most accurate information possible.

"It may be possible that this information was leaked from an insider with information that we just do not have yet. But we are certain that no other news group has been able to validate or substantiate this report. Our desire at GNN is to report accurately, and at this time, this so-called breaking news is merely rumor and speculation."

David paused as the anchor in New York asked him a question.

"So, in your opinion, why have the other news agencies been reporting this as fact?" the anchor, Calvin Owens, asked.

"I really don't want to give you my opinion. My opinion is not news. What *is* news is that this report is out there, but it has not been substantiated by any credible source, so as a result, that is the only news I can give you."

"Could you clarify that for our audience?" Calvin asked.

"Be glad to. The news here at Walt Disney World is that most of the news agencies have chosen to report that Chief Creative Architect Grayson Hawkes of the Disney Company is involved in the disappearance of President Tyler Pride.

Some have even gone as far as to say he kidnapped the first family. But they have no reliable sources to back their claims. We will keep working to find a valid source of information that will confirm or deny this report. Until that time, it would be reckless for us to report this story as truth. We promise to get back with you about any updates we might discover."

Calvin followed up. "Is there any official update that has been given by a credible source on the status of the president's whereabouts?"

"Not since earlier in the day." David looked back at his notes. "Most of the information that has been offered has come from unofficial streams of updates. But as we just reported, if we don't have confirmation, we would prefer to make sure what we report is accurate due to the extreme importance of the events of this day. To do anything else would be irresponsible. This is an unprecedented event of national importance. To create our own news or run with a false narrative is reckless and unhelpful. Credibility matters. We'll continue to seek the truth on our end."

"Thanks, David," Calvin Owens said, as the network cut back to the endless cycle of repeating the same information that twenty-four news stations were now forced to report to retain their viewers.

Allie smiled and mouthed one word, "Thanks." Her phone line was still open to the network, and she was immediately engaged in conversation.

John Ware stepped away from his camera. "That was good. It won't make some of the network powers that happy, but it should be enough to keep them at bay. Maybe we can get some confirmation on the story or someone to say it's not true."

"If we can't . . ." David shook his head. "If we can't, we will be the last ones to the party. And now that we've taken the stance of pushing back and implying this might be a false report—if it turns out to be true, I just made a serious mistake."

John scratched his head. "Who leaked the report that Hawkes was a person of interest in the president's disappearance anyway?"

"I'm not sure," David said. "To be honest, I imagine there are some who are very interested in what Hawkes knows or doesn't know. But I don't think he's a valid person of interest who is involved. That makes no sense." He paused. "However, it is troublesome that so many people took the bait and reported it. Some even reported the story as confirmed and ran with it."

Allie exited their truck, no longer talking on the phone. "Thanks! Good job," she said. "You did a good job walking the line and put some suspicion on the credibility of everyone but our network. It was a gamble, but if it pays off, we win big. If not, and the report turns out to be true . . ."

"Yeah, I know. We'll all be looking for new jobs," David said.

"Probably."

"Hey, hold on." John jumped into the conversation. "I'm just the tech guy. I didn't have anything to do with that report."

David smiled. "We'll make sure they know that."

"Nah, I'm just kidding. If we messed up, we messed up together." John looked at both of them. "We're a team."

"Allie, are you still trying to get me an audience with Juliette Keaton?" David asked.

"I've left messages, but right now she's not returning my calls."

"You know, I haven't seen her walking around the press area like she was earlier in the day." David looked out across the seemingly endless mass of news agencies spaced out over the landscape.

"I'll keep trying to reach her." Allie stepped away from them to place another call.

"Thanks," David replied. He was anxious to talk to Juliette. She had challenged him earlier, and he had taken the challenge. Although not completely convinced of a conspiracy, he now had to admit there was enough evidence to make him want to explore the information deeper. There was more evidence that pointed to a conspiracy than the news some of the other networks had been reporting.

He only had one chance to get it right, and he intended to do just that.

CHAPTER FORTY-EIGHT

President in the Hall

The number of the entrance was 1787. The two men entered the red-brick building that combined the historical look of the meeting houses in Boston and Philadelphia, where the US Constitution and the Declaration of Independence were signed. Still dripping wet from their swim in the Rivers of America, President Tyler Pride and Grayson Hawkes entered the Hall of Presidents.

"Seriously?" Pride said, as he slowly scratched his jaw. "This is the place we're going to hide and stay safe?"

"I said it was only for a short time." Hawk swallowed hard.

"The Hall of Presidents?" The president dripped his way across the blue carpet toward the golden circle in the center of the room. "Don't you think this might be a little obvious?"

Hawk realized that Pride was giving him a hard time, but he still felt the need to defend himself. "We'll only be here a minute. This is the fastest way to get where we're going."

"I've been meaning to talk to you about this," Pride said, gripping the handrail and looking at the Oval Office Seal of the president that was featured in the rotunda.

Hawk saw what he was looking at. "Mr. President, we have permission to use the Seal of the Oval Office. As a matter of fact, it took an act of Congress to let us put it here."

"What?"

"Yes, sir. The permission to display the seal here at the Magic Kingdom had to be approved by Congress."

"Well, at least Congress accomplished something at some point." Pride laughed at his own joke. "But that's not what I've been meaning to talk to you about."

Hawk looked at the soaked commander in chief standing next to the seal and shook his head in disbelief. "To be honest with you, sir, I didn't think when you visited the Hall of Presidents it would be like this."

Pride waved him off and strode around the room. He paused and looked at some of the paintings, then the display cases, which contained displays of three first-lady gowns, accessories, portraits, and artifacts. He took an extra moment to look at George Washington's tea caddy and George W. Bush's cowboy boots, which that former president wore during his inauguration.

Hawk watched as Pride examined pieces of history that he could now contribute to. He stopped in front of the black suit on display. Hawk knew it was one of the new additions to the display in the Hall of Presidents. Pride looked at the suit, back toward Hawk, then back at the suit. The suit had been worn by Pride at his own inauguration.

"What I wanted to talk to you about is my robot figure here in the Hall of Presidents," Pride said.

"We call them Audio Animatronics," Hawk said.

"Sure, I call them robots." Pride turned toward him. "That robot of me adds twenty pounds to my frame, don't you think? The hair is all wrong, and it just doesn't look that much like me."

Not sure whether he was being serious or not, Hawk waited for the expression on the president's face to change. It did not. He remained serious.

"Actually, people seem to think it does look like you." Hawk tried not to stammer. "Sorry you don't like it."

Pride finally relaxed his poker face and flashed a big grin. Hawk knew he had been duped and taken in by the gambler in that moment. He was kidding. The president continued to look around the room.

"I heard this attraction was Walt Disney's idea," Pride said as he continued to wander the room.

Hawk had already scanned the room to make sure the curtains were all pulled shut. He walked over next to the president and joined him in looking at the artifacts. "Walt was excited about an old film he made called *Johnny Tremain*. He was fearful that current generations were forgetting about the greatness of our Revolutionary period and our Founding Fathers."

"I am too," Pride said.

"Walt wanted to remind guests of all ages about the rich history of the United States. He was going to name the attraction 'One Nation Under God' and have the thirty-three presidents walk and talk for the audience. But as usual with Disney, his imagination was ahead of technology. Imagineers could only deliver wax dummies at that time, which was not what Walt Disney wanted, and the project was put aside until he could create the technology needed to deliver his original idea."

"Walt was a true patriot who loved his country," the president said. "He was awarded the Congressional Gold Medal in 1968 in honor of all he had done in support of the United States."

"Yes, he was." Hawk was impressed Pride knew that piece of trivia. "Walt Disney once said, 'If you could see close in my eyes, the American flag is waving in both of them, and up my spine is growing this red, white, and blue stripe.'"

Pride nodded. "He was a great American."

"Yes sir." Hawk nodded. "And so are you."

Pride looked Hawk in the eye. "I'm just not the typical politician."

"I agree with that."

"Politicians kick the can down the road and never get anything done. They try to look busy. They talk a lot, and they love to get in front of television cameras, especially during an election cycle. Then they do nothing. They don't solve problems, they don't compromise, they don't work together, and then they ramp back up as the next election cycle begins. They become very loud and try to get reelected, because they don't want to lose power." Pride shook his head. "We so need term limits."

"Why don't you make it happen?" Hawk smiled, already knowing the answer.

"Because Congress would have to pass a bill that I could sign into law that basically would kick them out of their jobs. We both know that will never happen."

"Mr. President, like I said, we aren't going to be here long." Hawk moved back toward the window and peeked out a curtain. "I don't know who to trust right now. But I have you with me, and I want to keep you safe." Hawk looked back at him. "But you have to tell me who I can let know."

"Hawk, since you found me and the Secret Service did not, the advantage we have is that you are able to stay one step ahead of everyone else. Because this is your world." Pride leaned against the railing in the center of the room. "I want us to keep that advantage."

"So I can't tell the Secret Service that you've been found?"

"No, I would prefer you didn't." Pride shrugged. "They are the ones who managed to get us kidnapped. The majority of the agents are patriots; they do a great job. The problem is that there are some I can't trust. As a result, we have to be careful around everyone."

"You want to stay here? You can be on permanent display in the Hall of Presidents." Hawk turned and walked toward the theater doors.

"Actually, I'm looking forward to seeing my wife and daughter again. So the quicker we can get out of this mess, the quicker I can get back to them, keep them safe, and do my job." Pride followed Hawk. "Where are we going next?"

"Some place where you can unravel this chaos. But you need to let me know how you want to do it." Hawk ran his hand through his hair. "I just don't know how big a mess we're talking about."

"I'm sorry you had to get involved." Pride patted Hawk on the back. "I just needed someone I could trust. And, of course, by now there are some in the Secret Service who are going to assume you are part of this plan. They will be looking for you to find me."

"Then I guess we can't let that happen." Hawk's chin jutted forward. "I can navigate the resort pretty well. We just have to be careful."

Hawk motioned for Pride to follow him. "We are headed down Stairway #10 into the Utilidor. Once we get there, we'll move out of the Magic Kingdom area."

CHAPTER FORTY-NINE

Watching and Listening

Jillian methodically made her way through Liberty Square. With Juliette close behind her, they hugged the buildings and darted, doorframe to doorframe. Stepping into the nooks and crannies off the main path, they eventually passed Ye Olde Christmas Shoppe and cut across the bridge that would take them past the Adventureland entrance back toward Main Street USA. Juliette had been the one who had pointed them in this direction, based on the clue Hawk had left them in the fireplace:

Walt's dad can watch and listen as he keeps them safe.

Juliette had convinced her this had to be a reference to Walt Disney's father, Elias Disney. Walt had been given his father's middle name when he was born, and his sometimes-strained relationship with his father had been the stuff many historians had attempted to understand and comment on. Juliette suggested to Jillian that Hawk had always said that most historians had no idea how Walt and his father got along. Walt had always been respectful of his father, although it was well documented that Elias could be a tough and sometimes stern patriarch.

"Now where to do we go?" Jillian said, as Juliette cautiously walked past the Crystal Palace toward Casey's Corner on the edge of Main Street.

"We have to find a reference to Elias Disney," Juliette said. She looked up toward the windows they could now see along the roofline of Main Street.

Jillian followed her gaze. Avid Disney fans knew all about the windows on Main Street. The names on these windows were more than just creative additions to make the surroundings seem authentic. They contained the names of some of the most talented people in the world of Disney.

Pressed against the wall in the alcove behind Casey's Corner, Juliette spoke quietly. "You know the deal with the windows on Main Street. They were put there to honor someone. Hawk knows all of them; I just know a few." She grew quiet for a moment before continuing. "I know that the window for Buena Vista Magic Lantern Slides features the names of Yale Gracey, Bud Martin, Ken O'Brien, and Wathel Rogers. That one window is loaded with Disney history. The special effects of the Haunted Mansion are part of the work of Gracey and Martin."

"And it was Gracey's painting that hung above the fireplace." Jillian remembered making the connection.

"Exactly. There are tributes everywhere. On the same window, Ken O'Brien was an animator who worked on Pecos Bill, some Donald Duck films, and Winnie the Pooh cartoons. Wathel Rogers worked on Audio Animatronics for the Enchanted Tiki Room and Hall of Presidents."

"So we're looking for a window to help us?" Jillian asked.

"Maybe . . . I think so. They all tell a story . . ." Juliette paused. "Though it's not always easy to get the whole story in a glance. Many windows have a lot to say about the people named on them. The window for former President and CEO Frank G. Wells features 'Seven Summits Expeditions' as a small nod to his mountain climbing hobby. It's the highest window on Main Street."

"Like a mountain?" Jillian asked.

"Right. And Walt Disney's name is at the start of Main Street, and at the end of Main Street, kind of like the credits of a film letting you know who is responsible for what you're seeing—in this case, the Magic Kingdom."

"So Elias Disney has a window on Main Street?" Jillian turned a corner and headed down the street, looking toward the upstairs windows.

"He must. I just don't know where."

They explored window after window, occasionally glancing behind them. Jillian knew it would not take long for the agents left behind in the Haunted Mansion to figure out they weren't there. She had no way of knowing if they would follow them to Main Street or not, but they had to stay on guard.

They came to an opening and small roadway that opened to their left off of Main Street. Jillian looked up and quickly pointed as she grabbed Juliette by the arm and pulled her off of Main Street into the short dead-end street.

"There it is. Elias Disney, Contractor, Established 1895," Jillian said. She pointed to the window with the lettering in blue, outlined in black.

"You found it." Juliette looked around them. "This is Center Street. It's one of the best kept secrets in the Magic Kingdom. Back here there are places to sit and watch the crowd on Main Street, but for the most part, no one ever comes back here. It's a quiet spot in the middle of Main Street madness."

"I know. Hawk and I have had ice cream here a few times."

"It's always been one of his favorite spots," Juliette said.

"But you also said it's one of the best kept secrets of the Magic Kingdom. That sounds like a Grayson Hawkes kind of place."

Juliette stood in the street and pointed to the window next to the Elias Disney window. "This has to be the right spot. Those windows next to Walt's dad are part of how this place came to be. Walt Disney knew the price of land in Florida would skyrocket once the public caught on to his plan to build his next big theme park here, so he purchased the land under several pseudonyms. Those two windows tell that story: M.T. Lott Real Estate Investments and the Pseudonym Real Estate Development Company." Juliette smiled. "This is definitely what Hawk was talking about."

"So the rest of the clue said, 'Walt's dad can watch and listen as he keeps them safe.'" Jillian went back to what brought them here. "Walt's dad could watch something, and I guess listen to something from his window up there."

Jillian turned and looked at the windows on display behind her. "Look up there. Those windows advertise private voice and singing lessons. There are also dance lessons offered." Jillian now had Juliette's attention, and she joined her in looking at the windows.

"Listen, you can hear some of those lessons happening right now," Juliette said.

Drifting down from the second story were the sounds of a voice lesson being given and notes from a piano being played. On a busy day, this would be hard to notice in the Magic Kingdom, but like so many things, it was a detail that was always there waiting to be discovered.

"Walt's dad can listen to the music from his second-story window and can probably see the dance lessons as well. It's the perfect spot for him to watch and listen." Jillian moved toward the store front.

"I think that's right. But I'm not sure you can access the second floor from the shop, can you?" Juliette said, and her words caused Jillian to stop in her tracks.

Reviewing what she knew about the shops, Juliette was right. The only way to access these offices was by entering a backstage area that would provide a way upstairs. She had been there before. These offices were located on Main Street, although none of the windows actually had a clear view of Main Street. There were various positions and departments that worked in these offices, but clearly what or who they were looking for was upstairs.

"Follow me," Jillian said, as she hurried to the end of Center Street. They pushed their way through the cast-member-only door and entered the backstage area. They stepped into the industrial, unfinished zone of Center Street. The concrete pad was cracked cement that stretched out behind the buildings of Main Street. Trucks, service vehicles, and other items necessary for the day-to-day operation were back here, and to their left was a staircase that would carry them to a second-floor landing.

Walking toward it, they heard nothing but the ticking of their heels on concrete. At the base of the stairwell, Jillian looked up with a knowing smile. There, behind the door on the landing, was their next stop.

CHAPTER FIFTY

Out of Sight

Hawk and Tyler Pride stepped out of the doorway into the tunnels below the Magic Kingdom. The Utilidor, or utility corridors, had been built for one main reason—to facilitate the unseen operations of the park without creating distractions for guests. Epcot had a much smaller version of this system beneath it, but the Magic Kingdom had an entire world below the theme-park level that most people would never see. Utilidors were entirely different from the onstage areas of the park and strictly utilitarian in style and decoration. Compared to the Magic Kingdom, to describe the underground tunnels as bland was an understatement.

Navigating the system was not always easy. Because cast members often got turned around, there were navigation signs throughout the tunnels to help directionally. Each different land had tunnels of a different color and different fonts to make finding a location easier. If they had not been set up that way, it would have been impossible for cast members to find their way through the concrete corridors, which carried a seemingly endless number of pipes along the ceiling, some carrying water, HVAC, and a pneumatic garbage system.

Their footsteps echoed softly off the walls of the Utilidor as they headed right after leaving the staircase. Hawk stopped suddenly. The president stopped behind him, and both remained silent.

Finally Hawk whispered, "I hear someone coming around the corner."

"Is there anyone supposed to be down here?"

"No." Hawk turned to move in the other direction. "Once you and the family disappeared, we locked everything down and emptied out the theme parks. That includes cast members."

They picked up their pace and jogged, trying not to make any noise as they ran. Running quietly was not easy, as every noise echoed off the concrete enveloping them. This section of the Utilidor wound back to their left. There were straight sections, then at various intersections, the tunnels veered off to the left or right, depending on where an employee needed to go.

"Hold it!" a loud voice echoed down the Utilidor.

They had been spotted. Immediately, Hawk and Pride broke into a run. Hawk tried to visualize where they were with his own mental map of the system. He knew most of the details better than most, but over time, he had not gotten down to the Utilidor as often as he used to. His familiarity was a little fuzzy.

The president ran stride for stride with the Disney CCA.

"I need to find a place for you to duck out of sight," Hawk said as they ran past the welding and carpenter shop on their left.

"I think it's a Secret Service agent chasing us. I saw the suit." The president sounded a little breathless.

"Is it a good agent or a bad agent?"

"Don't know which is which, and I didn't have time to get a good look at him."

They continued to run, with footsteps echoing behind them. Hawk had no idea whether they were losing ground or keeping their distance. But they couldn't continue to run around the Utilidor. They needed a plan.

Hawk knew they were getting ready to enter a straight stretch of hallway, and then it would take a turn to the left. Once they made the turn, they would be out of sight for a few moments. It would be the only time they would have.

"Up ahead, there's an elevator. When we run past it, hop in, and let the door close behind you," Hawk said as they ran.

"Where does it go?" the president asked.

"The Crystal Palace restaurant. But don't get out, just let it return you back here," Hawk said. "I'll come back to get you."

"What are you getting ready to do?"

"I'll keep running and drag our agent friend behind us deeper into the tunnels. I'll come back for you, so stay in the elevator. I can't lose you down here."

"That's your plan?"

"Best one I've got right now," Hawk said as he ran up to the elevator.

"Then we'll go with it." Pride pushed the button on the elevator.

The doors slid open, and he stepped inside. Before they closed, Hawk placed a hand on the door to stop it.

"There are no indicator buttons out here, go up and then come back down, but wait inside," Hawk said. "I'll come back for you."

"Go! Run!" The doors closed and Tyler Pride disappeared behind them.

Hawk now broke into a full-bore sprint. Legs pushing and arms pumping, he knew the agent or agents were very close. There was an intersection ahead, and he chose the right tunnel. The section of tunnel he entered was right below his apartment on Main Street. Then he came to another intersection. Sweating, he cut to his left without losing a step. The advantage he had, if there was any advantage, was that he was familiar with the tunnel system and what they contained.

A few strides further and he cut back to his right. The personnel offices were in front of him. The next doorway was unmarked and hid a storage area, usually full of water fountains, empty trash cans, and benches used along Main Street. Opening the door, he stepped inside and tried to control his hard breathing as he listened against it for the sound of someone in the tunnel. He heard the agent's footfalls, heard him slow, and knew the agent was pausing because he could no longer hear footsteps echoing in front of him.

Hawk guessed he would pause at the personnel section to see if they might have ducked in there. If he did, this was the only moment Hawk might get. He heard the door of the next area click open and decided it was time to move. Shoving open the door of his hiding place, he rolled around the corner into the personnel office, surprising the Secret Service agent. Hawk hit him with two open palms on his chest, driving him backward and flipping him over the desk behind him.

Hawk leapt to the desk and saw the stunned agent reach for his weapon. The Disney chief creative architect landed with a knee on the arm of the agent, preventing him from pulling out his gun. The agent on the ground threw a punch that landed on the side of Hawk's jaw. It was a glancing blow, but Hawk had been prepared for it. He jabbed toward the agent and connected with a more solid punch, causing the agent's head to turn to the side, stunning the guy. Taking advantage of the moment, Hawk grabbed the agent's weapon, popped out the clip, shoved it into his own pocket, and tossed the gun to the side.

The agent now struggled to get to his feet, but Hawk dove in to throw another series of punches. He led with a jab that connected, followed with an uppercut, and then ended the barrage with a hook. The agent fell to the floor again. Hawk reached over to the desk and rapidly pulled out drawers, looking for something, anything that might help. Gripping a roll of duct tape, he turned the agent over and quickly taped his hands together behind his back. Then he taped the man's legs and did the same at his ankles. The agent was coming around.

"What are you doing? Have you lost your mind?" the agent spat, struggling against the duct tape.

"Maybe, but you'll be all right. I'll send help," Hawk said as he leaped to his feet and turned out the light, plunging the agent into darkness. Back in the hallway, he glanced to his right and was heading back toward the president and the elevator when the idea hit. He stopped in his tracks, chased his line of thinking, and then decided it was the best plan he could come up with. Instead of picking up the president, he now made his way back to the right, toward the emergency station at the end of the next corridor.

CHAPTER FIFTY-ONE

In the Office Space

The hallway stretched before them as Juliette and Jillian slowly made their way to each office door and Jillian inserted the key they had found in the Haunted Mansion. They moved quickly and quietly, methodically trying the key in one door and then the next, looking for Kim and Mary Pride. As they searched, the soundtrack of inspirational Disney songs being played on Main Street USA drifted down the isolated hall.

The fourth office they approached had an unmarked, solid white door. Jillian slid the key inside and turned it. Juliette felt her heart jump as the lock clicked and the tumblers released the mechanism locking the door securely in place. Jillian looked back at her, and Juliette's eyes widened in anticipation.

Carefully pushing open the door, Jillian entered first with Juliette following close behind. Juliette looked over Jillian's shoulder and saw the remains of a meal. A box of Disney character cookies stood open on the desk. Two Walt Disney World cups with straws sat on the same surface. Napkins and empty Disney-themed boxes that had once contained food were now empty. Juliette knew this was the right place. But as they looked around, the office was empty.

Jillian turned her head to look over her shoulder and shrugged.

Clearing her throat, Juliette spoke. "Kim, it's me . . . Juliette Keaton. I'm here with Jillian Batterson. It's okay to come out. Hawk sent us."

A soft click sounded as the door to a storage room opened and the face of Kim Pride appeared around the doorframe. Smiling, she emerged from the closet. Her daughter Mary then exited from the storage closet behind her.

Juliette hugged Kim and then Mary.

"Hawk said you would come for us." Kim looked from Juliette to Jillian. "Or at least that's what he had planned."

"He didn't make it easy to find you." Jillian smiled at them. "He wanted to make sure you were safe."

"Now we need to move you to someplace even safer," Juliette added.

"Ah, about that," Kim said. "Hawk said to give you these."

The first lady reached into her pocket and pulled out a square black box and handed it to Juliette. It was heavier than it looked. Grasping it in her palm, she used the other hand to open the top. Inside, she saw polished-silver bars. Almost one inch in width and three and a half inches in length, the four individual bars had been engraved with words spoken by Walt Disney.

All of our dreams can come true if we have the courage to pursue them.

It's kind of fun to do the impossible.

The way to get started is to quit talking and begin doing.

If you can dream it, you can do it.

Juliette knew immediately what they were and what to do with them. While most people would look at them and think they were an expensive Disney collectible, she knew differently. These four bars were actually keys. They had been given to Hawk years ago by one of Walt Disney's original Imagineers, Farren Rales. They unlocked what Hawk had always referred to as "the bunker"—a place where he could monitor all the activity in the Magic Kingdom. Yet the bunker was so secure, all four keys, as well as a code, were needed to gain entrance.

Hawk had told her he'd never really used the bunker. At one time it had been the centerpiece of the secrets that had been left for Hawk by Walt and Roy Disney. Now as the keeper of those secrets, Hawk had found even more secure and obscure places to keep those things safe. As far as Juliette knew, Hawk had not been in the bunker for years.

Jillian reached for the unusual keys. Juliette handed her the items and watched as she inspected the bars closely. Juliette wondered for a moment if she knew what they were for but realized she did as she looked up and smiled.

"Of course," Jillian said. "Hawk wants us to put you in the most secure place in the Magic Kingdom."

Juliette tried to remember the code. After the bars were inserted into individual slots on the locking mechanism, the code had to be entered correctly on the keypad before the door would open. Quickly, she planned the best way to secret the pair in the bunker from their current position. It was underground but had an exclusive entrance and exit that was not part of the Utilidor tunnel system.

Suddenly, Jillian passed the four bars to Juliette and looked down at her phone. She scrolled through the text message and bit her lip as she read. Grim faced, she looked at the others in the room. "Juliette, you'll need to be the one to take Kim and Mary to their safe place," Jillian said. "I've been summoned to the conference room in Bay Lake Towers by Pat Nobles."

"The Secret Service is looking for you," Kim Pride said.

"Actually, they're looking for you. And we're obstructing their investigation."

"Will you tell them where we are?" Kim stepped back and pulled Mary behind her, shielding her with her body.

"Of course not," Juliette reassured her. "Not until we know who we can trust and who we can't. And hopefully by now, Hawk has found your husband."

"Whatever plan we follow is the one Hawk created to keep you safe," Jillian said as she headed for the door. "Juliette, you get them tucked away safe and sound. Unless you hear from me, I'll meet you back at Bay Lake Towers."

Juliette nodded as she prepared to leave. "Be safe and good luck."

"You too." Jillian paused and gave another reassuring smile to Kim and Mary. "We're so glad you're safe, and we plan to keep you that way. We promise."

As they watched Jillian leave, Kim turned to Mary and gave her a hug. "I told you everything would be all right. They're helping us, and Hawk will take care of your daddy."

Juliette stepped away to give mother and daughter a moment as they clung to each other. Her heart ached for this family. She couldn't even imagine the pressure they lived under each and every day as the first family. She also could not imagine the stress of this trip to Walt Disney World. What had started as a relaxing time to grab a few hours to play and have fun had turned into a nightmare.

"Where do we go now?" Kim Pride asked.

"I need to take you to the bunker," Juliette said. "It shouldn't be too tough. Hawk planned this out pretty well. We'll take the back stairway, which will lead us into a parking lot area. As long as the lot's empty, we'll be fine. We only need to walk a few feet and enter another building. From there, we just have to find the staircase to get you downstairs. Then you'll be all set."

"Is there anything to do there?" Mary Pride spoke for the first time since they had found them in the office.

"As a matter of fact, there is." Juliette patted her on the shoulder. "You can see everything that's happening in the Magic Kingdom from there. And I mean *everything*. You will love it."

Mary giggled. "Then let's go."

"Ready, set, go . . ." Juliette said as they moved back into the hallway.

Holding the four silver bars tightly in her hand, she felt her heart racing as she prepared to open the outside door. If the plan was going to fall apart, this was the moment it would tank. As long as the parking lot was empty, they had a chance. Slowly, she opened the door and peered cautiously outside. No one was there, at least no one she could see. This was the moment of truth. Once they stepped through the door, they were committed to their escape.

Motioning over her shoulder, staying on high alert, she beckoned Kim and Mary to follow. They left the safety of the office area and quietly walked down the stairs.

CHAPTER FIFTY-TWO

Call an Ambulance

Hawk stood in front of the metallic doors and pressed the call button. Immediately, the elevator doors opened, and just as they had planned, Tyler Pride was inside, leaning against the back wall.

"I thought you forgot about me," the president chided.

"I tried," Hawk retorted. "But you're difficult to ignore."

"That's part of my style. Are we in the clear?"

"Not yet." Hawk waved for the president to follow him. "So we need to keep moving."

"Good, I was getting bored looking at the Crystal Palace." Pride smiled as they moved back into the Utilidor.

Hawk sensed the president stop behind him and turned. Pride had been distracted by what he saw in front of them. The president pointed at the ambulance now sitting snugly inside the corridor with the engine running. Hawk smiled and motioned for the commander in chief to climb aboard.

"This is our ride out of the Utilidor," Hawk said.

The president slid into the passenger side as Hawk took his place behind the wheel. Checking the mirror, he noticed the president looking at how the ambulance filled up the Utilidor.

"There's not a lot of extra room in this tunnel anymore," Pride said.

"Actually, that's on purpose." Hawk glanced around to see if anyone was in the area. "The usual vehicles running through the Utilidor are golf carts and service carts. Only two gasoline-powered vehicles run down here. One is an armored truck that literally fills up the width of the corridor. It's used for a money drop, and there can be no one in front or behind it. The security benefits of not being able to get anywhere around the vehicle as it moves was an unintended benefit. This emergency vehicle is the only other gasoline-powered vehicle down here. Obviously, it's used for emergencies."

"Wouldn't the armored vehicle have been safer?"

"Probably, but I don't know where the keys are to it." Hawk shrugged. "Besides, I was right next to this one when I came out of the personnel office. I hope you don't mind, but I had to leave a Secret Service agent incapacitated."

"You fought with a Secret Service agent?"

"Yes, I had to . . . to keep him away from you."

The president nodded thoughtfully.

Hawk waited for a moment before he spoke again, carefully measuring his words. "Sir, you asked me to help you. But I don't understand why the Secret Service is after you or trying to hurt you."

"The Secret Service as a whole is not. As a matter of fact, we have some very dedicated and stellar agents." Pride spoke with an appreciation Hawk had not expected.

"But?"

"But there are some bad actors in the upper echelon who have strong ties to the political power brokers in Washington. They're the ones who planned this conspiracy against me. The problem is, I don't know which of the agents I can trust and who I can't. I have my suspicions, but I can't be sure."

"So you have a strategy for how to expose this conspiracy that will result in the bad guys getting caught and punished?" Hawk put the ambulance into gear and moved forward.

"That's my plan."

"And in the meantime?"

"We trust no one," the president said.

Hawk was struck with the loneliness Pride must be feeling. He was the leader of the free world, arguably the most powerful man in the world, and yet he didn't know who he could trust. And to make matters worse, they were willing to harm his family to remove him from power. That was a tough and desperate place to be, and sometimes extreme circumstances called for extreme actions.

The ambulance moved steadily through the Utilidor. Hawk found it more unnerving than he had thought it would be driving through the corridor. It was like trying to drive through a tunnel with a vehicle that barely fit through the opening. Any twitch, miscalculation, or turn of the wheel would cause the vehicle to bounce off the side or wreck into the wall.

He brought the ambulance to a rolling stop as he turned slightly to the right. The emergency vehicle cleared the corner, and he accelerated past a stairway that led up into Adventureland, and then he drove past the welding carpenter's shop. Now the tunnel would turn to the right again, so he repeated the slowing and braking procedure. This time, the angle was different, or he must have miscalculated the turn as he moved through it. The passenger window scraped against the wall. The president instinctively leaned toward him as the mirror broke off in the turn.

Once again, the Utilidor straightened out in front of them. The stairway to Ye Olde Christmas Shoppe was on their right, followed by the stairs they had used from the Hall of Presidents. Next they passed the Fantasyland Shop and approached the Character Zoo, which held the wardrobe that would be used by cast members to bring the iconic Disney characters to life for guests in the Magic Kingdom.

Now Hawk spotted a black-suited man in front of them rounding the corner. The agent spotted the ambulance and drew his weapon.

"Floor it!" Pride yelled. "He probably won't shoot."

"Probably won't shoot?" Hawk said as he sped up the vehicle.

"Well, let's put it this way. If he's a good agent, he won't shoot at me. But he'll probably shoot at you because you seem to have kidnapped me. If he's a not-so-good agent, he might shoot at me and then claim it was an accident. But I am going to go with he won't shoot because he won't know the best thing to do."

Hawk leveled his eyes at the agent with the drawn weapon and pressed his foot down on the accelerator. "You're not really inspiring me with confidence, Mr. President. You're basically telling me you aren't sure what's going to happen."

"Then we should find out." Pride shot a glance at Hawk and motioned for him to keep driving. "We'll know soon enough how it turns out."

The agent stood firmly in the middle of the Utilidor. Hawk figured the guy thought he'd come to a stop because of the weapon. Slowly, the Disney CCA eased off the gas pedal slightly.

"Don't slow down!" Pride barked.

Hawk instantly dropped his foot back on the accelerator and mashed it to the floor. The emergency vehicle bucked a little with the sudden increase in speed, but Hawk could see the motion had the desired effect. The agent flinched.

The movement was ever so slight, but he had raised his arm and shifted his stance. Once again, the agent drew the vehicle into his sights.

As the ambulance gained speed, the mirror on his side scraped against the side wall of the Utilidor, but he didn't slow down. They were now only feet away. The agent blinked and jumped into the protection of the doorway to the Character Zoo, giving Hawk a mere two inches to pass without hitting him.

The president laughed, and Hawk found himself smiling when suddenly the tunnel made a turn back to the left. The Utilidor only had one entrance and exit accessible for vehicles. They'd reach the main entrance of the tunnel system at the end of the next turn, but they were moving too fast. The ambulance bounced off one side of the Utilidor, causing them to careen off the other side. The ambulance slid at a weird angle, wedging itself into the tunnel corridor. It came to a shuddering and sudden complete stop.

At some point, the president had fastened his seatbelt, and his chest hit hard against the strap. Hawk had not, so as he was thrown forward, crashing into the front windshield. Momentarily stunned, stars and flashing lights filled his vision.

He felt the president grab his arm and pull him toward the now-open window of the passenger side. There was no room to open the door, but the angle would allow them to crawl out the window and back into the Utilidor. They had effectively blocked off and shut down the tunnel, trapping the agent they had almost hit behind them.

Hawk regained his senses as he followed Pride out the window of the vehicle. Once they landed on the concrete floor, Hawk staggered forward before regaining his balance. The Utilidor opening lay in front of them.

"There!" Hawk managed to say as he pushed forward.

"Mr. President, Mr. President, are you okay? Halt! Please halt!" The voice of the agent came from somewhere behind the ambulance.

"What do you think? A good guy or a bad guy?" Hawk said as they ran toward the exit.

"Not sure. No time to check." Pride matched Hawk stride for stride.

Together the pair moved to the end of the tunnel. Hawk skidded to a stop and looked outside. Once again, the coast was clear.

Turning back to the president, he spoke softly. "I know where we're going. I just have to figure out the best way to get you there. Do you trust me?"

"Of course," the president said. "Not that I have much of a choice," he added with a smirk.

CHAPTER FIFTY-THREE

Perspective and Reality

The glistening exterior of the Bay Lake Towers hid the intensity of the meeting happening behind the closed doors of the conference room in the office suite of Grayson Hawkes. Jillian sat at one end of the table and glanced around at the concerned faces of the people seated in the power chairs around it.

Sam Reno, the chief of staff, and Dana Brown, the president's press secretary, were on her immediate right. To her left sat Pat Nobles, the Secret Service detail chief. Agents she didn't recognize were both seated and standing along the edges of the room. Among that group, a stone-faced Agent Craig Johnson stood closest to the door. She assumed he was the guard to make sure no one entered who wasn't supposed to be here. Standing opposite her, an angry Jeremiah Stanley, the director of the Secret Service, leaned forward with his palms on the table.

"So let's review this again. Your boss, Grayson Hawkes, eluded the Secret Service by fooling them into boarding a gondola, which he later jumped off of, to hide the president's daughter?"

"That's what your agents reported," Jillian said calmly. "There's some security footage, but it's unclear where Hawk and Mary Pride went. They were not on the Skyliner when it arrived at the Caribbean Beach Resort. You are correct."

"That was after he eluded our agents in the Disney Hollywood Studios," Pat Nobles added. "Our team there was searching, but apparently Hawkes found the girl before they did and then decided to move her."

"Again, that's what you reported." Jillian looked at him coolly.

"Agent Batterson," Stanley continued, "I mean, *former* Agent Batterson, is there any reason you can think of that would explain why the chief creative architect of the Disney Company would hide the president's daughter from the United States Secret Service?"

"No." Her brows knitted. "But when you phrase the question that way, I would assume he has a very good reason."

Nobles snorted at her response.

"Are you aware that Hawkes has just been seen with President Pride in the tunnels below the Magic Kingdom?"

Stanley stood back up after he asked the question, which Jillian assumed was because leaning forward on the table had not intimidated her. She suppressed a smile. It was great news that Hawk had found the president and now was doing whatever he could to keep him safe.

"No, I wasn't aware of that until just now," she answered.

Stanley's voice rose in volume. "He nearly ran down one of my agents with an ambulance. Then he and the president ran out of the tunnel together."

"Interesting." Jillian raised an eyebrow. She wondered what Hawk was doing in an ambulance in the Utilidor.

Stanley frowned at her response or lack of it. She could tell he was trying to contain his composure and keep his cool. Agents often spoke of his explosive nature behind the scenes. However, the Secret Service head that the world saw on camera was composed and always in control. She could tell the tension of the situation had strained him to the max.

There was a disturbance by the door, and Jillian turned to see Agent Johnson talking to someone on the other side of it. Stepping back, he allowed Juliette Keaton to enter the conference room. As Jillian looked at her, Juliette gave her a slight nod. Jillian knew it meant she had gotten Kim and Mary to the bunker to hunker down until they knew what to do next.

"Come in." Stanley motioned for Juliette to take a seat. "We were just taking inventory of your boss's activity over the past few hours."

"About that," Juliette said, apologetically. "Hawk just texted me and said to tell you there's a Secret Service agent in the personnel office in the Utilidor that needs some assistance."

"Really?" Stanley reached out his hand. "May I see your phone?"

"Certainly." Juliette slid her phone across the table.

Stanley picked it up and read the message. As he did, he looked at one of the agents standing along the wall, and without saying word, sent some type of signal for him to go and check it out.

Jillian noticed that before he slid the phone back to Juliette, he slyly scrolled across her phone, probably to see if there were any other messages from Hawk. She knew he wouldn't find any.

"So, to add to what I said earlier, not only did Hawkes nearly injure one of my agents in the tunnels, he has also done something to another agent and left him in an office." Stanley glared at Jillian.

"Well, he did let you know where to find him." Jillian crossed her arms. "That counts for something."

"The something it counts for is letting me know that he has kidnapped the president of the United States!" Stanley yelled, his composure shattered, his face turning red. "And for some reason, that doesn't seem to bother you."

Defiant, Jillian pushed back from the table and rose to her feet. "You want to know what bothers me?" She glared right back at him.

"Oh, please tell." Stanley's voice dropped to a conversational decibel.

"It bothers me that on your watch the president and the first family disappeared. It bothers me that your team swooped in here weeks ago and made sure the resort was secure. It bothers me that you isolated me and my security team and kept us out of your way to make sure everything was ready. But somehow when the president arrives, you can't manage to keep him safe on a one-way monorail trip . . . with the entire world waiting to see him."

Jillian now moved around the table and stalked toward the Secret Service director. "It also bothers me that instead of trying to find the Pride family, you seem to be spinning your wheels worried about what Dr. Hawkes is doing, when in reality it looks like he has done what you couldn't—find our president."

Jillian felt her pulse racing and a tightness spreading in her jaw and neck. When she finished lashing out, the silence in the room hung like a heavy cloud waiting to burst into a rain shower.

Pat Nobles broke the silence by slowly and steadily clapping his hands together in faux appreciation. "That was beautiful. Do you feel better now?" His voice was snarky and condescending.

"Not really." Jillian turned on him with frightening speed, causing him to move back in his chair. "You're still here."

"It's become clear to me that Grayson Hawkes is the one responsible for making sure we can't do our job," Stanley interrupted. "He knows the resort better than we do, and he has managed to work around our security plans. I promise you Detail Chief Nobles does not miss anything in his security procedures and protocols."

Nobles nodded his appreciation to his boss. "So the question is, do you know where Hawkes and President Tyler are right now?"

"I do not." Jillian smiled as she gave her answer.

Juliette spread her hands as she placed them on the table. "What I would like to know is why someone told the news media that Hawk was your suspect and that he was the one who took the president. It seems to me that leaking such an uncorroborated rumor with no evidence to back it up would impede your investigation."

Dana Brown looked toward the head of the Secret Service. "It didn't come from us. But I was wondering the same thing. Who leaked that story?"

Stanley furrowed his brow. "We didn't release that information."

Sam Reno stepped into the conversation. "Somebody did. It didn't come from our office, so it had to have come from someone in your department."

"I can guarantee you, it didn't come from us," Stanley responded.

"Be careful not to guarantee what you can't deliver on," Jillian said. "You guaranteed to protect the president and that didn't work out so well for you."

Jeremiah Stanley's face grew red again. He opened his mouth to speak but was interrupted.

"If it didn't come from your department, at least that you're aware of," Dana said, "then you might want to ask yourself, who would have leaked that kind of inflammatory information? It certainly doesn't help you or the Pride family in this investigation. It opened up the floodgates for criticism and has sent the media into more of a frenzy than they were already in."

"There's been no leak in the Secret Service Division," Nobles said with conviction. Murmurs erupted around the room.

Stanley held up his hand for silence. "I want to believe we're all on the same team in this room and our goal is to find and secure the Pride family." He turned back to Jillian. "The last name of the dead couple we found on your property today was Grimsley. They arrived at the Fort Wilderness Campground in an Airstream camper."

The unexpected announcement caught her more off guard than she anticipated. She struggled to hide her surprise. "Thank you for the information. How did you discover that?"

Stanley smiled as though he was trying to read her reaction. "We're the Secret Service, and we really are good team players. I know you don't think so, but we're all trying to accomplish the same thing here."

Stanley waited, and Jillian could feel every pair of eyes in the room on her.

"Why do I have the feeling that you already knew that information?" Nobles injected himself into the conversation. "Did you know that and not share their name with us?"

Jillian's thoughts raced at lightning speed. She knew they would eventually discover the same information her team had discovered, but she had not expected to hear it from them yet. She scrambled mentally to come up with an answer.

"Why would I keep that from you?" When in doubt, answer a question with a question, she thought.

"Why indeed?" Stanley again smiled. "I have given you and your team far more leeway than I normally would. It seems my choice to do so has now become a problem."

"Let me ask you something." Jillian decided to go on the offensive. "You said that President Tyler was with Hawk in the Utilidor. Apparently, there were at least two of your agents looking for them in the tunnels."

"Yes, what's that got to do with anything?" Stanley took a slight step backward.

Invading his personal space, she continued, "If the president was trying to escape Hawk—because in your narrative, Hawk had kidnapped him—why didn't the president run to your agents? Why did he stay with Hawk? Did Hawk have a weapon? Was Hawk holding him captive in the ambulance?" Jillian flexed her fingers before drawing them into a fist. "And why did they run out of the Utilidor together? It would seem to me if the president was trying to escape, he would have run toward your agent, not away from him."

Jillian could tell she had Stanley's attention. "Maybe your perspective of what is really happening here is, in reality, not what is going on at all. And because you are so committed to believing and holding onto your perspective, then you are missing the real clues and the real problem." Jillian felt her pulse racing.

"Is that what you think?" Stanley leveled his gaze at her.

"Yes, it is." Jillian pointed her finger at him. "Your perspective and reality are two different things. You better decide which one you believe in."

CHAPTER FIFTY-FOUR

The American Adventure

The American Adventure is the quintessential Epcot attraction. It offers a brief history lesson of some of the highlights of America's finest moments. Now Hawk was transporting the president of the United States into this pavilion, with the hope of putting an end to this chapter of their lives.

The interior of the pavilion was brimming with history just waiting to be discovered. Hawk had the gnawing sense that together they were also making history, but exactly what kind was also waiting to be discovered. Using the back routes and maintenance pathways, Hawk drove the president to the rear entrance of Epcot in another vehicle he had commandeered. They walked the rest of the way. The president was looking around trying to get his bearings as they got ready to move inside. Even in the heat of being hunted and on the run, Hawk was amazed at how cool and conversational the president could be, even in crisis.

"What's your favorite part of this attraction?" Tyler Pride asked as they walked quickly, but quietly, to the cast members' back entrance of the American Adventure.

Hawk eyed the president. "No offense, Mr. President, but that's not the first question I'd ask if I was in danger."

The president grinned as though he was having fun. "Just curious. I trust you to get us out of this mess."

Hawk remained silent as he worked to pick the lock to open the door.

"Well?" the president said.

The question broke Hawk's focus. "Well . . . I suppose the exhibits that give guests a chance to learn about history they've never seen before."

"I like the Hall of Flags," President Pride offered without being asked. "I think most people glance at the flags but don't know what they're seeing. Are there still forty-four?"

"Yes." Hawk finally opened the door and let the president enter first. "We haven't changed it a bit."

"That's good," the president said, still sounding calm. "I don't think people really appreciate the number of flags that have flown over this nation. Every time a state was added, they sewed on another white star. Did you know that in 1889, a thirty-nine-star flag was created by people who believed the Dakota Territory would enter the Union as one combined state?"

Hawk tried to stay focused on his plan. "Uh huh. I did know that."

"Most people don't. Of course, that flag was never adopted. In 1890, a new flag was introduced with the correct number of stars—forty-three."

They sidled inside the rear access hallway of the pavilion. Weaving through the dimly lit corridor, the president continued to speak softly. Hawk thought the commander in chief seemed incredibly unconcerned for his safety and well-being. At any moment, the man could be assassinated. In contrast, Hawk's heart raced.

"The colonial Union Jack from the North American governors' ships—the Navy Jack—sported thirteen alternating red and white stripes under a rattle-snake with a warning, *Don't Tread on Me*." Tyler Pride smiled. "All our flags are magnificent, but my favorite is the Commodore Perry flag, bearing the infamous words, *Don't Give Up the Ship*."

Not wanting to scold the president, Hawk bit back a sarcastic retort and spoke over his shoulder. "I didn't realize you knew all those details, sir." After all, if thinking about American flags calmed the president, who was he to judge.

"People don't have any sense of how special those flags are. They mean something," President Pride said. "We can have differences, but the flag is a symbol of what unites us or what *should* unite us. The press incites people to think I'm overzealous about the American flag, but when we say the Pledge of Allegiance, we're making a commitment and honoring an oath that has been taken for generations. When that oath doesn't matter anymore, America as we know her will cease to exist."

Hawk pushed through the doors and emerged into the rotunda of the American Adventure Pavilion, breathtaking in size and beauty. As Pride walked past him and stared at the exhibit, Hawk was struck again by what an amazing, inspiring, difficult, and complicated personality the man who sat in the Oval Office had.

The president raised his hands and turned to Hawk with a wide smile. "Beautiful! Just beautiful." Pride sauntered through the space like any other guest might, taking in the sights. Slowly, he walked around the space, reading aloud some of the quotes on display.

> *"Bring me men to match my mountains. Bring me men to match my plains. Men with empires in their purpose. And new eras in their brains."*
> —Sam Walter Foss

> *"What Kind of man would live where there is no daring? I don't believe in taking foolish chances, but nothing can be accomplished without taking any chance at all."* —Charles Augustus Lindbergh

> *"Our way of living together in America is a strong but delicate fabric. It is made up of many threads. It has been woven over many centuries by the patience and sacrifice of countless liberty-loving men and women."*
> —Wendell Lewis Willkie

"I don't know how anyone could ever visit here, Hawk, and not leave proud of our American heritage."

Hawk nodded his head in agreement, wishing they had time for this patriotic moment. Instead, he brought them both back to the dangerous present. "Sorry to interrupt, sir. I agree with you, but right now someone is trying to harm you and your family. So first, let me show you the place I told you about to see if your plan will work."

They moved into a stairwell and climbed up the staircase that wound toward the next level in the rotunda. It led them to the area used by most guests to view the showpiece of the attraction. Bypassing it, they made their way to the next staircase that would take them to an even higher level in the pavilion.

"Hawk, I really wish you would have joined my administration. I think you could have made a real difference."

"You're doing fine without me, sir."

"All of us are expendable," Pride said, now serious. "America is bigger than any one person. But we can all make a difference. You should have taken me up on my offer."

Hawk continued to climb the next set of stairs, as the president followed. "I was flattered and did consider it."

"But you wish I was statelier, more presidential, right?" Pride paused on the staircase. "You get uncomfortable because you think I'm too tough, too mean, too nasty."

Hawk stopped and looked back. "I didn't say that."

"But that's how you feel." Pride smiled. "And I understand that, I really do. Not only do I understand it, I respect it. But we both know I'm not a good politician."

"I don't know about that, but you've done pretty well. You are the president of the United States after all." Hawk turned to continue upward, but Pride reached out and stopped him by placing a hand on his shoulder.

"No, I'm not a good politician. I'm a practical, no-nonsense, take-no-guff, and take-no-prisoner kind of guy. I always have been, and you know that." Pride shook his head. "Too many people are worried about being politically correct. I don't have time for political correctness. And to be frank, America can't afford the time either. Career politicians use it to manipulate, influence, and control people. It makes people afraid to disagree. I'll never score high on the politically correct spectrum."

"To be honest, President Pride . . ." Hawk hesitated. "I just think you could be a little nicer sometimes."

"You want me to be nice?" Pride sounded angry. "You be nice. My job is to defend the Constitution of the United States of America. The Constitution assigns me two roles—chief executive of the federal government and commander in chief of the armed forces. As commander in chief, I have the authority to send troops into combat, and I'm the only one who can decide whether to use nuclear weapons. As chief executive, I enforce laws, treaties, and court rulings. I attempt to establish federal policies, prepare a national budget, and appoint federal officials. I approve or veto acts of Congress. Nice is not in my job description."

"Fair enough, sir. You don't have to be nice." Hawk turned and jogged up the stairs into the magnificent American Adventure Parlor.

Most guests had never seen it and would never attend an event inside of it. Featuring colonial architecture and decorated in the colonial style with antique furniture, framed silhouettes, eighteenth-century prints, a cozy fireplace, and numerous seating areas, the parlor featured a living room looking out onto World Showcase, as well as a separate dining room. It was an expensive, high-end setting for conferences and receptions.

"Did I offend you on the stairs?" asked the president as they stepped into the parlor.

Hawk smiled. "No, you only confirmed why I didn't come to work for you."

Pride laughed. Hawk motioned for him to wait near the staircase as he angled toward the windows. He cautiously eased his body into position so he could see out glass to the exterior of the attraction. Seeing nothing, he moved to the next window and did the same. As he did, he listened to the president speaking in the background.

"Hawk, you used to be a preacher," the president said. "So you understand the way people have reacted to me as president. I was elected at a time when some were upset about the religious decline in America and the advance of secularism. Some even thought God would use me to change the direction of America. To be honest, I hate the division in America. So I hope I'm more of a restart button."

"I believe you sir, but right now—" Hawk strode to another window to continue checking to make sure they were not followed.

The president interrupted. "Some people don't like my past and think my character and conduct in my earlier years disqualify me for the office. I'm not sure that's historically defensible, but everyone can have an opinion. That's what makes America great. But what I'm doing today matters. One preacher said publicly that I was morally unqualified to be president. Granted, I've made lots of mistakes, but I listened to you preach, and you said we have all made mistakes, but there's forgiveness and hope."

"Mr. President, people will always have different views," Hawk said. Satisfied there was no one entering from the ground floor of the attraction, he now walked over to the doors that opened into the side rooms off the main area. As he did, he finished his thought. "But they need a leader right now."

"I agree," Pride said. Hawk could feel his eyes watching him as he secured the area. "I'm trying my best to be that leader. But the problem with a lot of people is they want a leader who will take them where they want to go, not necessarily where they need to go. You want me to be a leader who says things a certain way, who acts a certain way, and behaves a certain way. That's what you want."

Hawk flexed his fingers and sighed. They didn't have time for this conversation right now, but the president didn't seem to understand that.

Pride grew thoughtful, then continued. "In some ways you wish I was the moral rudder for our nation. But the truth is, I don't *need* to be the moral rudder for our country. But I do need to assure you the freedom to be one. You want me to defend your religious liberty so that you can change the world with the love of Jesus. If I do my job, and as a result you can do your job, we have a stronger nation."

Hawk thought about the president's words. He now moved back over to where the president waited and stood to face him.

"Aren't I a great defender of religious freedom?" Pride asked.

"Yes, sir, you are."

"Then you can do your job. Change the world, Hawk. But don't expect me to do it for you." Pride exhaled. "Pray for me, help me if you can, let me do my job for all Americans, and I'll let you do yours."

"Fair enough." Hawk was impressed and touched by his friend's honesty, but that sense of urgency in his gut burned. "Right now, let me do my job."

"Tell me what you need me to do," Pride said.

I need you to stop talking. But he respected the president enough not to voice his frustration. Instead Hawk answered, "Hide. Stay here and out of sight. No one knows where we are. The beauty of this pavilion is there are lots and lots of rooms. You should be safe here."

"You're in the driver's seat, Hawk, so hurry up and get everything set up. I want to see Kim and Mary again."

"I know that," Hawk said. "I'll be as fast as I can."

As Hawk turned to descend the steps, he paused. "Are you sure you want to do things this way?"

"Do you doubt my plan?"

Hawk grinned. "I know, let you do your job, so I can do mine."

"Exactly." The president smiled back.

Hawk took each step in rapid succession. He wished he had as much confidence as Tyler Pride seemed to have in what they were trying to do. If it worked, this would become a day people would talk about for years to come. If it didn't, history would also never forget it, but for a completely different reason.

CHAPTER FIFTY-FIVE

The Remains of Thunder Mesa

Jillian had received the text from Hawk in the stress-filled minutes of the meeting with the Secret Service. For now, the agency was determined to find Hawk, and when they did, they believed they would find the president. Juliette had assured her that she had gotten Kim and Mary safely secured, so now she needed to carry out Hawk's instructions. The text was another Disney-coded message. She had read it and reread it, and between herself and Juliette, she finally had a lead on what it might mean.

Find the remains of Thunder Mesa and then stop listening to so you can live with

Juliette had helped her figure out the destination based on the clues. Without her friend's help and knowledge of Disney history, Jillian would have been stuck. The remains of Thunder Mesa could be found in concept in a few locations within Walt Disney World. But the unused props and rest of the remains designed for Thunder Mesa could only be found in one place. They lived with the land in the Land Pavilion at Epcot. She headed there now.

The reference to Thunder Mesa concerned the props that were to have been a part of the much advertised, but never built, Western River Expansion in the Magic Kingdom at Walt Disney World.

Juliette had figured out the second part of the clue easily—the name change of the boat ride inside the pavilion. It had opened as Listen to the Land; the current version was known as Living *with* the Land.

According to Juliette, it was a surprisingly popular attraction in Epcot. Jillian had been extremely careful on her approach to the spot. She had taken the long way, walking in through the International Parkway entrance near the World Showcase. Clinging to the edges of the pathways, she had made her way through England and Canada, then cut over into the section of Future World that contained the pavilion.

Walking into the Land Pavilion, she saw the steam rising from the fountains lining the walkways below and their intricately designed mosaics. The look was meant to recreate the layered strata of the earth after a volcanic eruption. The double doors opened, and she knew she had to make her way down the stairs to the ground floor of the pavilion. To her right, signs pointed to the entrance queue for the boat ride.

Hurrying down the steps, she noticed the boats still ran constantly. Normally, a cast member would activate the boats once guests boarded, but now, the boats floated through the loading area and continued on into the attraction itself. She stepped over the queue railing and ran to the launch area.

After making sure she had not been followed, she glanced to her left and right to make sure no one lurked nearby. Waiting and timing it just right, she jumped into a moving boat. Sliding into the cool, plastic seat, she stayed on high alert for what might happen next.

Jillian floated into a raging storm. A narrator explained she was on a voyage of discovery and awareness. Simulated rain, thunder, and lightning crashed and flashed around her. Waterfalls raced over rocks and trees. The narrator explained the storm brought changes to the land that were beneficial to the environment. As a result, below the surface of the land, the roots of trees trapped water from flowing mud to create one of the most diverse living systems of our planet.

She peered into the darkness of the rain-forest storm but saw nothing and no one. The shadows created by the falling rain in the theatrical lighting cast shadows over the boat and audio-animatronic animals. She floated onward.

Her boat rocked gently along the waterway as it rounded a corner that carried her into a desert scene. Here, plants and animals survived because they had adapted to make use of what little water was available to them. Still, she could not see anything that would be considered another clue.

What did Hawk want her to find? Now the American prairie scene surrounded her, highlighted by buffalo on one side and a farm on the other. Looking up, she saw the rotating dining area where guests enjoyed their meals while giving them a glimpse into the attraction itself.

For her part, she was concerned about how the view above exposed her to anyone who might have spotted her entering the attraction. She kept her gaze fixed upward, looking for men in black suits. The boat now moved into a barn that was actually a theater, showcasing a seemingly endless series of pictures and movies displaying natural ways to use the land.

By this point in the attraction's journey, Jillian wondered whether she and Juliette might have missed the clue's real meaning. Then the narrator began to explain what was being shown on the screens.

"In Japan we're learning that by adding composted leaves and other plant material to our soil, we can reduce the need for fertilizer. In farmlands across America, we're learning that by plowing under vegetation containing natural fertilizers we can enrich the soil without the use of chemicals. In Saudi Arabia and Mexico, we're learning to produce food on desert seacoasts by developing and planting crops that thrive on saltwater. Here at Epcot, we're learning to reduce the need for pesticides by using natural predators like ladybugs and wasps to control pests."

Jillian slid to the side of the empty seat, knowing she would soon float into the Epcot Production & Research Center greenhouses. The greenhouses displayed the uses of biotechnology, crop production, integrated pest management, and aquaculture. The darkened barn theater was about to give way to the futuristic domed enclosure of the research greenhouse. The boat in which she rode would travel right through the middle of it. Just as it cleared the entrance into the greenhouse, a hand suddenly reached in and wrapped around Jillian's arm, giving her a sharp tug toward the side of the boat.

For a split second, she held her breath before letting out a slight gasp as she was pulled out of her floating carriage. The steady momentum of the boat left her feeling weightless for a moment when the person who grabbed her forced her up and out of the boat.

Reorienting herself to the unknown assailant behind her, she prepared to spin and attack as soon as her feet touched the ground. As her first foot found a solid surface, she began to pivot, ready to deliver a roundhouse kick to her abductor. Fists clenched, focusing all her force into the kick, she was mid-spin when she heard a familiar voice.

"Whoa, take it easy."

Hawk. Trying to stop her forward movement, she tilted off balance, and once again, she felt his hand steady her so that she didn't stumble into the flowing river.

Instinctively, she reached out and embraced him, pulling in close to him, relieved and glad it was him who had grabbed her instead of someone trying to do her harm. Hawk wrapped his arms around her and hugged her tightly.

Hawk laughed. "Wow, one minute you're trying to kick me, and the next you're hugging me. You are one complicated woman."

Gazing up at him, she laughed. "You have no idea, Disney dude."

Releasing her embrace, she stepped back. He looked good and apparently had survived his adventure. "I hear you've been busy," Jillian said.

Hawk motioned her to follow him. "Oh yeah? Who have you been talking to?" he said over his shoulder as they stepped into a backstage area.

"The director of the Secret Service, the national news media, the sheriff's department . . . you name it. You are the chief suspect in the kidnapping of the president." Jillian smiled. "You are on everyone's most wanted list."

"Nice to be wanted, I suppose." Hawk leaned against the doorway. "But I should get some credit for finding the president's daughter, wife, and the commander in chief himself."

"Oh, you are definitely getting some kind of credit." She rolled her eyes.

"You were able to find Kim and Mary?"

Jillian nodded. "Safe and sound, just where you left them. Juliette understood the clue you left with them and has them locked away and out of sight."

"Good." Hawk took a deep breath of relief.

"And Tyler Pride?" Jillian searched his eyes.

"Safe . . . for now." Hawk hesitated. "And he has a plan."

He glanced down and then rubbed his face with both hands before looking back at her.

Raising her eyebrows, she said, "I take it you don't like his plan."

"I think it's risky."

"For you to say it's risky, it must be a whopper of a plan!" Jillian wanted to know more.

"I'm not sure if it will work like he wants it to . . ." Hawk shook his head. "But I need to know how it went with Juliette's deep dive into a deep-state conspiracy."

"She found enough evidence to make her think it's real," she said. "At one point as she was researching the Internet, her laptop suddenly went dead—a total crash—like something had killed it. She also put an investigative journalist on the hunt and created enough suspicion to make him interested."

"So do you believe it's real?"

"I believe there's enough evidence, enough corruption, and enough greed for it to be real." Jillian raked her fingers through her hair. "I haven't been here that long, but I had almost forgotten how Washington really works. Got to tell you, I really don't miss it."

Hawk studied her for a moment. "I want you to know, I'm impressed that you figured out my Disney-coded clues."

"Hey, I am the head of security here, you know."

Hawk snickered. "So Juliette helped you?"

"Definitely!"

Hawk glanced toward the river, staring at it for a moment. Jillian followed his gaze and then looked back at him while his mind worked at warp speed.

Suddenly, he grabbed her hand and pulled her toward him as he jogged through the backstage area. Silently, she followed as he pushed his way through one door, and into a hallway. He led her through the labyrinth of the backstage area, then hesitated at a door marked Do Not Open.

"Did you notice the boats had quit running?" Hawk said.

"No." She had missed that detail.

"That means someone else is in here, probably walking through the attraction. I left the boats running automatically, which means someone turned them off and came searching for us. I don't know how long we've got, but this will get dangerous fast."

Hawk put his hand on the doorknob. "Once we open this, we step back into the attraction. If we are going to be spotted, this is where it will take place. I'm hoping whoever is searching for us will stay in the greenhouse. Before you arrived, I ran through the soft sand of the greenhouse toward the alligator-farming tanks to leave a false trail. Hopefully, that will buy us the time to get out of here."

"Good, let's go then." Jillian leaned against him, ready to follow. She had no idea where they were in the attraction, but Hawk did. That's all that mattered. Once again, his resourcefulness had caught her off guard.

They stepped cautiously out into the farmhouse scene of the attraction, standing in front of the dimly lit home. For the first time, Jillian noted it could be the house in a number of horror movies, considering the way the lighting illuminated it. The dog barked at them from the front porch.

"I hope the dog doesn't let anyone know we're here." She giggled quietly.

"Believe it or not, they say that dog is modeled after one of Walt Disney's pets."

"That's Walt Disney's dog?"

"Might be."

A chicken perched on top of the mailbox squawked. Again, Jillian made note of things she had never noticed before. The animal noises would cover any move they made. The letters on the mailbox read "B Jones RFD 82."

"The 82 means something, doesn't it?"

"Yeah." He whispered, glancing over his shoulder. "It's the year Epcot opened. There are details like that hidden in all of the theme parks."

A few steps beyond the mailbox, he stopped at the bottom of a tree. When he looked up into the limbs, she knew immediately what he was thinking and began to look for an alternative plan. She continued that search as Hawk spoke softly.

"I'll give you a hand and send you up into the tree. Climb out on the branches toward the rotating restaurant and then jump off. That will put us up on the exit level. We'll have a head start on whoever's down here, looking for us."

Jillian looked up into the tree. "You've got to be kidding."

"You don't know how to climb a tree?"

"I don't really *want* to climb a tree and then leap off into a rotating restaurant." She sighed as she squared off in front of him and waited for him to give her a boost.

Placing the bottom of her shoe into his cupped hands, she stepped up and he boosted her toward a branch. Reaching out, she grabbed the limb just above her, wrapped her hands securely around it, and started to pull herself up. As she did, she felt Hawk continue to push her foot upward. He practically catapulted her onto the limb.

Firmly wrapped around the branch, she glanced down at him. Pointing, he motioned for her to move toward the restaurant. Slowly, she scooted along, high above the ground. Hawk moved to the front porch, past the dog, and grabbed a chair. Bounding down the porch steps, he raced to the bottom of the tree and stepped onto the chair. Then he leaped upward and grabbed the limb Jillian crawled along.

"Will this limb hold both of us?" she said as she eased closer to the rotating Garden Grill Restaurant.

"I don't know. It's not a real tree." Hawk grunted as he pulled himself up and hoisted a leg over the branch to keep from falling back down.

"It's a lot farther to the Garden Grill from up here than it looked from down below."

"Get moving," Hawk whispered. "If *this bough breaks*, at least one of us needs to make it out."

A noise below caught their attention, and they froze. Below her, Jillian saw two men dressed in black fatigues moving along the shoreline of the attraction. She strained to hear their muffled whispers but couldn't make out a word.

Hawk pressed a finger to his lips to silence her. Duh, as if she didn't already know. But her legs betrayed her. They trembled from holding the same position too long. If she started shaking too much, it would cause the leaves of the tree to rustle, giving away their position.

Thank goodness, the men below did not break pace or look up, but rather moved out of the farmhouse scene below to enter the barn that led to the greenhouse.

Closing her eyes in relief, Jillian steadied herself and then pulled her legs up so her knees could rest on the branch beneath her. From a crouched position, she pushed off and extended her hand toward the Plexiglas side of the rotating restaurant. She grabbed the railing and threw her other arm over it.

Now dangling high off the ground, she kicked her legs and scrambled over onto a dining table. Rolling to her side and then off to the floor, she heard the sound of Hawk landing on the same table. He rolled off the side and crumpled next to her. They lay flat for a moment, neither one uttering a sound, as they listened for any noise below.

"I don't hear anything," she whispered in Hawk's ear.

Nodding, he crawled into the aisle of the Garden Grill and was up and moving again before she was ready. He slowed and waited for her to catch up. Cautiously moving along the side of the restaurant, they made their way to the exit and then clung to the walls as they slowly headed toward the main doors of the pavilion.

"Where are we going?" Jillian whispered.

"To help President Pride." They emerged from the exit of the Land Pavilion. "I didn't think we'd have any company in there. Follow me."

Silently, they crept down the sloped exit, which carried them through the layers of strata along the building to reemerge in Future World. Crouching low, Hawk raced across the open area. She stayed close on his heels. They slid through a set of double doors that deposited them inside a gift shop. Quickly stepping around the corner to make sure they were out of sight, Hawk turned and smiled at her.

"That was trickier than I thought." They both leaned against the wall and breathed heavily. "The Secret Service is pretty good at this game of hide and seek."

"I don't think they know it's a game," she said.

"It's a high-stakes game our gambler president wants to win."

"What does that mean?"

"It means we have to help him win." Hawk peeped around the corner toward the door. "President Pride was not going to announce a major policy on this trip to Epcot. He planned to make a worldwide announcement on live television to expose the deep-state conspiracy in our government."

Her brow wrinkled in surprise. "No way."

"Right in front of Spaceship Earth. He said no one else knew about it, except maybe Kim."

"And someone kidnapped them before he could expose the conspiracy," Jillian said. "Does he know who or how they figured it out?"

"No, but he's come up with a Plan B." Hawk grabbed her by both arms. "And we're going to help him make it happen. That's why I brought you here. No way could I put it in a text or call you. I couldn't even send a Disney code. I needed to tell you in person. You and I have work to do."

"All right, what's the plan?" Eager for the next chapter in the story to unfold, she felt her eyes gleam like a kid at Christmas.

CHAPTER FIFTY-SIX

Taking a Ride

David Walker lowered his head and climbed into the back seat of the Disney Security vehicle alongside John Ware. The driver nodded at them but said nothing as the car sped away from the media area of the Epcot parking lot.

Allie had passed on the news but had been vague, perhaps because the only information she had was what she shared with him. He and John had been given access to the interview they wanted. That was good news, but the remaining instructions had a cloak-and-dagger feel that had not impressed him, nor had it made him any more confident that this was what he had asked for.

The vehicle accelerated quickly, and the driver seemed quite familiar with the Walt Disney World roadway system. David was convinced the man was taking the shortest route possible, but he would have been more convinced if he knew exactly where they were going. The informational signs indicated they were entering the Epcot Resort area, but they continued to look out the windows for some sign of their final destination.

"Did you get everything?" David asked John.

John quickly checked the camera equipment bag he had hastily loaded up after they had gotten the word. He looked up and nodded in the affirmative.

"Good." David eased back into his seat.

The car made a left-hand turn and then another as they drove past the entrance to Disney's Boardwalk. David could see the security stand at the entrance, but the car sped past it and headed toward a gated entrance to the Boardwalk Conference Center.

The driver slowed the car then stopped at the closed gate, which prevented them from going any further. Their silent driver rolled down his window and looked directly into the camera. They waited. One minute passed, then another, and then another. Finally, David couldn't take the wait, which felt like an eternity.

"Is there a problem?" he asked, leaning forward over the front seat.

The driver remained silent. As a journalist, this didn't alleviate his rising angst. Finally, David heard an audible clicking sound and the gate began to rise, giving them room to pass.

Once inside, the car accelerated to the front entrance of the Boardwalk Conference Center, but the driver blew past the main doors and down to the end of the driveway. Stopping, the driver unlocked the doors, continuing to idle the car. Still silent, the man looked straight ahead and waited.

David looked at his cameraman and shrugged. Deciding this was the end of the trip, they opened the door and got out. John threw the equipment bag over his shoulder and David looked around, wondering which way to go. Just as they started walking toward the convention center, the automatic doors slid open, and Juliette Keaton walked out to greet them.

She closed her eyes for a moment and took a deep breath before reaching out her hand to shake David's in greeting.

"I have to admit, the ride over here was very . . . quiet," he said.

"I was told that you did some digging into the topic we discussed earlier." Juliette stood unnaturally still, as though she was nervous.

"I did." David wanted to know why she was so edgy. "I found out a number of things that might be incidental, perhaps coincidental, and some that were unexplainable—enough to give some validity to the deep-state conspiracy we discussed."

"Fair enough."

"I'm still not completely convinced." David shook his head. "Truth be told, I don't want to believe it. Because if some of the information is true, it undermines the stability of some of our most trusted institutions."

Juliette glanced around her before speaking. It was as if she wanted to ensure only the three of them were present. What or who was she afraid of? "Does it really undermine the stability of the institutions, or does it simply expose some extremely evil people who have seized power and are holding on to it with a stranglehold?"

David was impressed. In one sentence, Juliette had managed to summarize and reorganize some of his troubling thoughts since starting to dig into the alleged conspiracy.

"You could be a press secretary for the White House," he said, meaning it as a compliment.

"I was the face of the Disney Company for Grayson Hawkes for a number of years. I had to learn to think differently." She smiled for the first time since they had arrived.

"About Dr. Hawkes, I'm hoping I'll get to interview him," he said.

"Yes, about that." Juliette lost her smile. "I believe you will get the interview you want. Follow me . . . quietly please."

David looked toward John Ware, who repositioned the equipment bag as they walked down the sidewalk toward the entrance of the Disney Boardwalk Inn Resort.

Immediately, they were immersed in the charm and whimsy of turn-of-the-century Atlantic City. Following Juliette through the next set of doors, they crossed the lobby and headed toward the waterfront. Strung out like taffy along the glistening water of Crescent Lake, shops and restaurants that normally would have been brimming with activity were empty and dark. Moving quickly and silently as instructed, they continued to follow Juliette to their final destination, wherever that was.

Now stepping across the planks of the boardwalk itself, she slowed and allowed them to fall in step next to her. "Remember our conversation earlier about truth?" Juliette said, as she turned toward David.

"Yes, I've thought about it a lot," he said.

"Your ability to handle the truth will be extremely important." She motioned for them to move down the dock area.

Soon they arrived at the end of the guest queue line. Juliette reached down and unhooked the guard rope that would normally keep guests safely behind it. They walked through, and she allowed it to fall unconnected on the dock as they moved to the water's edge. They stood looking out over Crescent Lake at nothing but water.

"What happens now?" David asked. He turned and looked over his shoulder at John, who appeared just as confused as he was.

"You wait." Juliette looked out across the water and pointed. "It won't be long now."

"What won't be long?" David's eyes followed the direction she pointed in.

"Good luck, and please, be careful." Juliette walked away.

"Wait, what are you doing?"

"I'm leaving you here to wait."

"You're not going with us?" David asked.

"I can't."

"Why not?"

"I wasn't invited." Juliette continued to walk up the dock. "And it's safer if I don't."

"Safer? Safer for who?" David had never been so confused.

John tapped him on the arm and pointed in the same direction Juliette had pointed moments before. There in the distance, coming from around a corner in the lake, was a speedboat. He couldn't be sure, but he assumed they were taking another ride. What was up anyway? Turning back toward Juliette, he saw that she had increased her pace as she hurried away from the water, heading back to wherever she had come from.

"This is getting weirder by the minute," he said.

"I didn't think that was possible." John stared at the boat.

It decreased its speed, banked to the right, and then floated up to the side of the dock, coming to a stop with a gentle thud against the planking on the side.

CHAPTER FIFTY-SEVEN

A Trip Around the World

Water splashed as the boat edged up against the dock. Jillian kept the motor idling as the two passengers carefully stepped into the boat. Normally, a boat would be secured to the dock to make it easier for guests to come aboard. But she didn't plan on stopping for long. Every moment they remained in the open they might be spotted. Jillian watched as the camera operator stepped in first, followed by the reporter she had seen a number of times on television and then most recently here at the Walt Disney World Resort, David Walker of the Global News Network.

Walker's eyes opened in surprised recognition.

"Jillian Batterson," he said. "I didn't expect to see you."

"I'm not sure if that's a good or bad thing, but I am your driver." Jillian waited for the men to take their seats.

"No, no, no . . . I'm just confused about all the secrecy. I'm supposed to have an interview with your boss."

"Did you expect him to be driving the boat?"

"To be honest, I didn't expect to be on a boat at all," Walker admitted.

Jillian threw the boat into gear and felt the motor rev up, forcing her to lean back. The sudden forward movement pushed her passengers back in their seats. The Crescent Lake waterway ran along the front of the Disney Boardwalk Resort and provided water access not only to that resort but also to Disney's Yacht and Beach Club Resorts. The same waterway could carry guests to the Swan and Dolphin Resorts as well.

But that's not where Jillian was headed at full speed. The lake also provided access to Epcot on Friendship boats. Those boats weren't known for being fast, but they were air-conditioned. This was a back entrance to Epcot that opened up inside the World Showcase—the best path to the American Adventure.

Jillian had chosen the sleeker, faster security boat so she could cut the trip time in half and provide a quicker getaway if needed.

"I want you to listen to what I tell you," Jillian said, as the wind whipped through her hair. On another day, this would be an enjoyable experience. Not today. The stakes were too high. "We're going to enter the World Showcase, and I'll escort you to Hawk. Thanks to the Secret Service and all the media coverage, he's apparently the lead suspect in the kidnapping of the president and his family."

Walker corrected her as he leaned forward slightly. "For the record, that's not the way I reported it. As a matter of fact, I tried to distance myself from those reports."

"But you believe them, right?" Jillian glanced over her shoulder.

"I'm not sure. Let's just say I have my doubts."

"Well, you are the media. You'll probably tell whatever story you want to tell. That's the way it works these days."

"The media is not the enemy," David said, defending his profession. "At least not when they simply report the news and the facts."

"Does anybody really do that anymore?" Jillian asked. "It seems to me the media reports the news that fits their narrative because they're looking for a specific outcome."

"That's not news. Real journalism doesn't have a preconceived specific outcome. Real news reports the facts, adds little commentary, and gives listeners enough information to draw their own conclusions. At least that's what happens when it works right."

Jillian smiled to herself as she looked forward at the landing dock at Epcot. This was the journalist that Juliette Keaton had found to help unravel this story—the journalist that Hawk had insisted they find to help them with the president's plan. If he was being truthful, then at least they had made the right choice. If he was like the rest of the news pundits, this plan would turn out to be a disaster.

"Hold on, it's going to get bumpy," Jillian shouted over the sound of the wind. She waited until the last possible moment to cut power to the engine.

The boat hit the side of the dock hard, just as she had planned, and they scampered up and out of it quickly. After tying the boat to a piling, she motioned for them to follow her quickly. The entrance to Epcot was just ahead. They'd enter through the International Gateway and cross over the Pont des Arts-inspired footbridge. The spot was designed to be reminiscent of the Seine waterfront, complete with flower carts and street-side artists. Tucked away behind the Monsieur Paul restaurant in the France Pavilion was an alleyway where the Les Halles Boulangerie Patisserie stood. As they rushed down the alley, Jillian remembered asking Hawk what the name meant. He had told her it was a fancy way of saying bakery. She still wasn't sure of the exact translation.

The Eiffel Tower soared over them as they aggressively made their way through the France Pavilion.

"Wow, that looks like the real thing," John Ware commented, glancing up at the tower.

"That's because it was built off of the blueprints of Gustave Eiffel, scaled back for use in the World Showcase," Jillian said over her shoulder without turning.

Leading the pair through the pavilion, she entered the side door that would take them into the Palais du Cinema, where the *Impressions de France* film was shown throughout the day. The soundtrack of French composers reached their ears as they moved to the backstage area of the theater.

"Is this our final stop?" Ware asked.

"No, this is where we make sure we weren't followed." Jillian peered out the door they had just entered. "Take a seat and relax. I'll make sure the coast is clear." She paused and looked back at them. "Rest a little. When I get back, we need to keep moving fast."

Leaving the pair inside, Jillian hugged the buildings as she retraced their path through the cobblestone streets of the France Pavilion. Easing her way along, she made a dash for the center fountain and crouched behind it. Tense, her heart raced. She told herself to calm down. The plan was crazy enough to work, and they were almost there.

On watch, she saw no one enter the area. Her fear that the boat would be spotted or alert someone surveilling their activity seemed unfounded, but she remained wary. She'd rather they put more distance between them and their hunters.

Finally, she reentered the theater and motioned for the reporters to follow her.

"Can I ask where we're going?" Walker said.

"No." She opened another door. "You'll know when you get there."

Quickly, they entered the backstage area of the France Pavilion, an entire city that the general public would never get a chance to see. Disney wanted to preserve the illusion of being in another country.

Jillian would use this industrial backstage area to navigate through the streets and service areas. Moving quickly and forcing Ware to breathe a bit heavy while he carried his camera equipment, she was relentless in pushing forward. She took them in and out of warehouses, storerooms, maintenance areas, down side paths, behind berms, and then repeated the process all over again.

Thankfully, Jillian was familiar with this area and knew exactly where they were. They passed behind Morocco and Japan, and she was sure the journalist and his one-man crew had no idea where they were. This was the way she had wanted it, and she also hoped that taking this path would keep them under the radar.

The final path they would travel was a sidewalk carrying them to the back of a large industrial building. Although her traveling companions did not know it, they were about to enter the massive American Adventure show building through a rear entrance. The unmarked door was unlocked, as she had been promised it would be, but she knew once inside it would be dark. Anticipating this, she took out her cell phone and swiped on the flashlight feature with a touch of the screen.

"Stay close," she whispered. The trio hurried along darkened hallways illuminated only by the light from her phone.

Their footsteps echoed off the concrete walls and floor. Coming to the end of a hall, she turned, pressing her finger to her lips and motioned them to stay close and keep moving.

As she opened another door, an explosion of light almost blinded them. Jillian led them into the massive rotunda of the American Experience and rushed through the entrance to the American Heritage Gallery. They then turned to their right. As they did, they found who she had been looking for, just as planned.

"Hello." The smiling face of Grayson Hawkes greeted them. "Glad you could make it."

Extending his hand, the newsman said, "David Walker, GNN. Nice to finally meet you."

John Ware shook hands as well and set down his equipment bag, breathing heavily. Jillian stood next to Hawk, facing the media pair.

"Sorry for the circuitous route you had to take." Hawk smiled at Jillian. "I gave Jillian specific instructions on how to get you here. You were in very capable hands."

"She was an excellent tour guide," Walker said. "Dr. Hawkes, you're a wanted man right now. I appreciate you taking the time to talk to me, but I must admit

I'm surprised. Why do you want to do an interview with GNN right now? It seems you have more pressing problems."

"I don't think you understand, Mr. Walker," Jillian said, reading the surprise on the face of the journalist. "You aren't interviewing Hawk."

Obviously flustered and confused, Walker said, "I was very specific. I spoke to Juliette Keaton about this, and she assured me I was getting the interview I wanted."

"True, she did promise that," Hawk said. "Follow me, please."

The four of them moved back into the rotunda and climbed the circular stairs that wound above the floor below. Continuing to climb, they finally reached the third floor. Jillian felt a little sorry for the cameraman who had to lug around his equipment.

When they arrived at the American Adventure Parlor, the group crossed the thick carpet. Jillian dropped back and allowed Walker and Ware to follow directly behind Hawk.

"David Walker, Global News Network!" boomed the voice of President Tyler Pride. "Thanks for dropping by."

Jillian chuckled inwardly when both men's jaws dropped open upon meeting the president of the United States. She smiled and allowed herself to enjoy their confusion. It amused her more than she wanted to admit, because there was only one man more wanted and sought after than Grayson Hawkes in this moment—the president. David Walker had hit the jackpot, and he hadn't even bought a lottery ticket.

"Mr. President," Walker said, beaming. "I'm so glad to see you. I'm glad you're okay."

"Glad to see you too. Come on in." The president waved them to join him.

David turned back to Hawk and Jillian with a confused expression. He rubbed his hand down his face. He opened his mouth to speak but paused.

"You're not here to interview me." Hawk motioned for Ware to pick up his camera gear. "You're here to interview the president."

"This is the interview you really wanted," Jillian added. "It's the story that everyone in the world wants right now. You just didn't know you would be the one who gets to tell it."

"I can't stress enough how important it is that you get this started and over with," Hawk said, as they moved deeper into the room toward Tyler Pride. "There are a lot of people looking for the president."

"And Hawk," Jillian said, leaping into the mix.

"Yes," Hawk agreed. "And when they get here, I'm not sure what will happen. We're all in danger."

"Of course." David Walker nodded.

"I'll sit here in front of the fireplace," the president said. "Let's get this thing started. I have a story to tell you."

Jillian stood by Hawk as the reporter moved next to the president and his cameraman fumbled with the equipment, trying to set it up quickly. Satisfied they were almost there, he turned toward her, clasped her arms with his hands, and winked.

"Just the way we planned it." Hawk inhaled deeply. "You know what to do?"

"Yes." She turned quickly to move back down the stairs. "Tell them to hurry."

"You want me to rush the president of the United States?" Hawk said as he watched her rush down the huge spiral staircase.

"Yes, tell him I said so!"

CHAPTER FIFTY-EIGHT

The Power of Words

The historic significance of the moment filled the room like fog on a mountain morning. David Walker felt a flutter of nervousness as he quickly mapped out his strategy for the interview. Truth be told, this was not at all what he had expected. The promise of getting the interview he really wanted was correct, but this was one of those times when he honestly had no way of knowing what he really wanted until the opportunity presented itself.

It had practically arrived with an engraved invitation. He sat opposite the president of the United States, whom the entire world was searching for, because he was missing. Now he had the chance to talk to him, in front of a camera, and to hear what surely would be a story he would never forget.

"Are you nervous, David?" President Pride asked, snapping him from his thoughts.

He lied. "Uh, no sir."

"Good," Pride said. "Don't be. When Hawk told me you were here and wanting an interview with him, I told him Walker is a great journalist, always fair, and cares about getting the story correct. I wanted to talk with you."

"I appreciate that, sir." David hesitated. "You do realize the entire world is looking for you and wondering what has happened to you?"

"I do." Pride smiled. "And that's why I'm talking to you."

David felt John touch him on the shoulder. His cameraman gave him the thumbs-up sign that he was ready whenever they were. David glanced around the American Adventure Parlor, struck by the historicity of the setting itself. It was as if they had stepped back into time—a time when America was carving out her early beginnings and weaving the fabric of an amazing nation. Today, they would add another chapter to America's story.

Grayson Hawkes returned to the room. "I don't want to rush you," Hawk said, smiling. "But Jillian suggested you'd better get this thing started."

"She's right." Tyler Pride motioned for the GNN team to proceed. "I'm ready. Let's do this, Walker."

Ware held up three fingers and counted down the seconds. When he reached one, he pointed to David, giving him the cue that they were now officially filming. He knew if they made a mistake, they could always stop and give them some space to reedit later . . . if they had the time.

Looking at the camera, he said, "This is David Walker, and I am pleased to bring you a *Global News Network* exclusive. Today, I'm talking with the president of the United States, Tyler Pride. Right now, we are hiding in a secret location at Walt Disney World for his safety. As most of you are aware, the president has been missing. Later I will share with you some of the details that brought us together for this interview, but only when it's safe to tell those elements of the story."

David paused to give John time to broaden the shot and get both he and the president in the frame. John nodded almost imperceptibly, and David continued.

"Mr. President, I'm glad to see you are all right, and I'm sure the world is as well."

"I'm glad to be seen." Pride smiled. "It has been a pretty horrific few hours to be sure, but I am pleased to sit down with you and catch up the American people on what has been happening."

David nodded. "First of all, you were scheduled to give a speech in front of Spaceship Earth at Epcot, but when the monorail arrived, you and your family were missing. Where were you, and why weren't you on the monorail?"

The president leaned forward and locked his eyes on the lens of the camera. "Kim, Mary, and I climbed aboard the monorail at the Transportation and Ticket Center for the short trip to Epcot. As planned, we left on time, but shortly after we left the station, the monorail stopped."

"Who stopped the monorail?"

"The driver. We felt the monorail slowing down, and I asked if there was a problem. He told me there was no problem at all—that things were going according to plan." Pride's expression darkened. "I then asked him what plan he was referring to. He said, the plan I was about to become a part of."

"So you were completely unaware of the unscheduled stop. But where can you stop along the monorail line?" David asked. He already knew the answer because of the research and events of the day, but he knew those were details that many listeners had not yet come to understand.

"I wondered that too, David," the president said. "I had no idea there was some sort of maintenance tower along the monorail line between the Transportation and Ticket Center and Epcot."

"And that's where the monorail driver stopped?"

"Yes."

"So you're saying the monorail driver planned to make an unscheduled stop there without your knowledge?" David leaned forward.

"Yes," Pride confirmed. "It was carefully planned. The monorail stopped, the driver hit a button that released the door, and then two men stormed inside. I met them at the door because I knew something was wrong. I told Kim to grab Mary and run. As soon as the door opened, the hooded men, dressed in black fatigues, knocked me backward across the monorail."

"Did they say anything?"

"Yes. I punched one of them. Smacked him in the side of his head with my fist," President Pride recalled. "It caused him to stumble back, but not much. The other man said if I did something like that again, he would kill me, my wife, and daughter, and that it was in our best interest to come along quietly."

David waited as the president shared what happened. "I think they hit me with some kind of stun gun. I remember hitting the floor of the monorail, and I think they must have kicked or punched me. I'm a little bit fuzzy on the events after that. Best I can tell, they put a hood over my head, dragged me down a set of stairs, and shoved me into a vehicle."

"What about the first lady and your daughter?"

"They're in a safe place." Pride smiled. "I didn't know that for sure until a little while ago, but they've been found and are safe and secure."

"Where are they?"

"Safe." Pride tilted his head to the side. "You really don't expect me to give away their location, do you?"

"No sir, just asking." David nodded for the president to continue.

"Eventually, the guys who grabbed me tied me up and dumped me inside an attraction here in Walt Disney World."

"Where did they dump you, sir?"

"Well, I can't get too specific because I'm sure it will be investigated as a crime scene, but I will tell you it was inside the Magic Kingdom."

David was surprised at this information. He wasn't sure why. The entire account stretched his belief threshold, but the thought of the US president being dumped inside the most popular tourist resort in the world seemed extremely brazen.

"Where was your Secret Service detail during your kidnapping?"

"Great question." Pride now sat up straighter in his chair. "That's a question you should ask them."

David raised his eyebrows. "The Secret Service was in on your abduction?"

"Somebody had to leave an opening for my family to be abducted, didn't they? One of the reasons I wanted to talk to you is to explain what's been going on ever since my election. It actually started before I was inaugurated, after my stunning win, which surprised everyone."

"I remember."

"In the aftermath of my victory, I became aware of a group. I didn't know how many or how far reaching their influence might be, but they were shocked I had won. It basically unraveled their stranglehold on power in the inner circles of Washington politics."

The president slowed his words, seemingly to make sure he explained the next piece of information carefully. "These are high-powered individuals who are more corrupt and deep-rooted in our government than the American people could ever imagine. Think about it. How often do you hear of politicians and political appointees who enter office and begin their service to our country with modest means but, by the time they leave office, have amassed enormous wealth and power for themselves and anyone close to them?"

Pride cleared his throat. "That's how our government has worked for decades. It doesn't matter which political party is in power. It's the establishment who holds the power. And once I became the chaos candidate, they joined forces to make sure the establishment would never lose that power."

"That is a serious accusation, Mr. President," David said.

"Serious? So is kidnapping the president and his family," Pride countered. "These power brokers are scum. The scum has banded together against me and accused me of anything and everything they could think of. They are anti-American and don't care what the American people really want. They are establishment leaders in the FBI, CIA, NSA, Republicans, Democrats, government agencies, and judicial appointments. They are well placed, extremely powerful, and nearly untouchable individuals who will do anything not to lose control and power. I'm a threat to all of them and the control they have over our nation."

"Sir, you are talking about a deep-state conspiracy." David used the phrase that he had been reading, studying, and researching about, and for the first time he felt like there was enough evidence to move it out of the realm of possible and into the realm of reality.

"Yes, you could call it that. I prefer to call it a scum bucket that needs to be dumped," Pride said, summarizing it as only he could do.

"The American people are sick of celebrating the values of our culture and are even sicker that the elites, the establishment, and the media have pushed these false values on the average American. That's why I got elected. I was the only one willing to call out the nonsense and the lies." Pride let his words register. "And when I did, the media and the establishment did what a child might do when caught doing something wrong. They started to whine, gripe, and complain. Then they started to lie and scream about it. The lies got bigger, they got louder, they got crazier, and before you knew it they started believing their own lies. The scum thinks they're right and justified in eliminating me."

"Let me clarify. You are saying this group of people is trying to eliminate you as president?"

"You bet they are, and if they have to kill me, the ends justify the means in their worldview."

David sat silently, thinking of what to ask next. The president waited patiently for a while, allowing him time to process this incredible story, but the president was not a patient man. He got tired of waiting for him to speak and filled the silence.

"David, when I was elected, the economy was limping along. It was awful. The previous administration told us we should get used to it. That's the way it was going to be from now on. We had made horrendous international trade deals that robbed working Americans of money but lined the pockets of those who made the deals. We offered our enemies billions in payoffs under the guise of security, peace treaties, and defense.

"Our military was limited in what they could do around the world. They were demoralized, flying old planes, and their sacrifices were neither valued nor appreciated. Washington politicians have known about all of these problems for years. Shoot, they created the problems. They think that if they do nothing, things will miraculously get better. So no one does anything."

David's heart pounded in his chest. "And because you have waded into all of these areas, they are trying to eliminate you? Assassinate the president?"

"Yes, because I'm not willing to go along with the status quo. I'm fixing everything that's broken. The politicians, the power brokers, the insiders, and the media don't know how to handle it.

"So they attack me. A lot of people excuse their actions by saying they don't like my style and that I should be nicer. But when I suggest we enforce the law, the media—your colleagues—accuse me of hating the world. They accuse me of being a racist and every other *ist* they can think of when I suggest we enforce the laws that Congress passed. If they don't like the law, they have the power to change it, but they don't. They'd rather do nothing and blame somebody else.

"If I suggest we put the needs of our nation first and then figure out how to deal with the rest of the world, the detractors say that people won't like us. The only reason people like us is because they can run over and take advantage of us. The elite trample over the Constitution like it's the front doormat but get mad when someone dares to suggest our Founding Fathers knew what they were doing when they created it."

"You have evidence of this conspiracy against you?" David hesitated as he asked. He wasn't sure he wanted the answer. If the president had the evidence, the power structures would begin to crumble. But if he didn't have it, it would fuel the hatred against the president, which seemed to ignite with his very being.

"I do." Pride smiled. "I have documents. I have files. I have names of some of the players behind the scenes. I'm not accusing the rank and file of these government agencies with treason. Most of them are great patriots. They love their country, their families, and their careers. They go to work every day and do their jobs. But they don't understand that some of the people sitting at the top of these groups, those in positions of power, are more concerned about keeping their power than they are about what's best for our nation."

"Is this evidence something we can examine and share?"

"Indeed, it will be," President Pride said. "Right now, the evidence I have been collecting is being delivered to a source that will be sharing it."

"And that's the reason you were kidnapped?"

"Yes, because the scum figured out I was going to expose them. That's why I came to Florida in the first place. I planned to share the information I just told you in a speech at Epcot and then present the evidence."

"And the individuals involved in the conspiracy against you found out about it?"

The president's jaw tightened. "Either that, or they just got wickedly fortunate in their timing."

"So why did they kidnap you and your family? What was their endgame?"

"I was given a choice." Pride looked straight into the camera. "Resign the presidency and go away with my family back into the private sector or prepare to die and seal the death of my family if I refused to play their political games."

"If you resigned, what would prevent you from speaking out later?"

"The threat to my family," Pride said. "After all, they proved they could get to us. They snatched us out of sight as the whole world waited to see us arrive. They're not afraid of being caught. Which ultimately is why they are going to fail."

"And this interview is a part of that process?"

"Absolutely," the president said. "The elite think I'm arrogant, but the real arrogance is theirs to own. They forget I'm a gambler. I take calculated risks, not high risks I can't win. Calculated risks. You will air this interview, and some will believe it, but some won't. I'll show the evidence, and some will believe it, but some will not. Here's what will happen. People will either flee or fight." President Pride paused for a moment, but David knew he had more to say.

"The evidence will prove the corruption of law enforcement at the highest levels, felonious national security leaks by members of the intelligence community sworn to uphold, protect, and defend the Constitution, and crooked and criminal deals with foreign governments and organizations who have used and abused American goodwill for too many years to stop now."

"And so you were told to go away and keep your mouth shut about this conspiracy, or you and your family would be murdered?" David needed to clarify this. Because if everything the president said was true, this was an existential threat to the Republic.

Pride nodded, then smiled. "Yes, that was the choice I was given. I was left to think about it. What they didn't know was I had already become suspicious of their willingness to go to any extreme to hold on to power, and I was at work on a plan to get help."

"By exposing them in the speech at Epcot?"

"Yes." Pride leaned back in his seat. "And I knew who I could trust to help me and my family to ensure our safety."

"I, for one, am glad you are alive and well, Mr. President."

"And I appreciate you, David. I know you will give my story the fair and truthful examination it deserves and that the American people deserve."

"Mr. President, you don't have a lot of fans in the media and you have a lot of critics. Why do you think GNN's coverage of the threats against you will be any different this time?" He could imagine how the pundits and critics would spin this story.

Pride lifted his hands and dropped them to his knees. "I don't know for sure, but I believe that most Americans are tired of living in fear, tired of being bombarded with bad news, and want to hear the truth. I believe they're smart enough to recognize the truth." The president paused. "My critics have a meltdown every time I do anything. I can't stop that. I also can't stop them from lying and telling the story they want others to hear. I suppose it makes them feel more important than they really are, or maybe they believe they are that important. I'm not sure."

"So this is all about the truth?"

"Do you remember what happened in Chernobyl?" the president asked, surprising him.

"It was one of the worst manmade disasters in history," he said, remembering the meltdown of the nuclear plant.

"Right. Chernobyl was a tragic event, but it was not the global catastrophe that most imagined. The initial reports in 1986 claimed two thousand people were dead and predicted an unknown number of future deaths and other tragic events impacting people from Sweden to the Black Sea. By the year 2000, the *BBC* and *New York Times* estimated fifteen to thirty thousand people had died. Do you know the real number of deaths?"

"I'm guessing close to thirty thousand?"

The president pointed his finger at him for emphasis. "The actual number is fifty-six. That's a big difference."

"But aren't we talking about radiation, sir? There are long-term consequences of that kind of eco disaster," David suggested respectfully. A number of fifty-six sounded like a huge error.

"Fair enough, but the media reports are once again less than accurate. Estimates were large, but let me pick one of the lesser estimates of delayed death because of the accident. One source estimated there would be five hundred thousand deaths, when the actual number of delayed deaths was less than four thousand." Tyler Pride now leaned forward and looked past him into the camera lens. "A United Nations report in 2005 said the largest public health problem created by the accident was the damaging psychological impact due to the lack of accurate information. It reported that as a result of wild speculation, people gave endless negative self-assessments of health. They believed in a shortened life expectancy, which created a lack of initiative and dependency on assistance from the state."

"I didn't know that, sir." David jotted a note to verify the information later.

"I know you didn't. You just believed what journalists and government agencies reported, like so many people did." The president smiled as a father might smile at a son. "Check those numbers out for yourself and see if they are true. What I'm saying is that the greatest damage done to the people of Chernobyl was caused by false information and wild speculation, not radiation. We all know we need to control the dangers of radiation because it's definitely a health hazard. But Chernobyl suggests that false information can be a health hazard as damaging as radiation."

The president knitted his brow, and his eyes drilled into his. "Now hear me carefully. I'm not saying radiation is not a threat. Chernobyl was a serious event that should never have happened. But Ukrainians were told they were going to die when they weren't. They were told their families would suffer, that they faced a future of disease, deformities, pain, and decay. They were terrified, and they lived and are still living their lives based on lies."

"What are you implying?"

"Nothing and everything," Pride said. "I'm telling you that people in power need to operate on facts rooted in truth, not on the things we want to be true or think might be true. Facts are facts; truth is truth. We don't get to look at the world on a sliding scale. We must do what is right at the right time for the right reason." Pride then pointed at his interviewer. "And David, you have people who listen to you every day and hang on your every word. You have a responsibility to tell the truth to the best of your ability. I think you try to do that. I only wish some of your colleagues in the industry tried as hard as you do. The American people deserve that."

"I want to be known as a teller of truth." David swallowed hard. He had no idea whether what the president had just said about one of the most well-known nuclear disasters was true or not, but it did make a point and had the desired effect on him.

"*I* know. The American people need to hear from people like you. And they need to know that it is time to expose the scum who have quit working for the people and have decided that they love power and money and all of the control it brings."

CHAPTER FIFTY-NINE

The Imperfect Pavilion

Jillian exited the back entrance of the American Adventure Pavilion and decided to cut a path through the Morocco Pavilion to make her way back to the International Gateway and her boat.

The Morocco Pavilion offered plenty of nooks and crannies in which to hide and was detailed enough to create an authentic look and feel of the nation. Inspired by the cities of Marrakesh, Rabat, and Fez, it looked to her like the set of *Casablanca*, which Hawk had informed her also had inspired the design.

The exteriors of the buildings were plain. Why? Because the people of Morocco believed true beauty lay inside, so the interior decoration would always be more important.

The pavilion also featured tons of handmade tiles, all cut and placed in beautiful patterned mosaics. In each was always one chip or defect because of their belief that only Allah was perfect and could create life. So no living thing—human, plant, or animal—could ever be portrayed.

Jillian slid inside the lobby of the Restaurant Marrakesh, designed to look like a southern Morocco fortress, pausing to look out the windows to see if she had been followed or spotted. She planned to take her time, stay hidden, and carefully make sure no one had penetrated the area. The people who pursued Hawk and the president would be relentless. They were pros. She could not afford to make a mistake.

As she clung to the shadows in the lobby, she had time to notice an often-missed display of American history. King Mohammed Ben Abdallah was the first world leader to send George Washington a letter recognizing the United States as a sovereign, independent nation. A copy of the king's letter and Washington's reply inside this restaurant gave visitors another glimpse into American history.

Peering through a window, she saw movement in the shadows. A man dressed in black fatigues moved through the entrance gate of the pavilion. Another man, dressed the same way, moved toward the gate right behind.

Hoping their search of this pavilion would only be cursory, she could not be certain, so she decided to text Hawk a message in her limited Disney code. Staring at her phone screen, she couldn't think of a single phrase their enemies could not break. No time to think. Instead, she texted, "trouble in Casablanca . . . get out." He would understand that she was confident, but would their pursuers figure it out too soon? She focused on her job. Get back to the Bay Lake Towers with the small flash drive the president had turned over to her and Hawk.

Sliding her fingers into her pocket, she gripped the device that held information that would expose the conspirators' scheme to unravel the American election system and attack the Republic. As badly as she wanted to return and help Hawk and the president, she knew her task was vital. Torn, she waited for a moment, then exited the restaurant, continuing her mission and heading for the International Gateway.

She planned to move along the wall of the France Pavilion and hurry down the steps to the edge of the water. There she could board the boat and head back out of Epcot. Glancing behind her as she crept around the corner, she took the steps two at a time, watching her feet. It was then she heard a voice coming from the bottom of the steps.

"Nice night for a walk, isn't it?" Agent Craig Johnson stepped out of the shadows.

Jillian froze in place and quickly evaluated her options should she need to escape.

"Where you headed?" Johnson asked as he walked up the steps toward her. "Or maybe more importantly, where have you been?"

Jillian didn't answer.

"We've been trying to track your movements and those of your boss, but you guys are very, very good. It wasn't until we spotted Juliette Keaton leaving the Boardwalk that we moved into the area and spread out to find you. And now here you are."

"So? We work here." Standing two steps above him, Jillian gripped the handrail.

"I think you know where your boss is. I think he knows where the president is, or maybe he has the president with him."

"Yes, I guess that's what you think. I already spotted a couple of your agents skulking around up there. You're wasting your time, you know."

"Other agents?" Johnson moved up a step and Jillian reflexively moved back and up one to keep the distance between them. "I'm the point agent in the area. Where did you see them?"

"Back there." Jillian nodded toward Morocco. "Exactly where you sent them."

"I didn't assign anyone to that section."

"I don't believe you."

"Believe me." His brows knitted together in thought.

"Why should I?" Jillian said, backing up another step.

"Because it's the truth," he said.

Jillian struggled, trying to figure out whether to believe him or to flee. He seemed sincere, but this conspiracy ran deep.

"I didn't, Jillian," Johnson said softly.

Jillian realized there was nothing he gained by denying he had sent more agents into this area. Her instinct said he really didn't know about them.

Johnson scratched his chin and leaned against the railing. "I've been thinking about what you said earlier, when you implied that if the president was running from Hawkes, he would have run toward the Secret Service, not away from them."

"And?"

"And that makes sense. It got me thinking. Some things don't add up; they don't fit our protocol."

"Well, here's another one for you." Jillian took a step closer to him. Maybe she could trust him. "Where did the monorail driver get the gun he used to kill himself? His personal bag would have been inspected. If he had a gun, the Secret Service would have found it. Or is it possible that the unscheduled stop allowed the abductors to pass him the weapon? One way or the other, it was a huge gap in presidential protection procedures, and those don't get messed up by accident. Someone knows what's happening here, and they're staying one step ahead of you."

Johnson listened. His face showed no emotion as he seemed to process what she said.

"If you remember, Hawk offered to help find the president," Jillian continued. "But no one wanted his help. As a matter of fact, he was told to stay out of the way. Then, as you already know, he found the president anyway. Why would he offer to help the Secret Service find him if he was behind the kidnapping? That makes no sense, does it?"

"I suppose not." Johnson spoke into his wrist microphone. "Agent Johnson here." He looked up at Jillian and shook his head. "All clear so far. Are there any other agents in front of me clearing the pavilions?"

Jillian watched his expression grow dark as he listened to the answer in his earpiece.

"Roger that." Johnson looked up at her. "There are no agents in front of me clearing pavilions. Which means, whoever you saw is not supposed to be here."

Jillian looked back toward Morocco and sighed. She had an ally in Craig Johnson.

"Show me where they are." Johnson moved up the steps, past her, and into the France Pavilion. He paused and turned. "Are you coming with me or not?"

Making sure the flash drive was still hidden in her pocket, she realized she needed to follow Johnson and help Hawk and the president. She would deliver the flash drive as soon as she got the chance.

CHAPTER SIXTY

An Extraction Team

Juliette entered Hawk's office suite at the Bay Lake Towers, which had now become the unofficial control center for the Secret Service. They had commandeered the conference room and littered it with open laptops, maps, notepads, and an ever-growing collection of empty coffee cups. As she walked down the hallway toward the conference room, Jeremiah Stanley, Pat Nobles, Sam Reno, and Dana Brown blocked her way.

"Ah, Mrs. Keaton," Stanley said. "Your timing is perfect. We believe Grayson Hawkes is in Epcot, somewhere in the World Showcase, probably the American Pavilion."

"The American Adventure," Juliette reflexively corrected.

"Yes, make that adventure," Stanley continued. "We're headed there now. As long as you stay out of our way, you may join us."

Turning on her heel, she walked shoulder to shoulder with him and tried to not let her face register concern. How did they know where Hawk was? And what was their plan?

She decided to ask. "How do you know where he is?"

"Well, as you know, we're conducting an extensive search of the resort," Stanley said. "But we just got a puzzling inquiry from one of our agents asking about the location of our other agents. Apparently, there's reason for concern, and we're sending in a team."

"A team?"

"An extraction team," Nobles said, entering the conversation. "If President Pride is there, we plan to extract him from his captor and then apprehend your boss."

"So you still think Hawk is responsible for taking the president?"

"If he's with him and holding him there, yes," Stanley said. He then turned to Reno and Brown. "You two can accompany us to the site, but you will remain where I tell you until I instruct you otherwise. Are we clear?"

"Crystal," Dana Brown said in a tone that seemed to blend disdain and sarcasm.

Juliette saw Sam Reno shoot Dana a look of irritation.

"We appreciate you letting us tag along," Reno said to Stanley. "It will be important for us to connect with the president as soon as possible once he is safe."

Stanley glanced over his shoulder at them as they boarded the elevator to head to the lobby. "Of course." He smiled as they stepped on board, and the elevator doors closed behind them.

CHAPTER SIXTY-ONE

Time to Go

Hawk read the text, and his heart sank—*"trouble in Casablanca—get out."* He immediately understood what Jillian was trying to tell him. They were about to have company, and it wasn't the kind of company you wanted to hang around and visit with. Rushing into the parlor, he was relieved to find the interview wrapping up. All three men turned toward him.

"Mr. President, we need to get you out of here. *Now.*" Hawk wanted to sound serious, but not panicked. "Mr. Walker and Mr. Ware, I have a place for you to go, but I ask you to please stay out of sight until we know it's safe."

All three hurried across the room to meet him at the stairwell. The plush blue carpeting on the stairs muffled their steps as they charged down. Hawk hoped they could succeed in making it through the lobby and then weave back into the backstage area to the exit behind the World Showcase. Just as they reached the lobby, he saw shadows moving past the exterior windows. The bad guys were close. Their presence called for an abrupt change of plans and coming up with a fast plan B.

"Are you familiar with this attraction?" Hawk turned to Walker and Ware.

"Yes, I've been here before," David Walker said.

Hawk pointed. "Good. Head up that stairwell beneath all the flags and hide in the theater. Hunker down inside. We're about to have company, and I'm not sure who they are."

"I'd rather stay with the two of you."

"No," the president said. "Hawk is right. We don't know what's about to happen. You need to stay out of sight and remain safe. You guys need to help me get my story out."

Walker hesitated. Hawk knew he was torn because the journalist in him wanted to cover what was about to happen. Finally, his expression softened. He nodded.

"Yes, sir. We can do that."

"Thanks," President Pride said.

Walker and his cameraman ran up the staircase toward the theater. Hawk motioned for the president to follow him, and together they advanced across the lobby toward an unmarked door on the far side of the rotunda. Hawk planned to head down into the depths of the attraction and stay out of sight until he could come up with a better strategy.

When the American Adventure had been created, it was one of the most complicated attractions Disney ever attempted. The project had been created and controlled by a team of twenty-something engineers. They needed fresh thinking and ideas beyond the boundaries of what had been imagined before. This young team of dreamers had delivered.

The show they created featured an engineering monster and marvel that worked out of sight of the audience as they watched the show a floor above. They called it the War Wagon—a machine that carried the audience through history. The massive, four-hundred-thousand-pound lift carriage carried ten hydraulic lifts that elevated sets and animated figures into place on the stage. The lifts were fourteen feet high and extended that same distance out the top of the carriage.

The entire carriage rolled almost silently underneath the audience, allowing many different lifts to be raised in the same small space between the proscenium and the rear-projection screen. Moving left to right, the three ten-by-ten-foot lifts were centered, with a ten- by thirty-foot lift on either side.

The lighting fixtures were built into the carriage. As the show played out, each scene, including audio-animatronic characters, were lifted with each set into view of the audience. Then they would disappear and another magically appear. There was no stage floor. It was only a wide-open area where the War Wagon moved back and forth, and at the precise time shifted the appropriate stage into place.

Stepping into what most would consider the basement of the American Adventure, Tyler Pride and Hawk moved into a workstation area just outside of where the War Wagon was housed. From their viewpoint, it was almost like looking at a history museum with characters and scenes on display. Except, in this case, because of how they were positioned on the War Wagon, it looked

Jeff Dixon 335

more as if they had all been placed scene-by-scene in a storage facility. There were more than thirty audio-animatronic figures staged in settings that featured actual furniture, lights, lamps, and decorations from that particular period of history.

"Wow! Impressive," Pride said, looking around.

"Mr. President, I need you to wait down here so I can see who's snooping around upstairs. Hide among the figures if you need to. I'll come back for you when I'm sure we can get you out of here," Hawk said as he ushered the president onto the War Wagon next to an audio-animatronic Thomas Jefferson. The lifelike ex-president was seated at a table, working on the Declaration of Independence.

"Don't be long." Pride smiled. "Good luck."

"Thanks, but I don't believe in luck."

"You don't believe in luck?"

"No, sir. Life is too short to worry about whether you're lucky or not. I trust God has a better plan for us that has nothing to do with luck." Hawk smiled back over his shoulder as he walked away.

"I like that," Pride said. "We need to talk about that sometime."

"After you're safe." Hawk snuck away from the War Wagon back into the holding area and headed toward the exit door and the staircase that would take him upstairs.

He took the stairs two at a time and emerged in the rotunda. A man dressed in black fatigues came out of the historical exhibit, obviously searching for them. Hawk caught a glimpse of the man a split second before the guy spotted him. He looked like the man Hawk had fought at the Jungle Cruise, but with the outfit and mask it was impossible to tell.

The dark-clothed man ran toward him. Streaking up the staircase, Hawk ascended the steps beneath the display of flags and headed toward the theater. If their enemy followed, Hawk wanted to put some distance between himself and the president, which was a good thing.

Hawk's vision narrowed as he focused on the doors of the darkened theater. A hot flush washed over him as adrenaline poured through his system. Once he entered, he'd only have a matter of seconds to turn the tables on his pursuer. He'd made the mistake of underestimating him once, but not this time. His hands crashed into the door, opening it into the dimly lit theater. Glancing around quickly, he couldn't spot Walker or Ware, and he was relieved. They were in the thousand-seat theater somewhere, tucked away out of sight.

Hawk slid to his right and placed his back flat against the wall on the far side of the door, waiting for the intruder to step inside the theater. His heart hammered so loudly he could hear it in his own ears. Tensed and ready, he didn't have long to wait. The black-clad man stepped into the doors of the theater one step and paused. He turned his head away from Hawk, scanning his surroundings. This was the splinter of time Hawk needed.

Lowering his shoulder, he lunged toward his enemy and like a football player buried it into the man's rib cage. The force and momentum of his attack lifted the man off his feet and sent him crashing into the wall next to the entryway. Not allowing him time to recover, Hawk pounced on top of the guy and threw two fast and hard punches into his jaw.

The element of surprise had worked. The man was stunned, but he was strong. If this was the same guy from his fight earlier, Hawk knew he only had a matter of moments before the attacker would be back on his feet and coming at him. Not waiting, Hawk threw a punch toward his stomach, trying to knock the air out of him. The man groaned and rolled away. Hopefully, this was the opening Hawk needed.

Scampering to his feet, leaving the fallen attacker behind, Hawk knew he had to get the president out now. If the bad guy had brought help, he would need to come up with a plan C. Hawk raced back toward the steps and heard the doors behind him crash against the wall. His attacker had already regained his footing and was up and after him.

At the top of the massive stairwell, Hawk glanced back and saw his pursuer was up but wobbly. He weighed his options. Now what?

Hawk had never been in a fight until he assumed the position of chief creative architect of the Walt Disney Company. But once he became the keeper of Walt Disney's secrets, he discovered that on more than one occasion, learning how to survive in a scrape had been a helpful skillset to acquire. He'd never faced an opponent as resilient as this guy.

Whirling to face the assailant, Hawk checked his position at the top of the stairwell. The man in black fatigues grew steadier with each step toward him and now broke into a run. Hawk braced himself for the impact. Seconds before the man got to him, he dropped to his back, placed a foot in the air, and kicked the man in the stomach. The momentum flipped the guy into the air over Hawk's body to collide with the steps beneath them.

Hawk rolled to his shoulder and watched the man in black tumble down the steps. As he crumpled into an unnatural heap at the bottom of the steps, Hawk slowly stood and took a deep breath. His attacker lay motionless.

Hawk had just taken his first step toward ground level when another man in black stepped into view. He paused at the bottom of the stairwell and examined his fallen comrade, then looked at Hawk. The guy stepped over the injured man and raced up the stairs toward him.

Hawk ran back into the theater and sprinted toward the front of the auditorium. Since the resort had been locked down so quickly, the attraction was ready to run. Hawk slammed his palm on the green button, which fully darkened the lights in the theater and started the show sequence.

The voice that represented Ben Franklin uttered the words, "America did not exist. Four centuries of work, bloodshed, loneliness, and fear created this land. We built America, and the process made us Americans—a new breed, rooted in all races."

An audio-animatronic Ben Franklin sat behind a desk while an audio-animatronic Mark Twain dozed in a rocker next to the table. These two figures would serve as narrators for the show piece of the attraction.

Hawk wished he could have gotten through a message to tell the president he had activated the show sequence. He tried to guess what Pride had done as the first scene, featuring Franklin and Twain, had lifted into place. Hoping the president had adjusted, he tried to figure out a way to gain an advantage over this new attacker, using the darkness and sound that filled the hollow hall.

Running across the front of the theater, Hawk headed toward the exit. He had to protect the president at all costs. The Disney Company handled the ebb and flow of crowds better than anyone in the world of theme park design. It was an art form, duplicated and studied by organizations internationally. Hawk hoped the exit would draw this next invader in, but how would he deal with him on the other side?

He had very few options to defend himself or launch an attack. He needed to get creative. Then he saw it, a stanchion pole standing with barriers to keep the crowds flowing through the proper exit doors. Grabbing the stanchion, he hoisted it to make sure he could swing it. It was the closest thing to a weapon he was going to find. Plastering his back against the wall, he controlled his breathing and made himself invisible.

He waited and listened. Finally, he heard the steps of someone sneaking up the walkway toward the exit. His hands tightened on the barricade pole, gripping it like a baseball bat, feeling his knuckles turn white, getting ready to swing at whoever rounded the corner. Hawk saw a foot break into his line of sight and stepped out to swing the bat.

"Wait!" David Walker jumped back and knocked into John Ware.

Hawk twisted and turned mid-swing to stop the stanchion, nearly spinning him around with the force of the effort.

"I told you to stay out of sight," Hawk said, louder than he intended to.

"Sorry. We saw you and were following you out," Walker said. "Nice job taking out that guy back there."

"But there's another one on the way."

Walker and Ware looked at each other and shrugged.

"We didn't see anyone," Ware said.

"He's in the theater on my tail right now."

As Hawk finished his sentence, the next masked man in fatigues came around the corner. Unprepared, Hawk hastily used the stanchion as a jousting pole. Stepping in front of the journalist and his cameraman, he plunged the makeshift weapon into the chest of the next attacker. It connected hard and knocked him backward. When the man hit the ground, Hawk leaped on top of the interloper. Using a combination of punches, he stunned the guy, giving them another opportunity to escape.

"Get out of here," Hawk told the newsmen. "Go toward the main gates and get out in front of Spaceship Earth. Do what the president asked you to do." Hawk took a moment to explain. "Now that these bad guys know you're here, they'll be after you too. So move out."

Walker and Ware immediately crashed through the exit doors of the attraction at a dead run. Hawk jumped back on his feet, figuring that if two men had managed to find them, more were on the way. He needed to return to the president and try to get him out of this mess. He raced to the front of the attraction.

On the stage, a scene played out of Ben Franklin speaking to Thomas Jefferson in a loft. Jefferson was writing.

Franklin said, "Thomas, it is difficult to make thirteen clocks chime at the same time, but we must carefully justify the separation."

"Dr. Franklin, while you slept soundly through the meeting this afternoon, we did manage to justify separation," the audio-animatronic figure of Jefferson replied.

As the lights faded, Thomas Jefferson's voice began to read the words of the Declaration of Independence. "We hold these truths to be self-evident, that all men are created equal, that they are endowed by their Creator with certain unalienable rights, that among these are life, liberty, and the pursuit of happiness."

As Jefferson's words rang out, the stage set containing Jefferson and Franklin began to lower into the War Wagon mechanism below. Hawk jumped onto the set piece, landing next to Franklin. Grabbing on to the desk where Jefferson sat to help him balance, Hawk rode into the lower stage area with Jefferson and Franklin. Descending into the darkness below, he needed to find the president in the maze below—and fast.

CHAPTER SIXTY-TWO

Bad Company

Jillian pushed open the side entrance door to the American Adventure. Craig Johnson stayed on her shoulder, moving cautiously behind her into a room adjacent to the rotunda. She had made a judgment call that Johnson believed her and was trying to help. It was the questions he asked and the way he tried to put the pieces together that led her instincts to conclude he really wanted to protect the president.

The next door would open into the rotunda. They pushed into the lobby— the massive square room that surrounded the oval-shaped area with a dome-shaped ceiling.

"This is amazing," Johnson whispered as he turned in a circle.

"I know," Jillian said.

They made a slow circle around the perimeter of the room, passing the works of art lining the walls. Guests were always amazed at the depth and detail of these valuable masterpieces, created for and on display for the world to see in the American Adventure.

As Jillian walked by each one, she was struck again by the amazing story of the nation and the effort it took to create and preserve history. Her heart pounded, realizing she was playing a part in a historical moment, attempting to help save the president of the United States.

Rounding the last corner, she saw the bottom of the stairwell beneath the American flags on display. There, in a heap at the bottom, lay a masked man dressed in black military fatigues.

"Is he dead?" Johnson asked over her shoulder.

"Not sure." Jillian studied him from a distance. "He's certainly not moving."

Quickly, she crossed to the bottom of the stairwell and leaned over the man to check for any pulse in his neck. It was faint, but he was alive.

"He's unconscious."

Johnson pointed out the odd angles of the man's limbs. "Apparently, he broke a leg and an arm when he fell. Let's see who this is." He reached down and removed the black mask.

Jillian studied the guy's strong features and short-cropped hair, but she didn't recognize him. She could tell from Johnson's reaction he did.

"That's Gene Owens. The president fired him last year."

"Secret Service?"

"Yeah. He wasn't too happy with his performance review. Long timer. Didn't much like the new administration. He especially didn't get along well with Sam Reno, the president's chief of staff."

"Apparently, he didn't like President Pride much either."

Jillian removed Owens's weapon from its holster. Turning it over in her hand, she examined it closely. It was very different than any other firearm she had seen before in person.

"That is a serious handgun," Johnson said. "It's biometric. It will only fire when the hand of the owner is wrapped around it."

"I've heard about these, but I've never seen one." Jillian released the magazine and disabled the weapon.

"Every person's grip and hand placement have a pattern that's magnified through a unique bone and muscle structure, creating a combined physical and behavioral biometric," Johnson said. "The technology measures and programs the way each person holds the grip of the gun. In essence, you create a unique grip-print that depends on a person's hand size, finger length, and how much pressure the fingers exert on the gun. It's called Dynamic Grip Recognition."

"Which means I can't use his gun." Just in case the owner woke up and tried to use it though, Jillian handed it to Johnson, who tucked it in his back waistband.

"Exactly, but what is he doing here?" Johnson looked at her.

She smiled. "That's easy. This is Hawk's doing. I guarantee it." She stood up and stepped over the ex-agent and headed up the stairs. "He's in over his head. He just doesn't know it yet. He needs our help."

Jillian mounted the stairs toward the theater, with Johnson right behind. Moving cautiously and keeping her gaze forward, they made their way up each step until they had covered half of the stairs leading to the top. Suddenly, there was a flurry of motion above them and a man dressed in black, similar to the one they had just left at the base of the stairs, emerged on the landing just above them.

The man aimed a handgun at them. It looked exactly like the one she had just confiscated. Instantly pausing, she pushed against the wall. Agent Johnson reached for his gun and managed to raise it, but before he had the chance to squeeze off the first round, a shot rang out from above, hitting him in the shoulder.

The impact twisted him to the side into Jillian. They were both thrown off balance and fell backward. Jillian heard a second shot ring out and felt Johnson's body jolt again. He had been struck a second time. They tumbled down the steps, flipping over and over. She thought the fall would never stop. Finally, gaining a grip on the handrail, she slowed herself and reached out to stabilize the descent of a badly injured Agent Johnson.

The assailant at the top of the stairs had moved off after his second shot, so she examined the extent of Johnson's injuries. He was hurt badly, but she couldn't tell how serious. A gunshot wound to his shoulder bled, and his side oozed red in a spreading pattern across his crisp white shirt.

"I'll be okay," Johnson said as he pressed his weapon into her hand. "Take this and get the president out of here."

"You need to call for help," Jillian said as she grabbed his wrist and pulled the transmitter he wore toward his mouth.

"No," he gasped. "We don't know who we can trust. If I call for help, I don't know who might be listening or who will come."

Jillian knew he was right. After helping him scoot to the wall of the stairwell, she made him as comfortable as possible. She pressed his hand against his side to staunch the bleeding.

"Go!"

"I'm going," Jillian said, gripping his gun. She crouched down and moved away from him.

"Be careful," he said faintly as she ascended the stairs and stepped on the landing.

As she scanned the area, she could hear that the attraction was running inside the theater, with loud music and narration. Jillian smiled. Hawk must have been creating a distraction. And if there was one assailant, there must be more. She had to presume they were waiting inside the theater.

Tightening her grip on the handgun, she took a deep breath and then leaned against the door of the theater, pushing it open slowly. Cautiously, she stepped into the American Adventure and rapidly blinked her eyes, trying to adjust her vision to the theater lighting. Her stomach tightened as she caught a too-brief glimpse of Grayson Hawkes, Thomas Jefferson, and Benjamin Franklin disappearing from the stage as the show played on.

CHAPTER SIXTY-THREE

Stop and Wait

"I thought you were sending agents in to get the president. What happened?" Dana Brown asked Juliette as the group made their way across the International Gateway to enter the World Showcase at Epcot.

Juliette had thought the same thing but had not voiced her concern. She had been designated as the unofficial tour guide for Dana Brown, Sam Reno, Pat Nobles, and Jeremiah Stanley. At each juncture of their journey from the Bay Lake Towers, she had expected an army of agents, police, or security to join them, but it hadn't happened. They were nowhere to be seen.

As they had exited Bay Lake, the agents at the door and in the lobby had merely nodded at them, but not one had joined their group. Her assumption that a sea of agents would be flooding into the World Showcase had obviously been wrong. On one hand she was glad because of her concern for Hawk and the president, but on the other, there was something seriously wrong about such an urgent situation.

Silently, the group moved across the bridge into France before Nobles stepped up beside her. "Perhaps you should let me lead," he said as he took the point. "I'm not sure what we are about to run into."

"Have you heard any more reports from our forward agent?" Stanley asked.

"No, sir. That has me concerned," Nobles said as they moved to the edge of the Les Chefs de France, one of Epcot's overlooked gems.

Stepping inside the restaurant, they took a moment to overlook the streets below. The deserted restaurant, lined with tables covered in crisp white linens, had a light and airy interior. The location also gave them a bird's-eye view of any activity in the area. Stanley chose to address their small group here.

"It's really odd that we haven't gotten an update about what's going on up ahead," Stanley said. "By now, I thought we would have heard something else."

Nobles stepped away and busied himself on his cell phone as Stanley peered out the windows.

"In answer to your question from earlier, Dana, we do have a number of agents in the area." Stanley looked at her with condescension. "They are, of course, staying out of sight. But your assumption that we would have agents waiting for us was correct."

"So what's the plan now?" Juliette asked.

"We'll check on the status of the operation, but unfortunately, since we don't know what we'll face from now on, you will remain here."

"No, we won't," Juliette quickly replied.

"Yes, I'm afraid you will. We're in charge. I can't take the chance of you getting hurt, or worse, getting in the way of our extraction operation," Stanley said. "I had hoped to have a better update for you by the time we arrived here. We'll come get you as soon as it's safe."

"You just expect us to wait here in this restaurant?" Sam said.

"Yes, but I do need Juliette to let me know where we are directionally."

"I'm sorry?" she replied.

"What's between me and the American exhibit?"

"You have two more pavilions to pass through—Morocco and Japan. After that, you enter the American Adventure Pavilion area," Juliette said. "How do you know that's where the president is?"

"It makes sense, doesn't it?" Stanley said. "When your boss kidnapped the president, I acknowledge he's been creative in eluding us, but he's also been predictable. Where else would you find the president of the United States except in the American Adventure?"

Stanley stepped away from them and joined Pat Nobles outside the restaurant.

"What do you think?" Dana asked Sam, who stood next to her.

"I'm not sure," he said. "But I don't think this is over yet."

Juliette turned to the two of them. "So who do you trust? Is Stanley a solid guy or is he out to get the president? And what about Nobles? Is he on the up-and-up or is he involved as well?"

Dana shook her head. "I really don't know."

"President Pride told us he trusted no one and that we shouldn't either," Sam said. "Do you really think the president is with Hawkes in the American Adventure?"

"If they are, the only advantage they have is that Hawk is on his home turf," Juliette answered.

"Home turf?" Dana asked.

"Yes, the resort is his world. Hawk knows it inside and out. He has studied every square inch—the design, the secrets, and he has created some of those," Juliette said. "If he needs to figure out a way to level the playing field and restack the odds in his favor, then the Walt Disney World Resort is the best place for that to happen."

"So you think he has a plan?" Sam asked.

Juliette considered this. "He would probably tell you that he does, but the truth is, he tends to ad-lib and make things up as he goes. But he's incredibly resourceful and resilient. He's a force of nature that most people can't figure out how to stop."

"Let's hope so," Dana said as she watched Nobles and Stanley disappear from sight.

"It may take more than a force of nature to get him and the president out of this," Sam said.

CHAPTER SIXTY-FOUR

Out of Time

"**N**ow that's something you don't see every day," Tyler Pride said as he watched Hawk arrive inside the War Wagon.

Hawk smiled in spite of himself. The sight of him alongside Ben Franklin and Thomas Jefferson was not the usual way others saw him. But the moment of levity quickly grew more urgent.

"Mr. President, we have a situation," Hawk said.

"A new one?"

"No, same situation, just a little more urgent." Hawk jumped off the platform. He glanced up to see if he had been followed.

"There are men dressed in black, wearing masks, in the attraction with us. I got rid of two of them, but I don't know for how long and I don't know if there are more."

The audio-animatronic figure of George Washington on horseback in the snow lifted into position as he and Pride moved through the maze of statues. They stepped back as the narration played in the background and the figure of Fredrick Douglas, seated in a raft, slid into place, staged and ready to move upward into the viewing area.

"I don't know how to keep you safe, sir," Hawk admitted. "I need you to tell me who I can trust."

"Well, that's the problem, Hawk. I trust my inner circle—Sam Reno, Dana Brown, and the vice president. But Washington is full of lifers and liars who seem fascinated and fixated on holding onto power."

"This still seems unbelievable to me," Hawk said. "I don't always agree with everything you do or say, but you're my president and I support you."

349

"Ah, but you are like most Americans. You have a desire to get it right and want a better world for others." Pride slowed as they neared the edge of the War Wagon. "But when you hate a politician like me or a political party more than you love America, you go crazy and become unhinged."

"That's evil," Hawk summarized.

"You are correct."

The Civil War music began to play in the background as the attraction continued to operate. Hawk glanced behind them as the War Wagon once again slid another set piece into place. As he did, he noticed unusual movement beside a clump of soldiers who had been in the Revolutionary War scene with George Washington. A man in black slid out from the shadows, and Hawk realized they were not alone.

Shoving the president out of the way and into one of the scenes being staged, he turned and charged toward the unexpected assailant who had followed him down into the depths of the attraction. The man stepped out and braced himself for the impact. Hawk left his feet and turned his body into a human missile, only to realize the interloper had not only seen him but would be able to avoid him by stepping out of the way. Hawk missed and couldn't slow down his flight. Instead, he crashed into the Civil War audio-animatronic figures in front of him.

The paramilitary "soldier" quickly pounced on Hawk and pummeled him with punches that left him momentarily stunned. Hawk rolled on his side, raised up on one arm and threw an elbow at his attacker, slowing the onslaught. As the man stepped back, Hawk lunged toward the well-trained assailant and cut his legs out from under him, driving him to the ground.

Now it was Hawk's turn to throw punches. He had the upper hand when the man rolled to his side. Immediately, Hawk leapt to his feet and raced back to where he had left the president tucked away behind the top of the Statue of Liberty's torch—the finale of the show.

"Mr. President, we need to get out of here, now," Hawk said, trying to shake off the cobwebs.

"Not yet." Pride shoved Hawk to the side.

Hawk turned. His attacker had regained his feet and managed to sneak up behind him. The president punched the guy, hitting him squarely in the jaw. Hawk spun and followed up the presidential punch with a jab of his own, knocking the man down once again.

"Great punch, sir," Hawk said.

Reaching down, he pulled a pistol from the fallen man's shoulder harness. The weapon was so state of the art, he couldn't fire it. Tossing it deep into the War Wagon, he grabbed the president's arm and steered him to another set piece. A gas station rose into the air, leaving them below to step on the next set piece—a battleship.

Rosie the Riveter welded a piece of the vessel into place. On the deck, a crew member gazed seaward with a pair of binoculars. The radio played the Voice of America.

The scene was set at Christmastime, and the song "I'll Be Home for Christmas" played. The gas station blocked the view of the ship from the audience seats momentarily, but on cue, the station dropped to reveal the battleship they clung to. When the gas station disappeared, Hawk spotted a lone figure standing in front of the stage.

"Well, hello there." The smiling face of Jillian greeted them.

"It's good to see a friendly face," President Pride said.

"You have to admit, this is not the craziest thing you've ever seen me doing, right?" Hawk said as he jumped off the ship toward the solid frame of the stage.

"Oh, I'd say it ranks pretty close to the top." Jillian moved to the edge of the stage.

The president followed Hawk's lead and jumped to the edge of the platform and then stepped down into the theater next to Jillian.

"Are you okay, sir?" Jillian asked.

"Better than the guy we left down there in the hole," the president said.

"How bad is it?" Hawk asked her.

"Well, I've seen the damage you've done. We have a bad guy at the theater exit and one at the bottom of the steps. Agent Johnson has been shot and won't let me call for help because we don't know who to trust."

Hawk walked quickly toward the theater doors. In the background, the song "Golden Dream" was being sung as a series of images from modern history were displayed on the massive theater screens. He motioned for the pair to follow him. Making sure they were ready, Hawk cautiously looked out to see if the coast was clear. He saw no movement. They ran toward the steps, which had been part of the gun battle.

Glancing down, Hawk saw the attacker he had flipped down the steps. Farther beyond him, he saw Agent Johnson leaning against the wall, obviously injured badly, but watching them as they descended the stairs.

When President Pride, Jillian, and Hawk drew closer, the Secret Service agent straightened up, his words barely a whisper. "Good to see you, Mr. President."

"Craig, I'm so sorry you've been hurt trying to protect me."

As the president spoke to Agent Johnson, Jillian stole a moment to inspect Hawk. "Are you hurt?"

"No, how about you?"

"I'm good."

"We need to get the president to the Golden Dream," Hawk said. "We can keep him safe there until we figure out how to exit this nightmare. He doesn't know who to trust, and neither do I."

"The Golden Dream is the boat outside the pavilion, right?"

"Yes. There's room for him to stay out of sight there. I'll get our old friend Cal McManus to bring in the military if he has to, but we have to get the president out of here and make sure he's safe."

Jillian moved across the hallway into the rotunda and walked toward the front doors. Hawk tapped the president on the back, signaling it was time to go. Johnson saluted with his good arm as Pride stood to his feet and returned his salute.

He followed Hawk across the hallway and stepped into the rotunda. They were in the center of the domed room when the front doors cracked open. Jillian stopped and backed up. Hawk and the president pulled up short and waited to see who entered. In unison they all stepped back as a figure emerged from the doorway and entered the rotunda, allowing the door to close shut behind them.

CHAPTER SIXTY-FIVE

I Heard That

Juliette peered out the window in the direction Stanley and Nobles had left them. Dana Brown sat at a table next to her, while Sam Reno nervously paced behind her.

"I should have known something strange was going on," Dana said as she tapped her fingers on the table.

"What do you mean?" Sam asked.

"The president told us this was a trip that would change his presidency and make history." Dana sighed. "I thought it was just Tyler Pride being his usual confident self."

"He seemed more tense than usual when we arrived," Sam recalled. "I should have asked him about it or figured out that something else was up."

Juliette turned and looked over her shoulder. "Second guessing and playing woulda, shoulda, coulda is not usually healthy or very helpful. The president trusts you. If he wanted you to know what was going on, he would have told you. It sounds to me like he was trying to protect you."

The two presidential aides grew quiet at this thought.

Juliette turned back to the window, but she could no longer see the two Secret Service agents as they had moved beyond her sightline. Grabbing her cell phone, she held it up and pondered what to do or who to call. She wanted to call Hawk or Jillian but knew that was a bad idea. They had all agreed not to talk to each other over the phone. Her mouth felt dry and her mind seemed on an endless loop of worst-case scenarios where her friends and the president ended up hurt or dead. A gunshot halted her thoughts.

The explosion of sound was sudden and unexpected, yet distinct enough to cause all three of them to gasp.

"I'm not the only one who heard that, right?" Juliette asked, fixing her eyes on the street below.

Dana rose to her feet and stood next to Juliette. "It was a gunshot, wasn't it?"

"That's what it sounded like." Sam rushed to the window. "If it was, you two don't need to be standing next to the window. It isn't bulletproof."

Realizing he was right, Juliette tugged Dana's arm and pulled her deeper into the restaurant toward the kitchen. Sam followed, glancing back as they entered the kitchen through the swinging door separating it from the dining room.

"I think, under the circumstances, I'd like to go see what's going on," Juliette said.

"The Secret Service told us to stay here," Sam reminded her.

"Really? You want to stay here?" Dana asked.

"I didn't say that. I was just repeating what they said."

"Common sense would say we don't need to head toward the direction of a gunshot, but nothing about this situation seems very common anymore." Juliette looked at them. "You do what you want, but I'm not staying here. I'm going to look for Hawk, Jillian, and President Pride."

Juliette moved to the cast members' door on the back side of the restaurant. She stopped and looked at the pair.

"I know the back way out of here and through the other pavilions. I can get us to the American Adventure pretty much unseen."

Dana shrugged. "Then what are we waiting for?"

"Lead on." Sam Reno motioned toward the door.

CHAPTER SIXTY-SIX

Security Arrives

The man entered the room cautiously and stopped as soon as he saw them standing there. He was dressed in a shirt, tie, and dark pants. Slightly disheveled, eyebrows pinched together above reddened eyes, he looked at the three people in the rotunda and nearly broke into tears.

"I'm so glad to see you—all of you," he said.

Jillian stepped forward. "Joel? Joel Habecker? What are you doing here?"

Jillian had known Joel for the last three years of his employment at the Disney Company. He had quickly earned the respect of all of the cast members he had worked with and was a trusted member of Disney Security.

"I came to help . . . I think." He shuffled his feet nervously. "I mean, I *am* trying to help. I'm not sure."

"Take a deep breath." Jillian walked the rest of the way to him. "What is it you need to tell us?"

"You were spotted on the way into Epcot, apparently. I was monitoring some of the communication channels, and the report came in that you were spotted on a camera heading into Epcot. Then there were reports that other people were in the area as well."

"Other people?" Hawk raised an eyebrow as he asked the question.

Only then did Joel appear to notice the president of the United States standing slightly behind Hawk. He blushed.

"I'm sorry to be rude. Hello, Mr. President." Joel said.

"Hello," Pride said. "Please continue."

Joel turned his attention back to Jillian.

"The other people are agents I guess . . . maybe Secret Service, or police. They're all dressed in black. Every news channel is talking about how Dr. Hawkes has kidnapped the president and is being sought. I thought you should know. I didn't know how else to help." He looked at the floor. "I didn't know what to do. Our security teams have been asking for me to give them some task besides guarding the hotels, but I didn't know, so I came to help."

"Thanks, it's okay." Jillian patted him on the arm.

Hawk shot her a sympathetic look, but at the same time rubbed his arm with a slight shake of his head. She knew Hawk was uncomfortable with Joel's presence in the rotunda. She agreed.

"There's something else," Joel said.

"What?" Hawk asked.

"Someone has been shot. I'm not sure, but they might be dead." Joel was pale.

"Where?" Jillian asked.

"In the next pavilion over," Joel said. "In Japan."

"Show me."

Joel nodded and headed for the door. She motioned for him to wait and walked over to Hawk. He stood with arms folded and knitted brows. Jillian looked at Hawk and then at Joel.

"I'm not buying it," Hawk said softly. "It doesn't make sense." He never broke eye contact with Joel as he spoke to her. "You trust him?"

"I don't have any reason not to trust him," Jillian said. "He's worked with me for about three years, and he helped track down information about the Airstream at Fort Wilderness and the couple who was shot on the property."

"We have to get him out of here."

"Let me go check out what he said. I'll get him out of harm's way. It will only take a minute." Jillian tried to reassure Hawk. "Get in touch with Cal McManus and figure out where to hide the president."

Jillian made her way across the room and led Joel toward a side exit. They stepped into the hallway beyond the doors and moved along the corridor that would take them out the back of the gift shop and into the main walkways. This way, she could keep out of sight and see the agents Joel had mentioned. Her head swiveled from side to side as they moved quickly.

Joel motioned for her to follow him. As they rounded the corner, Jillian looked out toward the red torii gate in the lagoon. She knew from her world culture courses with Homeland Security that these gates were traditional in Japanese culture. Originally, they had been conceived as perches for roosters but had come to symbolize good luck and purification. Pausing, she held out her arm, stopping Joel.

"Where are we going?" she whispered.

"To the pagoda."

Jillian knew this was right around the corner from where they were located. Each floor of the five-story structure represented elements of earth, water, fire, wind, and heaven and had been patterned after a real shrine in Japan. She stayed low as they crept around the corner, her eyes continuing to search the surrounding landscape.

As they neared the edge of the temple, she could see the feet of a man lying on the ground, the upper part of his body obscured. She ran and turned him over. She let out a soft gasp as she rolled over the body of Jeremiah Stanley.

Blinking rapidly, she glanced over her shoulder at Joel.

"Do you know who this is?" Jillian asked.

Joel leaned over and looked closer. "Secret Service agent, I suppose."

Jeremiah Stanley had been shot. A blood stain covered his chest. Jillian checked for a pulse. There was none. Jillian felt her adrenaline surge, and her heart beat faster. She immediately knew she had to get back to the president and Hawk. If someone had shot and killed the head of the Secret Service, then every fear they had surmised had been correct. As her thoughts crashed together like tumbling dominos, she looked at the position of Stanley's body.

"Joel, how did you see his body from the pathway?" She turned to him as she spoke.

"Simple. I shot him here." Joel's answer echoed in her head as he slammed his fist down on Jillian's shoulder, driving her to the ground.

Jillian hit the pavement hard, but instinctively rolled her body slightly to soften the landing. Joel pounced over her, ready to rain down another blow, this one aimed at her head. Again she rolled, and his fist only grazed her jaw. Suddenly she remembered that in the Bay Lake Towers, the Secret Service had gotten the information about the Grimsley Airstream camper from someone in Disney Security. She had told Joel to take his time in sharing it with them.

Lifting a knee into him, Joel fell backward. He reached for his waistband in the small of his back. She knew he intended to shoot her too. Hauling herself quickly to her feet, Jillian shoved him to the pavement, where he fell on his hand behind his back. She wasted no time driving her knee into his chest. He groaned and rolled to his side, pulling his weapon out as he regained his feet. Instantly, she saw it was the same biometric weapon the other bad guys used. She lashed out a vicious kick toward his hand, and the gun tumbled and clanked off the pavement.

"Why?" Jillian unleashed another kick and knocked him off his feet. "Why did you do this?"

"Because I'm a patriot," Joel said. He rocked back up to his knees trying to regain his footing. His shy, almost apologetic persona had melted away. His mouth curled into a sneer. "I did it to save our country. Plus it pays pretty well to be a patriot."

Jillian delivered a whirling roundhouse kick. His head snapped back and whipped his body into a backbend that ended with him thundering to the pavement in a heap. Rushing to the queue-line barricade next to them, she extracted the rope used to control the crowds. Flipping Joel over, she drove a knee deeply into his back, jerked both of his hands behind him, wrapped the rope around them and then drew it down to his ankles, hog-tying him. He wouldn't be going anywhere soon. She picked up his weapon and tossed it as far as she could before returning to Jeremiah Stanley. She felt for a pulse again, confirming what she already knew. He was dead.

Gritting her jaw, she rose to her feet and hurried back to Hawk and the president.

CHAPTER SIXTY-SEVEN

Operation Marble Heart

Hawk ended the call to Cal McManus, the former sheriff, who had remained a good personal friend of his over the past few years. His call had been brief, but precise. He told McManus to send in whatever force he needed to rescue the president of the United States. Hawk realized that the request would stretch any type of rescue operation McManus had ever run before, but these were unusual circumstances.

Now he changed gears and began his plan to move President Pride away from the American Adventure and into another place that would be safer. There was no doubt their current location had been compromised.

They moved toward the back of the rotunda so they could exit through the rear doors. This would carry them once again into a backstage area, where they could navigate behind the World Showcase pavilions. As they reached the door, Hawk pulled up short and held his breath. The sudden stop caught Pride off guard, and he bumped into Hawk's back.

"What'd you hear?" the president said.

"Something or someone on the other side of this door." Hawk backed up. Looking from side to side, he tensed, getting ready to battle anyone who came through the door. Slowly, it creaked open, revealing Detail Chief Pat Nobles, who smiled broadly as he entered.

"Thank goodness, Mr. President." Nobles grinned. "I am so very glad to see you." He stopped smiling when he looked at Hawk. "And as for you, Dr. Hawkes, you're under arrest. Please put your hands behind your back and turn around."

"He is *not* under arrest," President Pride said. "He's the reason I'm still alive."

"But, sir, it's apparent he was involved in the plot to kidnap and harm you and your family."

"No, he's the reason my family and I are still alive." Pride pointed a finger at Nobles. "He did your job for you. He kept me safe. Your team allowed our kidnapping."

Nobles face fell. "My team? Who on my team?"

"There are folks working with you that are not so good. Scum. They're the people responsible for kidnapping me and my family."

"That's not possible, sir. Dr. Hawkes was last seen fleeing with your daughter."

The president moved across the rotunda and sat down on the bench facing the interior dome. Hawk took his cue from the commander in chief and followed him but remained standing.

"Are you all right, Mr. President?" Hawk asked.

"Fine," Pride said. He looked at Nobles, his brows drawn together. "What are you doing here . . . exactly?"

"Looking for you, sir. Ever since you disappeared."

"Really?"

"Yes, sir . . . really." Nobles took a step toward Hawk. "So, you have some explaining to do."

"I do?" Hawk said.

"Yes. You seemed to be the first to know the president and his family were missing. You seemed to be the one who was able to find them. And now, apparently, you're responsible for hiding the president from the Secret Service and every other law enforcement agency."

"Actually, Pat," the president said, "Hawk is working for me."

"Working for you?"

"Yes, I asked him for help. I became aware there were forces in play who had decided they didn't want me to remain in office. So they mobilized and implemented a plan to take me out."

"Take you out?"

"Out of office, for good."

"You mean, kill you?" Nobles shook his head. "Surely, no one close to you would do that."

"Only if necessary," Pride said. "The plan was to give me an option. If they were strong enough and connected enough to kidnap me from Secret Service protection, then they were strong and powerful enough to silence me. My family was the bargaining chip. If I left office and stayed silent about this deep-state conspiracy, they would let us live. If I chose to break my silence and expose the perpetrators, then my family and I would pay the price."

Nobles' mouth was now ajar. "Who would do that?"

"That's what I thought," Hawk injected. "Who would do that? It would have to be someone who was a Washington insider. It would have to be someone who had been a part of the government organization and infrastructure for a long time, and it would need to be someone who had a passionate dislike for a chaos presidential candidate."

"Chaos?"

"A candidate from outside the beltway—not really a politician. Someone politically incorrect and a threat to the power and prestige of political parties that have forgotten they represent and serve the people. Instead, they have decided it is better if people serve them." Hawk inched closer to the president. "You know the type, don't you?"

Nobles stared at them. Hawk could tell the man was carefully calculating and crafting his response. Nobles cleared his throat. "That is ludicrous. Are you suggesting I'm involved in this plot?"

"Not suggesting, implying is a better word," Hawk said. "I've been wondering why it is that I have been able to move around the resort as easily as I have. I would think that with the president and first family missing, a lockdown would really be a lockdown. However, it dawned on me that I never saw any real resistance to my movements.

"Oh, there was an occasional encounter when I seemed to cross paths with someone on a general search, but nothing too serious or intense. It's almost as if someone knew I'd find the president and the blame would fall on me." Hawk shrugged. "It took me a while to figure out someone wanted me to hide the president because it created a better narrative."

"And you think that was me?" Nobles narrowed his eyes.

"Then, of course, the entire world heard I had kidnapped the president and was now wanted in the case of the missing first family. And why not? The Secret Service lost them in my world and who knows my world better than me?"

Hawk's stance remained ready for any attack. "But you know what really threw me off? There were clues—just enough to help me be successful. Why would someone leave clues? It seemed pointless. That's why it took me so long to put the pieces together. I thought you would have been smarter than that."

Nobles smiled. He glanced from Hawk to the president and back to him. He laughed out loud, his laugh echoing off the top of the dome. Finally, he stopped and shrugged his shoulders.

"We had to have a way to communicate," Nobles said. "So we talked in code. It was a code that you figured out, but we realized you were the only one who could. And if you did, which you did, then you would become our number-one suspect."

Hawk knew that Nobles' confession meant they were in even more danger. He couldn't let either of them live. Nobles drew a handgun out of his belt and aimed it at Hawk, then the president.

"Don't make a move." Nobles locked his gaze on them, his hand steady. "You were just too smart, Hawkes, and figured out our code quicker than we antici-pated. That was the only part of the plan we underestimated. The rest worked pretty well. The president had announced a major policy speech to be delivered here at Walt Disney World, and we had the right people in place. Perfect timing."

"But I didn't come here to give a major policy speech." Pride stood to his feet.

"Really?"

"No, I had been collecting information about scum like you and your band of insiders that decided you couldn't let me remain in office. I told the voters I would clean up the government, and people like you couldn't handle that."

"People like me?!" Noble yelled. "I'm the patriot. I'm the hero. I've spent my entire career preserving a way of life for people who will never appreciate it. I've kept our nation safe from people like you who have no regard for the way things have to work, the steps that we have to take to keep us safe."

Nobles stepped closer to the president. "You're a buffoon who only cares about himself. You have no decorum, no style. You're a bull in a china shop and have broken America. You say you want to put pride in our country, but all you've done has disrupted, embarrassed, and weakened our nation. And as a result, you have to be eliminated."

Nobles leveled his gun directly at the president's chest.

The president straightened his spine and smiled. "Guess what? You failed. I've amassed the research, details, and evidence that will unravel your plans and those you have conspired with and made it available for the world to see."

Nobles sneered. "When did this happen?"

"Today." Pride watched the smile fade from Nobles' face.

"Tyler," Nobles said, "have you ever heard of the Marble Heart?"

The president shook his head no. Hawk watched as Nobles smile and cockiness returned.

"We called this Operation Marble Heart. The name came from a play that Abraham Lincoln had once attended at Ford's Theater."

"The theater where Lincoln was assassinated," Hawk said.

"Very good. You know something besides Mickey Mouse stuff," Nobles scoffed. "You know who the star of the play was that night? John Wilkes Booth."

"So what? So President Lincoln had seen Booth in a play at Ford's Theater," the president said coldly. "Is there a point?"

"Of course there's a point. There is always a point." Nobles paused. "That is something you just don't understand. Lincoln had attended with guests that night. One of them was a lady named Mary Clay. She noticed that twice during the play when Booth delivered some extra menacing lines, he walked closer to Lincoln and pointed his finger toward the president's face. When it happened the third time, she turned to Lincoln and said, 'Mr. Lincoln, he looks as if he meant that for you.' Lincoln just laughed and said, 'Well, he does look pretty sharp at me, doesn't he?'" Nobles sneered. "Have you noticed how many times I've looked at you that way? Have you noticed how often others have looked at you that way?"

"I have actually." The president laughed. "If looks could kill, you would have gotten me. But sadly, you've failed."

"I don't really see it that way, Pride," Nobles said flatly. "You are about to die. Notice I didn't call you Mr. President. You were never my president."

"Well, that is a shame. If you had been a better student of history, you might have pulled off this crazy plan. But just like your hero, John Wilkes Booth, you were sloppy. Ironically, you made the same mistake he did."

Nobles' face grew grim. "What mistake would that be?"

"The conversation you had with the vice president," President Pride said. "You mentioned to him in passing one day how much more of an honor it was to guard him than me. He thought that was an odd thing to say. He told me about it. I decided it was time to hold my cards close to my chest and launch my own investigation. Some things just didn't add up as I tried to get things done. I've had resistance since the day of my inauguration.

"One day I remembered my history and realized that John Wilkes Booth had sent a letter to Lincoln's vice president, Andrew Johnson, at his Kirkwood house. It was an attempt to drag Johnson into the conspiracy. Although history has suspected his involvement, he was never implicated."

Hawk watched Nobles closely. He seemed to grow angrier as the president spoke.

"Our vice president, Chris Ware, is an honorable man. A good man who is loyal. Statements like yours, even if they mean nothing, can't just be ignored in our political climate. Just like John Wilkes Booth tried to build a team of conspirators that unraveled around him, when it was all said and done, it was just him alone with the president that night in Ford's Theater." President Pride pointed at Nobles. "You did the same thing. Your grand team of conspirators has unraveled and failed. You're the only one left to carry out your plan. But I've already turned over all the evidence necessary to convict you. It is over."

"Yes, you're right about that, Pride. It is over." Nobles took one more step toward the president, the glint of the biometric handgun leveled at Pride's chest. "Sic Semper Tyrannis. Do you know what that means?"

Hawk knew. It was what John Wilkes Booth yelled from the stage of Ford's Theater after he had shot President Lincoln. He realized Nobles was ready to pull the trigger and kill the president. Time seemed to slow as Hawk almost heard the next few seconds of the clock tick away.

"Thus always to tyrants," the president said.

Hawk willed his body to move faster than ever before. He lunged and twisted his body so that it was between the president and the weapon aimed at him. Hawk heard the echo of a gunshot a split second before a searing pain exploded inside his body. His last thoughts were that he was falling on top of the president and there was pain.

CHAPTER SIXTY-EIGHT

Doing What It Takes

Using her shoulder to blast through the heavy doors, Jillian dashed inside America's Mansion, as Disney designers referred to the American Adventure Pavilion. On a dead sprint, she ran into the rotunda and heard President Pride say, "Thus always to tyrants." The words were followed by a single gunshot.

Skidding to a stop, her brain processed the scene unfolding in front of her. As had happened so many times in her training, in the midst of a crisis when others panicked, she saw events at a slower speed and could not only understand but react to them.

Pat Nobles aimed a gun at the president. Hawk threw his body in front of the president, protecting him from harm. The pistol had been fired. She watched in horror as Hawk's body absorbed the bullet. In a grotesque twisting motion, he had grabbed hold of the president and forced him to the ground, while taking the brunt of the bullet himself.

Jillian watched as Nobles shifted to change his line of sight. He then moved in for another shot, this one aimed to kill the president.

As she closed one eye and exhaled, Nobles came into laser focus over the end of the pistol that belonged to Agent Johnson. Jillian had drawn the weapon out of her waistband on the way through the door into the rotunda. Tensing her finger as she exhaled, she sent a single bullet flying through the air toward Nobles and ran forward to squeeze off a second round.

Nobles jerked to the side. A look of shock crossed his face, and then he frowned and sank to his knees. He once again raised his weapon to aim an unsteady arm toward the president, who was still protected by the body of Hawk.

Jillian squeezed off the second shot, striking Nobles in the side of the chest, jerking his body away from the other two men.

Simultaneously, he had fired his second shot, but due to the impact of her bullet, his had ricocheted off the roof of the dome. Jillian landed hard on top of him and leveled her gun to take a third shot. But he had dropped his gun and lay motionless on the floor, a red stain oozing from beneath his fallen form.

Kicking the pistol across the room, she turned and gasped. "Hawk!" she cried as she reached down and gently tried to roll him off the president. He bled from the wound in his back.

Tyler Pride cradled Hawk in his arms and carefully helped her lay him on the floor. Tears welled in the president's eyes.

"It happened so fast. He was suddenly there in front of me," Pride said in a choked voice. "Then we were on the ground. I didn't know he'd been shot."

Jillian felt for a pulse and could not find one. She leaned down and put her mouth next to his ear and whispered. "Don't you die on me, Hawk. Not on my watch. Don't you leave me."

"Oh no!" The voice of Juliette Keaton echoed through the dome of the rotunda. She ran over and knelt down next to them.

"He has no pulse." Tears streamed down Jillian's face. "He's gone."

Juliette reached down and touched Hawk on the cheek, her eyes also flooding with tears. She reached in her pocket and pulled out her cell phone, dialing 9-1-1.

"Let me help," Dana Brown said, joining them. "The president has emergency medical teams with him. They're close."

"I've already called them," Sam Reno said. "I put them on standby as soon as we entered Epcot."

Jillian rolled Hawk over, ripped the sleeve off her blouse, and stuffed it into the hole where the bullet had entered. Her first impulse was to begin CPR, but her training gave her pause. Although she was desperate to get some sort of vital sign from Hawk, she also knew that the force of beginning CPR would enhance how quickly he would lose blood. Covering the entry hole with pressure was the best first procedure. She leaned in and put pressure on the entry point. As she did, she now weighed the risk of beginning CPR.

She paused when Sam Reno reached down and grabbed her by the arm.

"Let me take over," he said. "You've been a federal agent. You know the drill. We have to secure the president. You are our best hope to do that right now."

"I'm fine," Pride said. "Let me help with Hawk."

The president worked to make Hawk comfortable as Jillian was once again trying to inspect where she had plugged up the hole in his body.

"We need to get a heartbeat, but if we aren't careful, he will bleed out. If the bullet hit the heart, we don't have a chance, but if he's in arrest because of the trauma, CPR might work," Jillian said, her thoughts and words running together rapidly.

"Let me take this," Sam said. "Secure the president, please . . . Agent Batterson."

Jillian paused, looking from Hawk to the president. Sighing, she nodded. Jillian knew what she had to do, what she must do, and she also knew it was what Hawk expected her to do. It was her duty, and duty called.

"Mr. President, we have to get you someplace safer. Now." She got to her feet, and the president reluctantly followed her lead.

Sam shoved his way in to take over Hawk's care. Dana leaned in to assist, and they prepared to start CPR. Juliette knelt to reinforce the patch Jillian had fashioned from her sleeve to stanch the bleeding.

In a flurry of motion, the front and back doors of the attraction slammed opened. With weapons drawn and aimed at anyone who dared cross them, the Orange County Sheriff's Department entered the pavilion. Cal McManus moved across the room, clearly in command. Behind them came a wave of medical personnel. They asked everyone to stand back and surrounded Hawk to work on him.

Confident Hawk was in good hands, Jillian took the president by the arm and led him to McManus.

"Mr. President, good to see you, sir," McManus said. "We'll move you to a secure location as soon as we get this straightened out. Jillian, or should I say, Agent Batterson, are you in charge?" He waited for her answer.

"Uh . . ." Jillian looked back at Hawk. "I guess so . . . Yes. I am."

Jillian stayed at the president's side as they were surrounded by armed guards. Dana Brown joined them as Hawk was now being attended to by the White House medical team. Jillian reached into her pocket and pulled out the flash drive the president had given them with all of the evidence he had been able to collect. She grasped Dana's hand, like she was giving her a handshake, and slipped the jump drive into her palm. Dana raised her eyebrows slightly but didn't say anything.

"Don't lose it. It has everything you need to back up the president's story," Jillian said. Then she hesitated and glanced over her shoulder. "Juliette?"

Juliette looked at her. She now stood watching the medical team work on Hawk. She grimly shook her head side to side, tears streaming down her cheeks. Juliette wouldn't leave his side.

Wiping her own eyes, Jillian turned and escorted President Pride through the doors of the American Adventure. An armored vehicle waited for them outside with the door open. The president ducked in first, she followed, Dana slid in, and then McManus. An armed officer from the Sheriff's Department jumped in with them. The door was closed, locked, and the vehicle sped away.

"Are you hurt, sir?" McManus asked the president.

"No, I'm fine. Because of Hawk." Pride nodded at Jillian. "He saved me. And so did you."

"I just want him to be okay," she said, weeping.

The president reached over and pulled her close. She buried her face in his chest and cried before finally sitting back in her seat. The armored car veered out of the back entrance of Epcot, turning down a service road. The driver accelerated.

"I know where we need to take the president." Jillian sniffed, trying to regain her composure.

"Name the place," McManus said.

"It's the same place that Kim and Mary are hidden away in." She then spoke to the president. "It's the safest place in the Walt Disney World Resort. I can take you there if you're ready to see them."

"I am, but I don't want to put them in danger. Before you take me there, do you really think we are safe now?"

"I'm sure we are, sir." McManus checked his cell phone. "According to what I'm seeing, we have teams fanning out all across the resort. Locking it down as it should have been when you first went missing. It's obvious someone did their best to leave gaping holes in your security."

"If this crisis is finally over, then take me to my family," the president said.

"Yes, sir." Jillian leaned forward to give the driver direction. As she did, she felt a hand tap her on the shoulder. She turned.

"Jillian, thank you," President Pride said. His eyes were reddened. "You're an excellent agent. Your quick thinking, instinct, and skill saved my life. Under the most horrendous circumstances, you've also kept my family safe. I can never express how much that means to me."

"You're welcome, Mr. President."

"And I want you to know, I really love Hawk. He was my friend." A tear trickled down his cheek. "Jesus said, 'a greater love has no one than this, that one lay down his life for his friends.'"

Without warning, a deafening explosion sounded. Their vehicle lurched on its side and turned over, not once, not twice, but three times. Inside the back of the armored car, she and the rest of the passengers, who were not belted in, tumbled inside the interior.

Jillian realized they had been struck directly on the side panel by another vehicle. The velocity of the impact told her it was intentional, and they were not as safe and secure as they had thought. Feeling the car come to rest upside down, she crawled through the shattered glass and around the bodies lying next to her. When she stuck her head out the shattered window, she felt a blast of tremendous heat. The car was now ablaze.

They had to get out before it blew up.

CHAPTER SIXTY-NINE

Someone Is In Charge

Craig Johnson grimaced as the medical personnel now swarming through the American Adventure worked to stop his own bleeding. He hurt but knew he would be fine, eventually. He looked over the shoulder of the doctor tending his wound to see them place the motionless body of Grayson Hawkes on a stretcher and roll it out of the rotunda. Surrounded by eight emergency medical personnel, they moved with a sense of urgency. He had heard the conversation, the shots, the aftermath, and the hollow words that Jillian Batterson had said about Hawk's condition.

He was dead.

Benny Wise, a former Navy SEAL and now a veteran Secret Service agent who Johnson had known for a number of years, knelt by Johnson's side.

"Craig, what happened?" Wise said.

Craig thought carefully about how to answer. What he knew about Wise was that President Pride had personally selected him to be part of the team guarding Fire and Ice. He was certain he had the trust of the president.

"We have some traitors in our midst," Johnson said. "Our team, our unit, is responsible for the first family's kidnapping. Pat Nobles tried to assassinate the president. I have no idea if Stanley is involved or not."

"Jeremiah Stanley was found dead in the pavilion next to this one," Wise said. "If he was involved, someone eliminated him. There's a lot of blood in the area. Don't know if all of it was his, but we didn't find anybody else nearby."

"Who's in charge of our team then?" Johnson asked.

"I suppose that would be you. You were the agent in the command center in contact with Nobles."

"But Nobles kept me out of the action, away from what was really going on." Johnson bit his lip to take his mind off the pain.

"It sounds like that was on purpose."

"Then we need to secure the first family and get them out of here." Johnson took a deep breath. "Use the contact we have with the Orange County Sheriff. Call in the army if you have to, but get the president out of here and do it yourself."

He was confident that of all the people in the orbit of the president, he could trust Benny Wise. Johnson winced as the doctor bound his wounds. A gurney was being rolled over to transfer him to an ambulance.

Wise leaned back in and whispered to Johnson. "We have a problem."

CHAPTER SEVENTY

The Never-Ending Nightmare

President Pride moaned and rolled over. He was cut and bleeding, but conscious. Dana also moved. She too was scraped but seemed to be coherent and aware. Cal McManus lay unconscious since he had been on the side of the vehicle that took the brunt of the impact. Dana crawled to the sheriff to check on his condition. The agent in the back with them lay still, and the condition of the driver was unknown.

Jillian reached back into her waistband only to find her gun was not there. After searching around her, she finally saw it lying next to the shattered window. She stretched out her hand and grabbed it, and then made sure there was a round in the chamber.

"Mr. President?" Jillian asked.

"I'm good. But we're not out of the woods yet. The car that hit us has us wedged in. "We need to exit out your side."

"I'll go first," Jillian instructed. "Once I give the all clear, get away from our vehicle as fast as you can. It's on fire and could explode."

"The sheriff is unconscious," Dana said. "I can't rouse him. He has a pulse, but he's not waking up."

Just then McManus coughed and opened his eyes.

"Strike that," Dana said with relief. "He's okay."

Jillian slid out of the car. The safety glass cut her as she dragged her body forward. Later, she could assess her aches and pains, but for now there was another challenge to face and overcome. As she cleared the car, she heard movement behind her. McManus was trying to squeeze through the opening. He had a gash on his head and struggled to gain his feet. She reached down to steady him as they crouched behind their overturned vehicle.

"Try to get everyone out, sir. Let me see if I can clear us a path." She looked up and saw flames licking the air from the front of the car. "It could blow at any time."

McManus reached back into the vehicle to pull the president out. Jillian slid around the rear of the car, away from the flames, to study the car that had hit them. The driver's side door stood ajar. The driver appeared to have exited the vehicle. But where to? She shuffled forward to change her position. Then she saw movement at the back of the car that had struck them.

"Are you still alive?" a voice said from behind the vehicle.

"Still alive?" Jillian said. "Who are you?"

"You don't remember me? I'm hurt."

Jillian looked through the smoke emanating from their burning armored car. She glanced back and could see McManus helping the president and Dana out.

"How about Tyler Pride? Is he still alive?" the voice asked.

"No, he didn't make it," she lied. "You finally did it. He's dead." She waited for the next response. Who was this person?

After a few silent moments that seemed to last an eternity, Jillian crouched down, trying to find an escape from the now-billowing smoke.

"You know, I just don't believe you," the person said. "I saw you leave the American Adventure. Tyler Pride is like a cockroach. He just won't die. Nobles should have taken care of him and wrapped up all the loose ends, but as usual, he messed up. Operation Marble Heart should not have been this difficult. Yet here we are."

"I asked you before, who are you?"

"I'm hurt, but still you don't recognize me."

Jillian moved to the other end of their vehicle. The president, Dana, and McManus crouched behind it. She motioned to the sheriff about the other occupants, but he shook his head. They had not survived.

Grimacing, she pointed toward a concrete road barricade less than twenty-five yards away. McManus nodded in agreement. The three others limped toward the barrier while she stayed at the back of their vehicle that was now almost engulfed in flames. The searing heat made her skin feel like it was melting, but from this angle, she could actually see behind the bumper of the other vehicle.

Suddenly, through the heat waves that blurred her vision, she saw who had called out to her. It was Joel Habecker. He had somehow managed to escape from where she had left him in the streets of Japan. Trying to ignore the pain from the intense heat, she closed her eyes a moment and then refocused. He leaned across the back of his car, intently staring at where she had been moments ago. Joel didn't know she had moved. The fire, although dangerous, provided her with the protection she badly needed.

Striking a shooting stance, she stepped out from behind the flaming vehicle. She decided to give him one chance, then she would fire.

"Joel, it's over. Drop your weapon and kick it toward me, or I *will* shoot you," she said, leveling her pistol at him.

"You're pretty tough and resilient." He smiled at her. "I'm impressed."

"Drop the weapon."

"Our boss really made this far more difficult than it needed to be. I thought my Disney clues would have kept the president hidden longer. But Hawk was too clever. He found him too fast, so we had to change our plans some. Now the world will think the Disney CCA plotted to eliminate the president, with the help of a few rogue agents.

"I asked you before, is the president okay? You said he was dead. I don't believe you. But I promise you, I will finish him now." Joel raised his weapon toward Jillian. "You won't shoot me. You didn't even have the right stuff to make it with Homeland Security. That's why you were so eager to come to Disney. This is a dangerous world, not some fantasy land."

Jillian watched as he took aim at her. She could see his eyes and knew the split second before he fired, he would close one to make sure his aim was true. That would be the moment of no return.

"This is not a fairy tale. There's no dream coming true for you today, Jillian. I *will* finish Operation Marble Heart."

"No you won't. Your fate will be the same as John Wilkes Booth. Your conspiracy has unraveled. You cowards have failed, and you will be remembered as evil men who were insane." Jillian smiled at him.

Joel's eyes widened at her words, then they narrowed again. Slowly he closed one eye as the other sighted down the barrel of his gun toward her. With her heart pounding, she inhaled and pulled the trigger on her exhale. Her shot hit its mark. She had aimed at the shoulder of his shooting arm, and it had exploded with the impact. His gun had fired, but wildly. She marched to where he writhed on the ground.

Jillian hesitated and her eyes widened as she could see more clearly through the waves of heat. He still held his gun. She raised her firearm to take another shot. But as she drew near, he put the pistol to his head and pulled the trigger—just like the monorail driver.

In the same instant Joel had taken his own life, the car exploded behind her. The compression wave drove her to the ground, where she landed several feet away. Slowly, she rolled to her side and glanced toward the burning wreckage. Joel's car had shielded her from the worst of the blast.

Cal McManus limped to where she lay on the ground. She gave him a thumbs-up to signal she was fine. Allowing her head to fall back to the pavement, she knew she was anything but fine. She was alive, and she had managed to keep the president alive, but she was not fine. She feared she would never be fine again. She felt tears sting the corners of her eyes, but she willed them not to fall.

Was this over? Was the president finally safe? Joel had been right about one thing—no dreams came true today. This was a day of nightmares. Hopefully, this nightmare had ended. But another loomed on the horizon. Hawk was gone.

CHAPTER SEVENTY-ONE

Hours Have Passed

Juliette stood in the empty hallway of Advent Health Hospital, leaning against her husband, Tim. Her sobs echoed through the hallway. As he hugged her, she knew he was trying to reassure her that things would be fine, but he didn't believe it and neither did she.

The double doors at the end of the hallway burst open and Jillian, Shep, and Jonathan Carlson walked toward them. Jonathan had arrived back from Disney Tokyo less than an hour ago and had been briefed on the chaos that had unfolded during his flight back.

As they greeted each other with teary-eyed hugs and hushed greetings, they huddled in the hallway, waiting for the news they dreaded.

"The word is . . .?" Jonathan asked for those who had just arrived.

"Still in surgery," Tim said. "It's been ten hours now."

"Prognosis?" Jon followed up.

"Not good." Juliette sighed, cutting off a sob. "Hawk has already slipped away three times, but they've managed to bring him back. The update we just got was not optimistic."

"Hey, but he's still with us," Shep said. "Hawk's a fighter. His pulse had stopped in the American Adventure, but the president's medical team managed to bring him back."

Tim nodded. "You're right. They did, and Hawk is tough and stubborn. So all things considered, the fact that he's still alive and in surgery is a good thing."

"Did the president and the first family fly out?" Juliette asked, directing her question to Jillian who had accompanied the Pride family to the airfield.

"Yes, Air Force One is on its way back to Washington." Jillian looked at each of them. "The agent in charge, Craig Johnson, sent Special Agent Wise to get them out of Disney. Cal McManus is with them, and there's a small contingent of agents on board. Two F-35s are escorting them back to Andrews Air Force base. No one is getting close to the president."

Jon shook his head. "I've got to tell you . . . this whole thing is unbelievable. A deep-state conspiracy. What a terrifying episode."

"Truly unbelievable," Juliette agreed.

"Well, people are believing it." Jon looked at each of them. "You don't know, do you?"

"Know what?" Jillian asked.

"The story about the assassination attempt, the conspiracy, and the evidence to prove it is broadcasting on every news channel. President Pride's interview with GNN has aired, but the reporter—"

"David Walker?" Juliette said.

"Yes, Walker and his cameraman also grabbed footage of what went down in the American Adventure Pavilion," Jon said. "It's been airing since its release. This is breaking news worldwide."

"They got it on camera?" Shep said.

"You really didn't know?" Jon said. "It's all there. The interview is scathing and thought provoking. The footage of Hawk fighting masked assassins in the American Adventure, the standoff with the rotten Secret Service agent, including his admission of the plot, and then Hawk jumping in front of the president and Jillian taking out the assassin. I bet every eye on the planet has seen it."

"They were supposed to have left the area," Jillian said, shaking her head.

"Who?"

"The reporter and his cameraman. Hawk had gotten them out of harm's way. They were supposed to have stayed hidden."

"Apparently, they didn't listen," Jon said. "Walker has been driving the story to make sure everyone understands what is true and why other media outlets have been less than honest in covering the Pride presidency. The president's press secretary has been outlining details and names. The implications will be far reaching."

"It's hard to believe there was such a thing as a deep-state conspiracy," Tim said. "How could this happen?"

"I don't know, but I believe it," Jillian said. "Hawk and the president talked at length about it. I couldn't have ever imagined something so bizarre and evil, but it's true. Hawk said we all need to learn how to disagree without being divisive. But tragically, those who seem to scream the loudest about diversity want their way so badly, they refuse to see the value and integrity in honest disagreement. They don't want diversity. They want to destroy anyone or anything that doesn't agree with them."

"We've traded diversity and tolerance for acceptance by destruction?" Shep asked.

"So it seems. There's no such thing as compromise for some; only compliance is acceptable." Jillian turned at the sound of the doors opening at the end of the hallway.

The small group turned as a lone doctor walked toward them. His face was grim, deeply lined, and glistening with sweat. He looked exhausted. He reached up and pulled off the cap he had been wearing in the operating room. After taking a deep breath, he sighed.

The doctor looked at them before speaking. "I'm sorry . . ."

CHAPTER SEVENTY-TWO

Ronald Reagan Once Said

Ronald Reagan was famous for his succinct, folksy one-liners. In the Reagan Diaries, he records the events related to the assassination attempt on his life, which took place on March 30, 1981. The diary entry was written nearly two weeks later, on April 11. He recorded his thoughts of the day:

> *Speech not riotously received – still it was successful. Left the hotel at the usual side entrance and headed for the car – suddenly there was a burst of gun fire from the left. SS [Secret Service] agent pushed me onto the floor of the car and jumped on top . . . I walked into the emergency room and was hoisted onto a cart where I was stripped of my clothes. It was then we learned I'd been shot and had a bullet in my lung. Getting shot hurts.*

Getting shot hurts.

Hawk was astounded at the sensation washing over him. It seemed as if he was in flight, soaring through a vast array of color and light. He was not afraid but acutely aware of everything happening around him. Yet it couldn't be happening. Suddenly, he was plunged into a sea of darkness and stood next to a twisted automobile that had veered off the highway into the trees along an isolated road. Knee deep in damp weeds, he could see the people inside the car and recognized it as one he had been driving years before.

With that realization, he was suddenly snatched out of the grass and was now looking out from the stage of the Celebration Community Church into the faces of old friends who waited to hear him speak. The sun streaked through the windows, and the room glowed in the light. He felt butterflies in his stomach as he rose to speak, as he always did, but then the light faded.

Now he was falling. Hawk tumbled through the air, dazzled by the freedom of flight, wondering what he might see next.

Getting shot hurts.

Darkness once again engulfed him. Then he was standing alone in a cottage that was built from the original concept of Walt Disney's *Snow White and the Seven Dwarfs*. The front door opened and Farren Rales, his old friend and mentor, walked in. Hawk reached out to embrace the Disney Imagineer only to close his arms around emptiness. Once again, he was in a free fall. Colors, shapes, blazed past at stupefying speed.

Getting shot hurts.

The free fall ended as he slammed down onto the top of a monorail car. Sliding across the slick white top, he tried to grab something to keep him from falling over the side. Rain stung his face, and the wind threatened to cut him in half. He could not slow his slide and was thrown off the monorail. He was now leaping off the top of Cinderella Castle, hanging onto a zip line that ran from the castle spire into Tomorrowland. A crowd below gazed up at him. He trembled. He had lived this moment before and knew he would land safely.

Getting shot hurts.

Now he was holding Kate Young. He felt her weight push against him and remembered this was the moment she had been shot. He knew it had hurt. But he had no idea how much until now. His eyes stung with tears, knowing he couldn't help her now any more than he could help her then.

Getting shot hurts.

Pat Nobles was aiming a pistol at Tyler Pride. Hawk knew the man was getting ready to shoot. He had to protect the president, so he jumped in front of the commander in chief just as the gun fired.

Getting shot hurts.

Hawk now saw the beautiful face of Jillian Batterson, who leaned over him. Her mouth next to his face, she was speaking to him. She was so worried.

"Don't you die on me, Hawk. Not on my watch. Don't you leave me," Jillian said as she touched his neck.

Getting shot hurts.

Hawk opened his eyes. He tried to focus on the blinding brightness of the light around him but could not. He heard the steady beat of a heart monitor and the ding sounding from a medical alarm next to him. Jerking his head to shield his eyes from the light, he focused on an IV pole that held more bags of medication and fluid than he could count. Then he realized they were connected to him. His arm ached. It felt heavy, and he tried to move it but could not. Turning his head to the other side, he saw a whiteboard. His eyes focused on his name, scribbled in black marker against the clean, white writing surface. *Grayson Hawkes.*

He was alive. The last conscious thought he'd had was trying to get to the president before Nobles fired the gun. Was the president alive? Had he managed to get there in time? What about Jillian? Was she safe?

A flurry of activity blew through the doorway into his room. Three nurses and a doctor strode in, a look of relief on their faces, he thought. Had they been worried he wouldn't survive? Why did he ache so badly and why was he having trouble moving? Then he remembered, getting shot hurts.

Although it hurt, he was alive. He closed his eyes and thanked God for his next breath.

CHAPTER SEVENTY-THREE

Medal of Freedom

The Presidential Medal of Freedom is awarded by the president of the United States. The Presidential Medal of Freedom and the Congressional Gold Medal are the highest civilian honors awarded by the country.

Officially, the award recognizes people who have made "an especially meritorious contribution to the security or national interests of the United States, world peace, cultural or other significant public or private endeavors." On this day at the White House, there had been two awards presented. One to Jillian Batterson and the other to Hawk for their heroic and selfless sacrifices in rescuing and saving the Pride family during the events that happened eight months earlier in Walt Disney World.

On September 14, 1964, Walt Disney received the Medal of Freedom from President Lyndon B. Johnson. President Johnson placed the medal on Walt and gave a brief statement.

"What America is to be, America will be, because of our trust in and of the individual and of his capacity for excellence," the president said.

What had made the Disney visit a bit confusing was that when the White House announced on July 3, 1964 that Walt would be a recipient of the Medal of Freedom, it came during the Goldwater campaign, and Walt Disney and his entire family were all united in their enthusiastic support of the conservative Arizona senator.

Walt was concerned that the invitation was a political ploy to surround the incumbent Democrat, LBJ, with people judged to be outstanding Americans for a powerful photo opportunity to be used during the election season. Walt was also distracted by more important things when the invitation arrived—the New

York World's fair opening, Disneyland, and the United States Lawn Bowling Championships, which Walt was participating in.

As he wrapped up the trip and made plans to stop in Washington, he decided to wear a Goldwater-for-president button as he received his award. Walt intended it to be a prank and a good-hearted joke. However, Walt did not know President Johnson held such opposing views from his on the political spectrum. So, in pictures of the event, you can catch a glimpse of the *G 64* button, a small campaign button that some supporters wore to events.

The mystery of history has created a number of variations of this story, but apparently President Johnson didn't have the sense of Midwestern humor that Walt had hoped. Disney never intended it as an insult to the office or the award, yet stories emerged that Lyndon Johnson had not enjoyed his subtle attempt at humor.

The ceremony for Hawk and Jillian took place in the East Room of the White House, the same room where Walt Disney had received his reward. President Pride was very kind in his words of appreciation for both Jillian and him. Hawk knew President Pride well enough to know of his love of history.

So, prior to their trip to Washington, Hawk had instructed the Disney Archives in California to find the lapel pin Walt had worn in 1964. He tucked it away, out of sight under his suit lapel. As the president got ready to present Hawk with his award, Hawk pulled his lapel back slightly so the president could see it. Pride burst into laughter, recognizing the pin and knowing the story behind it.

Standing in front of a distinguished audience, Hawk and President Pride both laughed, providing an amusing moment for all the guests to see, although onlookers had no clue what was actually happening.

Pride whispered to Hawk as he placed the medal on him. "Does this mean you're not going to vote for me?"

"It depends on who's running against you," Hawk said quietly.

The president once again burst into laughter as he hugged both Hawk and Jillian for their help to him and their service to the country. After a few photos, they took a moment to chat with some of the guests before being given a chance to freshen up for the press briefing.

The two were sent into dressing areas, with instructions to inspect their clothing. Jillian was told to freshen her makeup if she felt she needed to, and they were asked if either needed a hairdresser or assistant to help them. Hawk laughed this off and quickly inspected his black suit, open-collared white shirt, and dress shoes. Originally, he had been wearing a tie, but upon meeting the president prior to the presentation, he had immediately been harassed.

"You hate to wear a tie," Pride had kidded. "Don't wear one on my account."

"It will look better in the pictures," Hawk said.

"I'm telling you to lose it. That's an executive order."

So Hawk had taken off his tie before stepping onto the stage in the East Room with Jillian.

"You look beautiful," Hawk whispered to her. He thought she looked stunning in a perfect, form-fitting dress created by one of the Disney designers just for this event.

Now they were escorted back to the president's office. Jillian sat next to Hawk on a gold brocade sofa in the Oval Office. He glanced at Jillian, who fidgeted with her medal, her dress, and then her hair.

"What's wrong with you? You act like you've never been in this office before." Hawk grinned at her.

"I haven't." She exhaled loudly. "Have you?"

"What?"

"Have you ever been here before?"

"Of course I have," Hawk said, gloating a bit.

"When?" Jillian said in disbelief.

Hawk ignored her as Dana Brown entered the room. Hawk rose to his feet to greet her. Dana strode over, hugged them both, and then motioned for them to take their seats again.

"In just a few minutes, President Pride will be here and then we will escort you into the Press Room. With all that's happened, this will be the first time that most of the press pool will have seen you since we left Florida." Dana smiled. "I'll be back in a minute."

Dana left, and as soon as she had exited the room, Hawk turned to Jillian.

"I know this is probably not the best time to tell you I told you so, but I did tell you so." Hawk smiled at her. "Hopefully, you believe it yourself now."

"What are you talking about?" Jillian gave him a blank look.

"It . . . you wondered if you still had your edge, if you were still as good as when you were a federal agent. You wondered whether you still had . . . it. I knew you did. Remember? I told you so. I would think that after saving the life of the president on more than one occasion, you should be convinced you are not only as good as you once were, but you are better than ever." Hawk touched her hand as he spoke. "I'm proud of you and you definitely deserve any award they want to give you. You saved the president."

Jillian blushed. "You did pretty well yourself. If not for you, the president would be dead now."

"Actually, I got shot." Hawk motioned toward his back. "Did I ever tell you that getting shot hurts?"

Waving her hand in front of his face, she laughed. "Yes, yes, you have . . . more than once." Her smile dissolved. "Did you hear what the president spoke to me about earlier?"

"I did." Hawk grew somber and tilted his head as he looked into her eyes. "What are you going to do?"

"I didn't expect the president to offer me a position to join his Secret Service detail." Jillian looked down at her hands, which were clasped together in her lap. "I just did what I knew to do to keep him alive. I'd watched you get killed and knew I couldn't let you die in vain."

"I didn't get killed. I didn't die," Hawk said softly, then smiled. "Well, maybe I was a little bit dead for a few minutes, but I survived. You, however, saved not only me but the president. Like I said, you still have your edge. You're good at what you do and that's why the president wants you to come and work for him. He needs people he can trust."

"I love what I do now." Jillian looked up at him, searching for help.

"And you're great at it." Hawk still smiled. "But you have to decide what and where you want to be."

"I guess that depends." Jillian blushed once again. Tilting her head down to avoid eye contact, her dark hair fell across part of her face. "Where do you want me to be?"

The door to the Oval Office burst open, startling them both. The president, followed by Sam Reno and Dana Brown, walked into the room.

"Time to go," President Pride said cheerfully. "Ready?"

CHAPTER SEVENTY-FOUR

The Press Pool

Under the floor of the James C. Brady Press Briefing Room lies the original indoor White House swimming pool. The deep end sits under the platform and lectern end of the room, and the shallow end is where the cameras are perched. In between the two are the rows of chairs where members of the press sit during briefings.

Most people don't know that a stairwell behind the platform descends into the retired swimming pool, originally designed by Franklin Delano Roosevelt and used regularly by John F. Kennedy. The now-empty pool features autographs written on the pool walls by famous guests who've been fortunate enough to see it.

Part of exploring the White House with each new first family is the right of passage of walking down the steps and signing the walls. The dry old tiles of FDR's empty pool contain the autographs of Bono, Sugar Ray Leonard, prominent reporters, staffers, politicians, and Grayson Hawkes.

President Tyler Pride strode in from the side door of the briefing room followed by Jillian Batterson, Hawk, Dana Brown and Sam Reno. They had made the walk from the Oval Office and now faced the lights of the press as cameras instantly came to life waiting for their remarks.

The president stepped to the podium. "Thanks for being here. As usual, it's a busy day here at the White House. As most of you know, there have been some unusual events happening here in our nation's capital. A conspiracy to overthrow and disrupt our Republic has been exposed, and the ripple effect has been, well, devastating. Politicians, government officials, and even members of the media have been placed under scrutiny and many exposed and revealed to be either coconspirators or, at worst, willing participants in this plot to undercut and undermine the presidency." Pride smiled. "But this is a new day here in Washington and a new day in America. We are all learning to put the past behind us and move into the future, together."

Pride took a step back and looked at Jillian and Hawk before returning to the microphone. "Today, I awarded our nation's highest civilian honor to Jillian Batterson and Grayson Hawkes for outstanding service to this nation. They are true American heroes. They have graciously said they would take a few questions from you." Pride smiled slyly. "I know most of you were with me in Florida and you haven't seen these two since we were there. But be nice to them." Pride now grinned. "I promised them you would. Make Pride proud."

The reporters laughed respectfully. Pride stepped away from the podium, and Dana Brown pointed to the first reporter.

"This question is for Jillian Batterson." The reporter stood to his feet. "According to reports, a Mr. Joel Habecker was involved in this conspiracy to kill the president. He was one of your employees in your security division. Was there anything in his past that in hindsight you should have noticed about him?"

Jillian stepped up the lectern and grasped both sides with her hands. "No, not really. As you can imagine, we have gone back and thoroughly reviewed his personnel file, the background checks, and interview process. Apparently, it was his social media involvement and posts that led Pat Nobles and his accomplices to find him. Then it was nothing more than deciding on the right price to betray his country. He was already infuriated that Tyler Pride had been elected president and was posting his angry thoughts. The high-ranking conspirators found a Disney insider who could undermine and undercut our security system in such a way as to be undetected."

The follow-up question came quickly. "We've heard that you have been invited to join the president's security team here in Washington. Are you moving to DC?"

"I can't say yet. We're still in the negotiation stage." She smiled and stepped back.

"I love to negotiate and take a gamble," Pride quipped from the side, never stepping to the microphone. "If you'd like, later I'll give you the odds of her joining my team."

As the laughter that followed ebbed, another reporter was called on.

"This is also for Jillian," the female reporter on the front row said. "We've all seen some of the footage where you had to defend the president. Then, a short time later, you once again had to defend him when your car was struck.

Can you share with us what was going through your mind in both of those moments?"

Jillian looked down, swallowed hard, and then raised her head. "I just did what had to be done. You don't get a lot of time to think in those situations. You only have a split second to react. You just hope you have what it takes to react properly." She glanced at Hawk, then back to the reporter. "You don't get a second chance. If you react in the wrong way or miss your opportunity to act, then all hope is lost."

Dana Brown now called on another member of the press. A reporter stood from about halfway back in the seating area.

"This is for Dr. Hawkes," the man said.

Hawk slid in next to Jillian who started to step away. Hawk reached out and placed a hand on her back to keep her next to him.

"Go ahead," Hawk said.

"You were shot," the reporter said, stating the obvious.

"Yes, I was. And getting shot hurts," Hawk said.

"Don't get him started again," Jillian said, rolling her eyes.

Tyler Pride now stepped next to them, grinning. "All we've heard about is him getting shot. You would think by now, he would be over it."

Pride waited for the lighthearted, unscripted moment to pass. "The only reason we can laugh about it now is because he's fine. But I wouldn't be here if he hadn't thrown himself in front of me. I'm eternally thankful, and grateful to him."

Pride retreated a step, his eyes misty.

"How are you feeling?" the reporter asked Hawk.

"I feel good. Thank you for asking. It's taken some time, but slowly, each day, I feel like my old self . . . or older self."

Dana pointed to another reporter. This time David Walker from GNN stood to ask the question. It was the first time Hawk had seen him since their eventful time together at Walt Disney World.

"It's very good to see you again," Walker said. "We were extremely worried about you."

"Good to see you as well." Hawk smiled. "I know all of you have seen the footage that his team shot as the events in Florida unfolded. I tried to keep him safe, but he didn't listen to me."

Laughter filled the room. Walker looked at his colleagues and then continued. "I know what the official reports said, but how did you manage to find the president and the first family?"

"Well, the conspirators were confident they would not be caught. The mistake they made was leaving some coded messages for each other that I was able to understand and figure out. Once I had done that, they called an audible. I guess you could describe it that way. I hastily put another plan into place that gave me just enough time to find the president. They were able to implicate me as part of the kidnapping plot."

"When did you know what they were doing?" Walker asked as a follow-up.

"It dawned on me that it was too easy to do what I was doing." Hawk cleared his throat. "They were giving me too much space and too much room to maneuver. So I decided to work within the space they gave me and hoped I knew Walt Disney World better than they did."

Walker nodded and then added, "I think I was promised an interview with you in Florida, wasn't I? If so, I would still like to sit down with you."

Dana Brown now took the microphone from the stand near the front and asked the next question. "Dr. Hawkes, you said something to me earlier that I thought was important and inspiring. Would you mind sharing it here?"

Hawk thought for a moment. "You mean about changing the conversation?"

Dana nodded.

"Sure. As it has been reported and is well known, President Pride and I were friends before he was elected, and we are friends today. I was offered a job in his administration when he was elected, and I turned the job down.

"I am bothered by the tone of the conversation in the country that we all have been subjected to and maybe even participated in. I can disagree with my president, just like I can disagree with my friends, because that is how people relate. But I also can find areas where I can agree and stand alongside my president. However, it seems when we disagree, we have forgotten how to honor each other. Honor has never meant blanket endorsement; it means that we respect and value one another. Our conversations sometimes haven't reflected that, and we're guilty of messing that up. I know I have been at times.

"No matter how any individual voted in the last election, I believe, as a follower of God, that I need to pray for Him to bless our president. We can pray for him to be granted wisdom and health. We can pray that God would prosper his good ideas and change his mind on his bad ideas." Hawk glanced at President Pride, who nodded in agreement and laughed as he listened.

"We need to respect the office and the occupant of the office. No matter how you voted, Tyler Pride is your president and he is mine. And to say or think anything else is ridiculous. He is the American president."

Hawk looked across the room. "There's a time to vote. There's a time to campaign. And there's a time to debate important things. But through it all, let's be the people who can disagree on policy without being disagreeable. Our conversations need to be marked by kindness and respect. Until we can discipline ourselves to have conversations about the world we live in with honor, with respect, with prayer, and most of all, with love. Until we can have conversations like that, we don't really have anything to say worth listening to."

Dana nodded her head. David Walker still stood and threw out another question. "Does that mean you're going to take a job in the administration if President Pride asks again?"

Hawk looked back at the president who raised an eyebrow. Hawk turned back to the press. "Nope, I'm going to Disney World."

"Hey, I tried to get him to stay," the president said. "Thanks for coming today. That's all for now."

The three of them stepped to the side of the lectern and gave the press a moment to take pictures. President Tyler Pride stood to Hawk's left, and Jillian stood to his right. As the photographers and cameras captured the last few images of them standing together in the White House Press Room, Hawk turned his head to whisper in Jillian's ear.

"Hey," he said.

Jillian turned to him. She was savoring the moment, but at the same time, he knew she was relieved it would soon be over. Breathing deeply and letting out a gratifying sigh, she mouthed the word, "What?"

Leaning in close, so only she could hear, he said, "I want you to stay with me at Disney World."

It was the answer to the question she had asked him in the Oval Office. They had been interrupted before he could answer. He watched as she processed what he had just said. Jillian smiled at him—a dazzling smile that brightened the room more than the glowing lights all around them. Momentarily, he forgot where he was and realized that seeing her smile brought him joy.

Afterword

Each novel I have written has contained an afterword. A moment where I get to express to you my deep and heartfelt thanks for taking time out of your life to share an adventure through the world of Walt Disney with me. I hope that with each turn of the page you looked back and felt as if it was time well spent. Perhaps it was fun. Hopefully, there were a few smiles, a few thrills, and great escape into the world of Disney. One of the greatest compliments a fan of one the earlier novels gave me was that the story was "a vacation on the written page."

This story once again builds off of very real events that create the canvas that I have tried to paint a story upon: the kidnapping of Richard Nixon by Walt Disney at Disneyland, the shouting down of the Donald J. Trump audio-animatronic at the Hall of Presidents, and when Walt Disney was awarded the Medal of Freedom by Lyndon Johnson. All of those events happened just as I shared them with you.

I hope that if you are reading through this afterword, it means you have made it through each page of the story. If so, I want to make sure before we end this volume that you have a sense of how this story came to be.

It is easy to misclassify this fictional story as one with a political agenda. But you have to be fair; it does not really have one. There are certainly some characteristics of a certain fictional president that could be transposed onto a number of real presidents if you choose to do so, but remember the story also has an established lead character that is caught in the struggle where many people find themselves, not knowing exactly how to respond or how to react in the crazy, upside-down, and volatile political world we live in.

The climactic battle of the story happens inside the very real American Adventure at Epcot. I believe this is an attraction Walt Disney would have loved.

He dedicated Disneyland as a place to "the ideals, the dreams, and the hard facts that have created America."

When you think about America, there are some hard realities to deal with in a thirty-minute stage show that has to cover an expanse of over two hundred years. But the purpose of the show is to remind us of what America is all about. In the first official guidebook of Epcot, this is how it was explained:

> *If you ask yourself why they didn't include this, how could they possibly have ignored that, you won't be alone. The Disney people have themselves been asking the same questions for years, since they first conceived the show, subsequently reworked a thousand times. But chances are you won't be posing those questions at the end of the show. Chances are you will be too stunned by what you see and hear. And yes, inspired.*

The opening line in the attraction, and used in the novel, is borrowed from the work of John Steinbeck. *America did not exist.* The world is a tough and dangerous place, and there are a lot of very evil people out there who wish they lived in a world where America did not exist. But because America is real, there is hope for a world that desperately needs leadership.

Yet, America is still a very young nation in the grand scheme of history. There have been and will be mistakes and stumbling along the way. But America is also the greatest nation on Earth and a shining light to a world that needs a beacon to look toward and draw hope from. We are not perfect, but we are learning, growing, and becoming better.

The patriotic finale song of the American Adventure is called "Golden Dream." It is inspiring but honest about what it takes to make a dream come true. With phrases within that speak of struggle, hard times, tough decisions, and the beckoning call of change and progress, we are reminded that moving forward through time is tough, but worth it. That is the power of a dream. It just seems to me that the words of Ben Franklin in the American Adventure are a call to action and a powerful reminder of what America is all about. He says . . .

> *I may have invented these bifocals I am wearing, but I can assure you they are not rose colored.*

Liberty, equality, change, and being one nation under God is not easy. But it is worth the struggle. My fear is that the hyper-charged political climate of the day causes us to forget that. We shouldn't erase our past, we can't rewrite history, and we will never undo anything that has been done. Life does not work that way and neither does history. There is no such thing as a do-over. What does happen is that we learn, grow, and become better. So those themes of the American Adventure became the backdrop for the finale of this book. It is not by accident that this backdrop was chosen, because the message of the American Adventure resonates today like never before.

The thoughts expressed by Hawk and company do have some importance I believe. The need to learn to disagree without being disagreeable, the understanding that tolerance and acceptance are two different things and can exist side by side, the importance of how we deal with one another, what matters most, learning to care, the importance of religious freedom, and not forgetting that America is a gift, not just to her own citizens, but to the entire world.

I also believe that we need statesmen, not politicians, people who don't just talk about a love of country, but really do love their country more than political parties and their own power. There is a need for statesmen to care about the people. The way you know whether they love America and the Golden Dream is revealed in what they do and say.

So while there is chaos all around us, the great news is that each of us—real people—can make a difference and make the world a better place. I believe that is how God has created us and is the purpose we have been placed on this planet for. Let me encourage you to strive to always be the very best version of you.

As you think about the worlds Walt Disney imagined and created, know that they are not only an escape, but are meant to ignite within us a hope and a glimpse of what could be. And that ignites dreams within each of us. Each of us can have a legacy that touches and changes the world.

The other question that always seems to come up at the end of the story is what happens to Hawk next, and will we ever hear from him again? To be honest, each time a story has ended, I have thought that his adventure was complete. If you have been with him over a five-novel span, we have come a long way indeed. If this is your first journey with Hawk, then go back and tap into some of his other stuff. He has found a treasure trove in the world of Disney to explore. This time, I let Hawk tell part of the story from his viewpoint, but some of his other friends gave us a glimpse of the unfolding story from their eyes as well. Over the years they have all become fictional friends of mine. Letting you see things from their perspective was fun for me as a writer. So time will tell. Perhaps there will be more to come. Until then, let me again say to you—thanks.

I never take you as the reader for granted. I appreciate so much your response to the stories and your love of Disney. Thank you for letting me be a small part of that passion. Like you, I am a fan! And I also am a fan of yours—a reader who loves to use your imagination and make discoveries in a world that needs dreamers.

Blessings to you!

–Jeff Dixon

Bibliography

The following resources were invaluable in understanding the background, history, operation, and attractions within Walt Disney World. They are the sources that the author has adapted and used in this work of fiction. Because this novel blends fact with fiction, the term "faction" is an accurate way to move through the story. If there are moments where fact and fiction seem to blur together and the reader can no longer tell the difference, then the author has done what he intended. At the same time, if you need clarification as to what is real and what is not real, the following resources are invaluable in understanding the life, times, history, and legacy of Walter Elias Disney.

Barnes, Jeffrey. *The Wisdom of Walt: Leadership Lessons from the Happiest Place on Earth*. New York: Aviva Publishing, 2015.

———. *Beyond the Wisdom of Walt: Life Lessons from the Magical Place on Earth*. New York: Aviva Publishing, 2017.

Crawford, Michael. *The Progress City Primer*. Orlando: Progress City Press, 2015.

Denny, Jim. *Walt's Disneyland*. Anaheim, California: Writing in Overdrive Books, 2017.

Dixon, Jeff. *The Disney Driven Life*. United States of America: Theme Park Press, 2016.

———. *The Disney Code*. United States of America: Theme Park Press, 2018.

Fox, Mike. *Hidden Secrets & Stories of Walt Disney World*. United States of America: Mike Fox Publications, 2016.

Gabler, Neal. *Walt Disney: Triumph of the American Imagination*. New York: Knopf, 2006.

Gennawey, Sam. *Walt and the Promise of Progress City.* United States of America. Ayefour Publishing, 2011.

Ghez, Didier. *Disney's Grand Tour.* United States of America: Theme Park Press, 2013.

Green, Katherine and Richard. *The Man Behind the Magic: The Story of Walt Disney.* New York: Viking, 1991.

Hench, John. *Designing Disney: Imagineering and the Art of the Show.* New York: Disney Editions, 2003.

Imagineers. *Walt Disney Imagineering: A Behind the Dreams Look at Making the Magic.* New York: Hyperion, 1996.

Imagineers. *The Imagineering Field Guide to Epcot at Walt Disney World.* New York: Disney Editions, 2006.

Korkis, Jim. *The Vault of Walt.* United States of America: Ayefour Publishing, 2010.

———. *More Secret Stories of Walt Disney World.* United States of America: Theme Park Press, 2016.

———. *Walt's Words: Quotations of Walt Disney with Sources.* United States of America: Theme Park Press, 2016.

———. *Other Secret Stories of Walt Disney World.* United States of America: Theme Park Press, 2017.

———. *Secret Stories of Disneyland.* United States of America: Theme Park Press, 2017.

Kurtti, Jeff. *Imagineering Legends and the Genesis of the Disney Theme Park.* New York: Disney Editions, 2008.

Miller, Diane Disney and Pete Martin. *The Story of Walt Disney.* New York: Holt, 1957.

Moran, Christian. *Great Big Beautiful Tomorrow: Walt Disney and Technology.* United States of America: Theme Park Press, 2015.

Pedersen, R. A. *The Epcot Explorer's Encyclopedia.* Florida, USA: Encyclopedia Press, 2011.

Sklar, Marty. *One Little Spark*. Los Angeles, New York: Disney Editions, 2015.

————. *Dream it – Do it!* New York: Disney Editions, 2014.

Smith, Dave. *Disney Trivia from the Vault*. New York: Disney Editions, 2013.

————. *Disney Facts Revealed*. New York: Disney Editions, 2016.

————. *Disney A to Z: The Official Encyclopedia*. New York: Hyperion, 1996; updated 1998, 2006.

————. *The Quotable Walt Disney*. New York: Disney Editions, 2001.

Smith, Dave and Steven Clark. *Disney: The First 100 Years*. New York: Hyperion, 1999; Disney Editions, updated 2002.

Thomas, Bob. *The Art of Animation*. New York: Simon & Schuster, 1958.

————. *Walt Disney: An American Original*. New York: Simon & Schuster, 1976.

————. *Building a Company; Roy O. Disney and the Creation of an Entertainment Empire*. New York: Hyperion, 1998.

Vennes, Susan. *The Hidden Magic of Walt Disney World: Over 600 secrets of the Magic Kingdom, Epcot, Disney's Hollywood Studios, and Animal Kingdom*. Avon, MA: Adams Media, 2009.

Wallace, Aaron. *The Thinking Fan's Guide to Walt Disney World: Epcot*. Orlando, Florida: Pensive Pen Publishing, 2017.

Walt Disney World Explorer CD-ROM. Burbank, CA: Disney Interactive, 1996.

Williams, Pat. *How to Be Like Walt*. Deerfield Beach, Florida: Health Communications Inc., 2004.

Websites

These are *a few* of the author's favorite Disney news and fan sites that helped provide information and resources beyond the printed page.

Jim Hill Media, http://www.jimhillmedia.com.

Disney Pal, http://www.disney-pal.com.

Resort Information, http://www.mouseplanet.com.

Disney History Institute, http://www.disneyhistoryinstitute.com.